# Freeing Medusa

Elizabeth Andrews

This book is a work of fiction. The names, characters, places and incidents are products of the writer's imagination or have been used fictitiously and are not to be construed as real. Any resemblance to persons, living or dead, actual events, locale or organizations is entirely coincidental.

Protecting Medusa
*The Medusa's Daughters Trilogy, Book 3*

The current Medusa Katharine Rigas-Vardos spends a lot of time alone. All she wants is one hot night of male companionship. What she gets is a lot more than she bargained for.

Workaholic P.I. Hunter Phelps doesn't do relationships, but a one-night stand? Sure. Except one night with Katharine isn't enough, and when he tracks her down, he gets to save her life. He also discovers some old myths are true.

Hot sex evolves into tangled emotions, and Katharine vows to take on Athena and her Harvesters to end the curse. Hunter just hopes their quest isn't the end of the woman he loves.

This book is dedicated to everyone who would face the unimaginable for the people they love, even if it takes them to the ends of the earth.

And to my husband and sons, I love you!

# Acknowledgements

To the readers who have waited patiently all this time for this final installment in the series, my heartfelt thanks! I appreciate every one of you.

Big thanks to my monthly writing group, the 4th Thursday Writing Salon, Holly Bush, Allison B. Hanson, Natalie J. Damschroder, and Misty Simon, for the dinners, the writing talk, and the months we actually make writing progress. A huge additional thank you to Misty Simon for the extra pair of eyes on this as an alternative to kicking my ass, though I really appreciate both offers.

# THE LEGEND

Millennia ago, a beautiful young Gorgon made a fatal mistake, one her descendants still pay for today. She so angered Athena that the Goddess cursed Medusa, changing her lovely hair to snakes and causing her gaze to turn any living thing to stone. As if that wasn't bad enough, Perseus then set out to kill the unfortunate Medusa.

Perseus didn't know she'd already found a way to protect her descendants from some of the Goddess's curse: she created an amulet in the form of a golden goblet which would transfer from one Medusa to the next, either when she fell in love or died. This goblet prevents the curse from wreaking constant havoc on the women's lives, instead limiting it to once each month. And you thought you had PMS from hell.

Along with the Goddess's curse, Perseus's descendants have also followed the Medusas through the centuries, trying to take the amulet as they hunt, or harvest the Medusas. Over time, details about the goblet and how the curse passes from one Medusa to the next have been lost or forgotten. These Harvesters have so far failed to find the amulet, and, for several generations, have also failed to kill the reigning

Medusa. But they are persistent and are closer now to achieving one part of their task: killing the Medusa.

In recent years, one of their own fell in love with the Medusa he was destined to kill. Then her successor also fell in love, thus passing the curse on to another unlucky cousin. Now the Harvesters are even more determined to kill her successor, to satisfy the Goddess, and they will allow no one to stand in their way this time.

# CHAPTER ONE

**P**MS sucked. It sucked worse when one was the Medusa and had the curse of Athena multiplying PMS symptoms by about a million times the norm–plus snakes.

Katharine Rigas-Vardos groaned, lifting her face from her cupped hands. There was simply no help for it. If she didn't take the edge off before she went to Ramona's party, the first available man who looked at her wouldn't know what hit him. Especially since she'd stuck to her battery-operated boyfriends for two years. She pushed to her feet, abandoning the herbal tea her cousin Aleta swore was supposed to alleviate PMS symptoms.

Aleta wasn't the current Medusa, however, and her tea wasn't doing a thing for Katharine's problems. If it were going to work, it would've helped yesterday. No, that wasn't right. It would've worked last month when she tried it the first time. But she hadn't had the heart to tell her cousin. Aleta thought she was helping, and Katharine didn't want to disillusion her yet. She would, however, before Aleta sent any more of the useless tea. It tasted like dirt, but if it had done what Aleta swore it did, she'd have drunk gallons of it.

Her usual go-to of a shower with one of her

vibrators only eased the persistent PMS-fueled desires temporarily, but with a couple decent orgasms, she could function. For a few hours.

But it gave her time enough to get to Ramona's party and scope out the single males in the crowd for a likely candidate for one night of serious sex, the first in a couple of years.

Before the rest of the curse hit her.

After her shower, she dried her hair, then stared into her closet. This could take a while, she mused. These days, her clothing was purchased with protection in mind, not seduction. Lots of bootcut jeans so she could wear her dagger on her calf, or longer skirts to hide the hilt of the dagger if she had it in her boot or strapped to her thigh.

Not tonight.

Katharine pulled a black leather vest from its hanger and found a short, stretchy black skirt, then moved away from the closet. She stepped into sheer black lace panties and slipped the matching bra on, wincing slightly when she fastened it around her sensitive breasts.

She pulled the skirt up over her hips, then smoothed it. It reached only to mid-thigh, which meant no dagger. Right now, she could live with that. The leather vest paired nicely with the skirt, and she didn't bother with a shirt under it even though she knew it meant part of her tattoo would be visible on the back of her shoulder. No one could see the goblet or the snake, though, and if she got lucky, she figured the guy wouldn't care if she had one tattoo or twenty as he'd be getting lucky, too. *Very* lucky.

Mentally, she crossed her fingers as she moved to the mirror over her dresser. Her dark hair swung freely around her shoulders, and she decided to leave it alone. Some eyeliner and lipstick, and she was good to go.

She just hoped there was someone at Ramona's party who'd be willing to suffer through a long night in bed. She turned from her reflection. There *had* to be.

"YOU PROMISED, HUNT."

Hunter Phelps stifled a groan, wishing he'd been just a bit later getting home from his current stakeout. "That was before I spent half the week falling asleep in my car, Lance."

"Who are you spying on now?" His buddy Lance straightened, shut the refrigerator and turned back to him.

"Another cheat." Hunter leaned against the kitchen counter and folded his arms on his chest. "Guy with four kids and no brain whose 'late nights at work' are late nights at the office banging his young, blond secretary."

"Tough." Lance copied his pose at the fridge, his arms crossed over a neatly pressed blue shirt. "You promised me a week ago we'd hit this party. Ramona is hot, and I told her I'd be there."

"You can go without me." He knew that

wouldn't work. Not if he'd promised his friend, which he vaguely remembered doing.

Lance shook his head. "Go change. We've got to be there in half an hour."

Hunter looked at the clock. It was already well after eight on Friday night. "Why half an hour?"

"The party started at six, but I thought I was working later today, so I told her it would be closer to nine when I got there."

He shook his head at his friend. "You mean we could have gone earlier and got it over with?" He smiled. Lance was hopeless. He'd been this way as long as Hunter had known him, even back in boot-camp when they were eighteen.

The other man shrugged. "The later we get there, the less time you have to spend mingling. I know you hate going to these things. But her friends are pretty hot, too. Maybe you'll find one of your own for tonight."

Hunter's smile faded. "You're trying to pimp for me now?"

Lance frowned, disgust curling his mouth at the corners. "Hell, no. I just figured you've been celibate long enough."

Hunter knew a dig when he heard one. But he let it slide. His friends had been nagging him to start dating again for six months. No, longer, he realized. It had been a year since Tempest had moved to California for her promotion, and it had only been a few months before the guys had started trying to hook him up with sisters of friends or friends of sisters, or any other likely single woman who crossed into their orbits.

He pushed off the counter. "Where is this party? I can meet you there."

Lance was shaking his head before Hunter had finished speaking. "No. You can follow me, but if you don't go with me, I don't believe you'll actually show."

"What's with you, man?" He was too tired for this tonight. All he wanted to do was find something to eat and park his ass in front of the TV till he passed out, which wouldn't take long.

"You need to get laid, dude." Lance's eyes narrowed. "You haven't been any fun in months."

"I've been busy working, no time for fun." He set his hands on his hips, narrowing his own eyes and ignoring the voice in his head that reminded him his life philosophy these days of work, work, work kind of sucked.

"Nope. Shower and get dressed. We need to move."

Hunter gave in, shaking his head as he turned for the stairs to his bedroom.

"Hey, you don't have any beer, man!" Lance called up the steps after him.

"No time for grocery shopping," he answered, shutting his door behind him. He stripped off his clothes and tossed them into the hamper beside the bathroom door. He took clean jeans and a shirt from his dresser and headed into the smaller room. In ten minutes, he'd showered, dressed, and headed downstairs.

He found his friend parked on the couch watching a baseball game and drinking a beer. "I thought there weren't any of those left?"

"I found this one hiding behind some expired milk. You need supplies, man."

"Thanks." He clicked the television off. "I'm as ready as I'm getting. Let's go."

He steered his car behind Lance's pick-up truck, shaking his head. He always let his friends convince him to do this stuff, even when he didn't really want to. Probably because he hadn't relaxed otherwise in forever. Since he'd left his job as a cop with the county and opened the P.I. agency several years ago, he'd worked a lot more. The only times he'd not found an excuse to work were when his buddies had insisted he join them and actually shown up to make him do so.

He needed to do more of that.

Hell, maybe he *would* find some 'babe', as Lance would say, at this party. It was past time to get back in the saddle.

KATHARINE HAD HAD ENOUGH. Her skin tingled with need again, and her heart beat too fast. But she hadn't seen any likely candidates—even a desperate Medusa had standards.

Which meant it was time to go home and break out a couple more vibrators to appease her overactive hormones. *Dammit.*

She took another sip from her glass, smiling at Ramona from her post on the deck. Her friend danced with someone she'd greeted enthusiastically half an hour ago. She hated to interrupt, but it was time to go home.

Katharine sighed and shifted her shoulders, trying to loosen the tight muscles there. She turned her gaze over the crowd one last time, and her breath caught in her chest. *Him.*

He was gorgeous, in a rugged sort of way. His nose had been broken at least once, a dimple dented his chin, and he had the brightest blue eyes she'd ever seen, black hair dipping over one of them. His green shirt stretched taut over strong shoulders and a wide chest, then tucked into a pair of jeans that fit nicely on narrow hips.

Her heartbeat quickened in anticipation.

Then he glanced away from his conversation with a shorter man and caught her eye. A slow smile curved his mouth as his gaze slid down the front of her, making her skin heat, then back up, lingering on her mouth.

Her lips tingled hopefully.

She took a drink from the cup she held. Whatever frozen thing Ramona had given her was melting and slushy, but she still tasted the bite of alcohol as it hit her tongue.

He moved away from the couple he was with, toward her, and her temperature rose a few more degrees. His long-legged stride was confident and unhurried.

No, damn him, he made her wait, pausing

once to greet someone along the way.

She tightened her grip on the stem of the plastic cup and took a quick breath.

He finally stopped about two feet away, and she got a whiff of cologne, something musky that made her mouth water.

Her nipples tightened inside her vest.

"Hi." His low tone raised goosebumps on her arms despite the warm evening.

"Hi." She put out her right hand. "I'm Katharine Vardos."

He smiled again, a slow curve of his lips that made heat spread in her belly, from the inside out, until her panties were damp when she shifted her weight from one foot to the other.

He finally wrapped his long, strong fingers around hers. "Hunter Phelps. Nice to meet you."

Heat shot up her arm from where he held her hand, rising into her face. "Are you a friend of Ramona's?" She left her hand in his, her brain already imagining his long fingers elsewhere on her body. The mental images made her breathing quicken.

He shook his head, his thumb sliding across the back of her hand. "My buddy Lance is." His bright gaze dropped to her mouth again.

She inhaled slowly. "Are you a dancer, Hunter?" Blue eyes she could drown in, she thought when he met her gaze once more.

"Occasionally," he said, tightening his hold on her hand. "Was that an invitation?"

"Yes." *Oh, please let him say yes,* she thought.

He set his barely-touched beer bottle on the deck railing, then took her cup and set it aside, too. "Let's go."

Katharine swallowed at the look in his eyes and let him steer her to the improvised dance floor just off the deck.

The d.j. was playing something fast, but Hunter wrapped his arm around her back and drew her close. She set one hand on his shoulder and licked her lower lip when he clasped her other hand near his chest. She tried to concentrate on following his slow steps, but his denim-covered knees kept brushing her bare legs, and his fingers on her back traced a small circle, over and over, burning through her vest. She knew her panties were wetter now. Well and truly wet.

"So what do you do, Katharine?" he asked, his warm breath sliding past her ear.

"I write young adult books." Under her fingers, strong muscles flexed as he moved.

He tilted his head to one side. "Really?"

His knee slid between hers, distracting her for a second. "Mm-hm."

He bent nearer. "You smell good, Katharine." His lips grazed her ear, making her shiver.

She shut her eyes for a second. If he pressed a little closer, his wide chest would brush over her aching breasts. "One of my cousins mixes perfume oils, and she created this one for me." She slid her fingers from his shoulder to his nape, brushing the soft hair there.

He shivered and his eyes darkened when he met her gaze. "Do that again."

She held his gaze while she sifted through the short hair at his nape.

He yanked her closer, so their torsos were in full contact now, and she shut her eyes for a second when her nipples pressed tight into him. "Do you like playing with fire?"

She felt his arousal thickening along her belly, and her clit pulsed in anticipation. "Once in a while," she managed lightly, loving the soft, silky slide of his hair against her fingers, her palm.

His knee pressed higher between her thighs, and her breath caught. "Do you feel like playing tonight?" He bent closer to nuzzle her ear.

She sucked in a quick breath when his hand at the small of her back pressed her nearer to his erection. "Yes." Hell, she'd jump naked into the flames right now, her hormones were so happy.

"Did you drive?" He nipped at her earlobe, and she bit her lip to keep in her gasp.

"Yes."

"Too bad. I guess you'll have to follow me to my place then." He leaned back far enough to meet her gaze. "I was hoping to get my hands on you sooner."

Katharine slid her hand from his nape to his

cheek. "Sorry to disappoint. But it will be worth the wait." She stretched up on tiptoe to brush her lips along his, lightly. "I promise."

He didn't let her ease away, the hand at her back dropping to her ass to hold her right where she was, with his erection nudging at a spot low on her belly.

So close, she thought.

When he dragged his lips over hers, she felt the hot slide of his tongue, and she opened to let him in.

Her heart beat much too quickly, pumping blood into her swollen, achy breasts, down to where her clit pulsed inside her wet panties.

When he lifted his head this time, it took a moment for her to focus her gaze on his face. Hunger glinted in his eyes, and she slid her thumb along his wet lower lip.

"Let's go," he growled.

Katharine nodded, licking her own lip.

"Do you need to see anyone before we leave?" he asked as they left the dance area, the gravel of the parking lot crunching now under their feet.

"No." If she ever came up for air with her own dance partner, Ramona would figure Katharine had called it a night. His fingers tightened for a second at her waist. "There's me." She pointed to her car.

He steered her in that direction, his hip brushing hers with every step they took.

Each casual touch made her body ache more. And she wasn't sure all of it was due to her out-of-control PMS. More likely the opportunity to get her hands on a real live man for a change.

Hunter turned her in his arms again so his erection pressed into her belly. "My place isn't far." He held her gaze as his fingers slid up her side, over the swell of her breast until he could dip them inside her vest to stroke over her nipple. "Nice." His hard finger edged under the lace of her bra, back and forth, back and forth over the aching peak until she made a soft sound, shifting toward his touch. A little smile touched his lips, and he eased his fingers out of her vest. "I'm parked over there." He nodded toward his car. "See you soon." He drifted a teasing kiss on her lips while he rocked his hips against hers.

Katharine watched him walk away, trying to catch her breath. The back of him looked as enticing as the front, the faded jeans hugging his strong legs and tight ass. He glanced back when he got to his car, making her realize she needed to get into her own car if she wanted him. And she really, really did.

The eight-minute drive to his place seemed to take an hour. His taillights were a beacon the entire way through town, the red making her think of the heat between her thighs. When they stopped for a traffic light along the way, she dipped her left hand under the hem of her skirt.

Her panties were soaked. She bit her lip and rubbed her forefinger over her throbbing clit, much as he'd done with her nipple, rubbing back and forth, over and over, much too slowly to ease her need, even with the added friction of the lace. When the light turned green, she put her hand back on the steering wheel and blew out a shaky breath as she pressed her foot on the accelerator.

She hoped he was up for a long night, so to speak.

He pulled into the driveway of an older house, too big for just one person, she mused as she parked at the curb in front of the house. By the time she stepped out of her car, he was at the end of the driveway, waiting.

She put her hand in his outstretched one and let him lead her in silence to the front porch, lit by small carriage lamps on either side of the door. He unlocked the door and pushed it open, and she saw the glow of a light coming from the back of the entry hall, dimly illuminating a staircase on the right, a wide doorway on the left and the kitchen at the back.

Taking a deep breath, she stepped inside and heard him do the same as the door clicked shut softly.

She turned to face him, startled to find him only inches away. She hadn't heard him move once they came inside. Even in the shadowy hallway, she could read the intensity in his expression, and she relaxed a bit. That intensity was exactly what she wanted, that focus on her. At least for tonight. She lifted her hands to his shoulders, then slid them both to his nape, into his hair. His eyes shut for a second, and then his big hands pulled her against him, one tight on her ass, the other in the middle of her back. Yes.

"Do you want a drink?" he asked, his low tone raising goosebumps on her skin. "You didn't get to finish yours."

She shook her head, her tight nipples pressing into his hard chest. "No, thanks." She stretched to kiss him, lightly.

"Good." He slid his other hand down to her butt, too. "Wrap your legs around me, Katharine." He lifted her nearer.

She was suddenly glad for the stretch in her skirt as she wrapped first one leg, then the other around his narrow waist. "Oh, Gods," she breathed. Now she could feel the heat and bulge of his cock where she truly wanted it.

He nipped at her lower lip and turned to start the climb the stairs. "So wet already," he murmured, his fingers tightening on her ass as he carried her upstairs. "Just for me. I can't wait to touch you."

Katharine shut her eyes, her breath coming faster. She couldn't wait either. She slid her parted lips along his jaw, excited when his breath caught. He tasted good. A little salty, all male.

She was so busy kissing her way over his cheek to his ear she didn't notice when they reached the top of the stairs. She did notice, though, when he pressed her flat onto his bed, as the bulge in the front of his jeans pressed hard against her clit, making her hips jerk up to meet his. She realized, too, he'd turned on the light as they came into his bedroom

He groaned, and one of his hands slid down from her ass, along the sensitive skin of her thigh, dipping further, until he reached the wet lace between her legs. "Is that for me?" he said gruffly, one of his hard fingers sliding under the elastic and into wet flesh.

Katharine nipped his earlobe harder than she'd meant to when his finger slid deep, startling her. Gods, he felt good.

He lifted his head, forcing her to release his ear. "Can I make you come before I even get you naked, Katharine?"

The smoky tone of his voice made her body clench around his finger. "I was really looking forward to undressing you," she managed, tightening her inner muscles around his finger. That prompted him to press a second finger into her, stretching her before he stroked over a sensitive spot deep inside her.

"Oh Gods," she breathed, her head dropping backward.

Hunter chuckled, then withdrew his fingers, slowly. "You're right. We both need to be naked." He reached behind himself to catch her ankle, pulling it away from his back. She let her other leg fall to his side, too, trying to focus on breathing evenly as he eased backward, on not whimpering when his hips stopped pressing into hers.

He pushed to his feet, wincing, and her

gaze dropped to the front of his jeans, and her mouth watered. *All hers for tonight.*

She pushed herself up slowly, her head spinning a little with the rush of anticipation humming along her veins.

Hunter caught her hand and tugged her to her feet.

She yanked at his shirt, pulling it free of the waistband of his jeans, hearing his sharp inhalation. When she eased the shirt higher, it bared a well-defined abdomen, smooth skin pulled taut over his muscles. Her fingertips grazed his belly as she lifted his shirt.

He yanked it from her grasp, over his head, and she leaned closer to brush her lips across his chest. A fine sprinkling of crisp, dark hair tickled her lips and nose as she went, and then she found the little nipple she sought, rubbing her lips over it until he slid one hand into her hair and forced her head away from his chest. "Naked," he said darkly, reaching with his free hand for the top button on her vest.

Katharine let him unbutton her, slipping her fingers to his belt buckle and fumbling while he held her gaze. His hard fingers pushed her vest wide, and he made a strangled sound when he saw her bra. She smiled at that, reaching for the button at his waist.

He shoved the vest from her shoulders, and it caught at her elbows. He grabbed her wrists, forcing her fingers from his jeans, down to her sides so the leather fell from her arms. Then he released her hands and cupped her aching breasts against his hard palms.

She heard the soft sound escape her, and so did he, judging by the way his expression sharpened. Her fingers paused on the tab of his zipper when he pinched her tight nipples, then tugged lightly. Her body arched toward his as pleasure arced into her core.

He hummed something and bent to her collarbone, his open mouth leaving a warm, damp trail from the hollow of her throat to the slope of her breast.

Katharine sucked in a quick sip of air when his tongue slid over her nipple, over the lace of her bra. When she could focus her eyes a few seconds later, she tugged at his zipper, shoving his jeans from his waist.

They slid down his strong legs, revealing dark boxer briefs that barely contained his erection. Her fingers slid inside the soft cotton, his hard flesh searing hot.

Then his teeth scraped over her nipple, and her knees buckled.

Hunter caught her hips, keeping her upright as he nudged the lace out of his way so he could suck her nipple into his hot mouth.

She gripped his shaft tighter, trying to concentrate on just that, but the distraction of his mouth on her aching flesh made it a challenge. Against her palm, his cock pulsed, a sensation echoed deep inside her.

When he eased her backward again, pressed her flat on the bed, she drew him with her, her grip on his erection tightening. He groaned against her breast, his hips rocking into her caress. "You're not naked yet," he rasped, lifting his head. "So damn pretty." His gaze landed on her bared breast. Grimacing, he eased out of her grasp. "Shoes."

She shut her eyes, noticing how fast her breath came. Too quickly. Like her heartbeat. When she opened her eyes, Hunter was straightening, his bright gaze back on her body. He yanked at her skirt, and she shifted her hips to let him pull it off. Her shoes hit the floor with soft thuds.

He set one hand on her mound, making her breath catch. He held her gaze as he pressed lightly, and her hips arched up. He was so close to where she needed him to touch her. His blue eyes darkened as he bent nearer, tugging the lace down. Katharine heard it rip, but she didn't care, not when his fingers slid between her thighs.

"So wet." His murmur warmed her belly as he discarded her underwear and pushed her legs apart.

When his gaze dropped to see what he'd just exposed, she shut her eyes. Gods, let him touch her. Really touch her.

Someone somewhere heard her silent plea.

His hard thumbs pressed her folds open, and his tongue rasped over her clit.

Her hips arched up.

"Easy." His tongue slid along her wet flesh, up, up toward her clit again. "God, you taste good," he murmured, pressing his tongue deeper.

The pleasure coiled tighter in her belly and she tried to fight it, to make it last.

His tongue was magic. Licking, thrusting. The first little release washed over her in only a few minutes, leaving her panting and shaking.

Hunter rose over her then, satisfaction mingling with the heated desire in his eyes as he shifted her further onto the bed and wedged his knees between her own.

She found her arms heavy when she lifted them to stroke his thick erection.

"If you do that now, I'm done," he said gruffly, capturing her hands and setting them on the bed beside her head. "It's been a long time."

"For me, too," she admitted, noting the flash of pleasure in his eyes at her admission. Warmth curled into her middle and flared hotter when he lowered himself over her so his cock slid along wet folds. "Gods."

He shifted slightly so the head of his erection pressed into her. Steadily, slowly, until he was fully inside her.

Her body pulsed around him, and she sucked in a quick breath, eyes sliding shut. It wasn't going to take much to push her over the edge again.

"Katharine." He waited for her to meet his gaze before he bent to kiss her, lightly at first, then deeper, his hips still holding her pinned to the bed when she would have lifted against him.

It was torture, she mused when she could catch a thought out of the whirl in her head. The loveliest, most terrible torture, his big body stretching her, surrounding her, and his mouth teasing hers, stoking the need deep inside her.

When he finally eased his hips backward, withdrawing his lovely erection before thrusting deeper, she cried out into his kiss, pleasure erupting in her middle, white hot.

But he continued his slow strokes, pushing her higher. Beside her head, his arms shook with restraint, and she slid her hands up his back, along his damp skin. "Let go," she whispered along his lips.

Hunter groaned into their kiss when she bent her knees at his sides, digging her heels into the bed so she could better meet his thrusts. "We have all night."

"Yes, we do." She smiled at him, her heart pounding hard against his chest, his doing the same, both in the same crazy, too-quick rhythm. Staring into his bright eyes, she squeezed her inner muscles around him. The movement almost pushed her over.

It made him growl, dipping to catch her mouth roughly, his strokes into her willing body becoming harder, faster.

When she tumbled off the edge this time, he was with her.


THEY LAY, TREMBLING, ON THE rumpled bed for a long time, both trying to catch their breath, hearts only gradually slowing their rapid beating.

Hunter eventually realized he was crushing her into the mattress and rolled to his side, keeping her in his arms, his breathing still ragged. The soft woman against him was slick with sweat, his and hers, and her body occasionally tightened around him. He smiled into the side of her face. Hell of a way to end a drought.

Katharine took a long, slow breath, her fingers brushing his nape almost reflexively.

The touch sent warmth curling along his veins. His body perked up a little again, startling him. He was too damn old to be raring to go so fast. Maybe after his self-imposed celibacy, his body figured it had a lot of time to make up for.

Her breath slid out, leaving more heated tingles at the side of his neck.

"Are you okay?" He bent to kiss the corner of her mouth, then slid his lips along hers, just because he wanted to.

"Mm." She nestled closer, and he felt the swell of her breast pressing into his chest.

His cock started to thicken once more.

She made a startled sound and opened her eyes, tipping her head back to look fully at him.

He grinned at her. "You keep doing that and you'll be flat on your back again very soon."

Katharine smiled slowly, her grey eyes crinkling at the corners. "What if I want to be on top this time?"

Hunter rolled onto his back, bringing her with him, so now her knees rested beside his hips. "Have it your way."

She eased upright, the movement pressing her hips down harder over his, and braced herself with her hands on his chest. "Mm." Her gaze slid from his face to his torso, and her smile faded slowly as her eyes darkened. "If you insist," she murmured, bending to lick over one of his nipples.

His eyes slammed shut as his pulse kicked back into overdrive.

Helluva way to end a drought, he managed to think later, just before his release exploded.

They made love several more times, teasing and talking about nothing in particular in between, before they both passed out from sheer exhaustion, bodies still joined, legs and arms entwined.

Hunter had visions of more of the same in mind when he woke in the morning. He was disappointed to find his arms empty. Reaching across the bed, he found nothing but empty sheets, and as he pushed upright, he opened his eyes.

The only clothes strewn on the floor were his own.

He scowled. After all that, he hadn't imagined she might be gone when he woke.

Sighing, he shoved his hair back from his face and swung his legs over the side of the bed.

Well, not quite *all* of the clothes on the floor were his.

Grinning, he bent to pick up the scrap of delicate black lace. The panties he'd ripped in his haste to get them off of her. He lifted them and inhaled. The scent of her clung to them.

He squared his shoulders. Well, he'd have to find her to offer a replacement pair. And maybe another night like last night. Maybe more. Dinner. Movies. More of the easy conversation they'd shared in the wee hours when they were sated and relaxed.

He smiled as he set the torn panties on his night stand and headed for the shower.

It occurred to him as he showered that all he had to work with was her name.

He scrubbed one soapy hand at his back. He was a former detective, now a P.I. If he couldn't find her with just her name, someone should take away his license.

He'd settled at the kitchen table with his laptop and some breakfast half an hour later, intending to do a quick search for the sexy Katharine, when the phone rang. He sighed and grabbed it. Probably Lance calling to find out what happened to him last night. "Yeah?"

"Hey, boss man." His receptionist Mary Ann Renton. "I have some news for you."

"You know it's Saturday morning, right?"

She laughed. "Yeah. And so does Mrs. Baird. I told her weekends were double-time, and she didn't care."

Hunter sat back in his chair, pinching the

bridge of his nose and shutting his eyes. "What is wrong with Mrs. Baird today?"

"Seems the hubs told her he was heading to the office for a while, then fishing with 'the guys' after lunch. She of course thinks he's going to the office or somewhere to see the secretary and wants you to find out for sure."

"Damn." So much for tracking down Katharine this morning. "All right. I'll head to his office now. If she calls again, you should tell her she really doesn't need anything more in the way of evidence to get everything she wants in the divorce." He shut the laptop and set the paper plate holding his toast on top of it. He could eat in the car.

He'd have to search for Katharine later.

# CHAPTER TWO

Katharine curled into a ball in the corner of her sofa, a pillow and a heating pad stuffed against her cramping belly. Damn Athena. After thousands of years, one would think She might take pity on the original Medusa's descendants and end the freaking curse.

Or not. Miserable bitch.

She groaned into her knees when the next wave hit. She couldn't crawl into bed yet. She wanted to wait until after lunchtime when she could take another pain pill which would knock her out for a while.

Which left only one option.

She breathed through the rest of the cramp, then slowly got to her feet, hunched over like an old woman. She turned off the heating pad and headed back to her bedroom, carefully. A super-hot shower and a couple orgasms would make the cramps ease a little bit. After that, she should be able to make it till lunchtime.

As she stripped, she thought of Hunter. Probably one of those Hunter-induced orgasms from two nights ago would put an end to her cramps for a while.

"I hate You, Athena," she muttered as she stepped under the scalding shower, a vibrator in her hand.

By the time she got out, she felt a bit better, but it wouldn't last. It never did.

Which was why her cousin Phila had arranged for painkillers. They worked like magic, too. But when they knocked out her cramps, they also knocked her out cold for several hours. Which meant she depended solely on the alarm system and the protective warding she had set around her house to protect her from the possibility of someone from the Tassos family finding and killing her while she was defenseless.

She dressed slowly, frowning at her reflection in the mirror. She'd fastened her hair into a knot on the back of her head before her period had started, to contain the snakes, but one had escaped the knot and moved around at the back of her head. She glared at it, taking out the clip and rearranging her hair into a tighter knot, including the straggler. No more writhing.

A couple of Medusas ago, the cousin who'd had the curse then used to cut her hair mostly *off* every month when her period was approaching to keep the snakes at bay. Katharine was a little more vain about her hair, however–more like the original Medusa, maybe? She really needed to French-braid it, though, to keep it better contained for the three-day duration of her period and the curse's snakes.

A twinge low in her belly made her wince.

Too soon, dammit.

‘

HUNTER GROWLED AS HE SNAPPED more pictures of the cheating Mr. Baird Sunday afternoon. How many times could he possibly bang his secretary on the desk? At least get a motel room with a bed, for Christ's sake. Maybe try the sofa, or something besides the missionary position.

He sighed and sat back in his seat, glancing at his closed laptop. He'd considered several times opening it to do a quick search for Katharine, but when he left here, he had to go snoop around at someone else's place. Mary Ann had called him back a while ago about a new insurance job. Some idiot milking his workman's comp and the insurance company had had enough, especially when someone at his workplace mentioned seeing him bowling with his kids. With his 'injured' shoulder. *Dumb ass.*

No, Hunter decided. The Katharine hunt would be his reward tonight after he finally got done working.

He frowned. Working on a Sunday. No wonder Lance was so annoyed. Instead of locating the hot woman he'd spent Friday night with, he'd worked all weekend

Obviously, he wasn't charging enough for weekend work if he had all these people willing to pay the weekend rate.

Sighing, he lifted the digital camera again and snapped a few more shots. "Geez, Baird.

Use your imagination already," he muttered.

Evening couldn't come fast enough.

HUNTER HAD TO DO MORE DIGGING to find Katharine than he'd guessed would be necessary. After he found her whole name–Rigas-Vardos–it still took him several hours and finally a phone call to a friend at the DOT to get her mailing and street addresses. By then it was too late to show up at her door unannounced, or even to call. So in the morning, he checked in at the office to see what Mary Ann had on tap for him. Luckily, he had a couple hours free before he had to meet with a new client. Time to see Katharine.

He debated getting a gift certificate for a lingerie store to take along, to replace the underwear he'd destroyed, then decided that might be a little much, considering he was still virtually a stranger.

Instead, he picked up a fistful of daisies at a nearby florist and drove across town to the address his buddy had given him last night. A neat little one-story white house with an attached garage. Two narrow flowerbeds flanked the two steps to the front door.

And a tall guy in black shoved open a window at the side of the house as Hunter eased his car along the street.

Heart pounding faster, he didn't stop in front of her house, but parked down the street several houses–the way the homes were spaced on her street, it was far enough the guy wouldn't hear him and think he was coming to Katharine's. He left the daisies on the seat and sprinted back to her house, through her neighbors' yards. He peered around the corner of her house. The side window was open, and there was no sign of the man. *He was inside.*

Hunter's pulse quickened. No time to call the cops. He stepped up to the front door, noting the alarm company sticker in the front window. He didn't want to do damage to her door, though, or alert the intruder to his entry, so he pulled a set of picks from his pocket, jiggling one carefully in the lock until the latch gave. Then he stepped inside, holding his breath and hoping the alarm would take a few seconds before it went off.

There was silence through the little house. Maybe she hadn't set the alarm. He shut the door noiselessly, then heard a low voice.

Good thing he hadn't given up carrying. He whipped his gun out as he crept through the living room, past the empty kitchen and an office. He stopped when he got to the open door of the bedroom and leveled his gun on the dark man standing beside her bed with a wicked, slightly curved blade in his hand. In the open collar of his shirt, a gold pendant gleamed, something too small for Hunter to identify. A few feet from the other man, the curtain fluttered in the breeze coming through the open window.

"Drop it," he said evenly, hoping Katharine stayed right where she was, lumped beneath her blankets.

The guy jumped, startled, clearly so absorbed in his own plans that he hadn't paid any attention to the rest of the house. Good thing for Hunter, and for Katharine. Bad for the intruder.

From the corner of his eyes, Hunter saw movement on the pillow, but he couldn't take his attention from the intruder. He just hoped she remained still long enough for him to deal with this asshole.

"Do you truly want to stop me?" the other man said in heavily accented English. "From killing this monster?"

"No monsters here, buddy. Drop the knife. Now." He jerked his gun toward the rocking chair in front of the closet where the weapon wouldn't be easily reachable again. More movement on the pillow. In his peripheral vision, it looked like a couple of snakes. *That* couldn't be. He kept his gaze on the other man. "Do it."

The man's dark eyes narrowed, mouth tightening, his expression furious. "It is my duty to kill the Medusa."

Hunter thumbed off the safety on his gun. "If you don't drop your weapon now, I'm going to put a very large hole in you. One you will not recover from."

The dark guy muttered something Hunter couldn't understand, something foreign, and, after a few more seconds, tossed the blade away, but not where Hunter had indicated.

Instead, he threw it so it stuck in the plaster wall beside the mirror attached to her dresser. When Hunter glanced away from him to be certain the dagger hadn't done any damage to Katharine, the intruder lunged out the open window.

"Fuck." He strode to the window in time to see the back of the other guy vanishing around the neighbor's porch a few dozen yards away. He pulled his head back inside and froze.

Those *were* snakes on the pillow, several of them.

"Katharine," he said quietly.

"You should go, Hunter." Her voice was choked, hushed.

His gaze stuck on the snakes. They were in her hair. "Honey, there are snakes–"

"I know. You should go." She sucked in a harsh breath, and the lump of her under the blankets contracted.

His frown deepened. That could not be. The snakes were not just in her hair, they were her hair. His eyes widened, and his jaw dropped. "Honey, I think you'd better tell me." His racing mind called up the other man's words– "the Medusa."

But those old myths weren't real.

One of the dark snakes lifted its head from the pillow in his direction and hissed at him.

He blinked in surprise. "Katharine," he began, putting the safety back on his gun and then closing and locking the window with what looked like an undamaged latch. "Was he telling the truth? Are you the Medusa?" He couldn't believe he was even saying the words. It was insane. *Impossible.*

She was silent beneath the blankets, but the snakes still slithered on the pillow. He realized they could only go so far–just about the length of her hair. His jaw wanted to drop again, but he managed not to allow it.

"Are you all right? He didn't have time to hurt you, did he?" He moved closer, sat on the edge of the bed.

"No, he didn't," she whispered.

He frowned, watching her body curl tighter in on itself. "Are you sick?"

A humorless laugh huffed past her lips. "I guess you could say that." Another quick gasp.

He realized she was in pain. Serious pain. "How can I help you?"

"Please go."

"Not happening. This guy got in here once, and if I had worse timing, you'd have been dead when I got here. Tell me how I can help you. Do you have painkillers?"

Katharine sighed. "Yes, but I can't take one now. I did earlier, or I'd have heard the Harvester coming in and could've dealt with him myself."

Hunter's gaze slid to the snakes on her pillow, his mind working busily. If his very rusty mythology was correct, the Medusa turned people to stone with her gaze. He wasn't stone, and her gaze had been all over him Friday night. "You can explain the details later when you're feeling better. But right now you're going to have to let me help you."

A soft sound, like a stifled moan of pain came from under the blankets. "Are you always so obnoxious?" she asked after a moment.

He grinned at the blankets. "Only when you're being difficult. You weren't this difficult Friday night."

A short laugh passed her lips, quickly followed by another of those quiet moans.

His smile faded, and he stretched out one hand to touch her foot through the blankets. "All right. Enough arguing about it. Tell me. How can I help you?"

"I need to get into the shower for a while."

He waited.

"You could get some lunch together. A cup of soup or a couple scrambled eggs or something light. Nothing much."

He tried to follow her train of thought and failed. "How are you going to get yourself to the shower? You can't even stretch out in bed." And suddenly, he realized why she was curled into a ball. Cramps.

They must be bad to require pain pills.

"I can make it to the shower," she said, her tone grim. "Please go. It isn't safe for you to see me like this."

He sighed. "Fine. I'll find you some lunch, but I'm not leaving." Not without her anyway, but he thought he might wait until after she'd had her shower to tell her. He pushed to his feet and stood looking at her for another moment before he left the bedroom. As he moved toward her kitchen, he heard the rustling of blankets as she got up. Slowly.

Frowning, he searched her refrigerator for something quick to make. Not many options. He opened the tall cupboard beside the fridge. A pantry. He took out a can of chicken noodle soup and dumped it into a bowl, then decided to wait and put it in the microwave when she turned off the shower so it would be nice and hot.

While he waited, he paced from the kitchen into the living room, examining her window locks. Sturdy enough, but apparently the guy who'd come calling with the knife had something to unlatch them. And her alarm hadn't been turned on, or it would have started wailing after he'd opened the front door. Hell, if it were on, it should have gone off after the window was opened, because all of the windows he'd checked were wired into the alarm.

That thought made him stride to the front door and the alarm panel inside it. Nothing. The screen was blank.

He tested the light switch beside the door. The light overhead came on. So the bastard knew the alarm was on its own line and had only cut that one.

Hunter turned the light switch off and retraced his steps to her bedroom. He heard the shower and hoped she was all right. He'd bet anything she couldn't even stand up straight when she'd gotten out of bed.

He let out a slow breath and leaned against the doorjamb. When he'd thought all weekend about seeing her again, he'd never imagined anything like this.

Still, he couldn't deny the snakes. He'd seen them.

She'd called the other man a Harvester. There was sure to be a story there. He wondered if she'd be up to telling him some of it after her shower, then wondered how the debilitating cramps fit in with the Medusa thing.

Hunter was sure none of the mythologies he'd read in school mentioned anything like that. Or the Harvester. He figured it'd be a challenge finding anything on regular search engines.

The water shut off in the bathroom, and he went back to the kitchen and put her soup in the microwave. By the time he heard her incredibly slow footsteps in the short hall, the steaming bowl sat on the kitchen table.

"Hunter?"

"Right here."

She sighed. "I was afraid of that."

He grinned. She didn't know him very well. Yet.

"You'll have to close your eyes. Or go sit in the living room if you won't leave."

"I'm not leaving. And maybe you should shut *your* eyes and let me feed you."

She was silent for a moment. "I'd rather

you went in the living room."

He figured he could give her that one, since he had other plans for her after her lunch, and he was positive she wouldn't like them. Keeping his gaze averted from the hallway, he crossed to the living room and sat on the sofa facing the front windows.

Katharine moved into the kitchen, still walking slowly. When he heard a chair scrape across the floor, he glanced into the other room instinctively. She'd chosen a chair facing away from him. She'd also done something with her hair, some kind of complicated braid that made it impossible for the snakes to escape. He forced his gaze away from her.

There was silence from the kitchen for so long he wondered what she was doing. Finally, he heard the spoon clink against the side of the bowl.

He relaxed a little. "Guess you're wondering what I'm doing here," he said, trying to keep his tone conversational.

"Kind of."

He shut his eyes and smacked the heel of his hand on his forehead. "Shit. I have flowers in the car for you."

She huffed out a laugh. "You're kidding."

Hunter smiled. "No. I brought daisies. They'll have to wait now."

"You brought me flowers and walked into hell." Another laugh escaped her, though this one didn't sound as if she were truly amused.

"I brought you flowers and got to save your

life," he corrected her. He leaned forward until he could rest his elbows on his knees. "I didn't expect that, but it's a nice bonus."

"I'm afraid I'm not up for another night like Friday right now." She scraped the spoon against the side of the bowl. "A tad under the weather today."

Stung, he considered her words. "That wasn't why I tracked you down," he said after a few moments of silence broken only by her spoon clinking on the glass bowl. "I was hoping to talk you into dinner some night. Maybe some more dancing." *Had no idea I'd learn the Medusa was real.*

Katharine was silent for a long moment. "I'm sorry. I don't mean to be a bitch. I was already cranky, and now the Harvester's put a real crimp in my day. Hell, in my life." She dropped the spoon into the bowl. "Thank you for saving my life, Hunter."

"You're welcome."

"You wouldn't really have shot him, would you?"

He smiled grimly. "You bet I would."

"What exactly is it you do? I don't think we got around to that Friday night." She sounded a little worried.

"P.I. Used to be a cop." He watched her shoulders sag a bit, and he wondered if it was from relief or resignation.

"Bet you never ran into this sort of thing before, huh?" She hunched forward even more, and he realized her other arm was across her middle.

The shower hadn't provided very long-lasting relief. "You need one of those pain pills. Where are they?"

"Bathroom medicine chest. But don't bother." She sat straighter in her seat. "I can't take one now. Not with the Harvester in town. The heating pad will have to do."

Hunter pushed to his feet. "You can't stay here. He cut the power to your alarm system."

She started to turn toward him, then froze halfway, as if recalling the danger. "Bastard," she muttered after a few seconds, turning to face into the kitchen again. "I'll have to call the alarm company."

"You can call them, but you can't stay here." He set his hands on his hips. "He knows where you are, you have to get out."

She shook her head. "This is my home."

"And it's unsafe. I may not understand all the details yet, but I know you can't stay here. He said it was his duty to kill you, Katharine."

Her shoulders hunched. "I need to call my cousin."

He blew out a hard breath. "You're coming with me."

"I can't go with you." Her tone was a mix of astonishment and annoyance. "Don't you know anything about Greek mythology?"

"Yes, but not everything I need to know. Not yet." He studied her back, tight with tension, probably from the pain she was feeling and now her determination to fight him. "I'm sure we can find something to hide your eyes for the trip over to my place. Then you can take a pain pill and rest safely for a few hours, and we'll figure something out."

Katharine shoved to her feet, her chair screeching across the tile floor. "I am not going with you to your place." For a second, she appeared to want to turn around, but she didn't, gripping the edge of the table instead.

"You have a martyr complex?" He narrowed his gaze on the back of her neck.

She sighed. "I don't really want it on my conscience when you turn to stone. Plus I imagine a statue that size would be extremely difficult for me to get rid of."

He laughed, shaking his head. "Honey, you're not going to turn me to stone. Not even accidentally. Look at you."

She bowed her head, and he realized she was rubbing her belly surreptitiously.

"Sit down," he said gently. "What things can you absolutely not leave behind?"

"Don't."

He waited. He could wait as long as it took.

"I'll pack what I need."

Hunter sighed. "Katharine, don't be difficult."

"I said I'll do it." She sounded now as if she were gritting her teeth together.

He knew when to yield. She *had* agreed to go with him. Kind of. "Fine. I'll clean up out here after you go back to your room." He didn't want her too pissed off, not so she'd change her mind and insist on staying here. He could stay with her, but it'd be easier to protect her at his place now–the Harvester couldn't find her there. He returned to the sofa and waited, listening to her slow footsteps on the wooden floor toward her bedroom. Then he went to the kitchen, gathering the half bowl of soup she'd abandoned and moving to the sink with it.

There was a low rumble from the other room, and he realized she'd slid open her closet door. "Good girl," he murmured, rinsing the spoon and bowl off.

He paced from the kitchen into the living room and back, keeping an eye outside to make sure their friend hadn't returned. If the guy was smart, and he probably was, he'd wait until at least tonight before making attempt to finish the job.

Hunter thought about the alarm. This would be impossible to fully explain, but he had a buddy who worked on security systems. He pulled his cell out of his pocket and searched the directory for the number. "Hey, Warren, Hunter."

"Hey, man, how're you doing?"

"I'm good. I need a favor."

"Sure, what's up?"

He glanced toward the hallway, where he could hear dresser drawers opening and closing, slowly. "A friend had a problem at her place earlier. Someone cut the power line for her alarm system, then broke into the house.

How soon can you have someone repair it?"

"I can be there in an hour or so. I'm in the office today doing paperwork while the guys are out on a couple of job sites. Where are you?"

"I'm with her right now, but I'm taking her out of here in about ten minutes." He rattled off her address. "I can meet you back here to get you started." He just had to call Mary Ann and have her reschedule the meet with the new client.

"No problem. Sounds like the power source is an issue."

"Yeah. The system doesn't seem to have any back-up." Hunter didn't hear anything coming from the bedroom, and he frowned, moving toward the hallway, and covered the mouthpiece. "Katharine?"

"I'm fine," she said, sounding anything but.

He put the phone back to his mouth. "I've got to go, Warren. I'll see you in about an hour." He ended the call and walked along the short hall, stopping shy of her bedroom door and leaning against the wall, arms folded on his chest. "What's wrong, honey?"

"I've got to get some things out of the office, too." Pain edged her voice.

"Why don't you tell me what you need, and I can get that stuff for you?" He was sure she'd refuse, so when she sighed, his eyebrows shot up.

"I need the laptop. The case for it is on the floor next to the desk. There's a small file box beside the computer I'll need as well."

He went into the smaller bedroom, spotting the laptop and case right away. "What else?" He slid the computer and cord into the carryall beside a battery pack in a charger, then the file box, too.

"Um, my cell phone and charger." She inhaled unsteadily.

Hunter shot a worried glance at the wall. She needed the damn pain pill. He stuffed her phone into the bag, too. "And?"

"There's a small metal lock box in the bottom right drawer in the desk."

He slid the drawer open and found the box. It wouldn't fit in her laptop bag.

"That should do it."

He glanced around the office. There were some art prints hanging on the walls, a couple dictionaries on the desk, office supplies, paper, pens, tape. Nothing personal. He shot a quick look at the box in his hand. It must be deliberate, in case she had to get out in a hurry— grab this stuff and go.

He scowled. That was no way to live. Hunted like an animal. He almost wished he'd shot the Harvester earlier.

"Are you sure that's it?" He turned to the door with the things he carried.

"Mm-hm."

He frowned, moving to the living room with her necessities to drop them on the couch before he headed back toward the bedroom. "I'm coming in, Katharine."

He heard a soft sound, and, when he rounded the doorway, found she'd hidden her face in a pillow in her lap.

"What do you need out of the bathroom?" He scanned the open carry-on she had lying across the bottom of her bed. Not nearly enough clothing in there.

"I'll get the bathroom stuff. But I need another bag." Despite being muffled in the pillow, he still heard the edge in her voice, indicating the level of pain she was feeling had increased.

He turned to the open closet and found a small stack of tote bags on the shelf above the hanger rod. He pulled one out and unfolded it. Sizable. It should do. "Okay." He carried it into the bathroom and set it on the vanity, returning to the bedroom. "Go ahead." He walked to the opposite side of the bed and waited.

It took her a moment to get up, and his mouth tightened with annoyance. And worry. The woman was too damned stubborn.

Muffled sounds from the bathroom reached his ears, and he turned around, eyeing her bag. He hesitated a second before he dug in. She'd only packed for a day or two at the most. Until this Harvester was out of commission in some way, she couldn't come back here. He didn't feel guilty about pulling more jeans from her closet and dropping them into the suitcase, then yanking open a dresser drawer to find underwear and adding more of that, too. He tried hard not to look to closely at the tiny silky garments he'd grabbed before he tossed them into the carry-on.

"What are you doing in there?" she asked.

He smiled. "Helping you pack."

"I packed what I need."

"Uh-huh." He tugged another drawer open and found shirts. He added more of them to the bag, too. The next drawer he opened, though...*whoa.*

Vibrators. All shapes and sizes, different colors and textures.

He shot a wide-eyed glance at the wall dividing the rooms, then dropped his gaze back to the drawer. Mixed in the with toys were other things, like edible lotions and a set of nipple clamps.

Hunter's temperature rise a few degrees just imagining her using any of these things.

Before his body went too wild, he shut the drawer and tried to concentrate on the task at hand–getting Katharine safely out of here. "Do you have any scarves?"

A soft thud reached his ears from the next room, and he wondered if she'd banged her head against the wall in frustration. "Why?"

"To cover your eyes." While he waited, he tugged the Harvester's blade out of the wall for later inspection.

She was silent again for a long, long time. He imagined she wanted to tell him to go to hell. "There might be a couple in the bottom left drawer," she said finally.

He opened the drawer she'd suggested and

found a jumble of things. Hair accessories. Necklaces. Belts. Finally, tangled in the back with a necklace of tiny, rough gemstones, he found a black silk scarf. Holding it up, he frowned, pretty sure it wasn't heavy enough to keep her from seeing through.

It would have to do, as it was the only one he found. He shut the drawer and turned around to study the room. As with the office, nothing personal in the way of decorations. No family pictures or framed certificates. Generic art prints in cheap frames, mostly beach scenes. She apparently didn't want any trace of *her* to be found in case she had to get out fast.

"I'm finished," she said, her tone more subdued.

He started to turn around and stopped when he spied the hooded sweatshirt on the back of the rocking chair. Perfect. He grabbed it. "Okay. Close your eyes."

When he went into the smaller room, she sat on the closed toilet, eyes shut, mouth bracketed with tense lines that told him her pain level really had ratcheted up. "I've got a hoodie for you, so no one will know you're blindfolded under it." He helped her into it, then folded the scarf and wrapped it around her head. "Can you stand on your own?" He caught her hand.

She pushed slowly to her feet, and he tightened his grip on her when she swayed a little, not quite upright.

"I think we're okay for now, this Harvester

isn't going to come right back," he said. "I'm going to put you in the living room and pull my car in the driveway so we can load your stuff and you into it even faster, and without any of the neighbors seeing anything they shouldn't, okay?"

Katharine nodded once, and the lines around her mouth tightened as she inhaled.

"Did you pack the pain pills?"

"In the tote."

He picked up the bag from the vanity and slowly led her out of the bathroom, letting her sit on the foot of the bed for a minute while he zipped up her suitcase, then they made their way to the living room. "Where are your keys?"

"In my purse. Hanging behind the front door." She bent forward on the sofa, her head almost on her knees.

Hunter strode to the coat rack behind the door and grabbed her purse, adding it to the small stack of bags on the chair. "I'll be right back, Katharine. Don't go anywhere, all right?"

"Can't," she whispered.

His pulse beat harder in his ears. Not good. Not good at all. He let himself out of the house, making sure to leave the door unlocked behind him, then sprinted to his car. He backed it along the empty street until he could whip into her driveway. He didn't even care now if the neighbors thought it was odd enough to warrant being nosy.

When he stepped back inside, she was right

where he'd left her. "Will you take the pill now?"

"No. Not till we get there."

He glared at the top of her head. "Why not?"

"Just in case."

After what he'd walked in on earlier, he guessed he couldn't argue, but he didn't like it. "All right." He heard the grudging tone in his reply, sure she had, too. "Let's get all of this in one go, okay, honey?" He eased her to her feet and slid her purse strap onto her shoulder, then picked up her other things himself, hooking the tote bag and laptop satchel over the carry-on's handle. That left the box, which he tucked under his arm. "We'll go slow."

They did, as it took some effort just for her to cross the floor. It might've been faster for him to carry her things out, then come back for her, but they'd already lingered longer than he liked. He wanted to get her out. Now.

Hunter finally got her settled in the passenger seat, her things in the back, and slid into his own seat, starting the car again. "Ready?"

"If I have to be." A ghost of a smile touched her mouth. Even her lips were pale now, he realized. Her cheeks were paler than white at this point, and her lips were bloodless.

"Are you going to be sick?"

She shook her head. "No. I just need to lie down and curl up around the heating pad. I should've filled the hot water bottle."

He stifled a curse. "Can you make it across town?"

"I'll make it." The determination in her voice made him smile grimly.

He backed out of the driveway and put the car in drive. He didn't want to go too fast and attract unwanted attention. In case the Harvester was lurking around. But he wanted to get the hell out of there. He kept an eye on the mirrors, watching all the way to the other side of town, with several winding detours, to make sure no one was following them. When he pulled into his garage and the door shut behind them, he breathed a sigh of relief. "Stay put. I'll come around and get you," he said quietly, touching her knee lightly.

She'd stayed silent for the entire drive, her jaw clenched, alternately massaging her belly and bracing one forearm across it, trying to alleviate the pain from her cramps. She didn't answer him now, concentrating on breathing evenly through the latest rush of cramping.

She thought it was probably for the best he had blindfolded her. Otherwise, she'd have glared him to dust by now. Okay, maybe not dust, but certainly stone. She'd been trying to concentrate on her aggravation for the duration of the drive, rather than on the pain radiating from her core, but it hadn't worked.

She tensed now, stiffening against the cramps assaulting her. Her door opened a moment later, and one of Hunter's hands touched her shoulder.

"Careful." His hand shifted to the top of her head, making sure she didn't crack it on the car as she eased out of her seat.

When he scooped her into his arms, she reached blindly to hold on. She found his shoulder with one hand, her other slipping around the back of his neck.

"Easy." His warm breath brushed along the side of her face. "I've got you."

She sighed, biting her tongue.

Hunter's stride was easy, unhurried, and, after a minute, she realized they were climbing stairs. On the way to his bedroom. Despite the pain in her gut and her irritation over his I-know-best attitude, heat bloomed in her cheeks as she recalled Friday night.

He bent, easing her onto the side of the bed. "Are you ready for your pain pill now?" One of his hands brushed her jaw, which was still clenched, she realized.

She shook her head. "I need to make a pit stop first."

He picked her up again, startling her.

"I can walk," she ground out.

"I know. But it's easier this way." He was smiling, she heard it in his tone. He set her on her feet. "I'll wait outside the door."

Katharine released a slow breath, forcing herself to relax her jaw, and, after the door clicked shut, shoved the scarf off her eyes.

He'd even set her tote bag on the floor inside the door.

Tears stung her eyes at that unexpected kindness.

She was overreacting, she knew. Partly due to her overloaded hormones. Partly because she was angry she'd been unable to defend herself against the Harvester since she'd believed herself safe enough in her house to take the damned painkiller that morning, which knocked her out for hours.

She'd been the Medusa for more than five years now, and with her alarm system in place and no sign of trouble, she'd felt confident there after all this time...

She shut her eyes for a second, her fingers curling into fists at her sides.

None of this was Hunter's fault. All he'd done was save her life, not sic the Harvester on her when she was vulnerable.

That she was ultimately responsible for her near-death experience made her angrier. At herself. He just happened to be within firing range.

"Katharine? You okay?"

"Fine," she said shortly. "I'm fine." She took a long, deep breath, then released it.

When she'd finished washing her hands, she fumbled the blindfold back down over her eyes and reached for the doorknob, groping empty air.

"Coming in," he said, and she dropped her hand back to her side. "Okay?"

"Yes." His hard fingers slid over hers. "Thank you, Hunter."

He pulled her along with him, thirteen paces to the bed.

"For saving my life earlier."

"Not a problem." He made her sit, then loosened her shoelaces. "Nice blade," he said mildly, easing her boot from her foot.

She swallowed. "If I hadn't taken the pill earlier, I could've used it. Or turned him to stone, I guess."

"Well, you won't need the dagger here. I have a state-of-the-art security system, and nobody followed us from your place, so you're safe here." He took her other boot off. "You want to get out of the jeans and back into a nightshirt? Something more comfortable for sleeping?"

Katharine hesitated, biting her lip. It wasn't like he hadn't seen her naked already. Up close and personal. "Yes," she whispered.

"Okay. I'll go grab the rest of your stuff from the garage. Don't go anywhere."

"Ha, ha." Still, she smiled a little, listening to his footsteps on the stairs, the sound fading as he walked away from the entry hall. The room smelled like Hunter, she mused as she sat there on the edge of his bed. The same musky, spicy scent that had set her body humming Friday night.

She almost wished it were Friday night again. She'd much rather be in the middle of some seriously hot sex with Hunter than suffering through her cursed period.

On the other hand, she only had to suffer

through one more day or so of this, and then it would be over for the next month.

Hunter's footsteps sounded in the hallway downstairs, then on the steps, nearer. Her heart beat faster.

*Stupid*, she thought.

"Let me dig that out for you."

She winced, thinking of him rummaging through her clothing. She hadn't packed very neatly. On the other hand, he'd added things to her suitcase, which meant he'd already seen everything there.

"All right." His fingers caught the hem of her shirt and tugged.

Katharine hesitated, then raised her arms and let him pull the tee off over her head. She shivered in the cooler air. And again, when his fingers brushed her back as he unhooked her bra.

He didn't linger over her bare breasts, both relieving and disappointing her, but instead eased her nightshirt over her head, helped her get her arms into the sleeves, then pulled her to her feet so he could unfasten her jeans and tug them off, too.

Heat climbed her cheeks, competing with the jagged pain in her belly.

"All right. I'm going to get you some water, and you're going to take one of these pills." He brushed his lips over her forehead above the scarf, then pushed her back onto the edge of the mattress.

She rubbed the heel of one hand over her

belly, trying to concentrate on that rather than the nice things this sexy near-stranger was doing for her.

Then he was back, pressing a pill into her hand. She took it, swallowed it with a few gulps of water.

"Do you want the heating pad?"

"Thank you, that'd be great." She let him lift her into a different spot on the bed. It was easier than arguing with him. She could argue later, when she felt better. The heating pad settled over her belly as she lay down, and she sucked in a quick breath. Stretching out did nothing to alleviate her cramps, so she rolled onto her side, holding onto the heating pad.

She heard the click of the controls. "Would you turn it to high, please?" If she was going to let him help, she may as well tell him what worked best.

Another click, then the blankets came up over her, all the way to her chin. "Can I do anything else for you?"

She shook her head on the pillow. "It won't take long for the pill to kick in, and I'll be good for a few hours." Except she kept thinking about what had happened earlier, after she'd taken her last pill.

The mattress sank under his weight near her knees, and his fingers brushed her jaw. "Good. I hate that you're in so much pain."

Katharine smiled. "Good thing you're not a woman."

He chuckled. "I guess. I won't say I haven't

suffered pain, but not on a regular basis. And something tells me this isn't exactly a normal level of pain."

She hummed her agreement, feeling the warmth from the heating pad seep into her belly.

"I'm going to want to hear all about this later." He stroked her cheek this time.

She opened her mouth to tell him she wasn't sure he could deal with it, then realized he was already dealing with it, and pretty well, considering he'd witnessed the snakes on her head and still scared off the Harvester bent on killing her. "Okay." The painkiller was beginning to do its thing, making her thought process take longer than normal, she mused.

Hunter's fingers kept stroking her face, and she nestled deeper under the covers, a slow breath passing her lips. She didn't feel nearly as bad now. Pretty soon, she'd be passed out from the pill she'd taken.

She felt safe, safer than she had when she'd wakened to hear Hunter confronting the Harvester in her bedroom.

Her pain eased slowly, and consciousness faded.

"Sleep well," Hunter whispered, brushing a kiss on her cheek.

She smiled, she thought, but couldn't summon a reply. Instead, her sleepy brain called up images of him from Friday night, lovely, sexy images of the two of them in this very bed, and she fell asleep with pleasure floating through her head.

# CHAPTER THREE

Hunter sat on the edge of the bed until she was completely out, listening to her breathing slow. Then he sat a few moments more, watching her sleep, before he got to his feet and eased the heating pad out from under the blankets.

He needed to meet Warren at her place in a few minutes.

The reminder of what he'd stopped earlier made him frown as he turned the heating pad off and set it on the night table.

There were a lot of gaps in the published mythologies he'd read in school.

He tucked the blankets in around her snugly and kissed her cheek again. "I'll be back soon," he breathed, even though she couldn't hear him.

He took her bags from the foot of the bed and set them on the top of his dresser, dug into her purse for her keys, before he headed downstairs.

In ten minutes, he parked in front of her house, this time behind Warren's work van. If anyone was watching, they'd know exactly what was going on here.

Good. If the Harvester was watching, he needed to know Katharine wouldn't be an easy target again. Not that Hunter intended to let her come back here as long as she was in danger.

He met Warren at the front door, fumbling with her keys until he found the right one.

"You know," Warren said, scowling at her front window and its sticker, "this company's notorious for putting the systems on a separate line from the rest of the house with no back-up."

Hunter smiled. "You can fix it, right?"

"Of course I can. But your friend would be better off going with someone else." He set his toolbox on the hallway floor. "I'm going out to take a gander at this line."

Hunter let Warren go and tucked her keys into his pocket with his own. He looked around, as he might if he were stepping inside for the first time.

The living room walls held several more of the beach prints, but no knick-knacks decorated the room. The comfortable couch, with a coffee table holding an untouched Sunday paper. A remote for the television in the opposite corner. Two cushy chairs.

No personality, though.

He frowned, turning in a circle. There wasn't even a mailbox at the front of the house like the rest of her neighbors had, and he recalled his buddy saying her mailing address was a post office box.

The kitchen was clean, even after he'd made lunch, a napkin holder sitting in the middle of her table, and only a can opener and toaster sat on her counter.

Maybe Katharine didn't cook much?

He smiled, moving into the kitchen and peeking in several cupboards. He already knew there were sturdy dishes in one, and he found pots and pans in another, spices and cooking oils in yet another. She cooked. She just didn't keep a lot of unnecessary things sitting around.

Warren stepped back inside. "Your guy came in the through a bedroom window earlier. Footprints under the windowsill."

"I know. I was here." Hunter scowled.

"Big guy, too. Heavy footprints." His buddy's brow furrowed, and he rubbed his chin. "Your friend might want to think about getting a better system installed. This one was good ten years ago, even five it was decent, but there's better available now. This guy was pretty determined. The line he cut isn't easily repairable."

*Of course not.* Hunter sighed. "Do what you can. She can't come back here, not while this guy is on the loose anyway."

"Oh, I can fix it." Warren smiled. "I still remember how." He set his hand on his hips. "But it's gonna cost you."

Hunter shook his head. "How much?"

"I might need a guy to track one of my wife's in-laws. Her sister thinks the dumb ass is cheating."

"I can do that." He glanced around. He wasn't gaining much insight into Katharine here. "How long do you think this will take?"

"Couple hours." Warren shrugged. "I'll lock up and set the alarm with a new code when I'm done."

"Thanks, I have a new client coming to the office soon."

"Go. I'll fix things here."

Hunter shook Warren's hand and headed to his car. Nothing looked out of place in the neighborhood, no service people aside from the security company van parked on the street, no busybody neighbors peering out their windows. And no one hiding in any neatly trimmed bushes.

Maybe the Harvester had gone back to his hole to formulate a new plan.

It would have to be a damn good one to find her now.

Smiling grimly, he guided his car out of her neighborhood, keeping an eye on his mirrors as he went to the office via a very indirect route.

Nobody following him.

That bothered him during the two hours he spent at the office. If he was hunting someone, he'd've stuck around to see what was going on. At least for a little while.

Then again, he *had* forced the guy to leave his weapon. Maybe he needed to rearm himself before he felt comfortable returning. But he had to think she might not stick around.

Hunter didn't like that either. He would've had a back-up weapon.

Maybe the guy just hadn't planned on having to take out someone else, too—he'd expected to find her alone. Maybe the gun had scared him.

He was still pondering it when he got home a couple hours later, groceries on the seat beside him, along with another, smaller bag. He let himself in, then reactivated the alarm for the perimeter and all entry points to the house. Silence greeted him, and he hoped Katharine was sound asleep, under the influence of her painkiller.

He put the groceries away before he headed upstairs. She shifted under the blankets, her face pale, stark against the scarf. A soft moan passed her lips.

The pill must be wearing off. He glanced at the clock–it wasn't time for her to have another according to the label on her bottle. He lifted the heating pad and turned it back on, slipping it under the blankets to her belly. She curled around it, almost automatically, though the stress lines around her mouth didn't ease.

He sat on the edge of the bed and brushed his fingers along her cheek. "Relax," he whispered.

After a few moments, she inhaled unsteadily. "Hunter?"

"I didn't want to wake you." He didn't bother asking how she felt

"I need to get in the shower," she murmured, sucking in a quick breath.

"The hot water helps?"

"That, too," she said after a second.

He frowned, wondering what that meant.

"Okay. Sit up. Slowly."

She eased upright, and he took the heating pad away, then carefully picked her up.

"You don't have to–"

"Sh." He kissed her cheek lightly. "Let me help."

Her mouth compressed into a flat line, but she didn't argue.

He set her on her feet in the bathroom. "Can I get you anything right now?"

Katharine shook her head. "No, thank you."

He grinned at her polite tone. "I got some things for supper, so after your shower, we can eat before you have another pain pill."

Her shoulders tensed under the rumpled blue nightshirt, but she didn't protest.

"I'll come back for you in a little while, okay?"

She sighed, and he stifled a laugh as he left the smaller room, pulling the door shut behind him. She may be aggravated with him, but she wouldn't be rude.

He wondered how far he'd have to push her to make her change her mind.

Not, he thought, that he'd like her to take off her blindfold and turn him to stone.

KATHARINE WANTED VERY MUCH TO take the scarf from her eyes and turn Hunter to stone at the moment. She thought about it as she struggled out of her nightshirt. Then she realized he'd left her alone and yanked the scarf off. She needed to see to dig through her tote bag anyway.

She'd buried the vibrators in the bottom of the bag when she packed earlier, and she hoped he hadn't dug that far when he retrieved her heating pad and pills.

She pulled out the first one she found, smiling grimly when she saw it was the big ridged one with the short extension to stroke over her clit with each thrust. She finished undressing and stepped into his shower, adjusting the water temp to hot. Extra hot.

The scalding water was a shock for a moment, and she inhaled deeply, feeling the heat penetrate her tight muscles. There was soap in the shower, something utilitarian, but when she picked it up, it smelled like Hunter.

Her hormones came to attention, which would make this easier.

She lathered herself with Hunter's soap, taking her time and thinking of Friday night, so when she picked the vibrator up, her body was ready for it. The toy stretched her with each thrust, the ridges rasping over sensitive tissues with every movement. The first orgasm erupted in only a few strokes, but she kept going, keeping the thrusts steady, deep and hard, until the next wave broke, bigger, more intense. Then again, and this time, she slid to her knees under the hot spray, gasping in time with her racing heartbeat.

She eased the vibrator out of her shaking body and shut it off, dropped it aside to try to catch her breath.

At least her cramps had eased.

A grim smile touched her lips as she turned her face to the hot water, pushing to her feet.

It wouldn't last long, she knew. It just needed to last long enough for her to deal with Hunter. If only she knew what to do with him.

She was drying off when he tapped at the door. "Not quite ready yet," she said, heat climbing her cheeks.

"Okay. Just checking on you."

She shut her eyes and took a deep breath and continued to dry herself off. Even the clean towel he'd set out for her smelled like him. Must be something in the detergent.

She fumbled back into her nightshirt and was cleaning her vibrator when she heard him on the other side of the door again. She jumped, dropping the toy in the sink. "Still not ready."

"Are you hungry?"

She frowned at his conversational tone on the other side of the wood panel. "A little, I guess," she said after a moment to think about the question. She finished her task, dried off the toy and stuffed it back into the bottom of her tote, then fumbled for the black scarf. It wouldn't go on straight.

She growled.

"What's wrong?"

"I can't get the stupid scarf back on right."

"Close your eyes. I have something that'll work better."

Katharine dropped the scarf onto the vanity and shut her eyes, sighing as he opened the door. "What is it?"

"I found an actual blindfold."

She resisted the urge to open her eyes and look at him. "Do I want to know where?"

His warm fingers eased something over her head, and soft cotton brushed down over her forehead to her eyes, settling on the bridge of her nose. "Probably not."

"Tell me anyway."

His fingers adjusted the back of the blindfold. "A sex shop."

"Oh my Gods," she muttered, her face heating.

He chuckled. "I told you you didn't want to know." His hands settled on her shoulders. "How are you feeling?"

"Not too bad right now." The warmth from his fingers seeped through her nightshirt and into her skin, making hormones surge again. She ignored them. "What's for supper?"

He scooped her up against his chest, and she slid her arm around the back of his neck, felt him shiver. "There's a great little take-out place near the office, so I grabbed some of their soup of the day, then stopped at the grocery store for some other supplies."

"You don't keep food in your house?"

His movements changed, and she realized they were going downstairs now. "Yes, but I've been working a lot lately, so I needed to get groceries. You were a good excuse to do that."

Unsure if that was good or bad, she cleared her throat. "What's the soup of the day?"

"Creamy cucumber and dill."

Her mouth watered. "Sounds delicious." Her butt hit a soft surface.

"Sofa," he murmured. "It smelled delicious, too, all the way home in the car." He eased away. "I'll be right back with dinner." His lips grazed her forehead.

Her belly tightened, and she wasn't quite sure of the cause this time. Rather than worry about it when she was barely functioning, she listened to his footsteps fading away along the hall instead. She hadn't got a look in the living room the other night, so she wasn't sure of the furniture layout in this room. Really, the only rooms she'd seen had been the bedroom and the bathroom when she'd crept in to get dressed before she left.

Hunter's footsteps returned a moment later, and she inhaled deeply, the scent of the soup reaching her nose. His weight depressed the soft leather beside her, and he shifted. "Open."

Her stomach rumbled, and she opened her mouth rather than argue with him. She was hungrier than she'd realized, and the soup smelled fantastic. "Mm." She savored the warm liquid on her tongue, enjoying the melded flavors of the fresh herbs and vegetables. "That's amazing," she said after she'd swallowed.

Hunter took a moment to reply, and she realized he was eating, too. "It is. Open."

Katharine let him feed her, trying not to think of how intimate the act was and instead concentrating on the meal, which wasn't finished with the soup, but followed by fresh fruit salad. "Thank you, Hunter," she said quietly when she was sated.

"No problem."

She lifted one hand to the blindfold, touching soft satin on the outside. It fit snugly over her eyes, but not too tightly. "A sex shop?" she asked after a moment.

Hunter laughed, and the warm sound washed over her, making her body perk up a bit even though the cramps were tightening in her middle again. "Yes. I couldn't think of anywhere else to find one, and there happens to be a shop a few blocks from my office. I've passed it hundreds of times and never gone in until today."

"Gee, thanks." Heat rose in her throat and face, and she dropped her hand back to her lap.

"Only for you," he teased, "would I visit an adult toy shop." One of his big hands settled over hers on her leg. "You ready for another pill?"

She was, she realized. But she hated to take it now, in spite of the worsening cramps, when she was enjoying sitting here with him.

All the more reason she ought to take it and crawl into a bed.

"I can sleep on the sofa, instead of hogging up your bed," she said after a moment.

"Hell, no." He touched her cheek. "I want

you where I can keep an eye on you." His tone was still teasing, but she had the feeling he meant every word.

That made her nervous. And curiously excited at the same time.

She sighed, trying to concentrate on the nervous. "Okay."

He lifted her carefully, and she winced at the stab of cramping in her belly. "Getting worse again?" he asked near her ear, his warm breath washing over her skin.

She nodded, shutting her eyes behind the blindfold. "I'm sorry, Hunter."

"For what?"

"For you being stuck in the middle of this." She let her chin drop as he carried her up the steps. "You shouldn't have to play nursemaid and fight off killers you never even heard of."

The bed hit her back, but Hunter didn't move away, his wide chest half-covering hers. "I'm not stuck in anything, Katharine. I do what I want, and if scaring off murderers and keeping you safe is necessary, I can do it."

"You shouldn't have to."

She heard his quick, exasperated sigh. "I don't have to. Don't you get that? I could've just kept driving this morning when I saw him climbing in your bedroom window. I wanted to do this, to make sure you're safe." He touched the corner of her mouth. "Friday night was amazing, but I was kind of hoping we could play the dating game, Kat."

Her brain whirling at the rest of his words,

she didn't catch the shortening of her name right away. "No one's called me Kat since I was six," she said finally.

"Who was it?"

"A boy in my class. He only did it once."

"Did you hit him?" A smile sounded in his voice.

"Maybe." She couldn't stop her own smile. "He never talked to me after that, even though he was in my class for two more years."

Hunter brushed her lips with his, startling her. "Are you going to hit me?"

She shook her head on the pillow. "Not today."

He chuckled, the movement of his chest pressing into hers so heat shot from her breasts into her belly to mingle with the painful cramping. She must've made some sound, because he eased up, so their bodies no longer touched. "I'll get your pill."

She bit her lip, rubbing one hand over her belly, digging the heel of her hand in over the most painful spot.

"Here you go." He caught her shoulder to help her upright before putting the tablet into her hand, lifting the glass of water to her mouth.

Katharine sighed and let him ease her down. There was no point arguing. Not now, when her options were limited.

In another day or so, though...

Hunter's footsteps returned from the bathroom, and then he slid the heating pad over her belly, tugging up the covers.

"Thanks, Hunter. I really do appreciate your help." She did, no matter how bitchy she felt. No matter how worried she was.

His footsteps moved to the other side of the bed, and his weight pressed into the mattress. "Not a problem. I've never had the opportunity to rescue any damsels in distress before. I kind of like it." One of his fingers slid along her jaw. "It doesn't take the pill long to kick in, does it?"

She shook her head on the pillow. "Not usually."

He tucked the blanket higher under her chin. "Tell me about the Harvester."

She sighed, though this time in frustration with him. "He's only one of many."

"How many?"

She shrugged. "Thousands. My cousin is married to a man from the Tassos family, but he's not welcome anymore, so there's no way of knowing exactly what they're up to."

"Tassos?"

"It means 'harvester'. They're descendants of Perseus. They've been after us for centuries." His fingers brushed over the bridge of her nose, at the edge of the blindfold, and she shivered. "Their mission in life is to kill the Medusa and a real bonus would be to steal the protective amulet the first Medusa created for her daughters so the current Medusa would be miserable three days a month instead of all the time." She shifted at a particularly sharp cramp, trying to find a more comfortable position.

Hunter's finger slid over her cheek, lightly. "What kind of amulet?"

"Every daughter of Medusa is born with a snake-shaped birthmark somewhere on her body. But only the one chosen to be the Medusa will have her birthmark change into a tattoo that includes the amulet once the curse falls on her. It's a goblet. The Harvesters have been trying to steal it forever, but the only one of them who knows it's in our skin is my cousin's husband. If the Medusa dies, the amulet automatically transfers to the new Medusa." The beginning wooziness from the painkiller made her fingers and toes tingle. Pretty soon the rest of her would be feeling better, too, and her brain would shut down.

"Is that the only way a new Medusa is created? When her predecessor dies?" His finger slid along her lower lip now, warming it, making her remember what his kiss tasted like.

"Either death, or she falls in love, which is a challenge. Not many men want to date a woman who can turn him to stone just by looking at him, or who sprouts snakes on her head three days a month. So few, the family had forgotten it was a possibility until recently." The warmth from his touch on her lip spread into her chest, as the tingles of numbness started to climb her arms and legs.

Hunter's finger slid back and forth along her lip, as if he were recalling Friday night, too. "But it has happened, right? I mean, your cousin is married."

"Mm-hm." Her brain wasn't working so well now. She took a deep breath, inhaling the enticing scent of him. "You smell good." She rolled onto her side, facing him while keeping the heating pad securely against her stomach.

"So do you." His warm breath skimmed her mouth. "Is your pill kicking in now?"

"Mm." She smiled, wanting the taste of him on her lips. "You're a good kisser, Hunter."

"You're not so bad yourself," he said softly, his tone husky. "But I think we'll have to wait a little while before we do any more of that."

She shook her head. "Just a kiss. Please." Before she passed out and couldn't enjoy his nearness.

She heard him take a slow, deep breath, and the exhale warmed her chin. "Kat," he began.

She slipped one hand from beneath the blankets and found his chest. "Please."

A frustrated groan reached her ears only a second before his mouth settled over hers.

Gods, he tasted good.

His tongue slid past her lips, and she tightened her grip on his shirt, feeling his heartbeat quicken under her fingers. It matched her own. His kiss was incredible, hot, wet, demanding.

It was going to give her really, really good dreams tonight.

HUNTER KNEW WHEN SHE PASSED out—right in the middle of the kiss. He lifted his head, smiling. Perhaps he could do some research into the Medusa and Perseus mythology, but he didn't believe he'd find much on the current situation.

He touched her lower lip with his forefinger, listening to her even breathing. He suspected Katharine would be difficult about this when she felt better which would make protecting her a challenge.

He lay there, watching her sleep, his mind busy with the puzzle he'd stumbled onto. How had the Harvester found her when he'd had a difficult enough time with his sources? How did the curse choose which woman to claim? How would he keep her safe from the family bent on murdering her?

He finally pushed himself upright, tucking the blankets tighter around her, and headed into the bathroom to fill her hot water bottle. When he dug it from her tote bag, he discovered she'd packed some very interesting things in the bottom of the tote–a couple of her vibrators.

He hefted one, glancing at the shower. An orgasm might help with the cramps, he supposed. He put the toy back into the bottom of her bag and filled the water bottle with the hottest water he could get from the faucet. After he tucked it under the blankets to replace the heating pad, he headed downstairs to his computer, parking his butt in the chair at his corner desk and pulling up his web browser to search for Greek myths.

He spent a couple hours at it, never finding

anything but ancient stories, told and retold, along with photo galleries of artifacts related to the myth. Another search on the Tassos family only returned a few articles on an older man named Aristotle and his donations to several museums over the years along with grainy black and white photos. Nothing more.

Hunter sat back, staring at the screen. He hadn't really expected to find anything, but was still disappointed not to discover even a scrap of something useful.

He rubbed his chin as he pushed to his feet, then stretched. It would soon be bedtime, but he wanted to wait until Katharine woke again so he could get her another pill. Maybe she'd sleep the rest of the night after that.

He turned the news on and the computer off, and sank onto the sofa with a bottle of water. The local news didn't have anything interesting in the first ten minutes, so he turned it off and made the rounds of the house, checking windows and doors, and double-checking the alarm system. By the time he stepped into the bedroom, Kat was stirring, a soft moan reaching his ears. He frowned and crossed to her, smoothing one hand along her cheek. She shifted into his touch, her brow furrowed above the blindfold.

"Kat?" He kept his voice low, not wanting to startle her awake.

She murmured something he couldn't understand and rolled onto her side, curling tight into herself.

Time for a pill.

He went to the bathroom for the glass he'd left on the sink earlier, filling it with cold water and grabbing her pill bottle on the way back to the bed. "Honey?" He set the glass and bottle on his night stand and put one hand on her shoulder, lightly. "It's time for another pill."

Katharine took a long, shuddering breath, then turned her head, and he knew she was awake suddenly. "Hunter?"

"Right here." He helped her upright, noting the way her hand went to her belly. He took the now-cool water bottle away and tapped a pill onto his palm. "Here." He set it in her palm, then held the water to her lips.

That she didn't protest at all, simply took the pill, told him just how bad she felt. He suspected she wasn't a woman who took orders. Ever. He helped her lie down again. "Do you want the heating pad?"

She nodded. "Please."

"Okay, give me a minute." He took the glass and pill bottle with him into the bathroom, then returned and put the heating pad against her stomach before he turned it on. "All the way?"

She nodded, and he realized her lips were as white as her cheeks, compressed into a flat line with the pain.

Hunter wondered exactly how much of a bitch Athena was if She thought this was a suitable punishment several thousand years later for the descendants of a woman who'd bragged her hair was more beautiful than the Goddess's.

He settled Kat back into bed, noting the way she curled in around the heating pad. Then he kicked off his shoes and peeled off the rest of his clothes before he climbed into bed, too, facing her. The light from the night stand on his side of the bed made her look even paler, shining directly into her face. He slid his fingers along the side of her face, feeling her slight start at the unexpected touch. "Just me," he murmured.

She forced a small smile. "Thanks again."

"Who takes care of you?" he wondered aloud, brushing his thumb over her cheekbone.

"Me." Her whisper made her warm breath wash past his chin.

"Thank you for letting me help." He stretched over to kiss her forehead.

She sighed softly, and he continued stroking the side of her face until her breathing evened out, until there was a tiny bit of color back in her cheeks. Then he shut off the heating pad and turned out the lights, hoping she slept well. For a while, at least.

# CHAPTER FOUR

Elek clenched his fingers underneath the table. "You disobeyed a direct order, and now you have lost her?" He couldn't help the edge in his tone any more than he could control the surge of anger quickening his pulse. Putting his fist through the computer screen wouldn't be as satisfying as knocking his cousin to the floor, so he kept his fist on his knee.

Leandro's face darkened, his jaw tightening.

At least he didn't make excuses. Not that the Goddess would be happier. "I thought Great-uncle Ari was quite clear when the monster was located, the person who found her would wait to move in until after he'd notified us, so a team could be dispatched to be certain she did not escape. Was he unclear?"

Leandro scowled. "No," he said, low.

"Then why did you go alone?" Elek already knew the answer, but he wanted to know if his cousin would be honest.

Leandro remained silent.

Elek waited.

His cousin glared at him.

Elek unclenched his fist beneath the desk, concentrating on relaxing his fingers.

"I wanted to kill her. I almost did."

"But 'almost' isn't dead, is it, and now we don't know where she's gone," Elek replied, narrowing his eyes at the younger man. "You will turn all of your research over to Argos by four o'clock, and you will report here immediately to consult with Uncle Ari."

Leandro's scowl deepened. "But I–"

"Now," Elek said, his tone hard. "Your part in this hunt is finished." He touched a key on the laptop, and his cousin's face vanished. He pulled his cell phone across the desk and dialed Argos. "Pull everything from Leandro's computer and phone. I told him to turn over his research to you by four, but he'll delay. We need it now." He disconnected and took a deep breath.

Ari would be furious, and Elek understood why. But Ari's declining health made Elek cautious. He needed to broach this carefully. But he did have to tell his great-uncle, and quickly.

He shoved to his feet and strode to the window overlooking the meditation garden. He'd need not only Athena's wisdom to find the right words, but the self-control not to flatten his cousin when he arrived later.

Straightening, he headed down the hall to Ari's study. His great-uncle sat erect in his chair, reading intently on his computer screen.

"Uncle."

Ari lifted his head, brow furrowing. "What's happened?"

"I'm afraid I have bad news." Elek stopped beside the desk. "Leandro has disobeyed your order to notify us if anyone found the Medusa."

The older man closed his eyes for a second. "And now he has lost her." He met Elek's gaze, his own sharp. "Do we know where?"

"I have Argos pulling everything from his phone and computer now, and told Leandro to get here immediately."

Ari nodded. "Good. We must send a team to the area now, though if he's lost her, she may have left already. Do we know what happened?"

Elek couldn't stop his hands from curling into fists now. "He said he was in her house. In her room, and a man with a gun arrived."

Ari paled. "A man?" he repeated sharply.

"With a gun."

Ari sat back in his chair, his gaze shifting away. "We have to find her. *Now.* Damo, Milo, Baltasar, and Phillip to the town as soon as Argos has the details. And when Leandro arrives, make sure he's brought to me."

"I will." Elek studied the older man for a few seconds. "May I ask why the man worries you so much?"

For a moment, he thought Ari wouldn't answer. Then his great-uncle sighed softly. "If the monster falls in love, we must start all over. I fear the Goddess's anger if we fail yet again. It's been many decades since we last killed one of these monsters, never mind that we've failed for thousands of years to find and destroy the amulet that protects them. Surely we are allowed only so many failures before our family loses Her favor."

Elek understood perfectly. "I will speak to Argos and send the others as quickly as I can."

"Thank you." Ari waved one hand, and Elek took the dismissal.

Before the door closed behind him, he had his phone to his ear. "What do you have, Argos?" He strode toward his own office.

"New Jersey. Katharine Rigas-Vardos. She writes books for teenagers. Lives alone. Leandro is an imbecile."

Elek agreed. "Send me the details so we can get there ASAP." He shut his door

"Done. I'll dig more to find out about family she might go to if she had to flee. Please ask Ari not to send Leandro to assist me."

Elek laughed. "I think Leandro will be doing something far less fun. Thank you, Argos." When he disconnected, he opened the email Argos had sent and forwarded it to the cousins Ari had chosen and sat to study the information more closely.

He wished there was a photo. It would make the search easier. He shot off a quick message to Argos to have him find one. Surely as an author she had something. And if not, Argos could hack the DMV.

He frowned as he read. This one didn't fit the profile they'd been working from. She hadn't moved to a remote area when she became the Medusa, as her recent predecessors had. Instead, she'd moved into a medium-size town where she would have a lot of neighbors. Odd.

He made a mental note to ask Leandro why he had looked at her, because Elek's cursory read through of these notes didn't explain it. Then he picked up a pen to make a list of what would need to be done if the new team had trouble locating her. The Goddess must not be disappointed.

KATHARINE WOKE WITH SHARP PAIN radiating out from her belly and stifled the moan that wanted to escape. Because she realized Hunter was sleeping close beside her.

She didn't want to wake him. But, oh, Gods, this hurt.

She panted through the next vicious cramp and tried to think of something else.

It didn't work, of course.

The only help for this was a shower, a spectacular orgasm, and a pain pill.

She rolled carefully onto her back, trying hard to move slowly enough not to disturb Hunter.

"What's wrong?" he asked, his voice rough with sleep.

"Need to get to the bathroom," she managed, closing her eyes behind the blindfold in resignation.

"Okay." She heard him moving beside her, before his weight left the bed.

Damn. She pushed upright, biting her lip against the pain.

One of Hunter's hands settled in the middle of her back. "I can wait outside the door."

"I need to get in the shower," she whispered as he lifted her. Heat touched her cheeks.

"Okay." He carried her into the next room, setting her carefully on her feet. "Why don't you get undressed, and I'll come back in to help."

"I'm okay on my own." The heat flared hotter in her face.

He brushed his lips across her forehead. "I'll be back once you're in the shower, so keep that blindfold handy." He moved away, and a few seconds later, she heard the door shut.

Katharine shivered, trying to think of a way to dissuade him from coming back. She really needed to dig out one of the vibrators in her bag.

"You okay?"

She started, realizing she'd been standing there in thought for too long. "I'm fine." She shoved the blindfold up for a quick peek in the mirror. A few wisps of hair had escaped her braids, but they were short enough not to worry about snake potential. Color stained her face, and she knew that would only get worse if Hunter insisted on helping with her shower.

She turned away from the sink and stripped off the nightshirt, deciding she'd just deal with the shower and forget the relief she might find from an orgasm, much as she might want one.

She stepped into the shower and turned the water on as hot as she could bear it against her skin. Then she turned it up a little more.

"I'm coming in, Kat," Hunter called.

She tugged the mask back down over her eyes and set her jaw. The mask would likely be ruined. "I'm really fine on my own." She heard the shower door slide open anyway.

"I'm sure you are, but I want to help."

Taking a slow breath, she turned her face away from the sound of his voice. "I don't think you can help," she said after a moment.

"I think I can." Something smooth touched her hip, and she realized he'd found her vibrators.

Heat that had nothing to do with the scalding water raining down warmed her face. "I can do that myself."

"Don't argue with me, Kat," he said mildly. "This makes me feel not so helpless." He flipped the toy on and stroked it over the slope of her breast.

Warmth curled into her middle, though not nearly enough. She tried to focus on his words. "You're not helpless."

He chuckled, sliding the tip of the vibrator to her nipple, rubbing around and around until her breath caught. "It's how I feel. There isn't anything I can do to make this better except get you a pill every couple hours. I don't like it." The vibrator slid lower, to her navel, then back up to her other breast.

The pleasure spiraling into her middle

rivaled the strength of the cramps now. "You shouldn't have to worry about it simply because you were in the wrong place at the wrong time." She sucked in a quick breath.

Hunter growled. "I was in the right place at exactly the right time." He rubbed the tip of the vibe over her aching nipple, back and forth, until she sucked in a harsh breath. "I'm not at all upset about that. I'm more annoyed I can't just make this go away for you." He slid the toy lower again, this time over the wet curls between her legs.

Katharine squeezed her eyes shut tight. The anticipation was going to kill her.

"How's that?" he asked, his tone softer now.

"Better." She caught her lower lip in her teeth, her hips rocking toward the toy he held, as desire spread along her veins.

As if he knew what she was hoping for, Hunter slipped the vibrator lower, far enough to stroke over her clit. She gasped, and he repeated the caress.

"Please, Hunter," she whispered. "Don't tease me."

"This helps the cramps?" He eased the vibe lower, sliding it along her slick folds.

"Yes." She gasped when he pushed the wide tip inside her. "Oh Gods." Her hips shifted toward it, forcing the toy deeper.

Hunter made a strangled sound, then pushed it farther.

Katharine moaned, relief mingling with the

desire in her veins, overtaking the pain.

She leaned against the cool, slick wall, the hot water beating down on her side and front while Hunter thrust the toy deep, then withdrew it, his thumb grazing her clit with each stroke so the release burst quickly. "Oh, don't stop," she gasped out when he slowed his movements. She thought she smiled when he quickened his thrusts, but she couldn't be sure. She was too busy sinking into the pleasure. When she cried out sometime later, her legs giving out beneath her, she dimly heard Hunter's groan over the pounding water and her racing heart.

She felt him ease the vibe out of her quivering body, thankful the release had overcome the cramping in her belly, for now. That was the most important thing.

She could worry about the intimacy of the act later. When her brain worked again.

Hunter watched Kat sleeping later. His own body still throbbed with need, but he wouldn't disturb her rest to relieve himself. If his dick didn't start cooperating soon, he'd take care of it.

He thought of the way her body had bowed toward his hand with the strength of her orgasm.

That wouldn't help get rid of his hard-on. He slid one hand along the side of her face, pushing back a few short, dark wisps from her temple, apparently too short to change to snakes. Her sleep now was sound, and even by the time she'd taken her pill and crawled back into his bed, her cramps hadn't come back full-force.

Hunter liked her sleeping in his bed, probably far more than he should with a woman he didn't know very well yet.

But he kind of thought he may be able to remedy that part while he kept her safe from this Harvester. Or however many more of them there were in the vicinity now.

He frowned. He should've asked her if they hunted solo all the time or if they teamed up. He needed as much information as possible to protect her.

And in the meantime... He winced as he shifted and his jeans pulled tight over his erection. He needed to do something about that.

He rolled to his feet and sighed. He didn't want to jack off. He didn't want a cold shower, either.

Which left work as a distraction.

He padded out of the room after making sure she was tucked in tight and headed downstairs. He had pictures to print for Mrs. Baird and for the insurance company. Neither would take long and once they were delivered, he'd get paid.

For an hour and a half, he dragged out the typing up and printing of reports, checked his work email and cleared his inbox. By then his jeans no longer strangled his dick. He shut off the computer and the light before he made the rounds of the house, double-checking locks and the alarm. He didn't normally think too much about it when he was home alone, just did it when he got home for the night and forgot about it.

Now with Katharine here and in mortal danger, he wanted to be certain she was safe.

He turned off the stairwell light and walked into the bedroom. She wasn't really his responsibility.

But he wanted her. Even after the wild night they'd spent Friday, he hadn't had enough.

That worried him a bit. He hadn't dated anyone, even casually, since Tempest had left New Jersey last year. Not that they'd had been serious. Monogamous, yes, but their relationship hadn't been destined for anything long-term, even before her boss promoted her all the way across the country.

Hunter shucked his jeans in the bathroom, doing his best not to look at the vibrator lying on the vanity as he brushed his teeth. So much for no more hard-on.

He ignored the arousal stirring and climbed into bed, keeping a safe distance from Katharine as he did so. No sense torturing himself all damn night.

When he woke a few hours later, he was wrapped around her, and she was stirring, stifled sounds of discomfort rising from her throat. He kissed her temple. "Easy, honey," he murmured, setting one of his hands over the one she had clenched over her belly.

She sucked in a soft breath. "Sorry. I didn't mean to wake you."

"What do you want to do?" He hoped it wasn't another shower. If he had to see that again, he might have to kill himself.

"I just want to get up for a while. I need to use the bathroom."

"Are you hungry?"

"A little."

He shut his eyes. Relief mingled with the warmth coursing through him from every inch of the back of her touching the front of him. It was a lot of touching. He stifled a groan when her soft bottom shifted into his erection.

Katharine went still in his arms, and he winced, glad she couldn't see him. "I'm so sorry, Hunter," she whispered.

He shifted backward and rolled her to her back, wishing she didn't have the damned blindfold on. Wishing he could see her pretty grey eyes. "You have nothing to apologize for, Katharine," he said, smoothing a short wisp of hair away from her forehead. "Not a damn thing."

"Of course I do." Her lush mouth flattened. "I've got you in the middle of something that could get you killed."

"Don't go there again," he said flatly, pushing onto his elbow. "I am in this because I want to be. If I'd been a few minutes later, you'd have been dead when I got to your house, and I'd hate that."

Her lips pursed.

"Don't argue with me, Kat. I don't do anything I don't want to, and I'm doing exactly what I want right now." Well, that was a lie. He wasn't doing exactly what he'd like to be doing right now. But he'd have to wait. "Someone needs to keep you safe, and I'm the lucky guy."

"Yeah, lucky." Her mouth twisted.

He caught her chin when she started to turn her head away. "I am. I was lucky enough to meet you last week. And lucky enough to save your life." He brushed his lips over hers, lightly. "No matter what happens." After all, they hadn't spent enough time talking Friday night for him to know if she was even interested in any sort of relationship with a man other than the no-strings-attached sex.

He scowled. And what the hell was he doing, even thinking in terms of a relationship when they barely knew one another? He forced his frown away. "Now, what would you like for breakfast? I can it started while you get moving." He touched her lower lip with one finger. "I have eggs and bread. You like your eggs scrambled or fried?"

"You don't need to," she whispered, sounding choked.

He stifled another sigh. "I'm going to make breakfast, so if you have a preference, now's the time to let me know, Kat."

She shook her head, her lower lip between her teeth.

Instead of kissing her, he sat up. "Come

on." He scooped her up against his chest, then eased his feet onto the floor.

Katharine caught his shoulder, her fingers warm on his bare skin.

Hunter ignored that for the moment and took her into the next room. "I'll be back in a couple minutes to get you." He left the room before she could argue. Or before he said something he shouldn't.

KATHARINE STOOD IN THE BATHROOM with her head bowed for a long time, even after Hunter's footsteps on the stairs had faded away.

This was way too complicated.

She shoved the blindfold up off of her eyes and blinked in the sudden brightness. Her braids were still mostly intact, with only a few short strands loose around her face. Her face, though, was an unflattering pale shade. She frowned and turned away from the mirror to try to straighten herself out. When Hunter returned a few minutes later, tapping lightly on the closed door, Katharine squared her shoulders and tugged the blindfold back down over her eyes. "I'm ready." She'd deal with all the rest later.

She let him cart her downstairs and feed her scrambled eggs and toast, answering his casual questions in monosyllables. Then, when they'd finished breakfast, she kept her mouth shut while he carried her back to bed. She took the pain pill and nodded when he told her he was going to his office for a few hours and would be back by the time she woke up.

Finally, when she was woozy from the painkiller, her thoughts too scattered for her to do more than realize she was about to pass out again, Hunter's lips brushed hers lightly. "Sleep well," he whispered, his breath warm on her cheek. His heavy footsteps left the room.

Katharine smiled. His kiss was nice.

But she was putting him in danger by being here.

Her smile faded, and she tried to collect her thoughts, but the painkiller coursed through her system now. Too sleepy.

She'd deal with that later, too. Whatever that was.

When she woke at lunchtime, she felt so much better. She rolled onto her back, stretching cautiously. No more cramps. No more snakes, no more danger of turning anyone or anything living into stone again until next month.

*Thank the Gods.*

"Ah, you're up." Hunter's footsteps sounded on the floor, startling her.

"Hi." Her voice was rusty, she realized, pushing herself upright.

"Take it easy." His weight made the side of the bed sink lower.

"I'm feeling better." She tugged the blindfold up, blinking in the bright midday light.

Hunter looked good. Just as good as he had

Friday night, she realized. His dark hair was mussed, as if he'd been dragging his fingers through it, and his bright blue eyes held relief.

He'd be glad to be rid of her.

Katharine swallowed, setting the blindfold on the night stand beside the bed.

"I'm glad to hear it." He pushed a strand of hair away from her cheek. "You're still pale."

She shrugged, averting her gaze from his watchful eyes.

"You want to hit the shower? I have lunch ready."

She blushed, thinking of his assistance with her last shower. "Sure." Then she could get out of here.

He startled her by leaning close and brushing a kiss on her mouth. "We can talk about what we're going to do next."

Her gaze flew back to his, and her mouth dropped open. "'*We*' don't need to do anything," she started.

Hunter put his fingers over her mouth. "Don't. I don't want to argue with you before we get lunch."

She swallowed but kept her mouth shut. She could tell him later his temporary guardianship was over. She waited while he held her gaze for a long moment, resisting the urge to tell him now.

Finally, he nodded once and got to his feet. "I'll have lunch ready when you come down." He touched her cheek with one finger, then left the room.

Katharine shut her eyes for a second before throwing the blankets back. All through her shower, she kept replaying last night and their short conversation just now. He'd understand once she told him her cousins and their husbands were her best bet for safety.

She dressed quickly after dragging her comb through her tangled hair. She wanted to gather her things together, but all she could find were her bathroom tote and her carry-on. She frowned, wondering what he'd done with her other things.

Downstairs. He must have left the other bag and her box there.

She stuffed her things into the carry-on and the bathroom tote, and carried them down with her, leaving them on the landing at the bottom of the steps. The living room was empty, so she turned to the hallway and the kitchen she'd barely glimpsed last weekend.

Hunter was putting some chips in a bowl when she stepped into the room, and he smiled as he turned toward her. "Sit." He gestured to the table, where he'd already set plates with sandwiches, as well as small deli containers of cole slaw and potato salad.

Swallowing, Katharine dropped onto the chair, her stomach fluttering nervously.

"Don't wait for me." He set the chips on the table.

She picked up her sandwich and found tuna salad, starving in spite of her anxiety. By the time he set a plate of fruit on the table and sat, she'd eaten half her sandwich.

Hunter smiled at her.

She swallowed the bite of tuna salad in her mouth. "Thank you."

He shook his head and picked up half of his sandwich.

"I mean it. I really do appreciate what you've done for me." She set the sandwich down. "I don't want you to think I'm ungrateful. I know the Harvester would've killed me if you hadn't gotten there at just the right time." She tried to remember all the points she needed to argue, everything that had occurred to her during her shower.

"Katharine."

She lifted her gaze to his.

"Eat your lunch. We'll figure out our next step afterward." He smiled.

Her heart pounded harder in reaction to his smile, and she frowned. Leftover hormones, she thought.

Rather than argue with him, she forced her gaze back to her plate and picked up the rest of her sandwich.

Finally, Hunter sat back in his chair when he'd polished off his lunch. "Okay. Hit me."

She blinked at him. "What?"

"Give me your best argument."

That wasn't what she'd expected. She frowned again, pushing her empty plate aside and resting her forearms on the edge of the table. "I shouldn't need to convince you," she said after a moment. "You saw him. You heard how determined he is. And there are more like him. Lots more. All on the hunt, and because he found me, more of them will be looking specifically for me." She brushed her fingers absently over the smooth surface of the table. "My best bet right now is to hook up with one of my cousins or their husbands who've dealt with the Harvesters before. Then you'll be safe."

"You can't muster up anything better?"

Katharine glared at him, more annoyed when he just continued to smile at her. Only half a day ago, that look would've killed him. Now it didn't even make her feel better to know that. "I shouldn't have to convince you you're unsafe as long as you're with me."

He shrugged. "I'm not the Medusa. They're not interested in me."

*True.* She shook her head. "It doesn't matter. My cousin Philomena, who was the Medusa before me, had Harvesters target her family to try to reach her."

His shoulder jerked. "I'm not family. They have no way to connect me to you."

"Except for the one who saw you Monday."

"But he doesn't know who I am. I didn't introduce myself while I had him at gunpoint."

Her pulse quickened. "That doesn't mean he didn't wait around to see you leave so he could follow you or try to track you down."

Hunter shook his head. "Didn't follow. And he definitely didn't stick around after I made him ditch his knife."

Her frustration level jumped up. He wasn't understanding. Why wasn't he understanding?

Why did it matter? She was an adult and could do what she wanted.

"Don't even think it." His tone was mild, but something in his eyes made her hesitate.

"I'm not going to stay here and put you in danger," she said finally, working to keep the edge out of her voice. "I'll call my cousin and get some advice from her husband, then get out of your hair."

Hunter's smile disappeared. "No."

She covered her face with her hands.

"I'll talk to your cousin's husband, get his take, but you're not going off on your own."

She dropped her hands. "I can defend myself just fine, at least for the next four weeks," she pointed out.

"I'm sure you can. I'd rather keep you where I can see you."

"Why?"

His expression softened a little. "I know how to deal with guys like this. And I've already gotten you to safety. Oh, I have the new code to your alarm system, but you can't go back." He dug a piece of paper from his pocket and handed it across the table.

Katharine sighed. "You're going to be difficult about this, aren't you?" She took the paper and unfolded it, staring blankly for a few seconds at the numbers. She swallowed, wishing her brain was functioning more quickly. The residual effects of three days of painkillers hadn't yet dissipated.

"You'd better believe it." He set one hand over hers on the table, his fingers warm. "I'm in this thing now, Kat."

That's what she was afraid of. She looked away, her gaze catching on the fruit plate where the green grapes contrasted sharply with the whitish flesh of the apple slices.

"So," he said at last, giving her fingers a squeeze, "which cousin are you calling? Didn't you say there are two now who used to be the Medusa?"

Katharine rested her face on her other hand, shutting her eyes, and sighed. "Yes. Andi's husband is the one who was a Harvester, and Phila's husband owns a security firm."

"Really?"

She opened her eyes to find his gaze had sharpened with his tone. "Yes."

"I'll want to talk to him. Between us, we can come up with something to keep you safe."

She shook her head slowly, noting the stubborn set of his jaw. "You're serious."

"As a heart attack."

Katharine couldn't think of anything else to dissuade him. Maybe later, after the painkillers were completely out of her system and her head was clear...

But his expression told her he wouldn't be dissuaded. She swallowed. He couldn't keep her prisoner here. He had to go to work sometime. Then she could leave.

To go where?

She frowned at the thought and picked up a slice of apple. It didn't matter where, just somewhere safe. Away. Somewhere the Harvesters wouldn't find her. Or Hunter. She didn't want him in danger because of her.

He touched the back of her hand.

She looked up, wary.

"I want to help you."

"I appreciate that," she said after a second, slowly. "But you don't need to endanger yourself for my sake."

One dark brow lifted.

Katharine inhaled deeply. She didn't want to argue with him.

"I can see the wheels turning in your head," Hunter said with a crooked smile. "You aren't ditching me."

She set her jaw.

His mouth hitched a little higher on one side. "I know it's what you're thinking."

She exhaled carefully. "Just because you had the misfortune to—"

His smile vanished. "To what? Meet a really beautiful woman? To have seriously hot sex with her?" He leaned forward, and she realized he was still holding her hand. "I don't have any expectations here, Kat. I just don't want you killed when I can keep you safe."

Katharine met his blue gaze, debating with herself. "Can we fight about this later?" she asked finally. "I'd rather be able to do it with a clear head."

Though his mouth quirked faintly, his eyes

remained somber. "I don't want to argue with you about it at all."

She couldn't think of anything to say that wouldn't simply encourage him to continue the discussion.

"But we can wait until you feel more clear-headed to figure out details," he said, giving her fingers a light squeeze.

She frowned, tugging her hand free and linking her fingers in front of her on the table. "Thank you." It was terse, and she knew it, but she didn't care at the moment.

The man might be the sexiest thing she'd ever seen up close and personal, but he had a stubborn streak at least a mile wide, and she was pretty sure she didn't like it.

# CHAPTER FIVE

unter stuck close all afternoon, not giving her an opportunity to do anything foolish, as he was sure she planned to do the first chance she got. He sat on the recliner while she curled into a corner of the sofa with her laptop. Every so often, her fingers would fly over the keyboard, then she would simply sit and scroll slowly over whatever it was she was reading.

For a while, he studied some papers he'd brought home the day before, then he moved to his laptop, searching for Greek myths online. Eventually, she sighed and leaned back in her seat.

"What's wrong?" He lifted his gaze from his screen, away from a fascinating college paper someone had written about Perseus and Medusa, and noted the faint lines on her forehead. Whatever it was, she was aggravated.

Her mouth tightened for a moment before she blew out a quick breath. "My cousin's husband."

He set his laptop aside and rested his elbows on his knees. "What did he say?"

Her grey eyes were stormy when she lifted her gaze to his. "He wants to talk to you."

Hunter stifled the smile that wanted to

spread over his face. "Really?" He noted the slight narrowing of her eyes and realized he hadn't kept the smile from his tone.

"I told him it's not necessary."

"I disagree." He set his laptop on the coffee table and got up from his seat to join her on the sofa. "Which husband is this?"

"The security guy." Katharine's mouth tightened. "And it isn't necessary. I'm not staying here indefinitely and putting you in danger, too."

"I think that's my choice to make." He leaned over and looked at the screen on her laptop, where a short email had a telephone number after the signature. Hunter scooped his cell from the table and dialed the number, watching her expression darken still further. Right now, she could be as pissed off as she wanted.

She pushed to her feet and put the laptop on the coffee table, pacing away from him toward the fireplace.

"Hi, this is Hunter Phelps," he said when a gruff male voice answered the line. "I'm with Katharine."

There was a brief silence before he heard the other man sigh softly. "Did you have to wrestle the phone number out of her?"

He chuckled, watching her shoulders tense. "Not quite."

"I'm Ryder Ware, married to Katharine's cousin Mena. How'd you get involved in this?"

"That's kind of personal. Let's just say I

happened to be visiting at the right time to catch the Harvester entering her house."

The other man muttered something under his breath. "Damn," he said. "She didn't say he'd gotten into the house." He blew out a breath. "It's bad if they know where she lives. You can't let her go back there."

"Working on it." He watched her scowl as she turned to pace back again

"Work harder. She'll be stubborn and won't make it easy for you."

"I've noticed." He smiled as he watched her ass in her faded jeans as she strode across his living room.

"Ah, that didn't take long."

"No." He moved to stand in the doorway, blocking any attempt she might make to leave. "As soon as she felt better, actually."

Katharine glared at him over her shoulder.

His smile widened.

"Sounds about right. She hasn't made any actual attempt to go, has she?"

"Not yet."

"Good. I'll have Mena try to persuade her that staying with you is in her best interest."

"She mentioned you have a security company."

"Yes." Satisfaction tinged the other man's voice. "But there's only so much even I can do against the Harvesters."

Hunter's smile faded. "That doesn't sound good."

Katharine shot him a frown as she dropped

onto the sofa and picked up her laptop.

"These people are determined, Hunter. They don't stop, and there are thousands of them."

He considered the other man's words. "Is there any way to know which ones are in the area?"

Ryder sighed. "No. There are permanent addresses, of course, many here along the eastern seaboard, but they move all around on their hunt. Mena and Katharine's cousin Andi had Harvesters from across the country hunting her in Maine years ago."

Hunter didn't like the sound of that. "Makes this a bit more challenging."

The other man laughed, humorlessly. "An understatement. Keep her out of sight as much as possible. They have no way to connect her to you, do they?"

"No. I made sure we weren't followed when we left her house, and this relationship is still pretty new." He noted the way her shoulders stiffened at his words and wondered if she was more annoyed by his refusal to let her leave on her own, or his characterization of them as having a relationship.

"Well, it's a good start. I don't suppose you have any secondary identification, do you?"

Hunter lifted one eyebrow. "I'm afraid not. I used to be a cop."

Ryder laughed again. "Then you might have the right contacts to get some."

Hunter pondered, leaning against the

doorway. He had made some interesting contacts in his work as a detective, but he'd never imagined he might need to use any of their illegal services. "Maybe."

"If not, I can hook you up, as I got Katharine's when she became the Medusa. You'll probably want more than one new ID. Katharine should have brought hers with her."

He glanced at her bag on the table behind the sofa, at her small lock box. "I imagine she has." He ignored the quick, quizzical glance she shot at him.

"Good, because if you have to travel, you don't want them to be able to connect to you."

Hunter frowned. He had a lot to learn about dealing with the Harvesters. "I think we need to have a much longer conversation," he said after a moment.

Ryder hummed his agreement. "Give me your email. I can send you a quick and dirty history so you have a better idea of what you're looking at, then let me know if you have questions. I'm sure Katharine's told you some, but there's a lot more you'll need to know if you're intending to stick with her."

He rattled off his email address, thinking about the other man's last comment. To stick with her. He let his gaze slide over the top of her head, bent over her laptop now, black hair shining. He liked the idea, very, very much.

But she didn't want to hear that yet.

He dragged his attention back to his conversation in time to hear Ryder say, "I'll email you shortly. Call me if there are any new developments. I'll have Mena email or call Katharine, make her understand she needs to stay put. Andi and Kallan, too. She cannot go off on her own."

"I appreciate it." He finished his conversation and thumbed the phone off, his gaze sliding back to Katharine, who, despite her focused attention on the laptop, didn't seem to be actually reading whatever was on her screen.

He rubbed his knuckles against his lower lip, watching her for a moment. "I suppose you heard that."

She spared him a brief, annoyed glance. "You mean the two of you planning my life?"

Hunter stifled a grin. "You mean the two of us trying to keep you safe."

She made a dismissive sound, her mouth flattening.

He also restrained a sigh, pushing off the wall to move back toward her. As he walked, he heard her email program chime a new mail alert. He wondered if her cousin had also been listening to the conversation. "Your family wants you safe, Kat."

She didn't look at him, but when she got a look at the new email, her expression darkened even more.

Yep, from the cousin. "I can keep you safe."

She set her laptop carefully on the coffee table and pushed to her feet. "And I don't want you involved."

"Too late." He ignored the sting at her declaration. Not pain. Annoyance. The woman might be sexy as hell, but she was really pushing his buttons. "I *am* involved. I couldn't be anything else after saving your life."

She put her hands on her hips, drawing his gaze there for a second and making him remember having his own hands on her naked hips last week. Then he jerked his gaze back to her face. "I do appreciate that, Hunter," she said, her tone careful. "But I'm an adult, and I don't need a babysitter, no matter what you and my family are cooking up."

Hunter smiled. "A babysitter? Honey, I aspire to a lot of things, but babysitting you isn't on the list."

To his surprise, her cheeks flushed at his insinuation. She glanced away. "Perhaps I should tell you I'm not in the market for a long-term relationship," she said after a few seconds.

His smile faded. "Excuse me?"

More color tinted her cheeks, but she met his gaze again. "Maybe we should've had this discussion Friday night."

He lifted one eyebrow and folded his arms over his chest. Sure, he figured she hadn't intended this to be more than one night. But he'd hoped he might persuade her to extend one night to at least a few more. And not just in bed.

Katharine swallowed, but her gaze held

steady. "I don't want to hurt your feelings, Hunter, but I'm not exactly in a position to do a relationship. This curse is going nowhere, and now the damned Harvesters are in my hometown of choice, ready to kill me. I'm no prize."

Hunter laughed, his arms dropping back to his sides. "You need to work on your arguments."

Her eyes widened for a second, then narrowed in fresh annoyance.

"But I'd prefer not to argue with you right now. Ryder is emailing me info on the family history and the Harvesters, and we can figure out what we're doing next."

She sat again, dropping her face into her hands. "Why aren't you listening to me?" Her voice was muffled by her hands. Her hair swung forward, hiding her face from view.

He sat beside her and tucked her hair behind her ear so he could see at least a little of her face. "Kat, I am listening. I just don't agree with everything coming out of your pretty mouth."

Her head shot up, her eyes darkening.

Hunter's heart beat faster.

Her throat worked as she swallowed. "You shouldn't."

"Maybe not." Still, he leaned in and brushed her lips with his, lightly. Too briefly, before he sat back, denying himself the deeper taste he wanted. "The attraction isn't going away, Kat," he said after he cleared his throat.

"But I have some self-control. I can't promise you I'll never touch you or kiss you, but I can certainly wait until you're ready before we wind up in bed again." And he sincerely hoped she would be ready for that eventually.

For a long, long time, she sat there, her grey eyes sober as she studied him. She didn't smile, didn't look away. "I can't tell you I will be," she said at last.

He lifted one shoulder. "I'm okay with that." *Lies!*

For a second, he thought she might argue, one dark eyebrow winged up, then she set her jaw. "Maybe we should save this discussion for another day."

Hunter waited.

"I'm sure Ryder's sent you at least one email by now." She nodded toward his laptop.

She was wimping out.

He considered that for a moment. She'd had a rough couple of days, so he thought he'd let it go for now. He released a slow breath. "All right. Another day. But don't think I'll forget."

A ghost of a smile curved her lips, rueful. "I'm sure you won't."

He lifted his laptop and turned it to face him. Sure enough, there was new email from Ryder. He stifled a sigh. It wasn't the time for this discussion. Hell, he didn't even know exactly what he wanted in a relationship anyway. Well, okay, maybe he knew he wanted a relationship to be smoking hot, like the connection he'd felt with Katharine Friday night.

But he hadn't given thought to a serious relationship in a long time.

He needed to, before he pushed *her* into a relationship conversation.

In the meantime, he had his hands full trying to keep her safe, whether she liked it or not.

He clicked on the email, relaxing only slightly when she sat back with her own laptop.

Judging by the length of the email, Ryder's idea of 'quick and dirty' was a lot different than Hunter's own.

KATHARINE REALIZED SHE WAS NODDING off in front of the late news when the soft cotton of Hunter's shirt brushed her cheek right before she jerked up again. The tension hadn't left her since his earlier conversation with Philomena's husband Ryder, and it was exhausting. She sat upright, then realized Hunter's arm lay around her shoulders.

He smiled when she glanced up.

Warmth slid along her veins, reminding her of the ways he'd touched her Friday night, the heat those touches had generated in her. A blush climbed her throat to her cheeks. Still, she couldn't tear her gaze away from his.

"Ready for bed?"

At his words, the heat amped up a few more degrees. "I can take the couch now."

He was shaking his head before she

finished speaking. "I told you I can control myself."

"Don't you trust me to be here when you get up in the morning?"

His expression hardened. "That isn't it, Kat. Besides, you couldn't get out without setting off the alarm."

She felt her jaw clenching, and she pushed to her feet before she said something she'd be sorry for later.

Hunter caught her wrist, standing behind her when she would have pulled away. "It's for your safety, Kat."

"I think I understand how the prisoner thing works," she managed, her head thumping in time with her heart, slow and too hard.

"You know you're not a prisoner."

She tugged her wrist free of his hold and moved away. "You have a spare bedroom in this house, right?" She didn't care if it only had a bed. She just knew she wasn't sleeping in his again tonight.

Though he was silent, she knew he followed as she made her way up the stairs and along the hallway. She pushed open the first door across from his room and found it filled with stacks of file boxes and a couple of filing cabinets. She moved to the next doorway and opened the door. Completely empty. She stared. How could he have two extra bedrooms and no beds?

He didn't say anything when she turned around, trembling with anger. Just stood waiting.

Katharine tried to breathe more evenly, uncertain whether she was angrier at him for being so pigheaded, or for only having one bed in his entire house...or if she was angrier at herself for the way her body heated at the notion of sleeping in his bed.

"I can sleep in the same bed without touching you, Kat," he said softly.

She wasn't sure she could say the same, so she didn't reply. She stood there for another moment, breathing deeply, if not evenly, before she moved around him and walked to his room.

At some point, he'd brought her bag back upstairs, and she saw it on the floor at the foot of his bed. She grabbed it and carried it into the bathroom, shutting the door behind her, harder than she needed to.

Her reflection over the sink showed two flushed spots high on her cheeks and grey eyes dark with tumultuous emotion. She averted her gaze and jerked a nightshirt out of her bag. By the time she'd gotten ready for bed, she hadn't calmed down any, so when she walked out of the bathroom and found him in his boxer briefs and tugging back the blankets on the bed, her pulse spiked even higher.

Annoyance, she told herself. Nothing more.

She made her way around the bed and climbed into it on the opposite side.

Okay, and maybe some leftover hormones, she admitted when she saw the flex of his muscles from the corner of her eyes.

Hunter slid into the bed on his side and angled a quick glance her way. "Sleep well, Kat," he murmured, reaching for the light on his nightstand.

She dropped back onto her pillow and shut her eyes, listening to the soft click of the switch. "Good night," she whispered, blindly reaching for the blankets.

She opened her eyes at the soft rustling from the opposite side of the bed, her eyes adjusting to the faint light.

After a moment, Hunter stopped moving, his breathing slow and even.

"I'm sorry," she whispered.

"I understand." A rustle, then the mattress shifted a tiny bit. "I wouldn't be happy about being dependent on someone else either."

"It isn't even that." She rolled onto her side, facing his direction in the dark. "I don't like having decisions made for me. I've made it all this time on my own, safely. I haven't put anyone else in danger. And now, suddenly everything's changed."

Hunter inhaled deeply, then released the air, slowly. "It's not your fault, Kat. Sometimes shit happens, and the only thing you can do is change directions to get out of the way." He shifted a little, and she knew he was rolling onto his own side, to face her. "I can keep you safe. Between me and your cousins' husbands, we can make sure the Harvesters can't get at you."

"I'm sure you can." She considered her

words carefully. "But I'm not happy that if something happens to you, it'll be my fault. You're in danger by being with me now they know where I am."

"They don't know where you are right now," he reminded her. "They can camp out at your house, and they won't find any clues to your whereabouts."

Katharine sighed. "I need some time to wrap my head around this," she said after a moment. "It's not that I'm angry at you, exactly, but more at the circumstances."

"You're pissed at me, too." She could tell from his tone that he was smiling. "As long as you're safe, it's okay."

She stifled another sigh. "I am, thanks to you." She closed her eyes for a moment. "Good night, Hunter." She reached out one hand to touch his face. "Sleep well." She rolled away before she was tempted to lean closer.

He didn't say anything, but he didn't move.

She squeezed her eyes shut. Just because she was here now didn't mean she had to stay.

ARI WOKE FROM A FITFUL SLEEP WHEN his bedroom lights flashed on. He stumbled out of bed and onto his knees. "My Lady," he murmured, his heart beating much too quickly.

"Aristotle, your family has failed me once more."

Heat rushed to his face. "I know, my Lady, and I offer my most abject apologies." Goddess damn his nephew for letting the monster get away *again*.

"This must stop, Aristotle. Your family has failed at its mission for too long, and it cannot continue. I expect better from my servants."

Ari shut his eyes tight. "We will get her, my Lady."

"You must. Or your family will lose my favor forever."

His eyes popped open in horror and fear.

"If this Medusa is not eliminated, I will take drastic action, Aristotle."

He dared a glance in Her direction, and even without looking any higher than the gleaming folds of Her gown, he knew She was furious. Waves of angry energy rolled from Her.

"If this Medusa is not found and killed, your family will suffer my displeasure. Do you understand?"

Her displeasure would involve eliminating the Tassos family, he feared. "Yes, my Lady. Forgive me, my Lady, for this failure. I promise we will find and kill her." He bent his head lower, fear racing along his veins.

When only silence hung in the air, he opened his eyes once more to an empty room. It took him a moment to struggle to his feet, and then he had to steady himself on the edge of his bed for a few more seconds before he could cross to the telephone on his dresser. He pressed a button to dial a stored number, and lifted the receiver to his ear.

"I require a progress report," he said

unsteadily when a sleepy voice sounded in his ear. "The Goddess is angry."

He feared Her anger this time was more dangerous than ever before.

He feared failing at his task.

He feared the dishonor another failure would create.

He refused to fail again. This Medusa would die at the hands of a Tassos, as the Goddess had decreed. He would make sure of it.

KATHARINE BOLTED UPRIGHT IN BED, breathing hard, and Hunter shot up, too, suddenly wide awake, and caught one of her flailing arms.

"Easy," he murmured, "easy, Kat." He set his other hand on her back.

She went still, her breath coming too quickly. "Sorry," she managed after a moment. "Bad dream."

"Lie down." He loosened his hold on her wrist, gratified when she obeyed him, dropping back onto her pillow. He eased down beside her, stroking his hand along her arm, lightly, from wrist to elbow and back. "What was the dream?"

She took a deep breath and held it for a moment, then let it out slowly. "Athena."

Hunter exhaled, too. "You okay?"

He heard the movement her head made on the pillow as she shook it. "She's angry."

"You can tell that from a dream?"

"Not sure it's just a dream, exactly," she

said softly.

"What do you mean?" He let his fingers stay circled around her wrist, her pulse rushing beneath his forefinger.

"I know what a dream feels like." She went silent for another moment. "This wasn't a dream. This is something else. She was with Aristotle, and She's furious I'm not dead."

Hunter frowned in the dark, wishing he could see her eyes. "And?"

Another rustle of the blankets. Maybe a shrug, judging by the slight motion of her arm in his hold. "He's afraid. That's it."

He smiled at the frustration he heard in her tone, but only for a second. An angry Goddess couldn't be a good thing. Not when the Goddess in question had cursed an entire family into eternity. "Does She rely on them to do all the work as far as tracking the Medusa?"

Her breathing slowed. "Yes," she said after a few seconds. "Unless things have changed since Kallan was involved in the hunt."

"You'd think a Goddess would be able to give them an unfair advantage in their hunt."

Her pulse eased a bit under his fingers. "You would." She sounded as if she were seriously thinking about it.

"I wonder why She doesn't." Hunter rubbed his thumb along the back of her hand. If Athena wanted the Medusa dead so badly, one would think She'd give her Harvesters every advantage She could.

"Maybe She can't?"

It was definitely a question, he noted. Her tone was uncertain, plain even in the dark.

Hunter lifted her hand to his mouth and brushed a quick kiss across the back of her fingers. "I don't know, but we can try to figure it out later. Can you go back to sleep?"

Her fingers tightened in his hold for a quick second before relaxing again. "I can try."

He let their joined hands drop to the bed between them. "Try." He listened to her for a while, the tiny shifting sounds as she settled, her breathing slowing gradually. While his own brain raced.

Why wouldn't Athena help Her Harvesters? Why would She expect them to do all the work on their own?

Maybe She really couldn't find the Medusa herself because of the amulet.

He lay awake for a long time, thinking about the possibilities and what they might mean for Katharine, until his brain finally shut down from sheer exhaustion.

He jerked awake when Kat stretched in her sleep, and he realized he was wrapped around her, the soft curve of her ass snuggled into his groin, her breasts only inches from where his hand rested on her ribs. He shut his eyes for a second, allowing himself to savor the feel of her against him for another couple heartbeats before he eased away, putting a few much-needed inches between her cotton-clad butt and his strengthening erection.

He took a slow breath, but all that got him

was a bigger lungful of her scent. He rolled onto his back. The sheet and blanket weren't nearly as warm as Katharine.

She shifted beside him, rolling first onto her back, then onto her side to face him.

Hunter stifled a groan when her hand landed on his abdomen and her leg brushed his. Her fingers flexed along his belly, and he covered her hand with his own to keep her from sliding her fingers any lower.

A sleepy sound escaped her as she snuggled closer.

Torture. He shut his eyes.

Her knee rubbed along his thigh, higher.

His heart pounded harder, drowning out the quiet voice of reason in his head attempting to remind him she wasn't ready yet for more intimacy.

Her knee nudged at his erection, and the groan rumbled up from his throat this time. He slid away, until he could put one foot on the floor and get out of bed.

Kat's hand moved across the blanket for a few seconds, as if she were searching for something, then stopped, and her breathing evened out.

He shut his eyes for a heartbeat, before he turned away to gather clean clothes and head for the shower. A cold shower.

So much for keeping his hands to himself while she slept in his bed.

# CHAPTER SIX

atharine didn't look up when Hunter walked inside and shut the front door. She heard the soft sound of his finger tapping over the keypad, accompanied by faint beeps. Resetting the alarm on her prison. She stared at her laptop screen, though she was no longer reading the scanned page there.

"Are you hungry?"

She took a slow breath and released it, then finally lifted her gaze to his face. "Not really." He seemed relieved. He probably hadn't expected her to speak to him. Or maybe he hadn't expected she'd still be here. If she could've figured out a way to go without setting off his damned alarm, she wouldn't be. But every window and door in the entire house was wired into the system. She'd checked. Twice. If she set it off, who knew how many people would notice, and who knew how many Harvesters were in town now to notice, too. She could have tried drawing energy from the earth to knock out his power, but that worked better when she was in physical contact with the ground, so she'd ruled it out.

He took several steps into the living room, sliding one hand into his pocket, his gaze focused on her face. She took another measured breath, keeping her expression neutral.

Disappointment shadowed his eyes, but he held her gaze. "You should have some lunch with me."

"No, thank you. I'm reading some of the things my cousin sent me. Since I can't go anywhere."

His jaw tightened, but he didn't argue, turning to leave the room.

Listening to his footfalls in the hallway, she didn't feel as if she'd won that little skirmish. Just prolonged the battle. She shut her eyes and blew out a quick breath before refocusing her attention on her laptop and the decades-old journals Mena and Andi had emailed.

A few minutes later, Hunter returned with a plate of sandwiches and dropped onto the armchair closest to the sofa, putting the plate on the coffee table between them. "What are you reading?" He took a sandwich from the top of the stack and bit into it.

Katharine ignored the rumbling of her stomach. It was past lunchtime, and she hadn't eaten anything since she made herself toast after Hunter left for work. "Old journals." She lifted one shoulder and kept her eyes on her screen.

"From previous Medusas?" He moved from the chair to the couch, his weight depressing the cushion beside her.

She frowned at him. "Yes."

He leaned closer, and she sighed, shifting

so their shoulders didn't touch and angling the laptop so he could see the screen without getting nearer. Hunter lifted one eyebrow as he gave her a solemn, sidelong glance, then turned his gaze back to the computer. "How old is this?"

"About a hundred and fifty years."

"Have you found anything useful?"

She contained another sigh. It was a pretty lousy day so far–no way out of the house and nothing interesting in the scanned pages. "No."

He took another bite of his sandwich and scanned the screen slowly.

"If you want to read it, you can hold it, too," she said, annoyance sharpening her tone.

He shot her another sidelong glance. "I don't want to fight with you, Katharine."

She debated with herself for a few moments about whether or not she really wanted to go there right now. Probably not, but what the hell. "Then you shouldn't lock me in your house."

Hunter put the last of his sandwich in his mouth and took the laptop from her knee. When he'd finished chewing, he turned his head to look at her. "You know why your cousins' husbands think this is best."

"And you know I'm an adult. I could call the police, I suppose, and have you arrested for kidnapping."

He smiled. "Yeah, why don't you do that?"

Because all the cops in town were his friends. She was a moron. She glared at him. "I can't imagine why I found you so attractive."

His smile widened, and he picked up another sandwich.

She growled and shoved off the sofa. "Just leave the computer on the table when you go back to work," she said as she left the room.

Only where was she going?

She clenched her jaw as she strode toward the kitchen. She could at least get a drink.

When she'd drunk half a glass of water, she heard his footsteps in the hallway, heading her direction. "For the love of all the Gods, can't you leave me alone?" she growled without turning around. She rested the glass on the edge of the sink and squeezed her eyes shut.

"Apparently not," he muttered from several feet away. "Look, Kat, I'm sorry. Not sorry you're safe, but sorry you're unhappy."

"Not that sorry, or we wouldn't be having this conversation."

"Can we call a truce? I don't want to argue with you, and neither of us is going to change our position on this."

"I'm not sure that's really a truce, just me backing down." She opened her eyes to look at the window over the sink. She was beginning to be annoyed at herself now, for not letting it go. She knew her family wanted her safe. She knew Hunter would keep her safe.

But she hated not having a choice in the matter as much as she hated that he could be in danger, too.

Hunter was silent for a moment, and then

she heard his long exhalation. "Kat–"

"Don't. I get it." She put the glass on the counter and turned around, ignoring the way her pulse leaped at the sight of him standing there in his faded jeans and the black t-shirt that stretched across his wide chest and shoulders. "I don't like having decisions made for me. It isn't your fault you got stuck in the middle of this."

A muscle in his jaw jumped, but he didn't say anything.

"I'll do my best not to provoke any arguments. I can't promise I won't be cranky, though. How's that for a truce?"

"It's a start." He didn't appear mollified, though, fists clenched at his sides and mouth flat. "Will you go eat something now? I heard your stomach growling."

She flushed, embarrassed and annoyed all over again. "Fine." She grabbed her water and headed for the living room, sucking in a quick breath when he caught her wrist on the way by.

"I left you two sandwiches. And the journal still looks interesting, even if there isn't anything useful in it." He dropped her arm and turned away.

She stood there for a few seconds while he went to the fridge before she continued out of the room, back to where he'd left her laptop on the coffee table beside the sandwich plate. Warmth still drifted up her arm from her wrist where his fingers had circled it.

Chemical, she told herself, sitting and

reaching for a sandwich without even checking to see what was in it. Might even be leftover hormones.

She ignored his departure a few minutes later, accompanied as it was by more beeping from the alarm panel by the door, in favor of eating her lunch and continuing to skim through the journal, ignoring the dull ache at the back of her head.

She didn't really think the journal would have anything useful in it. If it had, one of her cousins would have seen it when they were scanning the old pages into their computers.

SHE FINISHED ONE JOURNAL AND STARTED on another before Hunter came back, bearing supper and groceries. She didn't protest when he made her take a break to eat the grilled salmon salad and chunky tomato soup, but then she went back to reading.

Katharine paged through the scanned documents, the thumping behind her eyes increasing until she couldn't focus fully anymore.

Hunter sat beside her just about when she thought she had to call it a day, holding out a glass of water and two aspirin.

"Thank you." She set her laptop on the coffee table and took them, then leaned back against the sofa and closed her eyes with a sigh.

"Had enough for tonight?" He caught one of her hands in his and rubbed his thumb across the back of it.

"I don't think I have a choice." A recurring theme.

"Okay." He released her hand, and she heard her laptop shutting down. "Come on, Kat." He recaptured her hand and tugged, so she sat upright, opening her eyes, and pushed to her feet. "Let me tuck you in," he murmured into her hair as he guided her out of the living room with his arm around her shoulders.

She didn't even argue that he was touching her. Or calling her Kat. When they got to the bedroom, she kicked off her sneakers while she unfastened her shorts. It wasn't until she climbed into bed wearing only her panties that she realized Hunter was standing motionless, a foot away, eyes dark, lips parted. Heat touched her cheeks, and she yanked the blankets up to her chin. *Oops.* Between utter exhaustion and the non-stop worry about their situation, she hadn't even thought about her nightshirt. She rarely bothered at home. *Not your home.*

He swallowed, dragging his gaze from her now-covered breasts to her face. "I'm not sure if I should be flattered or insulted," he teased gruffly.

Katharine kept her mouth shut, suddenly very aware of him so near.

He took a step closer and touched her hair. "You'll find something, Kat. But try to put it out of your head for now and get some rest."

Only now her aching head was full of memories of being in this bed with Hunter, both of them naked, sweaty, entwined. "Thanks," she managed. *Gods, let him go back downstairs.*

He did, without lingering. For that she was grateful. When he closed the door, she shut her eyes tight and curled onto her side. She just needed some sleep to make her head feel better. Stripping in front of Hunter was a slip she couldn't repeat, no matter how much the desire in his eyes tempted her. She needed to find a way to stay safe from the Harvesters that didn't put Hunter in the line of fire.

The scent of him surrounded her in the sheets, and she concentrated on blocking it out while drawing up healing energy from the earth. The concentration was difficult with the thumping in her head, but she kept pushing away the other thoughts trying to intrude. Like Hunter's mouth on her naked breast. No, warm healing energy, flowing up from the earth to her.

Hunter, buried deep inside her in the midst of explosive pleasure.

She growled and rolled onto her other side. "Not now." She concentrated on the visualization once more, breathing easier when she felt the gentle heat start at her feet, sliding up her legs to her spine, to the base of her skull, into her head to loosen the grip of the headache. "Thank you," she whispered, relaxing slightly. Now to concentrate on sleep.

Except she started thinking again, about how Hunter should never have been put in the middle of this. Why wouldn't her brain shut down?

Because of one night of the hottest sex ever, she'd put his life in danger. That'd teach her to pick up hot guys.

*Not funny.* She huffed out a breath and pulled the blankets higher around her ear. Hunter needed to stay safe. She knew the Harvesters wouldn't leave him alone if he got in their way.

She needed to make *him* understand.

Stubborn man.

*Sexy man.*

She growled and flopped onto her back. "Stop it. Go to sleep." Her head gave a twinge, as if the headache might be making a return. "No more." She tried to think of a way to relax and blank her mind, but it was too full of everything that had happened in the past week.

IT TOOK HUNTER A VERY LONG TIME to make his brain stop flashing the image of Kat sliding into his bed wearing only her panties. All that perfect, tawny skin, bare, tempting.

He tapped his pen on his desk, staring at the computer screen without actually seeing the words there. He didn't need to see them anymore.

Clearly, he'd been meant to meet Katharine Rigas-Vardos at the party, to discover her secret, to keep her safe, alive. The desire for more was unexpected, though not unwelcome. At least for him.

Kat, on the other hand, fought it. Hard.

He set his pen down before he tapped a hole in the desktop.

He understood her reasoning, mostly. But it was a bad idea to let her go out on her own where would-be-killers were hunting her. She didn't need her cousins' husbands to tell her that. And he knew he could protect her. If she left, would he see her again? He thought not, and the idea made his chest squeeze tight.

He focused on his computer in the hope of distracting himself before his body took complete control. He opened the new emails Ryder had sent and downloaded the attached files. A little light reading would be the perfect distraction from the nearly-naked woman in his bed.

He stifled a chuckle. Yeah, right. But he wanted to see what Ryder had sent anyway and now was as good a time as any.

Hunter stared at the computer screen for several hours, reading about the women who'd come generations before Katharine until he couldn't see straight anymore. Nothing. He could find nothing that hinted at ending the curse once and for all.

He scribbled a note to study Athena, to see if he could find anything about other curses she might've inflicted. In the morning, when he was fully awake. After shutting everything off, he headed upstairs. By now, Kat should be sound asleep.

Except, after he'd stripped to his underwear

and climbed into the far side of the bed, he knew she wasn't. Her breathing was too measured as she lay motionless.

Still angry.

He exhaled slowly, debating with himself.

"I don't want to be responsible for you getting hurt," she said before he made up his mind.

"My decision, my responsibility," he said evenly.

She rolled over, huffing with annoyance. "That's not true."

"Sweetheart, we can go around and around this again for the rest of the night, but I'm not changing my mind." He rolled to face her in the dark. "And I really don't enjoy arguing with you, despite the frequency we seem to do this." He held his breath and reached out, finding first her arm, then sliding down to catch her hand.

She let him, which meant a surrender of sorts, he imagined. Or she was simply exhausted. Finally she sighed and laced her fingers with his. "I don't like the fighting either."

"Relax, Kat. Close your eyes and get some sleep. It won't seem so bad in the morning." *He hoped.*

She didn't speak, just took a deep breath and let it out.

Hunter listened to her even breathing gradually slow until it was shallower and softer. Sleeping, finally. He relaxed, too, concentrating on her warm fingers in his.

When he woke early in the morning, he started to stretch, then froze. Katharine lay sprawled half over him, her naked breast pressed into his chest, her arm over him so her hand clung to his shoulder, and one leg resting on his. He swallowed, feeling the rush of arousal.

Then she stretched. And went perfectly still. She lifted her head and glared at him.

His mouth went dry.

She jerked away, moving to the other side of the bed, scowling.

Hunter thought he'd better keep his mouth shut. But he didn't think he ought to get out of bed right this second, with the erection he now sported. He took a slow breath and bent his leg, trying to think of something else. Work. What was he doing at work today?

Kat shifted several times on the other side of the bed, but he didn't look at her. Finally, she huffed out a quick breath and rolled to face away from him. At least she hadn't accused him of mauling her in her sleep, when, clearly, she was on *his* side of the bed, draped over him. Pointing that out wouldn't make this better.

He shut his eyes and dragged his thoughts back to work. He had some cheating wife to spy on today, he thought. Maybe. Some cheating spouse. Plus Warren's cheating brother-in-law. Maybe Mary Ann had something else lined up, too.

He lay there until he thought he could safely get out of bed. By then, her fidgeting had stopped, and her breathing had evened out again. She might have gone back to sleep. He hoped she'd gone back to sleep as he eased upright and slid from beneath the covers, pausing to grab clean clothing from the dresser before he made a beeline for the bathroom. When he emerged from his hasty shower, she was definitely sleeping, her mouth relaxed, one hand beneath her chin, fingers half-curled.

His remaining tension seeped away, and he headed downstairs. He thought it best to leave her right where she was. Maybe when she woke again, she'd have forgotten about this.

KAT TOOK OUT A JUICE GLASS, THEN slammed the cupboard. Obviously there was something wrong with her. Waking up wrapped around Hunter like she belonged there. Good Gods. It was a damn good thing he hadn't opened his mouth. Of course, he'd left the house before she woke up, leaving her a note on top of her suitcase to tell her he'd check in later when he had a chance.

*Smart man.*

She took her juice into the living room and fired up her laptop. No new emails from her cousins or their husbands waited. She scowled at the screen. She'd recently submitted the last manuscript on her publishing contract, so she didn't have a looming deadline, which meant...back to reading old journals. She sighed. It was better than brooding. Maybe.

By the time Hunter came home for lunch, she'd managed to distract herself by opening a different journal, a Medusa from the seventeen hundreds. That poor, unlucky woman didn't have the luxury of painkillers, or technology. But she lived quite a long time. Kat glanced away from her screen only when Hunter sat beside her and held out a plate.

"Oh, thanks." She took the dish, noting the skinny roll stuffed with chicken salad and a sliced apple beside it. "Thank you, Hunter." She shot him a sidelong glance, but his attention was on his own sandwich. "This looks good."

"It is. I get them from the deli near my office all the time." He finally glanced up. "Anything interesting in your reading today?"

"Some history, but nothing useful. No magic way to get rid of the curse, if that's what you mean." She took a bite of her sandwich. "Mm, yum." She chewed for a moment, her gaze sliding toward her laptop screen. "Have you heard from anyone today?"

He shook his head. "I didn't expect to. Did you?"

She lifted one shoulder. "I thought maybe they'd be in touch." She'd hoped they would. She wanted out. She wanted her life back. Okay, sure she knew she couldn't go back to her house. She'd deal with that, she'd have to start fresh somewhere. Or at least hide out where she wasn't putting anyone else in danger.

Hunter finished his sandwich and took a drink of the water he'd carried in with him. "I'm sure if they find anything, they'll let you know."

She frowned at the computer instead of glaring at him. That was the problem, wasn't it? *If.* She finished her lunch in silence, a little surprised he let her. "What if I went to stay with one of them?" she said finally.

He glared at her now. "Why?"

"They've been through this. They know what to do. Or at least how to evade these guys."

"And you'd be putting them in danger."

"They're family." She didn't want her family in danger either, and the danger would follow her, so going to family wasn't feasible. Katharine couldn't see any ideal solutions to this situation. Even if the worst happened and the Harvesters found her, killed her, the curse would simply move on to the next unlucky cousin. No one would ever be safe as long as they carried this curse.

Jaw tight, Hunter gathered their empty plates and went to the kitchen, silent and furious.

She watched him stalk to the front door a minute later, a muscle jumping in his jaw as he punched keys on the alarm pad.

"Don't do anything foolish," he ground out, and then he was gone.

She sighed and sat back against the sofa. "It

was only a suggestion," she shouted at the door even though she knew he couldn't hear her anymore. Cranky. He was cranky. She was cranky.

Probably because of the way she'd been crawling all over him in her sleep that morning, she admitted, closing her eyes. Good grief. A few more minutes, and her steamy dream might've become reality.

She sat up and reached for the laptop she'd set aside to eat lunch. Back to the journals.

AFTER THEY'D FINISHED A MOSTLY SILENT supper of meatloaf and baked potatoes, Hunter parked himself at his computer, irritated with himself and with Kat. She didn't protest, probably equally angry with him. Not arguing was a good thing, he told himself. They'd just agreed to a truce yesterday, though he was kind of surprised it lasted this long.

He had no new email from Ryder or Kallan and wasn't sure if that was good or bad.

Kat gave up on reading after another hour and paced around the living room a few times before she sat on the chair nearest to his desk. "I don't want to argue with you, Hunter. Really. But I've been thinking about this all afternoon. It would be so much safer for you if I wasn't here. What if the Harvester is still here in town and he happens to see you? He's not going to let you walk away."

He didn't look at her, staring instead at the scanned page on his monitor. A journal page from a hundred years ago.

"He'll follow you, or worse. I'd feel awful if something happened to you because of me."

He glanced at her finally. "And you think they aren't watching your family, too? That they wouldn't think you might turn to previous Medusas for help?"

A tiny frown creased her brow. Clearly, she hadn't considered that possibility while trying to come up with reasons to take off. Or she just hadn't come up with another option.

"That puts your family in just as much danger." He shoved away from his desk. It was his turn to pace the room.

"I don't want anybody in danger because of me," she started.

"And what if they find you? When you can't protect yourself again? Then what?"

She clenched her hands on her lap. "I die."

"Not if I can help it." He stopped walking and set his hands on his hips to glare at her. "I can keep you alive." This time, he would.

She shut her eyes. "You are a very stubborn man, Hunter Phelps."

"My mother used to tell me the same thing." It wasn't a compliment then either.

"Used to?" She glanced at him.

"She's gone." And Katharine was still here, alive, and he planned to keep her that way.

"I'm sorry." Sympathy softened her expression.

He didn't say anything, just watched her. None of the things crowding his tongue right now would prevent another argument.

"Think about it, please. I don't want to argue, but please. Ryder or Kallan could make sure I was safe, and you'd be protected, too." She pushed to her feet. "Think about it." She skirted him to leave the room, and he heard her soft footfalls on the stairs a moment later.

*'Think about it.'* Yeah, right. He clenched his fists at his sides and shut his eyes tight. No way in hell.

He forced himself to take several slow, deep breaths when he heard the bedroom door close, and he returned to his desk.

It took him a few minutes to push her plea from his head so he could focus on the computer screen. He didn't know who this previous Medusa was, exactly, in Katharine's family tree, but she hadn't had an easy time of it. A young man had been courting her, a young man she wasn't really interested in, until the curse struck. Then she wished fervently she'd fallen in love with him, with anyone, before her predecessor had died.

That made him pause. So she had known if she'd been in love the curse would've passed to someone else. Interesting. Ryder had mentioned in his email the family had only recently rediscovered that.

Ryder.

Hunter scowled at the screen. Let Ryder or Kallan keep her safe.

He pondered the idea for a long time, staring unseeingly at his computer.

He could get her to Ryder or Kallan, who'd both been through this. But if he let her go, he had a sneaking suspicion he'd never see her again, no matter what any of them might say.

Have his life back? Hell, Lance had been right when he'd said Hunter should get a life. All work and no play made Hunter a very dull boy.

Being with Katharine had made him realize he'd been missing out on a lot in his self-imposed exile, and he didn't relish going back now.

No, he was not going to hand her off to Ryder or Kallan. He intended to see this through, all the way. Maybe it wouldn't turn out well between him and Katharine, but that was life. Maybe it wouldn't turn out to be the biggest mistake he'd ever made either.

He grinned, sitting back in his chair.

Feeling slightly better, he returned his attention to his reading. Even though he'd made up his mind not to send her away, he didn't think telling her that tonight was conducive to keeping their truce. He could read until she was sleeping. Or until he couldn't see straight anymore, whichever came first.

# CHAPTER SEVEN

Too early in the morning, the warmth woke him. The sun wasn't quite up, though the sky was light when he opened his eyes. Hunter's brain registered those things, then came alert enough to realize the source of the heat on his right side: Kat.

He held his breath when she shifted, rubbing her cheek along his chest, a flutter of her lashes, and a slow stretch that had her full breast pressing into his side. And back to sleep.

He unclenched his jaw and released the breath he'd been holding. His groin throbbed, painfully close to where her soft thigh rested over his. At least this morning, she had a pair of pajamas on instead of only her panties. It still wasn't enough for him to forget what she felt like wearing nothing.

Served him right.

Nevertheless, he didn't think she'd appreciate waking again this morning to find herself wrapped around him. So he eased away, carefully. Slowly. Until he was clinging to the edge of the mattress and there were several inches of warm sheet between them.

KAT REACHED OUT AND CAUGHT his wrist without opening her eyes. "Where you goin'?" she mumbled.

"Shower," he croaked. *Cold.* "I thought you were sleeping."

"I was, till you started moving." She opened sleepy eyes and caught his gaze.

His mouth went dry. "I didn't mean to wake you."

She studied him thoroughly, making him even more aware of her fingers on his skin.

"You should go back to sleep for a little longer," he managed.

Her thumb rubbed along the back of his wrist. Light. *Deliberate.* "Kiss me, Hunter."

His too-quick heartbeat kicked up another notch. "Now I know you need more sleep," he teased gruffly.

Her fingers tightened on his arm even though he hadn't moved—only thought about it. "Please."

He had all kinds of arguments ready—not in gratitude, thanks; complications she didn't want; blah-blah. But he wanted to. "I don't want you to regret it," he finally managed.

She released his arm, but just to set her hand on his jaw. "I won't. I promise."

Far better men than he must have succumbed to far less temptation. He leaned closer as she did the same. For a long moment, he held her gaze, still debating with himself. Then, because he truly wanted it, he closed the small distance, catching her mouth. Gently.

This was how he'd imagined they might wake after that first night together. Sleepy, warm woman in his arms, kissing lazily, as if they had all the time in the world.

Her fingers slid from his jaw to his nape. In turn, he nipped at her lower lip, and when she opened to him, he hummed his approval.

One kiss turned into two, into ten, into fifty. By the time Hunter came up for air, he had a handful of Kat's breast, and she'd wrapped one leg around his hip to rock into his erection. He let go of her breast and wrapped both arms tight around her to stop her movements.

"Wow, sweetheart," he rasped into her hair, "that was a helluva kiss."

She squirmed against him.

"Stop it."

He felt her smile along his throat, right before she did it again.

Hunter groaned. "You asked for a kiss, Kat, not *that*."

She tipped her head back, a wicked glint in her eyes. "If I ask–"

He flattened her beneath him, giving in to the need to roll his hips against hers. Once. "No. Not now." He waited till she focused her eyes, gratified that he wasn't the only one on the verge of losing all control here. "I'm not just looking for a quick fuck now, and I'm not looking for gratitude or convenience."

A tiny frown line appeared between her brows.

"I won't say I don't want you," he went on

before she could speak. "It'd be a lie. But not this way."

"Are you going all relationship on me?" She didn't quite manage to keep her tone light.

"No. I wouldn't pressure you. You have enough going on right now." But he wanted to.

And she knew it, judging by the wariness clouding her eyes.

"What would you like for breakfast?" he asked, rolling off of her and stifling a wince. "Pancakes? Waffles?" Making breakfast gave him time for his hard-on to subside.

"It doesn't matter." She sat up and set one hand in the middle of his bare back. "Hunter?"

He shut his eyes. "Yeah?"

"I do appreciate what you've done for me. But I'd never–not out of gratitude."

He swallowed. "Good to know," he managed after a few seconds and shoved to his feet. The spot where her hand had rested felt far warmer than the rest of him as he strode away.

Katharine couldn't decide if she was more annoyed with herself for instigating something she shouldn't have that morning, or with Hunter for turning her down. Being annoyed with him would be stupid, and she knew she wasn't stupid, but what kind of man said no to that?

Of course, if he hadn't stopped her, she'd have real reason to be annoyed with him now, even if she *had* started it.

She chopped more vegetables into the strainer for rinsing. What the hell was wrong with her? This was the second morning in a row she'd been dreaming of their night together and had woken to find herself wrapped around him. Clearly, the issue was hers.

She ran some water over the veggies, then rummaged through the cupboards until she found the right size pot. The least she could do was make up her damned mind. Either she wanted him or she didn't.

Of course she wanted him. She already knew the chemistry they shared was smoking hot. She'd be lying if she didn't admit to wanting him. Still. But she knew she wasn't staying, couldn't stay, and it would be better for both of them if they didn't indulge again.

Satisfied for now, she puttered around the kitchen a bit longer, putting the vegetables into the pot for soup and setting it to simmer. And until suppertime, she could read. Maybe there was a way to get rid of the curse forever, waiting to be found somewhere in one of these journals, and if there was, she'd find it.

Several hours later, Katharine pushed off the sofa with a growl to pace the living room. Was there really no hope of ever getting rid of this damned curse?

Nothing in the centuries of lore her family had kept indicated the possibility. Nothing in the information Kallan had managed to pilfer from his own family pointed to any possible end, aside from the Harvesters annihilating the

Medusas if they ever got the amulet, and he was the only Harvester who knew the secret of that.

How could one Goddess be so vindictive because a girl bragged about her hair?

Katharine stared out the side window at the narrow patch of grass between the house and the extra-tall fence bordering the yard. Praying and making offerings to the Goddess hadn't worked for her family.

Maybe it was finally time to pay Her a visit and beg.

Hunter would never go for it.

That didn't mean she couldn't make the suggestion. But maybe she needed to butter him up first. She wondered if homemade soup was enough. Maybe not. Perhaps dessert, too.

HUNTER SNIFFED THE AIR AS HE stepped inside the house, automatically resetting the alarm system. Kat was cooking.

He wondered what she wanted. Stupid question. She wanted to leave.

She appeared in the kitchen doorway a half a second later, looking uncertain. "Hi."

He steeled himself. "Hey. It smells good in here."

One side of her mouth curved up. "Creamy vegetable soup, bread, and brownies."

Surely she didn't think feeding him would persuade him to let her go off on her own into the path of the Harvesters. He stifled a sigh and started back the hallway to meet her. "What's the occasion?"

"I got tired of reading old journals." She shrugged. "Are you hungry?"

"Starved." He was, since he'd missed lunch on his stake-out of the cheating wife, and he was curious to see exactly what she wanted.

"You didn't get lunch today." She returned to the kitchen, going to the stove to stir the contents of the pot there.

"No. I had to do some surveillance for a divorce lawyer." He sat at the table, his gaze sliding from her back to the golden brown loaf of bread that sat on his counter, and the pan on the back burner of the stove that must be the promised brownies. "Yesterday was a worker's comp case."

"Do you get bored sitting around, waiting to see if they're really doing what you think they're doing?" She shut off the burner and turned back to him. "Soup's ready."

"Let's use the dining room. I'll set the table." He got to his feet, noting the slight lift of her eyebrows. "What?"

"It's nothing fancy. Dinner, I mean."

It was his turn to shrug. "I hardly ever have anyone here to eat with me, so I never use the dining room. Hell, I'm hardly ever here to eat by myself." He took bowls from a cupboard and gathered silverware. "Indulge me."

Kat swallowed, and his gaze slid down her throat to where a hint of color began, creeping up to her cheeks, and he realized her mind had gone in a different direction.

He'd like that sort of indulgence. But not until she was truly ready for it again.

"Why don't you get the bread and some butter, and I'll dish up the soup. Meet you in the dining room," he said gruffly.

She did as he suggested, then disappeared. Hunter smiled grimly. If she thought feeding him was going to persuade him to let her loose into danger, she had another thing coming.

HUNTER GLARED ACROSS THE TABLE at her. "Hell, no." *Go to Greece.* "That's even crazier than going off on your own when the Harvesters are right here." He shoved his empty bowl away and got to his feet in a rush, his chair scraping the floor. Now he knew what she'd wanted and it was way worse than he'd expected.

"Hunter, praying to Athena and making offerings to Her hasn't worked for us, and as far as I can tell, no one else in my family has come up with anything, so maybe it's time to go to the source." Kat remained in her seat, her chin on her hands.

"Have you forgotten this Goddess has sent a family of killers after yours for thousands of years? I highly doubt She'll change Her mind if someone pays Her a visit. That gives Her direct access to strike you down." He unclenched his fists at his sides. "No. Absolutely not."

"It was just a thought." Her mouth drooped at the corners.

He dropped his head back to look at the

ceiling for a few seconds, trying to gather some calm. "I'm sorry, Katharine. But don't you think someone else might've considered the same thing over the years?" He lowered his chin so he could meet her gaze. "I'd guess they discarded the idea as much too dangerous."

She looked down at the table, to the remains of their meal. "I didn't mean to start another argument. It occurred to me earlier, and I had to suggest it."

He realized it was a last-ditch effort for her, the next thing to admitting defeat, which he didn't believe she'd do. He collected himself. "I'm sorry I overreacted. I think Ryder and Kallan might have done the same." He sat again and took a slow breath. "Do you want to talk about anything else?"

Her head shot up, and pink tinted her cheeks. "No."

He raised one eyebrow. "You don't want to talk about this morning?"

Her blush deepened, and she shifted her gaze to the brownie pan. "It's been a long time since I slept with a man," she said, low. "I'm not sorry I wanted to kiss you this morning."

His heartbeat quickened, and he considered her words. "So if I wanted to kiss you now, you might be okay with that?"

Kat met his gaze. "I might. But I don't know if it's a good idea."

He reined in the impulse to rush around the table and yank her from her seat to kiss her anyway. "You asked me this morning if I was going all relationship on you, and I said I wouldn't pressure you. I didn't say I wouldn't like to give it a try, though."

She swallowed, her gaze dropping to his mouth for a second before lifting again. "I know," she whispered, "but I'm not sure that's a good idea either."

"Why don't we? Maybe make this a full date night, in-house, though. You've made dinner and dessert, so I'll clean up. Let's see a movie next." He didn't know where the idea had come from, but he held his breath to see what she'd do.

"A movie?" Doubt colored her tone.

"Yes. Like a date, only safe here from anyone we don't want to run into."

She debated it silently for a while. Almost too long to bear. Finally, she nodded. "Okay.

Hunter took a deeper breath at last.

"I don't think you realize the mess in the kitchen from my cooking and baking, though, to say you'll do the clean-up." She smiled and got to her feet.

As she rinsed the soup pot, Katharine realized her hands were trembling. What the hell had she been thinking? A date with Hunter? Dates led to more dates and then relationships. She was hiding out from murderers which didn't bode well for a relationship.

But Hunter was the first man she'd met in years who engaged her on so many levels.

Since they met, he'd made her laugh, made her angry, made her curious. He made her want.

She couldn't help thinking about the want when she went back to gather their bowls and the leftover bread to put away. That alone was probably worth at least one date. Her fingers shook as she wrapped the bread in foil.

If she was going to do it, she may as well really do it. With the dreams she'd had the past two nights, some part of her was ready to give it a try.

Katharine set the empty bread plate on the counter and took a deep breath before she turned back to where Hunter was collecting glasses and silverware. His burgeoning smile faded when she set one hand on his arm.

"It's been a long time since I've attempted a relationship," she started. "And I'm pretty sure this is a lousy time to give it a try–" she set her other hand over his mouth when he opened it–"but I do know I want you, Hunter. Would you please kiss me?"

He smiled behind her fingers, then pressed a kiss on them before he nudged her hand away from his face.

"That wasn't exactly what I meant," she whispered, her pulse skipping in anticipation.

"It's a start." He set his hands at her waist. "Why don't you go pick a movie while I start the dishwasher?"

Her disappointment must have shown on her face, because his fingers tightened on her briefly.

"I'll kiss you everywhere you want later. Movie portion of this date first."

For a few seconds, she pondered trying to change his mind. Then she decided anticipation might be good for her, so she nodded. *Everywhere she wanted.* Her pulse quickened.

Hunter released her. "The cabinet in the corner has a lot of choices, or we can stream something."

Katharine went, listening to the clinks and rattles of the dishes behind her. The corner cabinet had several hundred choices, she discovered when she tugged it open. Lots of very guy action movies, some comedies, a few documentaries and television series, as well as a decent selection of thrillers. She spent a few minutes scanning the titles, then pulled a thriller out. It should have enough speeding cars and shooting to satisfy Hunter.

One of his eyebrows quirked up when he saw her selection.

"I remember liking it when it first came out," she said with a shrug. "What's not to like: hot couple on the hunt for a killer in Rome?"

He smiled. "It happens to be one of my favorites. Should I make popcorn?"

She shook her head. "After that supper? I'm not eating till well into tomorrow."

Hunter's gaze slid over her, and she swallowed. "Then I guess it's movie time." He set one hand at the small of her back to move her toward the sofa.

BY THE TIME THE CLOSING CREDITS were rolling up the screen, Hunter could barely stand the anticipation anymore. During the course of the movie, he'd eased her closer, then into his lap so he could wrap both arms around her and hold her tight. Now, with Kat's soft ass planted over his erection, he didn't want to move. Yet he wanted very much to move–deep inside her again. He didn't want to rush this, but he wasn't sure he was capable of finesse at this point.

She turned her face into the side of his neck, her breath warm and quick. "Can we start the 'kissing everywhere I want' now?" She punctuated the question with a small wriggle of her ass in his lap.

He caught her hips and gave her a push away from him. "I may follow it up with a spanking," he growled as she got to her feet.

She laughed. "I may let you."

He groaned at that mental picture and shoved to his feet, lifting one hand toward her.

She backed out of reach, her eyes dark. "Come kiss me, Hunter. Upstairs."

He let her go, just so he could follow and watch the sway of her hips as she climbed the steps. It felt like he'd been waiting for this forever. While he knew it might not mean everything he wanted, he'd take what she offered and hope like hell he didn't wind up hurt.

Kat waited for him just inside his bedroom, her cheeks pink, tight nipples pressed against her shirt.

"Hi." He reached out to touch her cheek, then slid his forefinger down to stroke her full lower lip.

"Hi," she whispered.

He stepped closer, so only an inch separated their bodies. "So where would you like me to kiss you first?"

Her eyes widened slightly, and her mouth curved. "Here." She rubbed her own finger along her lip, brushing his finger.

He bent to oblige her, feathering a soft kiss on her mouth. Once more, nibbling at her upper lip, then easing back to look at her.

Her lashes fluttered up. "Kiss me again."

He smiled and bent back to her mouth, diving in this time and startling a small moan out of her. She tasted so damn good. Her tongue met his, stroking, coaxing. He caught her waist and drew her closer, so her hard little nipples rubbed his chest. So his erection nudged at her belly.

Her fingers slid around his nape as she lifted into him, rocking her hips.

He needed to slow her down.

He lifted his head, realizing how hard his breath came already. "Where next, sweetheart?"

She dropped her head back, swallowing. "Here," she breathed, gliding her fingers along her throat toward the top of her shirt.

Hunter nuzzled and licked his way over the warm column, pausing occasionally for a little nip before he continued on his way. By the time he reached her collarbone, Kat's fingernails dug into his nape and the back of his shoulder. So, for good measure, he nudged her shirt just low enough to suck on her collarbone, lightly. Then he lifted his head. "Next?"

It took her a moment to open her eyes this time. She released her death grip on his shoulder and eased her hand over first one breast, then the other, her breath catching when she rubbed her nipples. "Here."

Hunter caught the hem of her shirt and tugged it up, off, sending it flying. "So pretty," he murmured, lifting one hand to skim his fingers along the top edge of the pink lace that didn't hide her breasts. Then he bent to press a light kiss in the center of her chest.

She made a small sound of protest, and he smiled before dragging his open mouth over the upper swell of one breast. Her fingers dug into his shoulders again. And he set his mouth right over the tight peak, sucking on the nipple, hard.

Kat cried out, knees buckling.

Hunter caught her, then walked her backward to his bed, lowering her and climbing over her to taste her other nipple, too. She lifted against him, and he raked his teeth over the hard little bit of flesh so she gasped. It took him a very long time to thoroughly taste both her breasts, and by the time he'd finished, a fine sheen of perspiration gleamed on her skin, and she kept trying to lift her hips, though his heavier weight kept her pinned between him and the mattress.

"Now where?" he asked, his mouth watering in anticipation as he pushed his torso off of her, still holding her hips pinned with his.

She slipped her hand from his shoulder, from the top edge of her bra until she could wedge it between their bellies, lower, until her fingers rested between her thighs. "Please, Hunter." She was hoarse already from the moans and cries that had escaped her, and he wasn't nearly finished with her.

Before he moved lower, he caught her mouth once more, lingering, and gave a slow roll of his hips against hers, enjoying the taste of the whimper that slid into their kiss.

Then he began kissing his way down her torso, teasing her breasts again, briefly, discarding her bra this time, on his way to her navel, liking the way she squirmed away from his mouth. He unfastened her shorts and eased them off, along with her underwear, nuzzling and licking and kissing his way from one hip to the other before he pushed her thighs wide. Wider, so he could settle between them.

"Oh, sweetheart," he murmured. "You're so pretty. So wet for me." He glided one finger along her swollen flesh, and her breathing hitched. He leaned in and let his tongue follow the same path. Sweet, salty, aroused woman. *His* woman. "Taste so good," he muttered, nipping at the inside of her thigh. Then he settled his mouth on her fully, dimly hearing her moan as her hips jerked upward. He slid his hands beneath her ass and lifted her exactly where he wanted her, controlling her pleasure completely.

She was so close. Again.

Hunter had teased her to the brink and back several times now. Katharine didn't even care that the begging she heard came from her own mouth.

Hunter's mouth was devious. Voracious. *Perfect.*

This time, though, when she felt the scrape of his teeth on her over-sensitized clit, he plunged two fingers inside her and a ragged scream burst from her as the pleasure exploded.

When she could think again, Hunter was kissing his way up the center of her chest, his erection burning a path along her knee, her thigh, as he moved higher.

"I think you killed me," she rasped, realizing her throat hurt from all the moans and cries he'd wrung from her already.

She felt his smile against her collarbone, then one of his big hands settled on her breast. Heat spread outward from the spot, and her nipple tightened into his palm. He shifted over her, settling between her thighs so the tip of his cock brushed her clit, which sent a hot rush of pleasure into her middle. "Maybe I can revive you. A bit of mouth to mouth," he murmured, lifting his head so he could brush her lips with his own.

She smiled and summoned enough the energy to lift one hand to his shoulder. "It might take a lot," she whispered.

"I think I'm up to it." He nipped at her lower lip as he shifted his hips to lodge the head of his erection in her wet folds.

A ragged moan scraped past her sore throat.

His tongue slid along her upper lip, then the lower. "I didn't intend for you to lose your voice, sweetheart." He reached down with one hand to ease her knee up and his weight pressed him a little deeper inside her.

She felt the stretch of her muscles around him. "Worth it," she breathed, shifting beneath him so he slid a bit further.

His smile against her mouth registered a heartbeat before he shoved deep, and she whimpered. He kissed her lazily now, his hips pinning her to the bed while he stroked and touched her with hands and mouth for an eon.

Katharine shivered when Hunter lifted his head just enough to catch her gaze.

"Come for me, sweetheart, like this." He rocked his hips from side to side, pressing tight to her clit.

She shuddered at the pleasure bursting outward from the tiny bundle of nerves, digging her fingers into his back. "Hunter."

He cupped her breast. "Right here, Kat." He slid the tip of his tongue along her lower lip and gave her nipple a tight pinch.

And the pleasure magnified a thousand-fold, just like that.

HUNTER HELD TIGHT, MOTIONLESS, WHILE she quaked and moaned. Her body fisting around his cock made it a real challenge to remain motionless, to rein in his need to thrust, to power deeper inside her. But he managed it. *Barely.*

When she finally opened her eyes, they were dark, a hint of surprise lurking in the depths. "Wow, you're still–"

He kissed her lightly. "Yes." He wasn't sure how much longer he could hold out, though. "You feel incredible around me."

The color in her cheeks deepened. "You feel pretty good, too," she whispered, her voice even rougher than it had been.

"You up for another round?" As he spoke, he eased his hips backward, then glided deep again, and her breath caught. "Kat?"

"Yes." She undulated beneath him so the tips of her breasts rubbed his chest.

He bent and caught one in his teeth, using the point of his tongue to tease a moan out of her. But he knew he'd never be able to make this last. Not as hard as his dick was throbbing now. He groaned when her inner muscles rippled around him. *Soon.*

He wedged one hand between them so he could stroke his thumb over and around her swollen clit.

At his first touch, a ragged cry escaped her,

and he thrust harder inside her. The urge to go faster built, pleasure spreading outward from his cock, his balls, along his spine. When she surged up into his next thrust, he lost control and pounded into her, faster. Harder, until his release exploded.

It was a long time before he could think, and when he managed it, he realized he was crushing her into the mattress, so he started to roll to his side.

"Don't move," she whispered, digging her fingers harder again into the back of his shoulder, her legs tightening around his waist.

He propped himself on his forearms. "I'm too heavy."

"I like it." She pulled, and he let her tug him back down.

He liked it, too, far more than he thought Kat would appreciate. So he didn't speak for a while, containing any danger from words he might blurt out when all of his brain function at the moment was concentrated between his legs.

She nuzzled the side of his neck some time later, and he rolled to his side, keeping her tucked close, then fumbling for the blankets. He yanked them up to cover her to the shoulder, and a quiet sigh warmed his throat. It took only a few minutes for her breathing to slow into a sleepy rhythm, and Hunter swallowed.

He'd never imagined *this* when he came home from work today. He'd never imagined it when she told him her harebrained idea during supper either. Not when he was so furious.

Yet here they were.

He stroked one hand over the top of her damp head, listening to her even breathing. If he wasn't so damned exhausted, he might pay more attention to the tingling of his nerves from the contact, to the pulse in his groin. She needed some sleep.

He smiled. He'd worn her out so thoroughly she'd lost her voice. And some savage part of him loved it.

Almost as much as the part of him that was thrilled she'd uttered the "R" word earlier.

What did that say about him, he wondered.

He wasn't sure he wanted to know, and his brain was too decimated right now to ponder deeply.

Maybe tomorrow he could figure it out.

# CHAPTER EIGHT

**K**at woke first in the morning and stretched, then realized she lay in Hunter's arms, her back to his front. He breathed evenly, slowly. Heat suffused her face and throat. She hadn't intended *that* to happen again, at least not so soon. She'd barely wrapped her brain around attempting a relationship, something she hadn't tried in years, and certainly not under conditions like these.

Clearly, there was something wrong with her.

She squeezed her eyes shut for a second, letting out a slow breath. Sex didn't have to mean anything.

But she was afraid that sex with Hunter meant something more than just sex.

So she didn't allow her brain to linger there. Instead, she eased out from under his arm and grabbed the first clean clothes inside her suitcase on her way to the bathroom.

Hunter still slept when she emerged ten minutes later, though he rolled onto his back, and the sheet slid aside to uncover part of his wide chest.

Katharine paused to admire the strong muscles there, then blushed when she saw the faint imprint of teeth on his shoulder. Dear Gods, she had lost all restraint last night and actually *marked* him.

She hurried on bare feet out of the room, trying to banish the image from her head, and down the stairs. When she came to a stop in the kitchen, she took a deep breath and held it for a few seconds before releasing it. Breakfast. And caffeine.

By the time Hunter came downstairs less than fifteen minutes later, she had bacon and eggs on the stove, bread in the toaster, and a cup of tea steeping on the counter. She glanced back over her shoulder at him, swallowing at the intent look in his sleepy eyes. "Breakfast is almost ready."

He dragged one hand back over his dark, wet head and studied her for a few more seconds. She knew he was seeing much more than she'd like. "You're up early," he finally said, his tone neutral.

She shrugged, one-shouldered. "I couldn't sleep anymore."

The intensity in his eyes deepened, but he didn't say any of the things she feared he'd say, the things she was sure were running through his head. "What's for breakfast?"

Katharine relaxed a bit, turning back to their meal.

By the time they'd eaten almost everything on their plates, she felt a bit better.

"What are you going to work on today?" he asked, taking the last slice of toast.

She pondered for a few seconds. "I don't know. I'm tired of reading those old journals and getting nothing helpful. Maybe I could ride along with you today." She didn't know what had made her say it, but she held her breath now.

He shook his head, one eyebrow quirked up slightly. "Nice try."

She frowned. "You don't think I'd be safe with you?"

"That isn't what I said."

"Sounds like it. If that's the case, then you ought to–" She stopped talking at the dangerous glint in his eyes.

Hunter set his toast on the plate and put his hands flat on the table beside it. "I know you understand there's at least one Harvester running around this town. Neither of us knows where or who he is, and, since this town isn't very big, the chances of running into him are better than you think. There is no way in hell you can go along with me, since I'm not just leaving here and going to sit in my office all day." He shoved to his feet, startling her. "I have to do some surveillance today, and a client to meet at his office, and it isn't safe, Katharine."

She swallowed. "I'm sorry, I didn't mean–"

He shook his head, disappointment turning down the corners of his mouth.

And she realized suddenly what he was thinking. A lump tried to clog her throat, and she swallowed around it with some difficulty.

"Hunter, I didn't–" *Didn't sleep with you so you'd let me out of the house. Didn't make you breakfast as a bribe.* She couldn't say it. The look on his face said he wouldn't believe her.

"I'll see you later."

She put her face in her hands and tried to breathe evenly as she listened to his footfalls from the kitchen to the front door, the beeps as he reset the alarm on her prison.

"This is why I don't do relationships," she muttered when she was sure he was gone. "I can't manage to get it right."

"You're just out of practice," he said from the other end of the hallway, then banged the door shut behind him.

She dropped her arms to the table and buried her face in them. Gods, she really couldn't get it right.

Katharine felt a little bit bad about what she'd said earlier to Hunter about letting her go. Not bad enough to apologize yet, though, since he'd left her a prisoner in his house yet again.

She sighed and put her head down directly on the table. Going through the same argument every morning was getting old. Yes, she knew the chances the Harvester had stayed in town were high. Yes, she understood he'd definitely called in reinforcements by now Of course, they didn't know who Hunter was, so she felt pretty confident that her chances of running into a Harvester while with Hunter were nearly nil–after all, they weren't looking for his car.

Then again, they did know a man had interrupted, so they'd now be watching for a couple.

She groaned and thumped her head on the table, and once more for good measure. Of course she had to apologize to Hunter.

HUNTER WATCHED MR. PARNELL GILCHRIST mowing his lawn and snapped pictures as the man raked up the loose grass clippings with no obvious physical difficulty, but his mind was on Katharine.

She hadn't tried hard to persuade him to let her go off on her own, though he hadn't realized it this morning, when he was already irritated and hurt after waking to find her gone from his bed when he'd hoped to kiss her awake.

Her half-hearted effort made him smile now. Even if he hadn't promised her family, he'd never feel right letting her walk into danger. And then her grumbled comment when she thought he was gone...whether she admitted it to herself or not, this was definitely heading into relationship territory. Probably what had interrupted her sleep so early in the morning. It was almost definitely what had triggered her stammered attempts to apologize to him. He owed *her* an apology for not letting her finish.

He snapped another picture of Gilchrist lifting a picnic bench and hefting it onto his supposedly-injured shoulder to carry it away from the house to drop near the fire pit at the back fence. That should do it.

Hunter put the camera down and started the car, heading for the office, where he emailed the pictures to the insurance office and copied them onto a flash drive that Mary Ann would also messenger to them.

"No new messages," she said when he stopped at her desk.

"Then I'm going to see a friend."

She smiled slyly. "Is this the same 'friend' you've been spending so much time with?"

"Yes." He stuck his hand in his pocket and found his keys.

"About time." She winked. "Don't do anything I wouldn't do." Knowing his secretary, that meant no limits.

Hunter actually felt himself blush, and he bit his tongue to keep from telling her it was way too late for the warning. "Thanks for the advice," he muttered instead, turning for the door.

He stopped on his way home and grabbed some takeout and a bottle of wine. When he stepped inside and reset the alarm, the house was quiet. He put his purchases in the kitchen before heading upstairs in search of Katharine.

He found her in the room he intended to eventually turn into an office. She'd shoved aside some of his file boxes to set up his folding card table against the back wall at the window. She sat on one of the matching metal chairs, fingers tapping swiftly over her keyboard. She didn't even glance up when he stopped in the middle of the room, as if she hadn't heard him. He squinted at her screen—not email, but work, writing work from the look of it. She finally stopped typing a minute later and sat back in the chair, then jumped as if she'd just realized he was there.

"Hi." He smiled—her hair was a tumbled mess despite the pen stuck in the falling-down knot at her nape, and she wore one of his denim work shirts over a white tank top and a pair of jeans with a ragged hole across her knee. She looked good in his shirt. He wondered what had happened to the clothes she was wearing when he left the house.

"I didn't hear you." Her pulse did a little dance at the hollow of her throat.

"I know. New story?" He took a step closer, another.

She nodded. "I've got about fifty pages. It's rough, but it's there."

That meant she'd been working for quite a long time. "Have you eaten?"

She squinted at the clock on her laptop. "I didn't realize it was so late."

"That means 'no'." Hunter held out one hand. "Come, let me feed you, and then you can go back to work if you want."

She took his hand, which surprised him a bit after that morning. Clearly, she was more agreeable when her mind was in work mode than when she had nothing occupy her but thoughts of escape.

It took until they were halfway through

their meal, and a good thirty minutes past his apology for jumping to the wrong conclusion over breakfast before she seemed fully present. He thought he'd have to repeat his apology later to be sure she'd heard it, and that the shrug he'd gotten earlier actually indicated forgiveness.

She peered at him over her nearly-empty wineglass and smiled. "Are you trying to get me drunk?"

Hunter laughed. "I should've gotten something stronger than wine then, shouldn't I?"

Kat smiled wider. "Maybe." She held out her glass, and he refilled it, watching her expression.

"Are you going to be able to write after two glasses?" He topped off his own glass, too.

"I'm done writing for today." She took a sip of the red liquid. "My brain needs a break." Her gaze landed on him again, and her eyes darkened.

Hunter lifted one eyebrow. He recognized the expression on her face, and his pulse moved faster. "You know, I can see what you're thinking, Kat," he said, then, when his voice came out in a gruff rumble, cleared his throat. He shouldn't be thinking what he was thinking in response to her expression either. Not until they got some things clear between them.

Her smile widened. "I'm sure you can." She took another sip and put her glass down. "I want to dance with you." She pushed to her feet and moved around the table toward him.

He remembered dancing with her. He remembered what came after dancing with her. His body went on full-alert, heart rate increasing, blood flowing south. When she held out her hand, he set aside his own glass and shoved his chair back. "Be sure, Kat," he warned her, holding his hand half an inch from hers.

She closed the distance, her warm fingers wrapping around his. "Let's dance."

He let her tow him to the living room, watched as she turned on the stereo and fed in several cds. The speakers pumped out a slow, steady beat beneath an enticing melody, and Kat turned back to him, intent gleaming in her bright eyes.

Despite his good intentions, Hunter knew he'd let her seduce him tonight. He'd developed a serious weakness where she was concerned. She might think it was casual, she might think this was temporary, but he knew better.

KATHARINE SLID HER HANDS UP HUNTER'S chest, smiling at the quick thud of his heartbeat beneath her palms. Then his hands settled on her hips and drew her closer. Close enough to feel his strengthening arousal against her belly. She lifted her gaze to his face–he knew where this was going and didn't intend to stop it.

Her own heart beat faster at the realization. She let one hand slip higher, into the soft hair at his nape, loving the tiny shiver that elicited. His eyes darkened still more, so she did it again. And again.

They swayed together through another song before she slid a kiss along his jaw. His breathing snagged.

"You smell good," she whispered against his skin.

"What are you doing, Katharine?" His fingers tightened on her hips.

"Tasting." She smiled. She stretched up so her breasts pressed harder into his chest. "Are you going to make me do all the work?" His erection rubbed along her belly as they moved, and she inhaled shakily.

"You know you don't have to do this, right?"

She tipped her head back. "I know. But I want to."

"That scares the hell out of you, doesn't it?" He slid his other hand to her nape so his fingers could rub her skin.

"Yes." She decided to be honest. She really didn't have any secrets left from him. "I sucked at relationships before I became the Medusa, so this is probably never going to work, but I want to be with you now. If you really want me."

"You know I do." The words were unsteady, his warm breath caressing her cheeks.

Katharine stretched further to brush a kiss on his mouth. He let her, keeping a firm hold on her, so she did it again, deeper this time.

He made a soft sound when she eased back, and she smiled at the dark flush on his cheeks.

"I should clean up our dinner stuff," she said softly.

"Screw it," he growled. "You're going nowhere but upstairs with me." His grip tightened.

She studied his face, the dark desire in his heavy-lidded eyes, the lines of his mouth that she wanted to trace with her tongue. "All right. Then it's my turn to kiss you wherever you want tonight."

He swallowed, and she felt his erection swell against her belly.

Heat slid into her core. "Come upstairs, Hunter." She eased back and caught the hand on her hip. She turned and pulled him with her, across the entry hall to the stairs, up to his bedroom.

He didn't try to stop her when she took her time with his shirt, dragging her mouth over his chest, his spine, along one of his arms. His muscles bunched tighter with each touch of her lips or fingers on his skin, and his breathing roughened.

Katharine undid his belt while she teased one of his nipples with her tongue, and she heard him swallow. She smiled. "Are you all right, Hunter?"

"Better soon, I think," he rumbled, one hand catching her hair back away from her face.

"Working on it." She nipped at his chest

and heard his choked breath.

By the time she had him naked, his chest heaved with his rough breathing, and his hands clenched at his sides. Gods, he was gorgeous. She stood back for a moment, admiring his long, strong frame, his wide shoulders, the lovely erection aiming for his navel. She trailed one fingertip along the side of it, and he shuddered.

"Maybe you'd better lie down for this," she murmured, wrapping her fingers around him.

He caught her hand and pulled it from his cock, his eyes smoky with desire. "Maybe I'd better. And maybe you'd better join me."

She smiled. "Certainly."

When he eased flat on the bed, she climbed up beside him, her fingers wrapping around him again. He hitched in a sharp breath.

"Are you going to make it through the kissing everywhere portion of the evening's program?" she asked, squeezing the thick length of his shaft.

"Doubtful," he wheezed, his hips lifting into her touch.

"That's too bad." She bent to lick the tip of him, and his groan made her smile. Gods, he tasted good. She went back for another lick, then opened her mouth over the wide head.

As his need rose, so did her own, and she squirmed with each suck on his cock, squeezing her thighs together to no avail.

Hunter pushed her hair away from her face so he could watch her, his eyes glittering with desire, and she took him deeper. "God, Kat," he ground out, his head dropping back onto the pillow.

She hummed a reply, which only made him lift harder into her mouth. He was so close. So was she, for that matter. She eased one hand between her legs, rubbing the heel of her hand over her jeans, against her clit, in time with each stroke of him into her mouth.

He startled her when he reared up, tumbling her off of him.

"Hunter," she started, trying to right herself.

"You need to be naked, too," he growled, yanking at her jeans, sending them and her shirts flying through the air. And then he was there, oh, Gods, right where she needed him.

She grabbed his shoulders to anchor herself. "Hunter, it was my turn to–"

He shoved deep, deeper. "Together, honey. This is what I want."

It was what she wanted, too. She wrapped her arms and legs around him and rocked to meet each hard thrust. "Yes."

He took her at her word, and moved faster, sending her flying in just moments. He shouted his own release, before he dropped to his elbows over her, his harsh breaths dampening her already-sweat-slicked shoulder.

Kat kissed the underside of his jaw, his chin, her breathing ragged and painful. "You're impatient," she said a few minutes later, when she could speak again.

"You're a tease." He nipped at her collarbone, then turned his head to look at her. "This is addicting, and I didn't have nearly enough of you that first night."

She blushed. Actually *blushed*. She didn't even know what to say. They were here together now, naked, wrecked from some seriously hot sex, and she was still flustered by his words. She must be even more out of practice than she'd realized.

He seemed to understand her problem, smiling a little as he gathered her close and rolled to his side. "When did you get this new book idea?"

The change of subject let her focus on something besides the hot naked guy still buried deep inside her, but it took her a few seconds to redirect her brain. She took a slow breath and used the hand that wasn't beneath him to shove her damp hair out of her face. "Um, while I was cleaning up the breakfast stuff this morning."

"Fifty pages seems like a lot for one day."

"It is, but I was writing fast." She tipped her head back to look at him. "How was your stake-out?"

"Successful." One of his big hands stroked up her spine, warm, possessive.

That should scare the hell out of her, but she resolved to ignore it for now. "Good."

He hummed his agreement. "I like dancing with you, Katharine." He grinned.

"It always leads here, doesn't it? No

wonder you like it." She smiled back.

"You should close your eyes for a while, honey. I'm going to want to do this again, but I think we both need a nap first." His fingers retraced their route along her back until they curved around her ass and squeezed.

Renewed heat bubbled up in her middle. "I'm not feeling very sleepy." She slid her free hand across his chest.

"You will be," he promised, rolling onto his back so she now sat astride him, and, inside her, she felt his growing arousal.

"Promises, promises," she said lightly, leaning down to kiss him.

KAT DIDN'T KNOW WHAT TIME IT WAS when she woke, but when she rolled over, she was alone in the big bed. She sat up, pushing her tumbled hair away from her face, and saw Hunter's dark shape on the chair in front of the windows. "Hey," she said softly, "what are you doing?"

"Had a bad dream and I didn't want to disturb you." One of his shoulders lifted.

"What did you dream?"

He blew out a long, ragged breath. He remained silent for so long she wasn't sure he would answer. She slid closer to the edge of the bed nearest to him. "Sometimes I dream about my family," he said finally.

"Brothers and sisters?" They hadn't discussed his family at all even though he knew a lot about hers. She wondered what had happened to them.

Hunter shook his head. "No, I was an only child. My parents tried for years to have a baby and couldn't, so they finally decided on adoption."

"Ah, so you were spoiled," she teased, leaning back a little on the edge of the bed.

He smiled. "No, not spoiled, but well-loved."

"Of course you were. If they went through all that to have you, I bet they were thrilled when they finally got you." She thought of her own parents, far away. Safe.

"When they died, I felt like an orphan."

Her gaze shot back to him. "What happened?"

He swallowed, looking at his hands linked on his abdomen for a second. "A break-in at the house one night. The guy hit Dad in the head with the butt of his gun so hard he cracked Dad's skull. Mom had a heart attack from the trauma and stress, and they both died in the morning at the hospital."

KATHARINE HEARD THE PAIN IN HIS words and slid from her perch on the mattress to kneel beside his chair, sliding her arms around his waist. "That's terrible." His heart beat irregularly under her ear. "I'm so sorry, Hunter."

One of his hands slid out from between them and stroked over the top of her head. "Thank you. It was a long time ago."

"But you still miss them."

"Of course. You miss yours, too."

"Not quite the same. I can see mine, talk to them."

"When did you last see them? In person."

She frowned and tipped her head back to meet his steady gaze in the faint light from outside for a few seconds. "Three years. It's been three years."

He slipped his fingers through her hair. "Maybe when we settle this, you can pay them a visit."

Katharine stretched up to kiss him, lightly. "Come back to bed."

He didn't argue, just pushed to his feet and tugged her up, too. When she slid between the sheets, he followed, turning her onto her side so she faced away from him, and then he wrapped himself around her, tight.

She swallowed, trying to imagine the dreams that woke him and drove him from his bed in the middle of the night.

He kissed the back of her head. "Go to sleep," he murmured, his warm fingers splayed across her belly.

She turned her head far enough to kiss him, catching the corner of his mouth. "You, too."

He huffed out a little laugh, but she didn't think he was really amused.

She shifted against him, not surprised when his body reacted to the slide of skin on skin, his cock gradually coming to attention, thickening against her ass. "Come inside me then," she whispered, her eyes stinging.

He made a sound of dissent into her hair, but she shifted once more, easing one knee forward so the head of his erection slid along the damp folds of her sex. He growled and jerked his hips to wedge himself inside her.

Kat lifted her hand to touch the side of his face, slid it back into his hair, and he began to move, gliding in and back out, slowly, gradually faster. Her release surprised her, because he suddenly slid his hand from her belly to her clit, which he pinched, hard enough to jolt her into orgasm, half a second before he grunted with his own.

When his breathing evened out a long time later, she knew he was finally asleep. Her heart ached for him. He must feel guilty for not being there to save his parents to carry around so much pain that it still woke him in the middle of the night. She shut her eyes against the burning and concentrated on the sensation of the big, warm man buried inside her, wrapped around her, on his slow, deep breathing, the regular thudding of his heart against her back.

She was in *so much trouble* here.

WHEN HUNTER WOKE, IT WAS still dark. She lay on her side facing him now, her warm breaths puffing over his arm. He sat up and switched on the light on his night stand, then turned to her. He watched her sleeping for a while—black hair spread behind her on the pillow, one bare shoulder exposed above the blankets. When he pulled the sheet higher, she nestled deeper beneath it and closer to him.

He could tell himself it was proximity, or convenience, but he knew those had nothing to do with the way he felt about her. He'd known it that first weekend even if he hadn't realized the enormity of it. The certainty wasn't like a punch in the gut, but a sense of calm and rightness settling over him.

He doubted she'd have the same reaction, however, if he shared his middle of the night revelations with her.

Stifling a sigh, he slid down under the covers and shut the light off before settling Katharine closer. She rubbed one hand over her cheek, then slid that hand over his belly.

"You okay?" she mumbled.

"Fine, sweetheart. Go back to sleep." He kissed her forehead.

She hummed a reply, settling back into slumber.

Hunter let the feel of her in his arms lull him back to sleep as well.

# CHAPTER NINE

Hunter left Kat asleep in his bed in the morning while he showered and dressed. When he headed downstairs, she was still out.

And no wonder, after last night. She was probably exhausted.

He went into the kitchen with no real plan, then he spied the box of tea she'd set out yesterday. He could make her some. While he waited for the water to boil, his cell rang. Automatically, he fished it from his pocket. Ryder Ware. "Hunter here."

"It's Ryder. I wanted to check in, see how things are going."

Heat touched the back of his neck. "Things are fine. No sign of any Harvesters."

"Mena thinks Katharine was unhappy last time they spoke."

"Of course she was. She just found out she was trapped while killers are hunting her."

Ryder laughed shortly. "Mena's asked me to arrange for someone to come and get Katharine."

"No." Hunter glared at the sink.

"My guys are trained."

"So am I. Would you have let someone else take that job from you when it was

Philomena?"

Ryder went silent for a long moment. "No," he said finally. "I didn't realize–"

"Neither has she yet, but I don't trust anyone else to do this. Besides, I thought your guys were all busy with actual work."

"They are. I thought you'd be ready... Never mind. You sure you're ready to drop everything and go if you have to?"

"If it'll keep her safe." Hunter relaxed a little.

"All right. Look, if you need anything, let me know. I'll check in again."

Hunter thumbed off his phone and stuffed it back into his pocket. Drop everything and go. He didn't think it would come to that, but what did he know? He'd never imagined anything remotely like this before last week. He was in purely uncharted territory now, but one thing he was sure of was nobody else would protect Katharine.

He scowled at the pan full of steaming water on his stovetop. He just had to make her understand he was the man for the job.

Piece of cake.

He laughed, shaking his head. *Yeah.* He fished a teabag from the box and dropped it into a mug and poured the hot water on top of it.

Maybe he could start by getting out of the house this morning without another argument.

KATHARINE PUSHED THE SEND BUTTON on the email she'd composed to her cousins and mother to let them know she was safe, then sat back against the sofa. She was tired of being cooped up, no matter how good the intentions of her family and Hunter. She wondered what she could do to persuade him to allow her a few hours out of his house. Probably nothing.

It was kind of silly to think Harvesters would still be in town after a week. By now they'd have figured since her house was abandoned she'd fled somewhere else. Right?

She considered that for a few minutes. Would she assume the same?

Her house had been shut up tight since Hunter's friend did the alarm work. If she were stalking someone, that would be too long to wait in case they came back. After one break-in and attempted murder, she'd assume they had run far away, and, after a day or two with no sign of them, she'd have to search elsewhere.

She tried to see some flaw in her reasoning and couldn't find one. Then again, she only wanted to get out of the house for a little while. If there was a flaw, Hunter would find it. She decided she'd give it a try later.

HUNTER STIFLED A SIGH, RUBBING ONE hand at the back of his neck to ease the muscles there trying to tighten up as she spoke.

"Please, Hunter. Being stuck inside is making me insane. Hell, just a ride to the park for a while. Something." She lifted serious eyes to his face.

He knew when she met him at the door that she'd ask. Trouble was, he didn't know how many more times he could deny her before she finally decided the hell with it and went anyway.

And he'd done a bit of surveillance on her house again today. There'd been no sign of anyone watching the place, not any of the times he'd driven by since Warren fixed the power source problem. He wondered if she might be right that they'd assume she'd fled to safety.

"You know I'm trying to keep you alive, right?" he asked after a few long moments of silence.

She nodded. "I know. I do appreciate it, but if I can't get out soon, I'm going to flip out." A ghost of a smile touched her lips, but he didn't believe she was joking.

He groaned and dropped his head back against the sofa where they sat. "God, honey, you're killing me," he muttered.

One of her hands landed on his knee. "I'm not trying to. If you think I should try to disguise myself, I will. I'll do almost anything you ask."

He rolled his head to look at her. "Really? Almost anything?"

Her smile this time was genuine. "You're such a man."

He smiled back, in spite of the tightening in his gut. "I hope I don't regret this, but okay. I'll figure something out."

She jumped to her feet, grinning, then bent

back to kiss him lightly. When she would have straightened, he caught her arm and dragged her down for a deeper kiss, gratified when he finally released her mouth and she remained where she was for several seconds, eyes closed and lips parted. Her lashes fluttered up, and her mouth curved in a gentle smile. "I promise I'll behave, Hunter."

"I'll believe that when I see it," he teased. "How about we rustle up some supper?"

Over dinner, they danced around the subject of her leaving the house with him, then, when Hunter frowned, she moved on to the story she'd been working on since yesterday, and to the email she'd had from a very pregnant, very tired and cranky Philomena who hoped her baby would come soon.

But after supper, she considered again how she might change her appearance to throw off anyone watching for her. The most obvious, and probably easiest, was to change her hair. She went to Hunter's desk and pulled open drawers until she found a large pair of scissors.

Katharine looked at them for a moment, considering. The Harvesters knew who she was and had most likely found a photo. Maybe a haircut wasn't a bad idea.

Except she really did like her hair—aside from the three-days-of-snakes thing.

She shut the drawer and turned away from the desk to find Hunter leaning on the door frame, arms crossed on his chest and a smile tugging at one corner of his mouth.

"Don't ask me to cut your hair."

She flushed. "I wouldn't. Ask you, I mean."

"Good. I like it just as it is. Cutting it would be a sin." He pushed off the doorway and moved toward her.

Katharine suddenly felt stalked. Her heartbeat quickened.

He stopped, not quite in arm's length. "Don't you think they'll assume you'd cut your hair first?"

"Or dye it."

His eyes narrowed. "I suppose."

"I'm not cutting my hair," she said after a few seconds.

He lifted one hand to catch the end of her ponytail. "Come sit with me."

It was her turn to frown. She didn't believe that was what he'd been thinking. When he tugged gently at her ponytail, she let him, setting her hands on his chest. His strong, steady pulse beat faster beneath her fingers. "I have a better idea."

He swallowed audibly.

She stifled a smile as she slid one hand down to tug his shirt free of his jeans, then flattened her hand on his warm skin. His muscles tightened under her fingers. "Mm." She rubbed her thumb in a little circle, brushing his belly button so he inhaled sharply.

"Kat." Beneath the sexy rumble in his voice was a question.

She let her other hand cup the growing bulge in the front of his jeans. "You need to be horizontal so I can taste. And maybe tease with this hair you seem to like so much." She squeezed, gratified when he rocked into the caress, his grip on her hair tightening. "Let's go to bed," she whispered, leaning in to brush his mouth with hers.

"You're already teasing," he growled, then released her hair to scoop her over his shoulder.

She laughed when he strode out of the living room to the stairs, shrieking when he landed a smarting swat on her butt.

"I think we might have discussed a spanking the other night," he said in a sexy rumble.

She sucked in an unsteady breath, heat dampening her panties at his words. "I don't remember agreeing," she managed, though she might seriously consider it.

He chuckled. "Maybe we can negotiate that, too."

Her entire body flashed hot with desire and anticipation. "We'll see."

Hunter dropped her to her feet and set his hands on his hips. "I think you mentioned something about me being horizontal?"

She inhaled slowly, reaching for the button on his jeans. "I think I did," she murmured, her mouth watering in anticipation.

HUNTER BEAT HER INTO THE SHOWER in the morning, and she wasn't sure if she should be as disappointed as she was when he walked out of the other room wearing only a dark blue towel, a trickle of water sliding down his abdomen.

Averting her gaze, she collected some clean clothes from her suitcase and took her turn in the smaller room, pondering this unexpected new relationship she found herself in.

Even before she became the Medusa, she'd never had a relationship where she lived with a man. There were guys she'd dated, men she'd slept with, but they were never in one another's company for days at a time. Hell, she'd never even gone on vacation or for a long weekend trip with her last serious boyfriend before the curse landed on her. Now she had literally moved into Hunter's house.

Katharine scrubbed quickly, and wiped the steam from the mirror with her towel so she could see to untangle her hair, frowning into the mirror. It wasn't like her to be so weak. She never had any trouble saying 'no' and meaning it when it came to men. Hunter was a whole new ballgame, evidently.

She dragged the comb through her hair, concentrating on smoothing away her scowl with each stroke. By the time she'd twisted her hair into a loose braid, she thought she'd managed some semblance of calm.

But when she stepped out of the bathroom and Hunter still sat on the foot of the bed, she frowned again.

He lifted one eyebrow. "What?"

She shook her head. "Nothing."

His expression conveyed his disbelief and

amusement over her response.

She started a slow count to ten.

"My game plan for today involves you coming to the office with me."

She stopped her second count on four. "Really?" Out of the house. *Finally!* Suddenly, she didn't feel so grouchy.

He nodded.

Katharine bent to kiss him, lightly, and found herself lingering. "Thank you."

His eyes had darkened a little, but he nodded again. "Sure." His gaze landed on her mouth for a few seconds before he pushed to his feet.

"When?"

"A bit later. First, I wanted to do some more reading, see if Annis left anything useful in her journals."

"Okay." If it meant getting out of the house for a few hours, she'd go through every bit of family lore all over, including the boring bits.

This time, he leaned in and brushed a kiss on her mouth. "Care to tell me now what had you so pissed when you came out of the bathroom?"

His mouth was distracting. While she watched him speak, she kept imagining the other places he had put his mouth on her. Could put it on her again. Heat bloomed in her middle.

"Kat?" He touched her cheek.

"Sex," she muttered.

"What?"

Her face warmed. "Nothing."

Hunter laughed and shook his head. "Oh, it's something, or you wouldn't have said it. You're mad about the sex? Not enough? Too much?"

She covered his mouth with her hand to stop anymore outrageous words from escaping.

He bit her hand, just hard enough to make her jump and yank her hand away. He didn't let her go, though, catching her hips and drawing her back in. "So you're annoyed we had sex?"

She shut her eyes, her blush intensifying. "I don't think I said that."

"You don't have to. You're angry with yourself? Me? Both?"

"Yes. No. Oh, hell," she muttered, dropping her chin and squeezing her eyes shut tighter.

"You're pissed it was good?"

"Oh, my Gods," she ground out, opening her eyes to glare at him–and found him suppressing a smile. "You are an evil man," she said after a few seconds.

"Pretty sure that's one of the things you like about me." He winked and gave her hips a squeeze.

"Sometimes." She watched his lips curve at her admission. "I've never been in a relationship like this before. And not in any sort of relationship for years. I don't know that I'm going to be any good at this."

His smile vanished. "I think we've already had this discussion."

"We have. But–"

It was his turn to cut off her words with his hand. "No buts. You're here for your safety, we like each other. When you're not in danger anymore, we can figure out what we're doing."

She didn't bite him, as he had her, but she inhaled deeply, drawing his scent inside her head. His eyes darkened with awareness, and the fingers holding her hip dug in a little harder. "You're still wearing your towel," she mumbled against his palm.

A wicked grin curved his mouth. "I was waiting for you."

Her pulse skipped. "A very bad man," she muttered.

Hunter bent as he removed his hand from her mouth and kissed her lightly. "You inspire me." He winked and released her, leaving her weak-kneed as he rounded the bed to his dresser.

She turned in time to see him drop the towel and bend to step into his underwear. Her mouth went dry at the sight of all those luscious muscles flexing as he moved. He winked at her again, over his shoulder, and she growled, marching for the door. Behind her, he laughed.

"What a jackass," she breathed on her way downstairs.

"I heard that," he called. "And I'm on my way down."

She quickened her pace, smiling in spite of herself.

AFTER LOOKING THROUGH SOME OF the old journal scans for a while, she got bored and rose to pace while Hunter continued to read. With a promised outing, she couldn't concentrate on reading the pages written in Annis's spidery hand, some of the pages so old and faded they were nearly illegible. Most of it was useless, daily notes her distant cousin had written. Occasionally, she'd written about one of the previous Medusas, but it was all information Katharine had seen in other journals, or heard from one of the aunts when she was a child. Maybe eventually one of the journals would produce something helpful.

She walked from one end of the living room to the other, pausing to glance out the side window.

"Honey, relax."

She met Hunter's gaze. He still sat at his desk. "Sorry. I'm antsy."

He smiled. "Fifteen minutes, and then we'll head to the office. I promise."

She nodded.

"Sit."

She shut her eyes for a second, then rounded the corner of the couch and sat again, clasping her hands on her lap. "Read." She tried hard not to tap her foot or jiggle her leg while she waited, but by the time Hunter finally rose, she was ready to leap out of her own seat.

He didn't say anything when she rushed to her feet, but she saw the smirking curve of his mouth. "Let's go."

She wasted no time giving him grief for his attitude, but grabbed her purse and walked with him to the front door.

"We should've discussed ground rules before now," he mused, wrapping his fingers around her arm.

"I'll do whatever you say. If you think there's a problem, I'll deal. Promise." He wasn't getting out of it now, not when she was inches from fresh air for the first time in too long.

He bent and brushed a kiss on her mouth. "I'll hold you to that." He punched some keys on the alarm pad, then several more before he opened the door and guided her out, his gaze shifting from side to side as they went.

Katharine took several deep breaths of the outside air before they got to the car, ignoring Hunter's wide smile when he ushered her into the passenger seat before returning to his own side. "What's on your schedule for the day?" she asked once they were underway.

"You."

She blinked. "What?"

He shot her a sidelong glance, his lips still curved. "I just need to check in at the office, and then I thought we could pick up some things for a picnic lunch at the park."

She stared at him while he steered the car around a corner. The park. He *had* been listening to her. "Thank you," she managed around the sudden lump in her throat.

He patted her knee, leaving his hand there,

and she covered his hand with her own, turning to look out the side window.

When he parked downtown, she glanced around. A small oval sign indicated the Phelps Investigative Agency was housed in the building to her right. She smiled and took his hand when he opened her car door.

An older woman sat at the desk in the small reception area, and she smiled when she saw them, though Kat noticed the curious glance the woman gave their joined hands.

"Mary Ann, this is Katharine. Katharine, Mary Ann's been with me since the beginning. Her husband was one of my teachers at the police academy." Hunter gave her fingers a squeeze while directing a squinty-eyed look at the other woman.

"It's very nice to meet you, Katharine." Mary Ann pushed to her feet and stuck out her right hand. "I'm glad someone is finally making this one take some time away from work. It's way overdue."

Kat blushed. "Nice to meet you, too," she murmured, deciding to leave the rest of that alone. She hadn't exactly planned on dragging Hunter away from his normal life.

As if he knew what she was thinking, he raised one eyebrow. "I need to check messages. Did we get payment on those last three jobs yet?" he asked, pulling Katharine with him into an open doorway nearby.

"There are three messages on your desk, and yes, we did. I've already taken care of it."

Mary Ann was easing back into her seat when Katharine glanced over her shoulder.

"Thanks." He shut his office door and turned to face her. "That wasn't so bad, was it?"

She lifted one eyebrow. "Really?"

He smiled and released her hand so he could round his desk. "Looks like I need to make a return call on this one, and then we can go."

"Whatever you need to do, I'm good. I'm at least out of the house." She moved around the room, touching the back of the nearest chair while he picked up his phone and started dialing.

Within forty-five minutes, they were in the park down the block, a blanket from his car trunk tossed over his shoulder, and a bag from the deli around the corner dangling from his fingers.

"I do appreciate this," Kat said, glancing up at him.

"I know. I'm sorry it's not something we can do everyday. Not until we know you're safe." He gave her fingers a gentle squeeze. "But this outing should make it a bit better, I hope."

When he stopped walking to survey the wide green lawn, she stretched onto tiptoe to brush a kiss on his cheek, smiling when he shot her a surprised glance. "Thank you, Hunter," she said softly.

He smiled and set down their bag. "Let's

get this spread out, okay?"

THEY HAD THEIR PICNIC, WATCHING KIDS running near the swing set nearby, the joggers weaving in and out among the elderly walkers, the young mothers pushing strollers. By the time they'd finished, all the tension had left Kat's shoulders and spine. She smiled at him easily, and Hunter's heart skipped a beat at the sight. "Having fun, honey?" he murmured, leaning closer.

"Yes, thank you." She kissed his cheek again, then his mouth, lightly.

The hairs on the back of his neck prickled, and he sat back, scanning the area.

"What's wrong?" Kat frowned, looking around, too.

"I don't know." He felt like eyes were on him, but when he studied their surroundings, he couldn't see anyone who seemed to be watching him and Kat.

"Time to go." She started gathering the remains of their lunch, stuffing everything into the bag they'd brought, and Hunter got to his feet, still searching.

He didn't find anything, not even a kid staring at them. But something felt wrong.

They made their way back to the car much more quickly than they'd walked to the park, and some of the tension was back, tightening the muscles of her back and shoulders under his hand. By the time he got her into the car, it was almost as if their outing hadn't happened.

"It's probably nothing. I don't see anyone," he said as he started the car, continuing to look around them.

"Maybe." But worry lined her forehead.

So much for good intentions. Hunter wished he'd held out and kept her at home. Just in case there actually was someone watching them now.

And if there wasn't? Then his instincts were rustier than he'd thought.

KAT DIDN'T SAY ANYTHING MORE ABOUT being stuck in the house the rest of the day or even in the morning when he headed out to the office, but Hunter wasn't surprised. The tension rolling off of her all evening was palpable, and she tossed and turned all night, despite his efforts to tease her into relaxing, or to settle her in his arms where she'd slept quite well previous nights.

He didn't worry when he went to the office. There was no way she'd leave the house today, with or without him. He checked in with Mary Ann, then headed across town to meet an insurance agent for payment on several jobs. He debated going right home after that, but decided he had time to head in to the office before he checked on Katharine.

Mary Ann shot him a look of disbelief when he walked in. "Why are you here? Shouldn't you be with that lovely young woman you brought in yesterday? Taking some time off?"

He grinned. "Just wanted to make sure we were good if I didn't stick around."

"Honey, you know I can handle this place. Go find her and take her something nice while you're at it."

"Yes, ma'am." He saluted and turned around, heading back out. She might be right about taking something nice to Kat, though. So he went down the street to the deli to get something for their dinner. He scanned the crowded sidewalk as he went, giving a second glance to the burly man in a windbreaker who stood behind him at the counter, but the man went across the street to his motorcycle and rode away.

Maybe some dessert, too, he mused, and strode to the next block.

After he stopped to peer in the bakery window, Hunter spotted the swarthy guy in a running suit following him. The man dropped to one knee to retie his sneaker, and when Hunter glanced at him, the man quickly looked away.

His pulse quickened. Dammit, he knew he shouldn't have let her out of the house.

He took a slow breath and turned back to the cakes and cookies in the display. He couldn't call her–the guy may have friends nearby with listening and tracing capabilities. To give himself a few minutes to figure it out, he went inside and bought some bread and a couple of pastries. While he was waiting at the checkout, he called the office. "Mary Ann, I need you to call home and let my friend know everything is set for our trip."

"Your trip, huh?" Mary Ann's voice didn't hide her curiosity.

"Yeah, tell her I'll be there in half an hour. I'll call you back soon." He hoped Kat understood.

When he stepped outside, the guy stood in front of the chain coffee shop at the corner, trying to appear as if he were thinking about going inside–and doing a lousy job, since Hunter caught his flash of relief when Hunter came into view. Terrible poker face on that one.

The Harvester also didn't manage to hide his annoyance when Hunter took an immediate turn into Gladys's gift store. While Hunter pretended to browse, he saw the other man walk past the front window, slowly. After he stepped beyond the window, Hunter headed for the back of the shop where he met Mary Ann's sister Gladys.

"Hi, Hunter."

"I need to use the back door, Gladys."

The older woman smiled in delight. "On a case? Go right ahead, dear. Good luck."

Unable to resist returning the smile, he went. "Thanks, Gladys."

The back door led to an empty alley, and he wasted no time breaking into a run toward his office, and the car. Once he was away from the office, he drove around town, making sure he wasn't being followed. While he drove, he dialed the office. "Me again."

"There's trouble? Your girl sounded spooked."

"Yes. I'm going to have to take some time off, and I'm not sure how long."

"You take care of whatever you need to do. I've been telling you for two years to take a damn vacation. I can handle the office in the meantime."

"Thanks, Mary Ann. I owe you."

She laughed. "Of course you do. Someday I'll collect, too."

When he screeched to a halt in the driveway another fifteen minutes later, he saw the curtain beside the door flutter. *Good girl. Of course she'd understood Mary Ann's message.* Inside, he caught her cold hand and dragged her past her packed bags a foot from the front door, up the stairs. "Let me get a bag, and we're out of here."

"How did he find you?" Resignation shadowed her eyes, and her shoulders slumped.

He shrugged. "Probably by chance yesterday when we headed for the car at the office, but now they'll be able to find the house, and since he lost me downtown, they're probably on the hunt." He kissed her lightly, then released her hand. "Grab some t-shirts out of the second drawer, please." He pulled a carry-on from the closet shelf and grabbed a handful of jeans and some shorts from the tall dresser.

Katharine was pale, strain lines around her

mouth and at the corners of her eyes. "If I go and you stay, we could throw them off for a while," she said as she folded his shirts into the bag, not meeting his gaze.

"No." He caught her wrist, lightly, and she flicked a quick glance at him. "I promised I'd keep you safe, and I can't do that by letting you go off alone." He watched her lashes flutter down briefly before she met his gaze and nodded once. "Come here." He pulled her into his arms and felt the tiny tremors shaking her. "You wanna fold my underwear, too?" he teased after a moment.

She sighed and tipped her head back so she could see him. "Do I look like your housekeeper?" Her attempt at a light tone fell a bit flat.

He bent and kissed her again, a little longer this time. "Come on. I only need a couple things and we're gone." He released her and went into the bathroom to grab toiletries, returning to find her smoothing the blankets on the bed. "Ready?" He dropped the last few things into his bag and grabbed her hand.

When they got to the door, he hesitated. "Let me get all the bags in the car first, okay? Make sure no one's made it here yet." He should've pulled into the garage. Idiot.

Kat swallowed and nodded, her gaze flitting to the window beside the door.

Hunter got everything loaded, surveying the street and surrounding houses. Satisfied nothing was amiss, he returned for Katharine, tucked her into the passenger seat and went.

He hoped his house remained untouched when they got back.

Then he wondered when they might get back. The Harvesters would only change the focus of their hunt if they killed the Medusa or the curse moved on to another cousin. Since he intended to keep her safe, it could mean some time away.

To protect her, he would gladly do it.

# CHAPTER TEN

"You're where?"

Hunter winced at Ryder's sharp tone. "On the expressway right now. I just wanted you to know we had to go."

Kat sat in the other seat, head against the headrest, her gaze on him. She was still too pale, but Hunter figured he could deal with that when they stopped for the night.

There was a sigh in his ear. "Damn, I should've known they wouldn't leave town even if her place was shut up," Ryder muttered. "What happened?"

"We went out yesterday. I felt like someone was watching us, but I didn't see anyone. I screwed up."

From the corner of his eye, he saw Kat straighten, frowning.

He patted her knee.

"Well, it can't be undone," Ryder said. "Don't tell me where you're going. I'll just say go somewhere for a couple days, blend in. At this point, the Harvesters have no idea where to start searching, which is good." The other man sighed again. "I'm sorry, man. This sucks."

"We'll be fine," Hunter said firmly. "We'll find someplace and hang tight."

"Good. I'll be in touch."

He hung up and tucked his phone away.

"You let him think this is your fault when it's mine," Katharine said, still glaring.

"I made the decision to take you with me yesterday. My call, my fault." He shrugged, easing the car onto the next exit. "Where would you never go?"

"What?"

"Where do you never go? Someplace they won't know to search. They found out you were the Medusa, so I'm sure they did homework. That means they probably have an idea where you might run if you had to. We already tripped them up with you staying at my place, because I wasn't on their radar." He shot her a quick smile. "Where don't you go? Ever?"

She huffed out a quick breath, turning her head to look out the window for a few moments. "The beach," she said finally.

"You don't like the beach?"

A sad smile touched her mouth. "I love the beach. I stopped going when I got the curse."

"Then you're overdue." He turned the car onto another ramp, heading east.

AN HOUR AND A HALF LATER, THEY CARRIED their things into a room at the motel Hunter had found–a room at the far end of the low building, where he could park the car directly in front of their door. There was a diner-style restaurant attached to the motel, and several others close by.

And they were only a block from the beach.

Katharine almost wanted to cry. He'd brought her to a place she'd loved and missed, even though it was her fault they had to flee.

She considered thumping her head against the wall. Repeatedly.

"Come here, sweetheart."

She turned her head just far enough to see Hunter sitting on the foot of the bed. He patted the spot beside him, but she remained beside the window. "I am so sorry to have dragged you into this." She looked outside.

For a moment he was silent. Then the mattress squeaked. A few seconds later, his hands landed on her upper arms, drawing her back against his chest. "You haven't dragged me anywhere. In fact, I'm pretty sure *you* may have been dragged a little today." His warm breath touched her scalp a second before his mouth brushed her hair.

"But your business–"

"Mary Ann's been nagging me for months about taking a vacation, or at least a day off. I think she has party plans for the office."

His joking didn't make her feel better. "And your house?"

"If they break in, the alarm will go off and the police will come to get them. But they won't break in. They're smart. They'll do some surveillance, realize we're gone, and leave the house alone. You need to try to relax." He gave her a tug, and she let him turn her, sighing. "We'll hear from Ryder in a few days."

She sat on the foot of the bed. "I didn't want you in danger, too."

He squatted in front of her and caught her hands in his. "I'm a big boy, Kat, I can take care of myself."

"I can take care of myself, too."

"Except for when you can't," he said gently.

Her eyes stung with unexpected tears, and she looked away. "That was low," she ground out. It was true, but the reminder still hurt. Because it was true, she already owed Hunter her life, which was *huge*. She pushed that away for now and took a deep breath. "So what's our plan?"

His jaw tightened a tiny bit, and if she hadn't been with him for so long now, she'd never have noticed it. "We're going to blend in here for a few days. See what Ryder and Kallan come up with."

She wondered which part he didn't like. "Okay." It was clear both of them needed a distraction. "What did you bring from the deli?" she asked, looking at the round table in the corner where they'd dropped the deli and bakery bags.

Maybe she could try to figure things out better after she ate.

HUNTER HATED NOT HAVING SOME KIND of plan. He always had a plan. Or he used to always have a plan. Until Katharine came into his life.

"Just go," Ryder had said.

So they sat on the beach the next day, blending with thousands of vacationers as if they weren't on the run from would-be murderers. He wasn't thrilled about sitting out in the open this way, but it seemed the Harvesters wouldn't expect it, even if they somehow stumbled on them.

Kat lay on her stomach, long legs crossed at the ankle as she faced the water, transfixed.

That was the only good thing he could see about this—her naked delight at being at the beach. Knowing she'd denied herself this pleasure for five long years to stay safe made him sad.

It also made him angry. How could anyone subject another human being to that—to reduce them to prey? Like animals, so every decision made was for their safety and survival, never for pleasure.

As if his tension had reached out to touch her, Kat turned to glance at him over her shoulder, her smile fading. "Thank you."

He forced himself to smile at her, to mentally shrug off his annoyance. "No one should have to give up something that makes them happy."

Her eyes turned somber at his words, and she rolled onto her side to look fully at him, making him wish she'd bought the orange bikini he'd pointed out when they went shopping earlier. Instead, she wore a purple, one-piece bathing suit that covered her from the top of her shorts to a reasonably modest spot on her chest. And over it, an unbuttoned denim shirt, to hide her tattoo.

Just in case.

That annoyed him all over.

Katharine let out a slow breath. "Sometimes things are important. Staying alive is important. The beach, not nearly so."

Hunter leaned nearer to brush back a wisp of hair from her temple, weighing her words. "Staying alive is important, but not much fun if you sacrifice all the things you love." He realized half a second too late what had just come out of his mouth.

Her gaze flickered away for a second, and she forced a smile. "Well, I'm here now. Who knows when that might happen again?" She rolled onto her belly and reached for her sunglasses, hiding her eyes.

He dropped his hand to the blanket, heart hammering in his ears. He'd said a little too much, and she knew it. *Damn.* He took a steadying breath and released it. She'd let it go, which was good. For now.

But he'd bring it up another day. Hopefully when they weren't hiding out.

Which made him aware again that they were hiding out from killers. He needed to be alert, but not too alert and draw unwanted attention to them. Fuck, he was out of practice. Surveilling guys trying to screw their insurance companies or cheating spouses didn't require the same level of attention he'd needed on the force.

He blew out a slow breath and set one hand on the back of Kat's calf, feeling her start. "Should've gotten you a bucket and shovel, too, to build a sand castle," he said gruffly.

A reluctant smile curved her mouth when she looked over her shoulder at him. "I'd only use the bucket to collect seashells."

"We can do that, too."

She shook her head. "Too many people now. It's best right after the tide goes out, like in the mornings."

He smiled. "We can do that, too," he repeated.

She laughed. "Maybe." She turned to face the water once more, but with less tension in her muscles.

Hunter felt a bit better. He let his gaze slide over the families and other couples and groups of kids around them on the beach. No one who stood out, who looked as if they shouldn't be there. Nothing to make the hair on the back of his neck stand up as it had the other day in the park. Still, he needed to stay on guard. He lifted his own sunglasses from beside him on the towel and put them on. Dark enough to hide his eyes, so no one knew he wasn't simply enjoying the beach but watching. Searching for potential danger.

Keeping Katharine safe. His new job.

THEY FOUND A TAKE-OUT PLACE A BLOCK from their motel later and carried fish and chips and sodas back to the room. Katharine couldn't believe she was actually enjoying herself. It seemed stupid, especially at a time like this, when she was on the run for her life. But she was at the beach with Hunter, they were having one of her favorite meals, and she felt good.

She decided not to question it. Hunter had made a good point earlier. What good was being alive if that was all you were doing? At this moment, she could enjoy herself.

She smiled across the little round table in their room at him, liking the way his eyes darkened when he met her gaze. "This is nice," she said, picking up a thick-cut piece of potato doused in malt vinegar.

His mouth curved slightly. "Almost like a date."

She laughed. "And neither of us has to do dishes this time."

He reached over to touch her cheek. "We could take a walk on the beach after we're done. Probably less crowded now with all those families heading for supper."

"Ah, a romantic date." Her pulse skipped. Stupid.

"When was the last time you had one of those?"

"I don't remember." That was true. Longer than five years. Her smile faded, and she lifted a chunk of hot, fried fish to take a bite.

"Then we should do it. Who knows when

you might have another?" He chose a piece of his own fish, watching her.

She wondered what he was thinking, with his blue eyes somber in spite of the smile curving his mouth.

His smile widened. "I have other ideas for after the walk."

She finished chewing her fish and swallowed, heat burning her cheeks. "Do you?"

"Oh yeah. I might even tell you about them while we walk." He took a big bite of the fried fish, still grinning at her as he ate it.

She flushed hotter and stuffed a fry into her mouth to keep from saying something dumb. She was being stupid. She'd already slept with him, figuratively and literally, multiple times, yet here she was, behaving like they were actually on a date and she didn't already know they would *for sure* be having sex later.

She didn't know what was wrong with her.

Hunter chuckled as he reached for his soda. "You're blushing, Kat."

She shut her eyes. "I'm aware," she muttered. She straightened in her chair and picked up her own drink to cool her down a little.

"Have you ever thought about sex on the beach?"

She choked on her soda, barely keeping from spewing it across the table at him.

And he laughed.

After she managed to swallow the soda, she wiped her mouth with her napkin, then narrowed her eyes at him. "You are a very bad man."

He reached over and stroked her lower lip with one finger. "You like that about me."

Heat slid into her middle. "Maybe we don't need a walk."

His grin grew. "Oh, we're going to take the walk, and I'll tell you all about what I'll do to you when we get back."

Her breath caught.

His smile faded. "I might even kiss you before we finish our walk."

Her nipples tightened. "I can't wait."

His eyes darkened. "Me neither."

She ignored the alarmed voice in the back of her head, shrieking that she was being ridiculous. Who knew how long this little break would last? She was at the beach with a man who wanted her. *Enjoy it for now.*

She could worry tomorrow about the Harvesters.

KATHARINE WOKE SUDDENLY, NOT QUITE sure why. Her heart pounded so hard inside her ribs, it must be leaving imprints.

Then Hunter shifted in his sleep, throwing one arm up. "Take cover, Bruce," he said hoarsely, urgently.

She frowned.

"God, no," he groaned, his legs thrashing. "I told you to get down...come on, keep breathing..."

Nightmare. "Hunter," she said softly,

catching his arm when he rolled toward her, "wake up. It's just a dream."

When she touched it lightly, his face was wet with sweat–and tears?

"Come on, wake up."

He rolled over her, then stopped, the tension in his body easing. "Kat?"

"Right here. You were having a nightmare." She cupped his jaw, rubbing her thumb along his stubbled cheek.

He let out a rough breath and put his face down in the pillow beside her head.

She smoothed one hand along his arm, the other over his damp head, over and over until more of the tension seeped out of him. He shifted slightly, his warm breath brushing her throat. "You want to talk about it?" she asked lightly. His heartbeat had slowed from a gallop to a much more sedate pace against her breasts. The pressure of his chest felt nice, but she ignored it.

He took a long time to answer. "No," he said at last, nudging her knees apart with his. "But I will." He settled his growing erection against the core of her. He inhaled slowly, letting the air out on a ragged sigh.

Katharine wrapped one arm around his shoulders and slid her other hand into his hair. She listened to his breathing as it evened out. It took a long time.

Finally, he took a slow, deep breath. "I've mentioned I used to be a cop."

"Mm-hm." She let him shift her a little so

he could put his face against her throat, one of his arms sliding under her pillow.

His warm breath washed the side of her throat on his exhale. "Bruce was my partner." He cleared his throat. "We worked together for about five years. He was a few years ahead of me in the academy, but we had mutual friends, so we knew each other for a while. I was best man at his wedding the year after we were partnered."

She swallowed, tightening her arm around him.

He remained silent for a few moments. "We were working a case, small time drug dealer." His arm tightened behind her. "We'd been digging and tailing him and working people around him for weeks. Our captain agreed we had enough to bring him in. Start working him for his supplier. Small fish net bigger fish."

She stroked his nape, biting her lower lip.

"Got our warrants and a couple of squads, and we went in late one night." She heard him swallow hard. "We always took turns on a bust, going in first."

Katharine felt him shiver, and she wrapped her other arm around him, too, tight.

"All the way over, he argued about who went first the last time. He swore it was me, so that made it his turn, but I knew he went in first on the last one, at a mobile brothel. We finally flipped a coin to decide, and I won." His breathing quickened. "He bitched the whole time we were parking the car and getting in position. He hated not being first. Always." Hunter shifted his shoulders, and she realized how tense he was, how tight his muscles were under her fingers. "One of the unis finally told him to shut up and quit being such a baby. And he laughed." He swallowed. "Laughed, then started the count."

She waited out this longer pause, her chest tight.

"The guy lived in a small apartment behind the garage his old man owned. We went in, me first, him next, and split inside the garage, just like we'd planned, one on each side, meet at the apartment door, and go in. Get the guy and be done. Easy." He shivered again, breathing harder. "Except the guy wasn't in his apartment. He was sitting in the dark garage office, in the back corner, and he had a gun."

She squeezed her eyes shut.

"He shot Bruce first, hit him right above his vest, and then he fired at me, missed." He swallowed noisily. "I shot at him on my way to Bruce, and he dropped. I should've made sure he was dead, but I went to Bruce instead. God, so much blood." He trembled over her. "I'd never seen so much blood. Bruce had one hand on his throat, but the blood was just pumping so hard...I knew the bullet must've nicked an artery." His heart pounded against her chest, too quick. "I couldn't stop it. Called back-up in, and then for an ambulance, and I tried...fuck, I tried." He sucked in an unsteady breath. "He was gone before the ambulance got to us. God, he had his wife and two babies. It should've been me. If I'd let him go in first, maybe..." He buried his face against her tighter.

Tears burned down her face. "I'm sorry, Hunter," she whispered.

"My fault. It was my fault." His trembling was full-on shaking now.

She shook her head, tightening her hold on him even more. "How was it your fault?"

"It was."

"It wasn't." She brushed a kiss on the top of his ear. "It wasn't."

Katharine held on until he stopped shaking. Her pulse drummed in her ears, in time with his heartbeat against her chest.

Hunter's breathing took a long time to even out, and he never relaxed her grip on her.

"You know it wasn't your fault," she whispered finally, stroking his sweat-damp nape.

"I was in the lead–"

"How does that make this your fault? You went in different directions after you went inside. Partners, Hunter. You were equals, right?" She felt his shuddering breath against her chest and nuzzled her cheek along his hair.

He evidently couldn't argue, so he pulled her closer yet.

"I bet he'd hate you feeling guilty after all this time," she murmured, doing her best to ignore the growing ache in her breasts, pressed tight against his hard chest. "What if you had died? Would you want him to carry unnecessary guilt around for years?"

His head came up at last, though all she could see in the dark was the glitter of his eyes. "But I didn't die. And he had a family."

"So it would have been better for you to die? What about your parents? Would it have been better for them to lose you?"

He made a frustrated sound. "I didn't mean that."

"That's what it sounded like." She kept rubbing his nape, the back of his shoulder, his damp hair. "That it would've been better for your parents to lose you. I don't think they would've agreed," she said softly.

His breathing roughened a bit. "You should try a little of that logic on yourself, you know," he rasped.

She swallowed, forcing a tiny smile. "I was saving it for you," she said lightly.

He bent and kissed her, hard.

She parted her lips, letting him take what he needed. In a matter of minutes, he'd thrust deep inside her, each rough stroke sliding along her clit and sending her spiraling out of control before she realized she was so close. She choked out a cry when her release surprised her, and Hunter growled seconds later as he came, too.

Katharine panted beneath him, a bit shocked. "Gods," she wheezed, "I think you've killed me."

Hunter laughed and buried his damp face

against her equally sweaty neck. "Are you all right?" he asked a few minutes later, when they were both breathing more evenly.

"I'm fine."

"Are you sure?" He lifted his head again. "I think I was pretty rough."

She smiled in the dark and touched the side of his face. "In case you failed to notice, that worked for me."

He rubbed his stubbled cheek against her palm. "Oh, I noticed," he growled, shifting so his breath touched her lips a second before his mouth. "Thank you."

She let him roll them to their sides and gather her closer once more, tightening her arms around his neck. "Anytime," she murmured, closing her eyes. He'd been carrying that guilt around for a long time. She wondered if he'd ever be able to let it go.

He exhaled roughly.

"Are you all right?" she whispered, tipping her head back to look up at him. In the dark, she could only see a shadow where she knew his face was.

"Better now."

Not really an answer. She shifted so she could tuck her face to his wet throat.

"Go back to sleep, Kat. I'll be fine. No more nightmares tonight."

"Do you dream about him often?"

One of his big hands slid along her spine. "Not anymore. Not as often."

"When did you quit? The job, I mean."

"About six months after he died."

"I'm sorry, Hunter." She kissed him, felt him swallow.

"It wasn't the same, and I knew it never would be." He blew out a slow breath. "The internal investigation concluded it wasn't my fault, it was no one's fault except the shooter. But I didn't agree."

Still didn't, she thought. "Didn't you have to go to counseling?"

"Yeah. I went to as many as they required for me to get back to work. It didn't help."

"You have to let it, and you probably needed more than the required handful," she said before she realized she meant to speak.

He reared back, and she imagined he was glaring down at her in the dark.

"Sorry, I didn't mean to...well, it's probably true, so I won't apologize. You have to let the guilt go, not carry it around with you forever. You aren't perfect, none of us are." She bit her lip, wondering if she'd said too much.

"What did you study at school?"

She blinked, then smiled a little. "I only had one psych class in college, if that's what you're asking. I was an English major. But people watching is essential for writing."

He grunted and returned to his previous position so her face was against his throat. "I don't need a shrink."

"Hm."

He sighed.

"You can't save everyone, Hunter."

"I can save you."

She swallowed. Would that make up for not being able to save his partner? Probably not. Penance in one's own mind often loomed far larger than the imagined transgression.

Unless you were a descendant of Medusa. Then the penance was much worse than the original offense.

She squeezed her eyes shut. Stupid Athena.

ELEK SCOWLED AT THE EMAIL ON his screen. "Goddess damn them," he muttered, shoving away from his desk to pace. Milo reported no one had been to the monster's house in days. Now the man's house was locked up tight, and even his office seemed to be in limbo, as his secretary said they were on vacation and would schedule new appointments soon.

They were gone. A week to find them, and they'd disappeared.

He dropped back in his chair. He needed to be logical. A man couldn't shut down his business indefinitely. Maybe he'd taken her somewhere else and would return soon so they could continue their surveillance and hope he'd lead them to the Medusa once more. Force him to.

Waiting was not his strength. He preferred action.

He rose again and headed for Argos's work space.

His older cousin hunched forward in his seat in front of three monitors. Elek paused at the doorway, trying to decipher some of the gibberish on one screen for a second before he quit.

"What's up?"

He crossed the shadowed room to the desk. "Milo's had no luck. The man is gone, too."

"Sit."

He glanced around and found another chair near the door. He moved it closer to the desk.

"What do you know about the woman?" Argos kept tapping at his keyboard, never looking up.

He shrugged. "She writes books. Lives alone. She hasn't gone to any known family members' homes."

His cousin slanted a glance over that implied there should be more.

Elek shook his head. "She wouldn't go to family and put them at risk. None of them do when they run."

Argos nodded once, returning his gaze to his work. "And?"

"She would go somewhere new. Somewhere different. Which means we have nothing to go on. They're never stupid enough to use a credit card along the way." He frowned. "What about the man?"

His cousin smiled. "Nothing on his cards yet."

"Why are you smiling?"

"Because they left in his car."

His pulse skipped. "Do we have a tracker on it?"

"No, there wasn't time."

"Please don't make me play a guessing game." He leaned forward in his seat.

"The highway department has cameras in New Jersey."

"And you hacked in." Elek felt his own lips curve. "Where did they go?"

"Well, they started out heading west, then turned around and headed toward the shore."

"Can you be more specific?"

"They eventually exited the highway near Atlantic City, but because I haven't found them on any cameras in town, it appears they didn't go there. Nothing on the interstate cameras since then either, so they stuck to smaller roads. But it gives us a starting point."

Elek wished they had more to go on, but it was better than nothing. "Thank you, Argos. Let me know if you find anything else." He got to his feet and returned the chair to where he'd found it, heading for his uncle's office. They needed to send more cousins to scout the beach towns around Atlantic City. They had to find some trace of her before she vanished completely.

# CHAPTER ELEVEN

Katharine fingered the shell in her shorts pocket. They'd been here blending in with tourists for three days, and she was starting to get antsy. Nervous. It wasn't a long time, but it felt like she'd been hiding for an eternity.

Counting the time she'd spent at Hunter's, it *had* been a while since she'd been home.

And Ryder hadn't yet reached out to them since they'd been here.

That was what bothered her, she thought, staring at the expanse of blue water stretching before her. He probably didn't have any news.

Hunter's hand landed on her shoulder, and she shut her eyes. "What are you thinking?"

She shook her head. "I'm being stupid, but I feel like we've been here too long."

He remained silent for a moment. "Let's check out and go," he said at last.

She tipped her head to look at him. "I should get on a bus away from here, and you should go home."

His jaw tightened. "I can't protect you like that."

She glared at him. "You're not responsible for me."

"Let's go back to the room if we're going

to fight about this."

His mild tone made her narrow her eyes even more. "I am not arguing–"

He smiled a little, which pissed her off. "Let's go back to the room, Kat. You can give me hell there where we don't have an audience." His chin dipped, and she turned to find a curious brown-eyed boy watching them from a few feet away, a plastic yellow shovel and bucket in his hands.

She met Hunter's gaze again, more annoyed by the smile crinkling the corners of his eyes. "Let's go," she muttered.

He turned her from the water's edge with his hand on her shoulder, and they strode up to drier sand, and then across the wood slats of the narrow boardwalk to cross the street on the way back to the motel. She kept her mouth shut, stewing.

She didn't know how to make him understand her concerns. And she didn't know why Ryder hadn't contacted them yet. Surely he had some ideas by now.

She bit her lip as Hunter slid the keycard into the slot on their door. She didn't want to argue. Really. She just didn't want him in danger. The Harvesters were after her, not him.

When the door shut behind them, she took a deep breath.

"Why don't you sit?" he said before she could speak.

She hesitated, then dropped onto the foot of the bed while he sat in one of the chairs at the tiny round table in the corner, resting one ankle on the opposite knee. His casual pose was deceptive, she knew. If he needed to, or wanted to, he could be at full attention in a heartbeat. She jerked her thoughts back from that direction. This wasn't about sex. This was about her being responsible for herself and keeping him from harm.

"Go ahead. Hit me with your best shot."

She frowned at his light tone. "This isn't a joke, Hunter. Do you have any idea how many of my ancestors these men have killed over the years?"

"I can probably ballpark it after reading the things your family's sent."

She sighed. "They changed their tactics with my cousin Philomena. They would've used her mom and nephew to get her if they thought they could. They tried to kill her *and* Ryder when they crossed paths early on. It wasn't just about killing her, it was 'get her however we can and kill anyone in our way'."

He smiled. "He mentioned that."

"There are a lot more of them than of you. And you have no good reason to make yourself a target this way. These men are dangerous."

"I'm sure they are. So am I."

She blinked. Why was he so stubborn?

KATHARINE WATCHED HIM, RATHER LIKE she might study a strange animal, he thought. "I don't understand why you'd do this," she said finally. "You have a home, your own business. A life."

Hunter resisted the need to sigh, but barely. "You're not safe, and I'd never send anyone out alone when I could keep them safe."

"So you have a knight in shining armor complex."

He glared at her. "I don't. But I have a vocal conscience."

She narrowed her own eyes. "Believe me when I tell you I'll be fine."

He shook his head. "No can do."

She shoved to her feet.

"And I've promised your family I'll protect you."

She froze, looking poised to stomp away. "I don't suppose you'll feel any remorse for playing the family guilt card, will you?"

He smiled, knowing he'd just won another skirmish. "None."

"Of course not." She shut her eyes for a second. "How about the guilt I'll have if anything happens to you?"

"Not a bit." He settled deeper into his chair. "You still don't trust me completely. I'm okay with that," he continued when she shot a sidelong glance at him. "I know I'm capable, and you will, too, eventually."

"How many men have you killed?"

He blinked at her, then cleared his throat. "That I know of?"

Kat folded her arms on her chest, her grey gaze leveled on his face.

For a moment he considered not answering, then reconsidered. "Probably a couple dozen, minimum when I was in the service." He shrugged, one-shouldered. "Two in the line of duty as a cop, counting the guy who shot Bruce." He remembered the expression on the first guy's face–it broadcast the man's intent even better than the weapon he'd held as he stood in a shadowed alley, desperate not to go back to the jail he'd been released from a few days earlier. "I would've put a bullet in that guy in your bedroom, Kat, if he'd made the tiniest move in your direction. He knew it, too. It's why he went out the window instead of sticking around." Hunter dropped his foot back to the floor.

She didn't appear to be convinced.

He pushed to his feet. "Are you angling to be restrained?" he asked lightly. "I do have handcuffs, you know."

Her eyes widened, and her mouth dropped open. "What? Of course not." Color tinted her cheeks, and he imagined she was pondering the possibility. "No," she said more firmly, shifting her gaze away.

"Let me know when you change your mind." He kept his tone light, moving toward her.

Kat glanced at him. "Don't stalk me."

He smiled. "Do I look like I'm sneaking?" He reached out and caught one of her wrists, pulling her closer despite her reluctance. "I was trying to be up-front. If I'd been sneaking just now, like that, you should send me back to basic training for a refresher."

She gave a tug at her wrist, but he held on, just enough to keep her where she was. "Hunter."

He let his smile widen. "I understand trusting me with your life is a lot different than trusting me with your body." He enjoyed the color deepening in her cheeks. "But please try."

She studied his face for a few long heartbeats. "You know it's got nothing to do with you personally, right? I don't trust many people," she said at last.

"I know." He leaned closer, bending to rest his forehead against hers. "Give it a try."

She sighed. "I can't make any promises, but I'll try."

His heart bounced harder in his chest as a burst of relief shot into his veins. "That wasn't so hard, was it?"

She rolled her eyes and gave him a shove, but he wrapped his other arm around her back, and her eyes widened a little. "Hunter–"

He kissed her, just a brush of his lips over hers, still holding her gaze. "Thank you." And when he released her, he was gratified to see the way her eyes darkened. "Now pack your things and let's get out of here."

She turned away, cheeks pink, and headed to the bathroom.

He let out a slow breath. He was a bit surprised she hadn't asked again sooner about going off on her own.

Hunter considered the accusation she'd hurled at him. Just because he wanted to do the right thing didn't mean he had a knight in shining armor complex. If that were the case, he might have actually saved Bruce.

And even if that were the case, he wasn't here now with Katharine for that reason. He was here because he knew he could keep her safe. And because he wanted to be with her, but she wasn't ready to hear that part.

He relaxed a bit. Let her think he had a hero complex. Maybe she'd realize the truth eventually.

KATHARINE STARED OUT THE WINDOW AS they drove along winding roads, further inland at her request. It seemed like a good idea, getting away from the beach, as much as she loved it. The past few days would have to hold her over until she had another chance, maybe another five years down the road.

Assuming a Harvester didn't find and kill her before then.

She scowled. *Think positively.* They wouldn't find her. How could they? She was nowhere near home, and even though they'd figured out she was with Hunter, they had no way to locate them now. She rested her chin on her hand. They'd been careful since leaving town, hadn't used any credit cards. She had a cash stash in her lock box, and she also had access to bank accounts with credit cards under names that matched her alternate passports if she needed them. So they should be fine.

But that nervous sensation niggled at her, like she was forgetting something.

Hunter touched her shoulder. "You okay?"

She nodded. "Yeah, just thinking."

"How far do you want to go?"

"Up to you."

One of his eyebrows lifted. "Trusting me?"

She smiled reluctantly. "Enough to decide where we should stay tonight."

"Hm. Maybe you'll let me decide what we should have for supper later, too," he teased.

Katharine sighed, feeling her smile widen. "Maybe." She did trust him to keep her safe. That didn't mean she had to like the reality of it.

She didn't.

His hand slid away from her shoulder, down so his fingers brushed her breast. Startled, she glanced over, but he had his eyes on the road ahead. Her body still reacted to the caress, her nipples tightening. She took a quick breath and settled into her seat, looking forward. "You *are* a very bad man," she said mildly.

He chuckled. "You like it."

She did. That was the problem. She liked him. If something happened to him because of her, she'd never forgive herself. Assuming she was still alive after the something bad to castigate herself for letting him get so involved. Her smile faded.

She needed to talk to her cousins.

HUNTER WATCHED HER AFTER THEY checked into a new motel, where their view was not the ocean but a truck stop across the road, her fingers tapping across her keyboard. He didn't think she was working on the new book. Almost certainly, she was reaching out to one of her cousins.

He hadn't heard from Ryder since they'd left home either. True, it had only been a few days. But he'd expected at least a check-in. Maybe he should reach out himself. As he thought it, his phone buzzed. He swiped his thumb across the screen and smiled. "Hi."

Katharine's head came up, her brow furrowing when she saw him on the phone.

"You're both safe?" Ryder asked.

"Yes. No sign of trouble."

"Good. I have some news. We've done some surveillance at Ari's house, and there's been a lot more activity in the last twenty-four hours. Lots of arrivals and departures, and we've heard some chatter today as they're coming and going. It seems like they're conducting a search fanning out from Atlantic City."

Hunter frowned.

"If you're there, you should get out."

"We're not."

"Were you near there?"

He noted when the tapping stopped from Kat's laptop. "Not too far, but never in. We got off the highway before there. Shit." The highway. There were cameras on the highway. "Fuck."

"Highway department cameras," Ryder murmured, coming to the same conclusion. "Well, they've got a good hacker at their disposal then."

Hunter scowled. He should've thought of it himself, and since they'd found him in town at home, they knew enough about him to find out about his vehicle. "We're going to need to get a rental car," he said slowly. He glanced to where she sat with her computer on her knees.

"I can make that happen. You just tell me where and when."

She set her laptop aside, her frown deepening.

"Somewhere with long-term parking nearby, I think."

"I can have someone pick your car up and get it away so they don't find it and have another starting point to where you guys might be."

She pushed to her feet, and he pointed at her computer. She brought it with her and sat in the other chair at the table.

He turned the screen to face him, and brought up a state map. "Train station. Airport. They'll have long-term parking. Trenton, I think."

"Tomorrow?"

"Yeah, that's probably good."

"I'll reserve it, all you'll have to do is sign for it and go. Give me a little while to set it up, and I'll send you the details."

Hunter looked away from the screen to Katharine. Worry shadowed her eyes. "Sounds good. Anything else we should know?"

"Not at the moment."

"Okay, thanks." He ended the call. "You have good instincts, Kat."

"How did they narrow the search area?"

"Highway cameras, we think."

She bit her lower lip. "Hunter–"

"Let's not have this argument again. You're safest with me." He reached over to touch her hand where it rested on the table. "I should've told him we want a sports car."

"Too conspicuous."

"The Harvesters would never expect it," he said lightly, smiling at her. "Are you hungry? We didn't stop for lunch."

She shook her head.

She needed a distraction, he thought. "Why don't you come over here?"

Her eyes widened slightly. "You're kidding."

He grinned. "I never kid about that. You look like you need to be kissed."

Katharine sighed.

He pushed to his feet, then bent nearer to her, nuzzling her temple, her cheek, her jaw. She tipped her head to let him, and he smiled, inhaling the fresh scent of her shampoo. "See? Much better, and I haven't even kissed you yet." He tilted her chin up so he could brush her mouth with his. "Come up here." He tugged on her hand, pleased when she rose, setting her free hand on his shoulder. "That's right," he breathed against her mouth. "Let me help you relax."

His own body wasn't relaxing, though. Now he was fully aware of her against him, and he wanted more.

She met his gaze, her lips slightly parted. "I'm not going to forget, you know."

He laughed. "You might for a few minutes." He set his free hand on her ass and hauled her closer. "Now kiss me back." He nipped at her lower lip, then opened his mouth over hers.

It seemed a good distraction for them both.

Katharine stretched, noting the soft sheet rubbing over her arm, the warm man behind her, and opened her eyes. The sunlight that shone into the room around the blinds was still bright, but the angle of it had changed. It must be near suppertime. Hunter had done a pretty good job distracting her earlier.

And she'd let him.

She smiled faintly. He was persuasive. She stretched again, before easing toward the edge of the bed.

"Whoa!"

She stopped moving and looked over her shoulder.

His bright eyes were wide with something like shock.

"What?"

"Your tattoo. The color is different."

She frowned. "Tattoos don't change–" She shut her mouth with a snap. *Holy shit.*

"The goblet is silver."

She shook her head, alarm threading along her veins.

His startled expression didn't change, so she shoved herself off the bed and strode into the bathroom, where she parked her hip on the edge of the counter and twisted so her shoulder was visible in the big mirror, craning her head around to get a good look.

The cup *was* silver. Goosebumps rose on her skin.

Gods, she couldn't be falling for Hunter.

She shut her eyes and covered her face with one hand, pulse hammering in her ears.

She needed to be honest with herself–if the cup was silver, there was no '*if* she was falling'. But she didn't think she could trust her heart. She'd spent the last five-plus years preparing herself for the very real possibility of dying at the hands of the Harvesters or at least spending the rest of her life alone–after all, what man could be expected to fall for a woman who could unintentionally kill him once a month? It was unrealistic to believe it could happen a third time in just over a decade after not happening for generations. And the Harvesters had grown more aggressive, more determined.

It simply wasn't fair of the Gods to make her hope.

She took a deep breath and closed her eyes for a moment before releasing the air slowly, concentrating on letting some of the stress go, too.

But when she opened her eyes, she knew it remained, along with that sneaky thing trying to settle in her heart.

Hope was too dangerous.

So she wouldn't. When the opportunity presented itself, she'd go–taking Hunter out of the Harvesters' line of fire.

And hope Hunter would eventually understand and forgive her.

The decision didn't alleviate the churning in her belly, just added to it. She turned on the faucet and rubbed some cool water on her face. The scratchy hand towel on her skin gave her something else to think about for a few seconds.

But when she opened the door, Hunter sat on the edge of the bed. Waiting. Expectant.

She swallowed hard, heart thudding hard against her ribs. He'd read the things her family had sent, so he knew what the color change meant. She swallowed again.

"Come here," he murmured, holding out one hand.

She hesitated, then crossed the floor to sit beside him.

"Take a breath, Kat." He wrapped his fingers around hers.

She realized she was holding her breath, and she inhaled slowly.

"Once more."

She shut her eyes and repeated the measured inhale-exhale several more times.

"It's going to be okay."

She opened her eyes and looked down to where his long fingers wrapped around her hand, stomach churning hot acid. She wanted to agree with him, but the lie stuck in her throat.

It wasn't okay, and she didn't see how it ever could be when she was going to hurt them both to keep him safe.

HUNTER DIDN'T LIKE THE SHADOWS IN her eyes as they sat in a corner booth at the motel diner the next evening. She picked at a grilled cheese sandwich and cup of tomato soup, but ate almost none of either. She hadn't eaten much the night before either. Earlier in the day, they'd dropped his car in the long-term lot at the nearby train station and picked up the rental Ryder had arranged for them. The rest of the day, they'd spent poring over old journal scans from her cousins.

He didn't know why they'd bothered. He knew what it meant that her tattoo had changed colors. So did she. He hadn't mentioned it to Ryder when he'd let him know they'd messengered the car keys so his guy could collect it until they could safely reclaim it. No, for now, that was for him and Kat only.

And she didn't want to discuss it. But she sure was brooding about it.

He stuck another bite of meatloaf in his mouth and watched her tear off a small piece of bread from her sandwich. "Is that even still warm?" he asked after a second.

She put it in her mouth. "Mm-hm."

He tamped down the urge to smile. "I'm thinking about dessert. There's some lemon meringue pie in the dessert case. What about you?"

She shook her head.

"You know what else I'm thinking about?"

She glanced over for a second, then away. "What?"

"You and me, and a hot shower."

Her gaze lifted from her plate to his face, her cheeks coloring faintly.

"You're awfully tense. We didn't run into any problems this morning with the cars. So maybe a nice hot shower, and then a back rub." He watched her blush deepen. "And then..."

Her eyes darkened. "And then...?"

He grinned. "We'll see."

A faint smile touched her mouth at last. "Tease."

"Oh, for sure there'll be plenty of that."

She put her sandwich down. "Promises, promises."

Better. He'd work on her more when they got back into their room.

Which didn't take long. He decided against the pie after all, and in under ten minutes, they were back in the room. He shut and locked the door behind them. She stopped walking in the middle of the room, almost quivering with the tension in her muscles.

"WHAT ARE YOU THINKING ABOUT so hard?" he asked without meaning to. He pushed off the door, debating whether to give her space or push her.

Kat hesitated for a second before she shrugged.

He frowned. That hesitation meant something, and he wanted to know what. "Tell me."

Her wide-eyed gaze swung to him for a second, unguarded enough for him to see pain shadowing her grey eyes. Then she looked away again. "I don't want you endangered, too," she said finally. She folded her arms over her middle, shoulders stiff.

Hunter's brain took a few seconds to process her words, and when it had, his heart began beating in double-time. He forced himself to take in a deep breath. Just because she cared enough to be so worried didn't mean she was happy about it. He crossed the floor and turned her to face him. "Sweetheart, I'll be fine. I'm certain my training is a few grades above theirs, and I have added motivation to keep you safe." He waited until she lifted wary eyes to his face, ignoring the voice of reason in his head pointing out what a terrible idea this was. "I'm in love with you, Katharine Rigas-Vardos. They're not getting you, because you're mine."

She didn't squeeze her grey eyes shut in time to keep him from seeing them fill, and when she did close them, two fat tears rolled down her face.

He was pushing his luck by telling her, but she needed to know why he was with her, and it wasn't because of some fucking knight-in-shining-armor complex.

He wrapped his arms around her, pulling her closer. He hadn't meant to blurt that out, but he wouldn't take it back now. It was true. "It's going to be all right." He noted her shiver. "I think I promised you a hot shower. It'll warm you up." He rubbed one of his hands along her spine.

She took a slow breath and nodded. "Okay."

He turned her toward the other room, keeping her tucked into his side. She faced him when he flipped the light on, and she tugged the hem of his t-shirt up, startling him for a second. He yanked the shirt off, then reached for hers.

When he had her naked, he turned the water on in the shower, adjusted the temperature, before he shucked his jeans. "Come on."

Still silent, she obeyed. He frowned as he followed her into the tiled stall and under the warm spray of water.

KATHARINE SHIVERED AGAIN, AND he made the water hotter.

"Better?"

She turned to face him, a sad little smile

tugging at one side of her mouth. "Kiss me, Hunter."

He bent and brushed his lips over hers.

She slid her hands around his neck to keep him close when he started to ease back. "For real," she whispered.

He smiled. "Eventually." He reached out blindly for the little bottle of shower gel on the soap ledge, flipping the cap to squirt some of the citrus-scented liquid into his hand. Holding her gaze, he lathered up, then put his hands on her, one on her belly, the other at the base of her spine. He swiped up, around, so the suds spread to her sides. He rubbed his hands over her ass, her hips, to her breasts, along her arms.

Back to the tight, dark nipples that brushed against him with her quick, ragged breaths. "Turn around, Kat," he murmured, ignoring the throb of his dick against her belly.

It took her a moment, but she turned, bracing one hand on the tiled wall. He stepped closer, sliding one soapy hand to her hip, and the other between her thighs.

Her breath caught, and her hips rocked toward his fingers.

He pressed nearer, so his erection rubbed against her ass. "Are you wet for me, honey?" He rubbed the heel of his hand over her clit.

She whimpered, hips pressing into his palm.

He stroked down the inside of her thigh, and she widened her stance. He smiled, briefly, sliding his hips away, then back toward her, his cock slipping over her slick skin.

"Hunter."

"Are you wet?" He traced his fingertips back up her leg.

"Yes."

He rewarded her response with a gentle stroke of his fingers over her sex.

She made a frustrated sound, and he grinned.

"Let's rinse." He reached up with his other hand to adjust the direction of the shower head so it sluiced soap from their bodies.

She started to turn around, but he caught her hips and held her still.

"Hang on." He dipped a little, then forward so his cock slid between her legs.

She braced herself on the wall again. "Please, Hunter."

He slid his hand from her hip to stroke her clit before he continued down, parting her slick folds with his forefinger. "Oh, Kat. You're so wet." He stroked in, just a shallow foray. A tease. He eased his hips forward so his cock could slip inside her.

She rose onto tiptoe, hips tilting back to meet him.

"That's right." He squeezed his eyes shut as the sensitive head of him pressed into her. Hot, tight. "You feel so good."

She whimpered, and he rubbed up to her clit, making her whimper once more.

He eased back a little, then pushed deeper on the next stroke. "Fuck."

One of her hands landed on his hip.

He held still, trying to gather some self-control. When he thought he'd mustered up a bit, he withdrew again, then glided forward, deeper yet, held there.

Her inner muscles tightened around him.

He groaned, pinching her clit between his finger and thumb. More silky moisture coated his erection, and she gasped. He sank into her fully, and his lungs pumped harder. So good. Even better now he'd bared his emotions. "Oh, yes." He stroked her harder, feeling her quiver. "Come for me, honey." He rubbed, circled, pinched, faster, slower, until she sobbed for breath, and her hips rocked back and forth between his fingers and his cock.

"Hunter!"

He nipped at her throat and slammed his hips hard into her. Once. Twice. Three times, at the same time he gave her clit a sharp tug.

She cried out as the release exploded, and he let go of his tenuous grip on his self control, thrusting faster until he came too. "God, I love you."

Kat shivered against him, and he gathered her closer, his heart hammering in his ears. Her fingers dug into his hip, her breaths almost sobs.

Hunter wished now that she was facing him instead of the shower wall. "You okay?" he managed.

She reached back with her free hand and brushed her fingers along the side of his face.

"You're a scary man, Hunter Phelps." She tipped her head back and to one side so she could look at him. Tears glimmered in her grey eyes. "You make me want more," she whispered.

His heart pounded against the inside of his ribs so hard his chest ached. "You can have as much as you want," he promised.

Her smile was shaky, but her kiss, when she pulled him down, was sure.

And when they stumbled out of the bathroom later, fumbling with their towels on the way to bed, Hunter tasted her wants in her kisses, felt it in her touch. Unexpected, but so right.

He wanted more of it. All of it. And he would stand between her and an army of Harvesters to get it.

He whispered it to her, over and over, as they touched and kissed, for hours, bodies moving together. By the time they passed out, he hoped he'd persuaded her he meant it, but he couldn't think hard enough now to be sure.

# CHAPTER TWELVE

In the faint pre-dawn light, she listened to his soft snores, her eyes burning. *It was time.* She eased out from beneath the blankets, silently pulling on the clothing she'd left on the chair yesterday. All she needed was her laptop bag. While Hunter showered yesterday morning, she'd stuffed some clothing in it, and the contents of her purse, which now included ID, cash and cards from her lock box.

Until he really looked, he wouldn't know anything was gone. Her stomach twisted, making her glad she hadn't eaten much last night.

As quietly as she could, she eased her laptop bag onto her shoulder, and then opened the door just enough to slip through, pulling it shut behind her without a whisper of sound. She swallowed around a lump in her throat and walked away from the room. Away from Hunter.

This was the best thing she could do to keep him safe.

Katharine held her breath all the way to the next block, half-expecting Hunter would come running up behind her, demanding to know what the hell she thought she was doing. When he didn't do that or come screeching up in the rental car for several more blocks, she relaxed only slightly. She still had to worry about Harvesters.

She walked as fast as she could without drawing attention to herself–though it was too early for much traffic on the street. When she reached the bus stop they'd passed on their way to the train station yesterday morning, she relaxed a little more.

And when the bus finally began moving, she ignored the stabbing pain in her chest and reminded herself Hunter was safe now. It was the only thing that mattered.

She repeated it to herself over the next hour, as the bus stopped and started, picking up and dropping off commuters, to the last stop. Then she got on the next bus, which carried her further.

She rode to the furthest point on the route, two towns away, where she got off with a handful of others who all hurried away from the bus stop. On their way somewhere. She didn't have to be somewhere right now. But she needed to find somewhere to be, somewhere to figure out her next step. Taking a deep breath, she walked from the stop, keeping an eye out for anyone who seemed to be watching her. About five minutes later, she saw a library, and according to the sign on the door, they were already open.

She meandered among the books for a while, trying to breathe past the tension banding her ribs. Finally, she settled in a quiet corner with her laptop and connected to the wifi. She needed to find a place to stay, so she started a quick search. If this town didn't have a motel, she'd have to get to one that did.

This one did. Several, in fact.

Relief loosened her chest enough to take a slightly deeper breath. She studied her options, finally choosing the one closest to the bus route, for when it was time to move on. It had a small restaurant connected, there was a bakery close by, and it was a few blocks from here. She shut her eyes. It would do.

She jotted down the address and made a short shopping list. She'd abandoned her toiletries, so she'd need replacements. Another quick search, and she found a drug store also near the motel she'd chosen. She could get some snacks and drinks, too, while she was there. Feeling only slightly better, she tucked her list into her pocket and opened her email. Philomena had sent a new journal the other night, and Katharine hadn't had much chance to look through it. Or at least not when she could focus on it. Now seemed like a good time.

HUNTER FELT A LITTLE HUNGOVER WHEN HE woke–fuzzy, not quite a headache, but not well-rested despite his exhaustion after the marathon of lovemaking. He smiled and rolled onto his side, then realized he was alone in the bed. He jerked upright, listening over his quickening heartbeat. Nothing. No sound or light from the open bathroom door.

He shoved the blankets away and shot out of bed. The door was locked but no longer dead-bolted.

Where the hell had she gone?

Panic made his pulse hammer in his ears.

He glanced at the corner where their bags lay–her small suitcase sat there, unzipped, with a sweater sleeve sticking out. In the bathroom, her toothbrush rested beside his.

Maybe she'd gone to the motel office or the diner.

He retraced his steps to the bed, yanking on his rumpled jeans and shirt and shoving his feet into his shoes.

The panic magnified when she wasn't in either place. Hunter returned to the room, breathing slowly to try to settle his pulse. It didn't work, but he kept trying as he stepped inside, leaning on the closed door for a few seconds.

And studied the room, putting himself back into his cop shoes. He'd missed something. He just had to figure out what.

He pushed off the door and went to the small collection of bags in the corner. Flipping up the lid on her suitcase, he studied the contents for a few seconds before digging through her clothes. He'd packed more things in her bag than this, he knew he had.

His heart ricocheted off his ribs again. He ignored it and reached for her purse, which was extremely light—empty, in fact.

He curled his fingers into fists to keep from shouting. Anger and fear bubbled up from his middle.

Her laptop bag was gone. Which meant she had only the things she couldn't do without, and she'd left with no intention of returning.

Which was why he didn't feel the slightest bit guilty about activating the GPS tracker he'd put in her phone. As soon as she turned it on, he'd know exactly where to find her, and when he did, she was getting that spanking they'd talked about the other night.

Hunter wanted to check out of the motel right now and go, but he didn't know where to go. So he stayed and brooded and paced, alternating between guilt for telling her how he felt so she ran, anger that she thought he couldn't keep her safe, and gut-cramping fear she'd crossed paths with a Harvester who'd killed her.

He didn't say anything to Ryder, when the other man texted to let him know they'd gotten the car keys and would pick it up later in the day. Just thanked him for his help.

He debated with himself all day over whether or not he should ask for help with Kat, too. She may reach out to her family. But probably not, especially if she thought they might alert him to her whereabouts. And she'd never put them in danger by going to them.

Finally, sick of the silence from his phone and tired of pacing, he dropped into one of the chairs at the little table and opened a journal to try to read and distract himself. He quit after about fifteen minutes. The journal was from a hundred and fifty years ago, and as far as he could tell, held nothing useful.

He closed it and instead pulled up a map of the area.

How far would she go? Which direction?

He knew it wouldn't be east. As much as she loved the shore, she knew the Harvesters were looking for her there, so she wouldn't go back.

Probably not south either, because it would be too close to home, and chances were good they'd kept someone in the area in case she returned.

That left west and north.

He stared at the map, but nothing obvious leaped out at him.

His head ached. His chest ached.

She had left him.

After he'd blurted out his feelings. What had he been thinking? He knew she wasn't ready.

Fuck. He squeezed his eyes shut. He was an idiot.


ON THE SECOND MORNING, SHE DECIDED she probably ought to check her phone, in case anyone in her family had tried to reach her. Then she was getting on the shuttle bus to the local farmers' market and afterward onto another bus to the next town, or the one after it.

That antsy feeling had been winding through her system since last night.

She turned on the phone, scrolled through a few text messages, including one from Philomena to call her. She bit her lip. Better to get it out of the way. She hit dial and took a few slow breaths.

"Hey there! You have excellent timing, the baby is napping."

She smiled. "How is she? How are you?"

"I'm fine. Tired. And she's beautiful." Her cousin laughed. "What about you?"

"Still alive."

"That's good. Ryder likes Hunter. You know he had to do a background check, right?"

Katharine winced. "Really?"

"Of course." Her tone wasn't the least bit apologetic. "He's perfect to protect you."

She bit her lip.

"What's wrong?"

"I hate putting him in danger."

"He can take care of himself and you, trust me. We like you alive, you know."

"I know." She could tell Philomena about the goblet changing color. Or she could keep her mouth shut. She hesitated.

Too long evidently. "Katharine? Are you there?"

She considered hanging up on her cousin, but she restrained the impulse. "Yes."

"You need to stay with him."

She flushed, grateful it wasn't a video call. "You don't trust I can take care of myself?"

It was Philomena's turn to pause. "Ryder and Kallan believe Ari is truly desperate this time. These men are coming and going from the Virginia estate all the time. We want you safe. That means staying with Hunter."

She sighed and crossed her fingers. "Fine." She felt only slightly bad about lying to her cousin. If Philomena knew the truth, they'd be on her as fast as they could manage and more people she cared about would be in danger.

"Oh, damn." Philomena sighed. "I thought she'd sleep longer. I need to get the baby."

Katharine's eyes stung. "Give her a kiss for me."

"I will. Talk to you soon."

She touched the off button and shut her eyes. It seemed very unfair that one angry Goddess should ruin a family into eternity.

Best she hadn't gone to any of them. They were all safe, and now so was Hunter.

She opened her eyes and squared her shoulders. It was time to catch the shuttle, wander around the market for a while, maybe get something healthy to eat for a change, and then onto a bus to somewhere different.

WHILE HE SAT IN THE MOTEL COFFEE SHOP in the morning, he watched the car idling across the street. The driver wore a ball cap, hiding his face, but Hunter had no doubt it was a Harvester. How the hell had the guy found him? Frowning, he balled up his napkin and put some money on the table, heading for the restrooms and the rear exit door he knew was nearby. While he made his way back to the room, his phone chimed out an alert. Relief rushed through him, making his vision swim.

She hadn't actually gone too far, he realized when he could focus enough to read the message. Just over an hour north and further inland.

It took ten minutes to pack their belongings, check out and get underway. By the time he got behind the wheel of the rental car, he was sweating, pulse pounding with adrenaline, and he'd almost forgotten about the Harvester. *Almost.* He kept a periodic eye on the rearview to make sure the other car wasn't behind him. The other man must have counted on not being recognized, on Hunter just carelessly leading the way to Katherine.

When he got to Centertown, he was a little surprised by the heavy traffic. Then he realized he'd seen about a dozen signs on his way in, advertising the weekly farmers' market for today. He'd bet Kat knew about it, too.

He stopped first at a convenient motel and checked in, dropping all of their bags in the corner before heading back out in search of the blip on his phone that was Kat.

He wasn't prepared for the size of the place. A sign before the first parking lot boasted that it sprawled over five acres, a lot of area to cover. He sat in the car for a few minutes, watching the blip. She wasn't moving very fast, often stopping for minutes at a time.

That'd make it easier to get to her. He tried to tamp down his hurt and anger, to slow his spinning thoughts–what would he say to her first? Finally, he climbed out of the car into the full midday heat and headed off on his hunt.

And when he found her...

KATHARINE SWIPED THE BACK OF HER HAND over her sweaty forehead. This had been a bad idea. She should've realized half the county would come to the market. But the librarian had begun to pay attention to her yesterday, and she didn't want that. She didn't want anyone paying attention to her. Here she could blend into the crowd and no one would notice one woman with a backpack among hundreds of others.

But after an hour and a half of being shoved and bumped and crushed, she'd had enough. If one more baby stroller rolled over her foot, there'd be bloodshed, and that was no way to remain unnoticed.

Katharine worked her way out of the flow of bodies toward the open doorway she spied ahead. It wasn't until after she'd gotten outside that she realized she was on the opposite side of the complex from the bus stop where she'd arrived. "Dammit," she muttered, eyeing the rows and rows of parked vehicles. She could either walk all the way around the sprawling buildings in the hottest part of the day, or she could go back inside and fight her way through the crowds to the other side. Neither option appealed, but the lack of people outside finally won, and she began the long walk to the other side of the buildings.

It was so hot outside, she wondered after a few minutes if she should've stayed inside. The top of her head felt burned, sweat dampened the back of her shirt beneath the strap of her bag, and she wished she'd stopped at one of the stands inside for a drink before coming outside.

She stopped walking, brushing her hair away from her face. She'd have to get a drink before she got on the bus. And maybe later, after she'd checked into a different motel in a new town, she could find something alcoholic and frozen. She took a slow breath and started walking again, but got only a few steps before she couldn't move. Her heart stopped beating for a painful moment, feet frozen in place.

*A Harvester.*

Her gaze caught on the small gold scythe pendant around his neck, hanging out of his shirt as he bent to the bumper of his car.

*Oh my Gods.*

She forced herself to breathe. He hadn't seen her yet. She swallowed hard and shifted to blend in with the other shoppers, but there weren't any at the moment, just a couple of people heading in different directions for their cars. Panic made her pulse race in her ears. She took a casual step to the side, then turned around.

Right into a solid chest.

Strong hands caught her shoulders and she

lifted her gaze, inhaling his familiar scent.

*Hunter.*

His expression was hard, and she saw the anger flash through his eyes.

"Harvester," she whispered, wedging one hand between them to push uselessly against his ribs.

His stormy gaze swung away from her face, then paused before it met hers again. "You need a serious spanking," he muttered, sliding one hand to her nape and yanking her closer.

His mouth claimed hers, though his kiss wasn't as punishing as his words implied.

Katharine wanted to enjoy the caress, but her brain was too aware of the other man nearby, the one intent on killing her.

Hunter nipped at her lower lip, startling her. "Kiss me back," he breathed. "He's about to turn this way." His tongue swiped over the same spot before sliding into her mouth.

She let him lift her into the kiss, his hard hand cupping her ass so her belly pressed into his stirring arousal. *That* got her attention. Heat sparked inside her.

He kissed her deeply, as if he hadn't in too long and needed to make up for lost time. Her heartbeat quickened even though she knew the kiss was for show, a distraction for an audience.

His hard fingers at her nape were gentle, slipping through her damp hair as his tongue teased hers.

Katharine tried to concentrate on the nearby

danger, but her senses were on overload now. Too full of Hunter to be concerned with the Harvester who probably hadn't seen her.

It seemed an eon before Hunter lifted his head. She couldn't quite focus her gaze on his face, or make her breathing even out.

"He's gone," Hunter murmured after a moment.

Just like that, her brain snapped back into focus. She swallowed with some difficulty at the fierce look in his bright eyes.

"Come with me." His grip on her nape firmed, and he turned to tuck her into his side. To any casual observer, they'd look like any other couple there. But the tension running through her was matched in him as he guided her through the parking lot toward the rental car.

"How did you—"

"Stop." His tone was hard, furious. "We will discuss this, but not here. Not now." He unlocked the car and gave her a nudge into the passenger seat.

She decided it was best not to argue, sliding in and fumbling the seatbelt into place while he strode around to his own door.

Hunter remained silent as he drove, but she knew his anger bubbled close to the surface, from the muscle that jumped in his clenched jaw, to the white knuckles gripping the steering wheel. It was a wonder steam didn't pour from his ears like an old-time cartoon character.

Katharine set her own jaw and kept her

mouth shut. When he was ready, he'd let her have it. And right now, she felt like she deserved it for almost walking right into a Harvester.

HUNTER KEPT HIS FINGERS CURLED AROUND the steering wheel. Tight. He knew if he let go, he was going to grab Katharine and not let *her* go. And he was afraid if he touched her now while that dangerous mix of anger and fear still rushed through him, he might be rough. She may actually get the spanking he'd threatened her with in the parking lot. He knew for sure if he touched her now, he was going to rip off every shred of clothing she wore right before he buried himself deep inside her.

That scared the hell out of him.

When he'd finally caught sight of her at the market, he'd been both livid and relieved. When he reached her and she'd whispered, "Harvester," his heart had stopped beating.

She'd wisely kept her mouth shut since he manhandled her into the car, but he knew that was temporary.

He steered the car into the motel parking lot and swung into the empty space in front of his room. *Their* room.

Katharine glanced at him, her grey gaze wary, and he took a deep breath. His heart still pounded too fast. "Don't move," he managed.

It pleased him that she obeyed for a change, and he wondered what that said about him as he went around the car. He pulled her door open and held out one hand to her, his fingers trembling.

Her cool fingers slid over his palm, hesitantly, and he wrapped his around her hand, pulling her from the car. He didn't meet her searching gaze as he steered her into the room, his knees still weak, before he finally released her. Already his nerves had come alive, arousal buzzing along his veins, damping the anger. He took her bag and put it on the table in the corner.

He needed to hold onto the anger a little longer.

Katharine stood just inside the door, her gaze following him as he returned to her. He had so many things to say to her, he couldn't decide where to start.

"I'm sorry, Hunter," she said softly.

He grabbed her upper arms, cutting off whatever else she'd been about to add, and stepped her back against the metal door. "You're sorry? Do you have any idea how scared I was when I woke and you were gone?" He gave her a quick shake before he could stop himself, his frustration and worry and anger and hurt and fear from the past several days boiling up out of him all at once. "I kept hoping you weren't going to cross paths with anyone trying to kill you."

She lifted one hand, grazing his jaw with her fingertips. "I know," she whispered. "I'm so–"

Hunter yanked her up onto tiptoe and away

from the door, then slammed his mouth over hers to stop the rest of the unwanted apology.

Gods, the taste of her... She opened for him, her fingers sliding around to brush his nape.

He gave her ass a sharp swat, startling her into moving against him. He repeated the smack, and this time a tiny moan slid into his kiss. With no conscious effort, he had them both naked and he stumbled backward to the bed, pulling her down onto his cock, still kissing her.

KATHARINE RODE HIM HARD, AND HE peppered her ass with more stinging slaps, until her release made her cry out, the movement of her hips slowing. He rolled her beneath him, gritting his teeth as her body fisted around his erection, and pounded into her harder. Faster. Until she cried out again, her body bowing up beneath him, slick with sweat and her orgasms, and he finally let go of the last tiny thread of his control, collapsing over her, his breath painful gasps.

The grip of her fingers on his back eased, and he realized he probably had scratches, or, at the very least, deep crescents from her nails.

It was all the thought he was capable of currently.

When her warm fingers slipped through the damp hair at his nape several minutes later, Hunter managed to roll to his side, though he didn't release her.

"You scare me," she murmured against his

throat. "*I'm* scaring me."

"Why?"

It took her a few seconds to reply. "When you tell me you'll protect me, I believe you. But I want to do the same for you, and that meant going, keeping the Harvesters away from you."

He reared back far enough to glare into her flushed face. "You are not leaving."

She didn't disagree. Nor did she agree, he noticed. Instead, she dragged her fingers through his hair. "I don't want anything to happen to you."

"The only thing that's going to happen is you're going to get another spanking."

The flush in her cheeks deepened.

As arousal stirred, he rolled her under him and braced his weight on his elbows. "I need you to promise, Kat."

She met his gaze, hers sober and shadowed with fear.

"I mean it. You need to promise me now you won't take off again, that you'll let me keep you safe till this is settled." He didn't add "and beyond," as he wanted–there was no need to send her running already.

She licked her lower lip, her gaze sliding to the side.

*"Promise."*

"Hunter..."

He withdrew from her heat and flipped her over beneath him. Her uptilted ass was still pink from his hand. "Kat." He smoothed his palm over her warm skin, and her breathing quickened. "Mm," he growled, "you liked that, didn't you? Promise me." He watched his fingers against her skin, noting the way her hips shifted into his touch, the way her thighs parted wider for him. "Sweetheart, I can hold out longer than you can." He let the head of his erection brush along her wet sex and felt her shudder. Okay, that might be a lie, but he wouldn't admit it now.

She lifted toward him, but a quick swat stopped the motion. Katharine glanced back over her shoulder, grey eyes dark with need.

"Promise, and I'll make it good," he rasped, rubbing his thumb over the curve of her ass at the same time he angled his cock down to stroke her clit.

Her eyes fluttered shut for a second. "I promise," she whispered on a rush of breath.

Relief pounded through him, and he rewarded her–and himself–with a strong thrust deep inside her. "Good girl," he muttered, bending over her to nip at the back of her shoulder.

"I don't want anything to happen to you." She lowered her head so her forehead pressed to the rumpled blanket.

"Nothing bad is going to happen," he promised, easing his hips backward, then gliding still deeper on the return, so she gasped, her body clenching around him. "Oh, so close already, sweetheart." He reached beneath her to find her swollen little clit and gave it a pinch that had her muffling a scream in the blankets while she came.

Hunter didn't give her time to catch her breath, just quickened his pace, pushing her higher. By the time he finally let go, she was begging, whimpering and gasping.

And he simply started all over a few minutes later. He had her back safely *and* he'd gotten her promise to stay.

Eventually, his brain was finally clear enough to consider how much he'd needed her to promise. She might not want to admit it yet, but she was his. The silver cup on the back of her shoulder was a strong indicator of that. The emails he'd gotten from Ryder talking about the emotional triggers for the color change for her cousins had been definite.

Kat exhaled slowly, then her stomach rumbled.

Hunter eased out of her reluctantly. "I'd better feed you if we're going to keep this up the rest of the day." He watched her roll to her side, noting the fresh flush in her cheeks.

"The rest of the day?" One dark brow winged up.

"At least," he said lightly, skimming his fingers over a fresh bruise on the inside of her hip–about the size of his thumb.

Her gaze followed his caress, and the color in her cheeks deepened.

"How about Chinese?" he asked after a moment. "I saw a delivery menu on the desk when I checked in." He shoved off the bed before he leaned down to kiss the spot and lost control again.

She nodded, pushing onto her elbows. "Are you going to let me properly apologize to you?"

He froze with his hand over the pile of menus. "Not yet," he finally managed, closing his fingers on the heavy paper.

She sat up further, now resting her ass on her heels, her expression somber, but she didn't argue when he handed her the menu. Just looked disappointed and chagrined.

He realized, too, as she shifted and her hair slid back over her shoulder, that he'd marked her collarbone, too. Like a damn high school kid, he mused, marking his territory.

It only took them a few minutes to decide on and order their food, and then Hunter set his hands on his hips. "You haven't asked yet how I found you." Might as well get it out now.

She paused in the middle of dragging her fingers through her tumbled hair, her gaze narrowing on him.

"Don't you want to know?"

It took her a moment to respond, and he knew her quick mind was working. "I have to assume some sort of tracking thing," she finally said, her voice flat. "Because you didn't trust me to stay." She pushed off the bed and grabbed the first shirt she found, which happened to be his. She yanked it on anyway, glaring at him all the while.

He shook his head. "And you proved me

right." She looked damn good in his t-shirt, which only reached to her upper thighs. He dragged his gaze back to her face, where disappointment and hurt flickered briefly.

"It wouldn't occur to you that my leaving had nothing to do with whether you could protect me or not, and everything to do with me protecting you." She set her hands on her hips, which made the hem of the shirt lift a little.

"We've been over that," he said, distracted by the length of her bare legs. "They're after you, not me. I'm perfectly safe." Now probably wasn't the time to mention the man he believed was a Harvester at their last motel.

The knock at the door of their room stopped whatever had been about to come out of her open mouth. She glanced around for her dagger, which had wound up on the night stand, and he turned for the peephole. "Food," he said shortly, glancing back to see her scurry into the bathroom, clutching her dagger as the shirt flapped up just enough for him to catch a glimpse of her ass. He tugged on his jeans, stuffing in his burgeoning erection, and took out his wallet, then opened the door to pay the delivery guy.

Kat emerged from the other room a minute later, still disgruntled. He noticed she'd strapped her knife onto her thigh again, and his heart beat faster. Apparently a woman armed with a deadly weapon and no panties was a total turn-on for him. He ignored his body's reaction for now and spread the carry-out containers across the table, setting her bag on the floor.

She sat, her lashes shielding her very expressive eyes, and reached for an eggroll.

"I'm not sorry about the tracking device," he said, watching her freeze, eggroll halfway to her mouth. "If he'd realized who you were, the Harvester wouldn't have cared how close I was or how many other shoppers were around. He'd have tried to kill you."

After a couple more seconds, she took a bite of the roll, no doubt to keep in an angry response.

He smiled grimly and grabbed the other eggroll.

"Do you suppose it's a coincidence he was at the farmers' market?" she asked after she finished her roll.

*Good question.* He finished chewing and swallowed, thinking. "Probably not."

She examined the contents of the small white cartons between them, finally chose one, still not looking at him. "I wonder if they're getting help from Her now. More than their special talents, I mean." She snapped apart a pair of chopsticks and dug into the kung pao chicken. "Or if it was luck."

Hunter considered that as he started wrestling his own chopsticks into submission. "Why not just tell them exactly where to find you then?"

"I think it's part of the protection in the amulet. I don't think She's able to pinpoint."

That wasn't especially reassuring, as, apparently the Goddess could still narrow down to a small area if She was actually helping the Harvesters now. It was too close for his comfort.

Kat finished her meal in silence, and Hunter let her, his own mind busy with the possibilities as he ate, tasting nothing. Too many possibilities. If Athena was giving the Harvesters more aid, She must be determined to find his Medusa. "I'm not letting Her have you," he said finally, startling her into meeting his gaze across the table.

Her lower lip wobbled, a tiny quiver before she caught it between her teeth, and her eyes went soft with something that made his heartbeat race.

He shoved to his feet and caught her wrist, pulling her out of her chair, too, into him. He was a little surprised she let him, and he gathered her close, feeling her breath quicken. "Come back to bed, sweetheart," he whispered, stroking one hand down her spine, lightly. He urged her to turn, stopped her beside the bed to pull the shirt off over her head, and, while he unfastened and dropped his jeans, she removed her dagger and climbed onto the bed, watching him with that emotion still shining in her eyes.

He took his time with her, tasting and touching her everywhere until she was begging, shifting restlessly beneath him. Over and over, until they both passed out from sheer exhaustion.

# CHAPTER THIRTEEN

For a while, in the dim light from the bathroom, Hunter watched her sleeping, noting the dark smudges beneath her eyes. She hadn't been sleeping well even before she took off, and clearly she hadn't slept much the last few nights either. Maybe he'd exhausted her thoroughly enough for her to sleep through the rest of the night.

He doubted he'd sleep as soundly, however, even as tired as he was.

Kat shifted, and he gathered her closer. When he closed his eyes, he could still see the Harvester behind her, interest flitting through his eyes until Hunter had bent to kiss her. Even then, the other man had hesitated before getting into his car to leave, and Hunter couldn't be sure whether it was because he'd recognized her, or because he'd thought she was attractive

They'd check out tomorrow. Put more distance between them and this latest Harvester.

In the meantime, he needed to catch up on a little sleep, too.

He smoothed one hand down her spine, and she moved closer still, her fingers sliding over his hip. Despite knowing they both needed the rest, his body came to attention.

Kat's breathing hitched, and she tipped her head back, sleepy eyes opening. "Already?"

He huffed out a laugh. "Non-stop, sweetheart. Go back to sleep."

Her fingers slipped inward from his hip to close around his burgeoning erection. "I'm not tired now." She squeezed, and his eyes crossed. "Touch me, Hunter," she whispered.

He didn't need to be told twice, easing his hand around from her spine to cup one breast. The tip was already hard, nudging at his fingers when she arched into his touch. He wedged his thigh between her knees, and she wrapped one leg around him, giving him access to the slippery, hot core of her. He let her guide him home, then rolled her beneath him.

She slid her hand up his back, nails digging into muscle. "Hunter."

"Slow, Kat. You rush me too much." He rocked gently back and forth, smiling for a second at the disappointed sound she made. Until she clenched her pussy around him. He swallowed a groan and slipped one hand between them to find her clit. He used his thumb to stroke her, in counterpoint to his slow thrusts. The pleasure built, more gradually this time. When he couldn't bear anymore, he bent to catch her mouth and quickened his pace.

*So good.* He growled when the release burst free, and she gasped with her own, her body bowed beneath him. "I love you," he whispered. He didn't even care about his big mouth right now. The words needed to be said.

Katharine's fingers dug harder into the back of his shoulder, but she didn't protest.

Smiling, he buried his face in the side of her sweaty neck. That would do for now.

KATHARINE SWALLOWED BACK THE LUMP in her throat as she eyed the shiny cuff holding her to the headboard in the morning. Of course he wouldn't trust her to stay even though she'd promised. She'd proven he couldn't.

The shower cut off in the next room, and she shut her eyes, rolling her head on the pillow so she faced the empty space on the bed beside her. After a few minutes, the door opened, and she imagined him padding out wrapped in one of the towels.

Another second, and he touched the side of her face. "I'm sorry, Kat."

She squeezed her eyes shut tighter, ignoring the brush of his fingers on her wrist as he unlocked the handcuffs. "I promised I wouldn't go," she ground out.

"I know. I'm sorry."

But he wouldn't trust her word. A tear burned down the side of her face toward the pillow, and she yanked her arm from his loose grasp, curling into a ball beneath the blankets and willing her breathing to remain even.

His weight behind her made the mattress dip.

She moved away, eyes stinging, and realized she was still nude beneath the blankets, her body sore in intimate places, and she swallowed a painful sob.

Hunter caged her between one strong arm and his body. "When I got up the other day and you were gone, I was furious. And more afraid than I've ever been," he choked out. "If something happened to you–" He swallowed noisily, then again. "If something happened to you, I'd never forgive myself. Or you, for not trusting me to protect you. I'm in love with you, Kat, and you left."

She blinked, but the tears blurring her vision didn't go away. His warm, ragged breath flowed along her scalp and nape. Even through the blankets, she felt the quick beating of his heart against her back. 'Love' was scary.

And impossible. She'd given up on any dreams for a happily ever after when that curse landed on her head, so to speak. No family for her, no picket fence, no white wedding dress.

But, Gods, she wanted Hunter, and not just to appease her cursed hormones.

Another hot tear slipped down the side of her face. She bit her lip to keep in the sobs crowding in her throat.

"Don't cry, sweetheart," he whispered, pressing his face into her hair.

The first sob burst free, and she pressed one hand to her mouth to keep in the rest.

Hunter moved over her, wrapping both arms tight around her so her face rested against his throat. "I never want to make you cry." His soft words only made it more difficult to keep the tears under control.

She bit her lip harder, trying to distract herself from the idea of crying. It didn't work. Scalding tears slipped from her face onto his warm skin. When he hugged her tighter, she could no longer stop the sobs from escaping.

Hunter murmured to her, holding her securely against his heart, occasionally brushing his lips over her hair, until she finally ran out of tears and lay limply in his embrace, her breaths eventually evening out.

"You're scary," she rasped out, throat sore from her sobbing. She worked one hand free of the blankets and swiped her fingers across her wet cheek.

"So are you, sweetheart." He smoothed one hand over her hair.

"I don't know what to do about this. Us." Katharine inhaled deeply, then released the air in a rush.

"How about just letting go? Some things we have no control over." Hunter tipped her chin up, no longer allowing her to hide.

"Gods, I'm a mess," she muttered, shutting her eyes.

"Kind of." He sounded like he might be smiling.

She didn't look. "I need a shower. Maybe an ice pack for my eyes."

He laughed, then pressed a quick kiss on her mouth. "No ice packs here, but maybe a cold washcloth."

"It'll have to do." She opened her eyes and met his gaze. "I am sorry, you know."

His smile vanished. "I know."

"And not just because of that spanking."

One corner of his mouth kicked up again. "You loved every second of *that*."

Her pulse beat faster just thinking about it. "Maybe."

His eyes darkened. "We don't have time for that before check-out." The gravelly tone of his voice made it clear he'd like to do it anyway.

Kat swallowed, suddenly very aware of her nudity beneath the blankets. "Then you'd better let go so I can get a shower and we can make check-out time."

Instead of releasing her, though, Hunter leaned in and pressed a kiss onto her mouth, holding her gaze. "Maybe I need another shower," he murmured.

She touched his cheek. "I'll be fast. You can wash my back tomorrow."

A ghost of a smile curved his lips. "Spoilsport." Still, he released her, pushing off the bed and adjusting the towel slipping low on his hips.

Exactly as she'd imagined. Her heart skipped a beat.

"You'd better stop looking at me like that if you really want a solo shower," he warned her, holding out one hand.

She took his hand and sat up, dropping the blankets as she slid out of bed. "Hunter–"

He shook his head. "Go on, sweetheart." He kissed her lightly, then gave her a little push toward the bathroom.

She smiled and let him, but when she heard the way he sucked in his breath after she'd passed him, she stopped and turned back. "What?"

His blue eyes were wide as they lifted back to her face, and her pulse quickened. "The amulet's changed colors again."

Her feet didn't want to move, and her heart beat too fast.

He stepped closer, then behind her, his fingers gliding over the back of her shoulder. "Pink," he breathed in answer to her unasked question. "Like the inside of a seashell." His finger outlined the rim of the goblet. "It was still silver last night, Kat." He flattened his hand over the tattoo and moved around to embrace her. "You're shaking, sweetheart."

Because she was scared as hell.

Her mind raced almost as fast as her heart. That color-change was far more abrupt than the last one–after reading Andi and Philomena's additions to the family lore, she knew what it meant. She wasn't ready for it. For him.

HUNTER HELD HER CLOSE, FINALLY EASING BACK onto the edge of the bed and pulling her onto his lap. He smoothed one hand up and down her spine.

His emails from Ryder and Kallan had been crystal clear about what the color changes meant when they'd been with Andi and Philomena. The trouble right now was he didn't know if Kat was shaking with fear or excitement. Likely fear. He might've already given in, but she wouldn't let go so easily. Not after years of this curse and giving up on a different future.

He inhaled slowly, continuing to rub her back, hoping to soothe away some of her distress. Her shaking had subsided to intermittent shudders, but her breath still came too fast. "So I was thinking about leaving this little town and heading for someplace more populated, to make it harder for them to find you," he said. "How do you feel about Philly or New York?"

She took a slow breath, then released it, just as slowly. And repeated. Then she tipped her head back enough to look at him, her face pale. "A needle in a haystack?"

He nodded.

She considered it for a moment, her gaze holding his. "In that case, it should be New York."

Hunter relaxed a little. Not a bad distraction, he thought. "We can turn in the rental car at the station and go in on the train."

She nodded, easing to her feet, then leaned down to brush a kiss on his mouth. "Thank you, Hunter," she whispered before moving toward the bathroom.

Of course she knew what he was doing. He watched her go into the other room, noting the way her shoulders had relaxed. And the small bruises on her very fine ass–spaced right about where his fingers would have been countless times since yesterday afternoon.

Heat climbed the back of his neck as she shut the door behind her. He'd behaved like an animal in the last twenty-four hours.

Then again, he had his own war wounds–the scratches down his back and the faint bite mark on his chest. He grinned and pushed to his feet to get dressed.

KATHARINE GLARED AT THE REFLECTION in the mirror. Stupid, cursed pink cup. It hadn't changed in years, and now twice within a week? She touched it, lightly. It didn't feel any different. She'd never have known it was a different color if one of them hadn't seen it. She knew what it meant.

She just wasn't sure she was ready to go there. *Love.*

She turned away from the mirror, rubbing at the back of her neck, a bit sore from craning around to study the back of her shoulder for so long. Falling for Hunter–it would certainly solve the problems from her curse. But she'd rarely taken the easy way out of anything. Not that being with him was easy.

He thought his way was the best way, all the time.

She rubbed at her neck again. Sometimes it was.

He was bossy.

Okay, so she might be difficult occasionally. That didn't mean he got to be in charge.

At least not all the time.

She sighed, then realized she hadn't brought any clean clothes in the bathroom with her. Too freaked out about her stupid tattoo.

She got a quick shower, using the tiny sample products the motel supplied, before she emerged from the smaller room, wrapped in her wet towel.

Hunter glanced over from his laptop, and one dark eyebrow winged up.

"Don't say a word," she muttered.

One corner of his mouth curved, but he didn't speak while she yanked clean things from her carry-on and put them on, flushing under his scrutiny.

"We should get breakfast, then head out," he said as she combed her wet hair. "We'll avoid the commuters, too, leaving after breakfast."

She glanced over at him. "And then what?"

One of his big shoulders lifted. "I don't know yet. I mean, besides the usual, find a place to stay." He sighed. "I don't like not having some kind of plan."

She didn't disagree with that right now, not with the Harvesters everywhere they turned around. "Well, since Mary Ann thinks you're on vacation, maybe that's the plan for now."

His eyes narrowed. "Play tourist in New York?"

She mimicked his half-shrug. "We could sit in a hotel room indefinitely, I suppose, but someone in the hotel might find that odd."

Hunter didn't speak again, eventually turning his gaze back to his computer screen, and she let him ponder while she combed her hair. When she finished, she crossed to the table, picking up her laptop bag, and then her carry-on, putting both on the bed so she could repack everything.

"We need to find a laundromat," she said as she sorted clean from dirty clothes.

He grunted, and she assumed it was an agreement. He'd run out of clean clothes soon, too.

Finally, she had her things back in order.

"Are you hungry?"

She glanced over and found he'd closed the laptop to watch her. "Starving, actually." Her stomach rumbled at the notion of food. Yesterday afternoon's meal had been a long time ago.

He smiled. "Okay. Let's get breakfast in the motel diner and then hit the road. The train station's pretty close. I'll text Ryder to let him know we're leaving the car."

Katharine nodded. "We can figure out our game plan on the train, starting with finding a place to stay and a laundromat near it."

Hunter pushed to his feet and stretched. "Okay."

Her gaze caught on his strong arms as he put them back down, and she swallowed. Powerful. He could probably best a lot of other men in a fight. Yet he knew how to be gentle. She dragged her attention away, back to her bags.

"We can do that again later," he murmured, "no time now."

She flushed hot. She needed to practice her poker face.

One of his hands slid into her back pocket, and he gave her ass a squeeze.

She looked up and found him smiling.

"Did I hurt you?"

She shook her head, heat spreading from her face to her throat.

"Good." He squeezed again. "You keep looking at me like that, and we're not going to get checked out on time."

She shut her eyes, and he laughed, bending to brush a kiss on her mouth. "You're awful," she ground out.

"And you like it." He released her. "Let me grab the rest of my stuff, and we'll get breakfast."

She sighed, then zipped her suitcase. She did like it, that was the problem.

She just didn't know what to do about it.

HUNTER COULDN'T REMEMBER WHEN HE'D last been to New York. It was a lot to take, which was why he only visited occasionally. Kat seemed enthralled, though, as they strolled along Broadway. It made him smile, seeing her so relaxed for a change.

She glanced at him and squeezed his fingers. "This is fun. I haven't been here in ages."

"What do you want to do? See a show? Get on a tour bus?"

She shook her head. "Let's just walk for a while. We can stop if we see something we want to check out, or walk forever."

He'd be okay walking forever if it was with her. "When was the last time you had a real vacation?"

"Almost seven years ago. My sisters and I rented a house on Cape Cod for two glorious weeks. Before Damaris had kids, before Tabitha was married, and Odessa had just graduated from high school." She smiled up at him. "And the next year, Philomena fell in love and I got this, and I haven't been able to spend time like that with my sisters since."

"Really?"

Her smile faded. "I could have, probably. But I didn't want them in danger if a Harvester found me, so I haven't."

"What about your parents?"

"We video chat once a month or so." Her smile disappeared altogether. "I miss them."

He didn't point out she was well on her way to getting rid of the curse. She knew that, but he didn't think she was ready to give her emotions free rein.

She looked up again. "I know what you're thinking."

"Do you?"

"Of course." Her fingers tightened on his. "But what if I could make this curse go away altogether?"

He frowned. "How do you think you can do that?"

She hesitated, and his stomach sank. "Go to Greece. Talk to Athena."

Fuck, this was what she'd been thinking about on the train while staring out the window. "You might as well take out a sign in Times Square with a 'Here I Am, Strike Me Down' message on it," he growled.

They reached a street corner and had to stop to wait for the walk signal. "I don't want to pass this on to another cousin. None of them should have to live this way, hiding away to avoid the Harvesters."

The signal changed, and they stepped off the curb with other tourists. "I don't think it's the best idea," he started.

"It might be the only way to do this, Hunter. To end it forever." After they'd crossed the street, she stopped and turned to him. "Don't say no without giving it some thought. I'd have to plan how to get there, how to do it..." She set her free hand on his chest. "Think about it."

His heart beat too hard against his ribs. He couldn't agree to her going to Greece. It might not just be the end of the curse, but the end of Kat, and he couldn't let that happen. He held her grey gaze for a long moment and finally made himself nod, knowing he had to.

A sad smile touched her lips. "Thank you." She stretched up to brush a kiss on his mouth, and he caught her nape with his free hand, holding her there for a real kiss when she started to ease back. Her dark lashes fluttered up when he released her, her eyes dark. She cleared her throat. "What would you like to see?"

"Why don't we get on one of those tour buses after all? Be tourists for a little while. We can find some good pizza later, and then..."

Her cheeks turned pink. "Ah. That sounds like fun, especially the 'and then...'."

And he could work on his arguments for why going to Greece was a bad idea. It would take some heavy persuasion.

In the meantime, he had the woman of his dreams in his arms, and he knew she was falling for him, too. "Let's see where this bus goes," he said, gesturing to the double-decker bus parked ahead.

Kat touched his jaw. "Let's just get on and be surprised."

He smiled. "Why not?" Now wasn't the time to argue or plot. They could do that later. Now was for a break, a chance to catch their breath, and to pretend there weren't men hunting her, like they were any other couple on a vacation.

He wanted more of that, and he'd do anything to get it.

*Fuck.*

Which meant if she was persuasive enough, he might have to consider her idea.

# CHAPTER FOURTEEN

*atharine.*

Aristotle cursed the name. How had she escaped? With all the nephews he'd sent to the New Jersey shore area, somehow she and the man managed to elude them.

Perhaps she was more witch than her ancestor. With the extensive training he put his family through, especially in the last few years since they'd failed to kill the two previous Medusas, she must have an advantage he'd never considered.

That wouldn't matter to the Goddess.

He shut his eyes and took a slow breath. They simply had to widen the search area. He opened his eyes and sent a quick message to Elek, then turned to the window behind his desk. There were a few hours until the summer sunset, but fatigue pulled at him. His body was failing.

He scowled at the garden below. He could not leave this unfinished. His legacy. No, he needed to oversee this to the correct conclusion: the death of this Medusa. It would redeem him, at least in his own eyes, for his brother's betrayal. The Goddess would never know the truth about Iphis, and Aristotle could die with his mind at ease, even if they failed to locate and destroy the amulet.

"Uncle."

He turned to greet Elek. "We need to expand the search area."

His great nephew nodded, a faint frown creasing his brow. "Of course. How many more cousins do you want me to reallocate?"

"Bring Ajax for sure. I think another four for now, until we can pick up their trail. I will leave the choice to you on which four."

A hint of surprise flitted across Elek's face. "I will work it out right away, Uncle."

"You're a good boy, Elek." Aristotle smiled a little. "And you're doing a good job."

The younger man blinked, then smiled. "Thank you, Uncle Ari."

He gestured toward the door, and Elek nodded and strode from the room.

He was a good boy. And when they found and killed this Medusa, Aristotle would feel good about putting him in charge. He had proven biddable, thoughtful, and smart. And he wouldn't have to bear Aristotle's secrets. He would be able to lead without fear of someone learning of such betrayal. A fresh start for Athena's Harvesters. Elek could lead the hunt for Medusa's daughters, to destroy the amulet protecting them.

But they had to find the monster first.

He turned back to the window. The Goddess would be satisfied this time, if it killed him.

He hoped it didn't, but he was smart enough to know his time was limited. He just needed enough to accomplish this one last thing, to atone for his brother's betrayal.

AFTER FINDING A HOLE-IN-THE-WALL PIZZERIA that served the best pizza she'd ever eaten, Katharine and Hunter made their way back to their hotel, also tucked away from the main tourist drags. They'd gotten off the train and located a laundromat nearby first thing, then checked in here before their touristy afternoon. She knew Hunter had been brooding about her idea to take the fight to Athena, though he hadn't said anything since they got on the tour bus.

Now he sat on the sofa against the wall, the television on but muted.

She felt a pang in the middle of her chest. He'd been doing his best to protect her for weeks, and what had she done? Insisted on going out when she knew there were Harvesters in town, left him behind and gone off on her own, and then suggested a trip to a Goddess who would most likely strike her down as soon as she set foot in Greece. Sounded pretty idiotic, laid out that way.

Maybe the first one, she admitted to herself. It had certainly been selfish and arrogant, assuming she could go out without being found in their hometown. But going off on her own had been for his safety. The Harvesters wouldn't hesitate to kill him if he got in their way. Going to Athens would be the end of it, one way or the other.

She hoped it would only end the curse and not end her as well.

He settled further into his seat, and she smiled. No more worrying about Athena tonight. She crossed the room and sat close beside him on the sofa, setting one hand on his knee.

"What are you watching?"

He shifted to put one arm behind her across the back of the couch. "I don't know. I think a detective show."

"No sound?" Katharine slid her fingers from his knee, slowly, finally coming to a stop several inches from his groin. And then she dragged them back to his knee, noting the growing bulge at his crotch.

"You're playing with fire, Kat," he ground out when she started back up his thigh.

She smiled. "I know." This time, she scraped her nails along the fly of his jeans, gratified to hear his breathing catch, before she retraced a leisurely path back to his knee.

Hunter shifted on the couch, spreading his knees farther apart.

She obliged him by cupping his erection on this pass, lightly, briefly.

"Honey."

She leaned closer and brushed her lips along his ear so his breath rushed out, while she rubbed the heel of her hand over taut muscles high on his thigh. "How about if we get you naked so I can play?" she whispered, then nipped at his earlobe.

"Anything you want," he rasped.

She noticed he didn't move, though. So she did, standing and holding out one hand.

He took it, his cheekbones flushed already and eyes at half-mast, then slowly rose.

Katharine slid her gaze down, past his wide chest, lifting too quickly with his labored breathing, to the solid bulge in the front of his jeans. "I can't wait to taste," she whispered.

Heat flared in his eyes, but she turned away, towing him behind her to the bed. When she released his hand and faced him, he yanked his shirt off.

She smiled at his impatience, then reached for his belt. "This part is mine," she told him, watching his eyes darken still more. She leaned in to press a kiss in the center of his chest, inhaling the scent of his skin–soap, a little sweat, and underneath, Hunter. She took her time undoing the belt, kissing her way across his chest to one little dark nipple. When she scraped her teeth over it lightly, he growled, his hands landing on her hips. She grinned, then tugged at the button on his jeans.

His quick, warm breaths beat on the top of her head.

She didn't make him wait longer, easing the zipper open and sliding her fingers in to stroke him.

His grip on her tightened.

She tipped her head back. "This will be

easier if you're on the bed," she murmured.

He bent to catch her mouth, his kiss rough.

She wrapped her fingers around his shaft and squeezed gently, feeling her inner muscles clench, too. He groaned, lifting his head after a moment.

"Tease."

"Oh, I will tonight," she promised, stroking her thumb over the head of his cock before she released him and gave his jeans a push.

He sat on the foot of the bed, and she knelt in front of him to untie his shoes so she could pull his jeans off the rest of the way.

"Mm." She lifted her gaze to his erection. "You need to move up and stretch out."

He pushed to his feet instead, yanking the blankets down before he eased onto the bed.

Katharine smiled again, crawling over his strong legs, then bending to kiss the side of his shaft.

Hunter's breath rushed out. "You weren't kidding about the tease, were you?"

"Nope." She licked up to the broad head, over it, watching his chest rise and fall a bit faster.

"Be prepared for some payback."

"I can't wait," she whispered, then opened her mouth over him. Warmth spread into her chest, and she feared it had nothing to do with desire.

IN THE MORNING, THEY LAZED IN BED for a while, and then Hunter got in the shower.

Katharine opened her laptop to check out the latest journal files her cousins had sent. One from several hundred years ago, and another from Annis, who'd been the Medusa before Andi and lived to a ripe old age. Gods, how many journals had Annis kept? Maybe the older one would be more interesting, since there'd been nothing helpful in the newer one.

Sixteen hundred and eighty-seven. That was a long time ago. She wondered if that Medusa, she squinted at the flowery handwriting, Margaret, had ever considered traveling to Greece to the temple of the Goddess? Or if any others had thought about it? She knew attempts had been made to apologize to the Goddess and been ignored, but those had all been done from a safe, respectful distance.

She stared at the screen, mind racing. It had been thousands of years. If she took her case to Athena, would the Goddess finally feel forgiving? Or would the Her anger last an eternity?

Hunter came out of the bathroom along with a rush of steam, and she clicked on download to save the journals to her computer to read later. She ignored the way her pulse quickened at the sight of his bare chest and looked at her screen again. No new email, though. She wondered if Kallan or Ryder had emailed Hunter.

Hunter swiped his towel across his chest and dropped it as he reached for a clean shirt.

Kat's gaze followed his swift movements as he tugged the t-shirt over his head, soft red fabric covering all the lovely muscles she'd touched and tasted... She frowned and forced her gaze away. She needed to consider a plan, an actual plan for this, as opposed to her flight earlier in the week with no plan other than to get away so Hunter would be safe.

Getting to Greece. That wasn't an issue. She had more than one passport, and the Harvesters didn't know about those, so they wouldn't have any idea she was traveling, even if they'd hacked airlines, too.

Hunter would need something, though. He'd never let her go on her own, and honestly, she'd rather have him with her. His presence made her feel safer. She wondered how long Ryder would need to get him good ID.

Then once she got there...go to the Parthenon.

Sounded simple enough, but it was a safe bet there were Harvesters in Athens. Probably even working near or at the temple.

She did a quick search for the Parthenon.

It was wide open, though there was ongoing reconstruction work. That would continue for years if they were to restore it fully. She studied the temple, trying to imagine the giant golden statue that used to be housed inside it. The structure was impressive even as a ruin, but it must have been spectacular when it was built originally. She clicked another link that took her to a 3D reconstruction.

How beautiful. She admired the painted friezes and sculptures.

Hunter's hand landed on her shoulder, and he sighed.

"Just looking," she said, glancing up to find his mouth set in a flat line.

"Plotting."

"I promised not to go anywhere without you."

He pulled out the other chair at the table. "I'm still thinking."

She smiled and reached over to touch his jaw. "I know. I'm trying to think ahead."

"That kind of trip will require more than just thinking ahead, Kat."

"You'll need another ID."

He frowned. "What?"

"They know who you are, and if they've hacked into any airlines to monitor travel, you can't use your own."

He opened his mouth, then shut it again. "That's illegal," he said at last. "The hacking and the ID."

Her smile widened. "So is murder, but they don't care. Besides, I have more than one ID in case of just such a situation. Ryder will take care of it for you."

His eyes narrowed. "Good thing I'm not a cop anymore."

She leaned over and brushed a kiss on his sulky mouth. "Good thing." She sat back. "I got a couple new journals in my email to read."

"You want to stay in today?"

She considered that. "Maybe this morning. It looks like a beautiful day. We could go for lunch and check out a museum or something this afternoon on your vacation."

"Your vacation, too. First one in seven years, you should make it count." A ghost of a smile touched his lips.

"True. So reading this morning, and sightseeing later?"

He nodded. "Maybe I got more reading material, too."

"Probably."

He went for his own laptop.

Katharine dragged her gaze back to her screen. Side-stepped that argument for now, but not forever, she knew.

THEY BOTH READ FOR A FEW HOURS, occasionally turning their screens to share something interesting or funny, but Hunter didn't find anything actually useful in the one he was skimming, and neither had Kat.

"Are you hungry yet?" He shut his laptop.

She glanced up, her gaze unfocused. "Kind of."

He smiled. "Go get a shower, and we'll find something to eat and figure out what we want to see this afternoon."

"Okay." She shut down her laptop and collected clean clothes.

He opened his browser to search for restaurants nearby, then expanded the search area a little. Lots of museums in the city, and most of them had restaurants close by. He had a short list of options by the time she stepped out of the bathroom, still toweling her hair dry.

"That looks interesting," she said, pointing at one of his top choices.

"And Chinatown's not too far, so we could start with lunch there, and walk to the museum afterward."

She smiled and brushed a kiss on his cheek. "Sounds good. Let me comb my hair, and then I'm ready."

He grinned at her back as she returned to the bathroom to hang up her towel. She was one of the most beautiful women he'd ever met, and probably the most low-maintenance.

Kat turned off the bathroom light a few minutes later, her wet hair combed into a sleek ponytail. "What?"

He shook his head. "Just enjoying the view."

She laughed. "Not quite like the night we met. I didn't pack any make-up when we rushed out of my place."

"You don't need it." He shut the laptop and pushed to his feet.

"Ah, but we're in New York, so I'm way under-done."

He tipped her chin up and held her gaze as he bent to kiss her lightly. "You're good as-is, I promise."

"You're a tad biased." She patted his cheek. "Let's go, I'm starving."

They headed out of the hotel and caught a

bus into Chinatown, where they moseyed in and out of several shops and through a street market before they chose a restaurant. Only a couple other tables were occupied, and they didn't look like tourists. They certainly weren't Harvesters–young couples, a table surrounded by older women. Hunter didn't fully let down his guard, but he didn't have any prickling sense of being watched. Not like at home after their picnic, or at the beach after Kat fled and the man sat in his car outside the motel diner. Maybe his needle in a haystack idea wasn't terrible.

If he were organizing the search and realized his quarry had vanished, he would expand the search area.

The good news was they couldn't be found by watching for his car on highway cams anymore.

*Shit.* He eyed the dumplings in his soup. Maybe this wasn't his best idea ever. New York had cameras everywhere, but unless someone spotted them...

Kat touched his wrist. "What's wrong with your soup?"

He realized he was scowling. "Nothing." He took a slow breath and released it, trying to make his frown go away. "Thinking about the cameras all around the city."

"Ah." She rested her chopsticks on the edge of her plate, her gaze locked on his. "They probably wouldn't look at them without reason. They'd need a big team to monitor so many round the clock. Not a good use of their resources. Even with thousands of them, they'll want to maximize their time, and staring at street video for days without knowing the person they're hunting is even there isn't productive. Better to have boots on the ground."

*Smart Katharine.* "I thought of that, too."

A faint smile curved her lips. "Then relax. And maybe we can buy some baseball caps at the stand we saw on the corner." She winked, maneuvering her chopsticks to get another bite of her noodles and shrimp.

Relax. It sounded like such an easy thing to do. But not since he'd encountered the Harvester in her bedroom. "How has your family done this for so long?"

She glanced over for a moment, then looked at her bowl. "We've been lucky for a long time," she said after a few seconds, meeting his gaze again. "And survival is a strong instinct, the need is enough to make people do things they don't want to do, wouldn't do otherwise. Like live on their own, away from the people they love. Stop doing things they enjoy to stay safe and off anyone's radar."

He realized he was clenching his jaw and forced himself to relax it. Being forced to live that way was wrong. He considered the color of her amulet.

Kat sighed. "You're not relaxing at all, vacation man," she teased.

He picked up a dumpling from his soup. "I have a lot to think about."

Her warm fingers on his wrist made him look at her. "I know," she whispered. "Me, too."

Warmth spread up his arm from her touch, making him feel a bit better. At least he wasn't the only one pondering their future. Or whether they had one. He smiled and put the dumpling into his mouth.

She smiled back and returned to her own bowl.

When his phone rang, he started. It hadn't rung in days, and he'd nearly forgotten about it, aside from habitually putting it into his pocket and keeping it charged. He pulled it out and glanced at the screen. "My buddy Lance." He thumbed it on. "Hey, Lance," he said, setting his chopsticks down and reaching for her hand.

"Where the hell are you?"

"What?"

"You're not home, the office is closed. Where are you?"

"I told you I might take some time off." He rubbed his thumb across the back of her hand, watching her cheeks turn pink.

"God, you're with *her*, aren't you?"

Hunter smiled. "Yeah."

"Hell. Are you kidding?"

"No, I'm not kidding. She's the one." He watched her eyes widen slightly, and the color in her face deepened. "Lance, I need to go. I'll call you later." He tapped to end the call without waiting for his friend to reply. "You know that, right?"

She swallowed. "You were pretty clear," she said softly. Her fingers tightened reflexively on his.

Hunter relaxed. "Good." He released her hand and lifted his chopsticks again. Satisfaction settled into his gut. "This soup is probably the best I've ever had."

Kat laughed. "You've never been to Chinatown before, have you?"

He shook his head. "We should come back here. On our next vacation." First he needed her to fully trust him and her own feelings. Then they could get rid of the curse and the Harvesters hunting them.

One thing at a time.

After lunch, they did buy baseball caps at the stall up the street. It didn't really ease his concern about the cameras, but she was right–unless the Harvesters knew they were in the city, there'd be no point wasting time looking at cameras here.

They took their time walking to the museum, pausing to admire some of the older buildings along the way, mixed in with newer architecture. Kat snapped a few photos of City Hall on her phone, smiling and seemingly carefree. He wished they actually were an ordinary couple on vacation–he wouldn't have to worry whether men with murder on their minds lurked around every corner, to worry about losing her if he didn't keep his wits sharp.

She tucked her phone away and turned to him, her smile fading. She stepped close enough to rise up and kiss his cheek, then tucked her hand in his once more.

He took a slow breath as they walked. Just for now, he told himself, just for now, relax a little. He could keep alert and not be so tense. He repeated it to himself for the first half hour that they explored the museum. Until he forgot and simply enjoyed Kat's reactions to the exhibits. Enjoyed being with her. No worries about keeping her alive, no wondering if she would trust herself.

Just him and the woman he loved.

When they finally left the museum, it was suppertime. Hunter pondered as she stood beside him on the steps, stretching. "Are you hungry?"

She shrugged. "I'm not starving yet, but if we head in the direction of our hotel, maybe we'll see something."

He considered the idea. It was still light, easier to see if anyone showed undue interest in them, even with the wicked storm clouds building in the southwest. "Okay, let's walk." He caught her hand, and they descended the stairs to join the other pedestrians.

"Maybe we can find someplace small like our lunch choice. The food was amazing." She swung their joined hands between them as they walked.

Hunter's chest ached. He wanted more of this. When she looked up, he smiled. "It was. So we're hunting for a hole in the wall for dinner."

Her fingers tightened on his. "Unless we see something else that looks good first." She laughed.

Not only more, but the rest of his life, this was what he wanted–Kat, her hand in his, no worries.

After a twenty minute walk, they reached a stretch of restaurants and stopped to study menus in the windows. She wrinkled her nose when they'd seen the last one, so they kept going, past the little cluster of restaurants and into a small patch of shops and offices. They meandered with no urgency, chatting, pausing to peer in store windows, and he kept a small part of his attention on the darkening sky as the towering clouds rolled closer.

"We could just find something to take back to our room," she said, turning toward him from the furniture display at an antique shop on the corner where he stood at the window of the restaurant two doors away, half-studying the menu.

He opened his mouth, and then his blood ran cold. He'd always thought that was a cliché, something people said for effect, but when he saw the big dark man striding purposefully toward them from the next block, he felt it happen. "Shit."

She sobered in a flash and turned to see

what he was looking at. "Oh, hell."

Hunter jogged toward her, catching her hand, and they started to run, away from the Harvester, who had to pause when the traffic started moving, blocking his crossing. They wove around others on the sidewalk, and he resisted the urge to glance back. When they got to the next corner, they had to stop for traffic, and his heartbeat quickened. Forget crossing. "This way." They rounded the corner, and when they reached the next one, he stopped, raising his free hand to hail a cab–before he looked and discovered the Harvester was only a few yards back. The other man was on his phone. He must be calling for back-up. *Fuck.* "Come on." He dragged Kat off the curb and into the slowing traffic to cross the street.

She kept pace with him, giving his fingers a squeeze. "We're still good."

Evidently the guy behind them didn't care who he ran into, as there was a chorus of protests in his wake, some indignant, some curses.

Hunter couldn't believe he'd been so stupid. In a city this size, the Harvesters would want to cover as much ground as possible, so there were probably more of them even if they didn't know their quarry was here. He ducked across another street, Kat's pace steady beside him, but he saw several cabs approaching and flagged down the first empty one. He gave Kat a push inside and slid in after her.

The cabbie reset his meter. "Where to,

folks?" He eased the car into motion.

Hunter couldn't think of a single place.

Kat leaned forward and murmured something to the older man, who whipped the cab into the left turn lane, cutting off a bus.

Hunter frowned. She leaned closer, her hand on his knee, breath warm on his jaw.

"Empire State Building," she whispered. "We can catch a train to the hotel."

He took a slow breath, then another. He'd screwed up. Big time. He clenched his hands on his knees and squeezed his eyes shut.

"We're fine," she breathed, putting her other hand against his face and pressing closer along his side. "We're fine."

But what if they weren't? He opened his eyes and met her gaze. "I'm so sorry," he said, low. He noticed that lights were coming on in the buildings they passed, and the storm clouds made it seem more like night than early evening.

She kissed him, lightly, but held his gaze. No fear in her grey eyes, just trust.

The car jerked to a stop, and the driver muttered something.

Hunter turned his head to see traffic stopped ahead of them for several blocks. "We'd better get out." He saw Kat nod, and he fished some money from his pocket for the cabbie.

They left the cab in the middle of the clogged street, hand in hand, and jogged to the corner, then headed for the subway sign on the next block. Thunder rumbled overhead.

Except a cab screeched to a halt behind them, and Hunter's heart jumped into his throat when he saw the big man shove open the back door.

"Son of a bitch," he muttered through clenched teeth, yanking on her hand as he broke into a dead run. He wasn't sure where they were, or where they were going. He only knew he had to get her to safety. But there was no crush of pedestrians to blend into here, just darkened offices and a few storefronts mixed with big block buildings. Dammit.

Ahead of them, another cab stopped, and two men got out, focused on him and Kat.

He veered around the corner when they reached it. Maybe if they headed back in the other direction, he could find a way to lose them. Where there were more people.

Halfway to the next corner, he felt a jerk on his hand, heard a muffled sound, and then she was gone. He whirled in time to see the big man drag her into an alleyway.

"Mother fucker!" He started back toward the alley, and the other two rushed around the corner at him.

He would die before he let them kill Katharine.

The thought provided a burst of pure adrenaline with the fear and fury already coursing through him, and he charged at the bigger man, fists clenched. "Not today, asshole," he growled, ramming both fists into the other man's throat, taking him by surprise. The big guy went down, hands clutching at his neck. Fat raindrops began to spatter onto the sidewalk.

"Your turn." He grabbed the other one's shoulder and bashed him against the bricks of the nearest building. Not getting her. *No fucking way.*

# CHAPTER FIFTEEN

Katharine struggled to free her right hand, but the big guy tightened his grip on her wrist behind her back, sending pain shooting up her arm. Her head throbbed from the Harvester back-handing her so hard she hit the rough block of one of the tall buildings flanking the entry after he'd grabbed her, making her see stars. The alley was dark, the tall buildings at the nearest opening and whatever lay further ahead mostly blocking the dusky light from outside. She blinked to try to adjust to the dimmer light.

If he got too far in here, he'd kill her, and the others would get Hunter. She jerked against his grip, ignoring the fiery pain in her arm and shoulder. His fingers pressed harder into her face, keeping her from yelling and obstructing her quick, panicked breathing.

"Where is the amulet?"

She bit his hand, hard enough to taste blood.

He yanked his hand away from her face, muttering something she didn't understand, before he punched her hard in the ribs, startling a cry from her when the pain registered. Then he locked his arm across her throat a second later, preventing her from moving away to avoid another blow and cutting off her air.

*Shit.* Black dots danced at the edges of her vision.

"Where is the amulet, monster?"

Katharine rammed her left elbow back into the man's ribs as hard as she could. He barely grunted, and his arm tightened still more across her throat. In this position, she couldn't reach her dagger. Or breathe. And her right arm was going numb, pinned behind her.

She dug her fingernails into his forearm, a small part of her brain noting the rain falling onto them, but his grip only loosened long enough for her to gasp in a quick breath. Out of ideas, she rammed her head backward into his face.

The satisfying crunch of his nose breaking was immediately followed by his yelp, and he released her, cursing.

She sucked in a deeper breath as she spun, grabbing her dagger with numb fingers and wrapping them tight around the hilt. When he stepped toward her again, blood dripping down his mouth and chin from his now-crooked nose, fury glittering in his eyes, she shoved her blade under his ribs. The force of the movement sent pain shooting up her arm as lightning flashed overhead, illuminating his face for a long moment.

His eyes rounded, and he sputtered, between the blood flowing from his nose and now more from his mouth, and then he fell backward, off of her dagger, thudding to the pavement. A few wet gasps escaped him before he went silent.

Katharine bent forward, trying to catch her breath. Running footsteps behind her had her straightening despite the black dots still swimming in her vision, tightening her grip on her dagger again. But it was Hunter, eyes widening as he skidded to a stop.

"ARE YOU ALL RIGHT?"

"I'll be fine," she managed. "He won't, though." She sucked in a slower breath, trying to calm her erratic pulse.

He eased closer, sliding his hands over her, careful.

"Nothing broken," she rasped. "Just bruised."

He took her dagger and wiped it clean on the dead man's shirt, then tucked it back into her sheath. "The other two are unconscious for the moment," he said finally, "so we need to move." He undid her ponytail.

"We're just leaving him here? What are you doing?"

"My only concern is you. Let his cousins deal with him. And you have blood on the back of your shirt, your hair will cover most of it, and the rain will help, too." He put his arm around her waist and herded her toward the other end of the alleyway, out into the full downpour of rain.

In the rainy dusk, no one would notice the bruises she knew she sported now. She let

Hunter steer her into the growing dinner time crush of people ahead on the sidewalk and kept her head down. Eventually, she supposed she'd feel bad about killing the Harvester. But right now, she was breathing through a sore throat, her head hurt, her jaw hurt, and her ribs ached where he'd punched her. Killing him didn't bother her at all right now.

"We'll get supper delivered to our room," he said as they hurried to the bus stop halfway up the next block. "We're done for today."

Katharine didn't care about food. Right now, all she felt was relief–she was alive, and so was Hunter. That was the only thing that mattered.

ELEK'S GUT TIGHTENED AND TWISTED, and Ari's face paled. "When?" Elek bit out.

"Ten minutes ago. We need more eyes here. Yannis's head injury needs medical attention." His cousin's voice had a rasp to it, testament to the throat hit he'd taken.

Ari's head bobbed.

"We'll take care of it."

"There's something else," Ajax said slowly. Reluctantly, Elek thought.

His heart sank. How much more bad news could Ari handle? "What?"

"I think someone's gone rogue, or they're not where they should be. I sensed another of us in the area when we were chasing them. But I lost track of him."

Elek's pulse skipped.

Ari frowned. "How close in the vicinity?"

"Very. Within a block, probably less. In the aftermath, I didn't sense him anymore."

Elek scowled, too, his mind working madly. A traitor? Again? Or Kallan, helping the monster? But he wouldn't have hidden, he'd have joined in the fight, surely. "Thank you for telling us, Ajax. Your additional help will be in touch shortly." He disconnected the call, then met his great-uncle's troubled gaze. *One thing at a time.* "I'll have Argos run a check to see who is not where they should be. Who do you want to send into New York to Ajax?"

His great-uncle sat back in his chair, swallowing several times before he cleared his throat. "I need a few minutes to think about it."

He hesitated, but when Ari waved one hand at him, he rose and left the room.

Another cousin dead at the hands of these monsters.

And Ari appeared unwell.

He stopped in the doorway of his office. The older man had been growing weaker for months. How many more set-backs could he endure in their quest to kill the monster?

Elek sat in his chair, thinking he could take a few minutes to look at the photos on the family website of their art collection–that always made him feel better, seeing the statuary and paintings of Perseus defeating Medusa–and automatically opened his email. He frowned when he opened the email from

Argos labeled 'You need to see this'.

The body of the email was empty, so he clicked on the attached file, and a photo opened. A man with familiar features.

His phone buzzed, and he answered it. "Yes."

"This is the man with the Medusa." Argos.

He made the image bigger, bigger still.

"He looks like you."

Elek studied the image filling his screen–Argos was right, the man did look like him. Too much to be coincidental.

The shape of the face and eyes. Elek had seen those exact things every day growing up–on his father's face. Now he saw them each time he saw himself in a mirror.

He wondered if his father knew he had another son–and who the woman had been. The man was just slightly older than he, so there hadn't been much time between Hunter Phelps's mother and Elek's own.

That didn't shock Elek. His father still screwed any willing woman.

But another son...one actively working against them... Elek didn't know if Ari could bear knowing that part. His great-uncle looked frailer every day, and Elek wasn't the only one who'd noticed how many of the small white pills Ari was popping.

Since Ari was a much better father-figure than his own father, Elek felt protective of his great-uncle.

He sighed and shoved to his feet. Ari

should know, but it had to be couched carefully.

He wondered if Phelps knew.

Surely the Medusa had realized...

Or Kallan.

His fingers curled tight.

"I don't think we should mention that to Ari right now."

"Yeah, I just got Ajax's text. How did he take it?"

"Not well." He looked at the photo on the screen. "We'll have to tell him eventually. Not tonight."

"Good call. And you can break that bad news. What do you need from me right now?"

"Find out if anyone is in New York who shouldn't be. Ajax said he sensed another of us nearby, and there shouldn't be anyone else there yet." Except for Phelps. He hoped it was only an overeager cousin out of an assigned area, and not this man with Harvester gifts.

"Okay, I'll let you know what I find out."

"Thanks." He disconnected, his gaze drawn back to the computer screen. It was too late to appeal to Phelps with a familial tie. He was too involved with the monster.

His gut knotted.

This was suddenly more complicated.

ARISTOTLE STEWED, STARING OUT THE window for about ten minutes. How had he failed these boys? Why did they continue to fail at their appointed task?

One woman and one man against three of his nephews, and his family had been bested once more.

He scowled down at the garden. Yes, the man had military and law enforcement training, but the monster? She did not. Yet he would bet anything that she was the one who'd killed Lysander. Ajax said it had been a knife wound, and he knew the Medusa's spawn carried blades. Had used them previously.

He returned to his desk and dialed Elek. "Find out who is closest to the city right now, and send three of them to take care of Lysander and to help Ajax. I will call in reinforcements from outside the area."

"Of course, Uncle Ari."

He replaced the receiver. He would have to call Lysander's wife, but he would wait until they retrieved the body. Now, who to call in to help scour the city?

Athena appeared in front of his desk in a flash of light, and he stumbled out of the chair, onto his knees, bowing his head. His heartbeat fluttered out of rhythm. *Not now.* "My Lady."

"How is it you continue to fail me?"

His heart beat too quickly, and perspiration popped out on his forehead, the back of his neck. "I beg forgiveness, my Lady."

"I do not feel forgiving, Aristotle. I am disappointed and angry. These monsters still live, safely protected by the spell of the first, while my chosen Harvesters repeatedly fail to do their duty. I begin to believe my favors are better bestowed elsewhere."

Ari shut his eyes against the rising panic. "Please, my Lady. We will kill the Medusa. I promise You we will."

"You have promised the same more than once in recent years, Aristotle. Your failures continue to blacken my name."

He fell onto his hands at Her feet, bowing his head further. "Please, my Lady. A little more time, I beg You."

"You do much begging today, Aristotle. It is unbecoming for one of your stature."

The thumping of his heart in his chest and ears nearly drowned out Her irritated sigh.

"One last opportunity, Aristotle. If your family fails, the consequences will be dire."

"Thank you, my Lady," he murmured, but he knew She was gone. He remained where he was, forehead nearly touching the floor and sweat running into his shirtfront.

He understood the Goddess's fury. His family had let Her down too many times.

When he felt able, he pushed to a sitting position and fumbled for the pill box in his pocket, slipping a tablet into his mouth. His body may be giving out, but his mind was not. A few moments later, he struggled to his feet and back to his chair, trying to steady his breathing.

He thumped his hand on his desk. There were no acceptable excuses. Aristotle lifted the phone from his desk and pressed a button, listening to the electronic beeps as his call went out. "Timo, I need you to bring your brothers east. Ajax and Yannis have also failed to kill the monster, and Lysander is dead." He didn't wait for a response, but dropped the phone back onto the desk, rubbing his other hand in the center of his chest.

He had no time for heart palpitations. He needed to ensure this was done.

KATHARINE ATE SOME OF THE PASTA HUNTER had ordered, but she was still wound too tight from her brush with the Harvesters. They were too close, and now they knew to watch city cameras and would bring reinforcements.

She paced the room, unable to think about anything else, barely noting the rain lashing the window, the steady rumbles of thunder and quick flashes of lightning outside. What if they'd killed her? What if they'd killed Hunter? Had the man seen them earlier and followed them, or happened on them by chance?

Hunter finally reached out and caught her wrist. "Come here."

She sighed. "I'm sorry. My brain is going a hundred miles an hour."

He studied her for a few seconds. "I can help with that."

She blinked at him. "I don't think that will help," she said after a second.

He smiled a little. "I bet it might." He tugged on her wrist, and she let him reel her in.

"Not in that kind of mind-set right now." Still, she didn't protest when he eased her onto his lap.

"We can work on it," he murmured, leaning in to kiss her throat.

She didn't argue, but her mind continued in another direction.

Until he pushed her skirt up past her knees and pressed his hand between her thighs. Her body reacted immediately, heat and wetness rushing to her core.

"Open for me, honey." He nuzzled a sensitive spot beneath her ear, and she automatically parted her thighs so he could ease his fingers inside her panties.

"Oh!" Her breath rushed out when he stroked over her clit, lower to part her damp flesh.

She felt his smile against her neck, but when his long finger eased inside her, she didn't care if he was thinking 'I told you so'. She didn't even care that he was distracting her with sex. The distraction was working.

He didn't waste time teasing, just went right for all the spots he knew made her hotter, desperate, and then pushed her right off the edge into a hard, fast orgasm. And while she trembled against him, he picked her up, carried her to the bed and undressed her.

She panted, shivering as the cooler air brushed over her sensitive skin, watching him strip. His blue eyes were dark, his intention clear, and when he dropped his jeans, she lifted one hand to him. He took it, pressing her thighs apart with his knees. "Open."

She obeyed his order, parting her legs even more, and he shoved deep inside her with no preliminaries. "Oh, Gods!"

Hunter bent closer, catching her mouth before he began to move.

The next release surprised her, it burst so quickly, and he quickened his pace until he groaned with his own orgasm, collapsing over her.

Katharine wrapped her arms around him, and his hold on her tightened, too. They were alive, thank the Gods, she thought, squeezing her eyes shut. His rough breaths warmed her sweat-damp skin. Thank the Gods. She relaxed a little, and he rolled them onto their sides. "Don't move," she whispered.

"Not goin' anywhere." His rumbled words vibrated on her collarbone, and she smiled.

Eventually, she relaxed her grip on him and eased back. He let her go, and she realized he was nearly asleep. She headed into the bathroom, then paused for a quick drink of water on her way back to the bed. He'd rolled onto his stomach, his face buried in his pillow. She climbed back onto the bed beside him.

Her brain wasn't rushing non-stop anymore. He'd been right about the distraction. She smiled and stretched out on her side, propping her head on one hand and slid the other along Hunter's damp shoulder, her gaze following her fingers over his muscles.

When she reached the back of his neck, he shivered and shifted a little, so his other shoulder lifted, and she squinted at the faint mark there. She pushed onto her elbow to get a better look.

"Where you goin'?" he mumbled into the pillow.

"Nowhere." Her heartbeat quickened, and she sat up to lean nearer. A birthmark, faint, but still visible. She traced her fingers over it. Shaped like a scythe. Her pulse skipped. "Hunter, do you know anything about your birth mother? Or father?"

He rolled onto his back, squinting at her. "What?"

She swallowed. "You have a birthmark."

A frown line appeared between his brows. "I know. It used to be darker when I was a kid. I used to pretend it was a tattoo."

"It's shaped like a scythe."

He stared at her for a few moments before her meaning penetrated his sleepy brain. Then his eyes widened, and he sat up in a rush, shoving out of bed to head for the bathroom.

Katharine scrambled over the rumpled bed to follow.

He stood in front of the large mirror over the sink, twisted to examine the mark on the back of his shoulder. He touched it with one fingertip, scowling. "I don't know anything about them," he said, staring into the mirror. "My parents weren't sure, but thought she'd been unmarried. They tried to find out more when I was ten, thinking I'd ask questions some day, and they wanted to have answers.

But they couldn't find anything–the courthouse records room had been damaged when a pipe burst years before. Some files were too wet to save, and of course my birth records were in that section." He met her gaze, his troubled. "You don't actually think–"

She stretched to brush a kiss on his mouth, holding his gaze. "I think we have to see what Kallan knows." She framed his face with her hands. "It doesn't change anything."

"Easy for you to say," he muttered, gathering her close and resting his chin on the top of her head.

She didn't argue. For her, it really didn't change anything. Even if his birth father was a Harvester, Hunter was *not*.

For him, it would be huge.

After a few minutes, he leaned away. "I know it's late, but..."

"We should call him," she agreed, letting him turn her back to the bedroom.

He rifled through his pants for his phone, and thumbed a few buttons once he had it.

Katharine glanced at the clock–eleven-forty. She winced. Still, she thought this might qualify as an emergency.

"Kallan, it's Hunter. I'm sorry to call so late, but something's come up." He dropped onto the side of the bed, his free hand rubbing his nape.

She climbed onto the bed behind him, gently moving his hand aside so she could massage the tight muscles there–muscles that had been lax five minutes ago.

"We're both fine, had a Harvester run-in earlier. But..." He glanced at her over his shoulder. "There's an old birthmark on the back of my shoulder, and Katharine thinks it looks like a...a scythe."

"Way to skip over the good parts," she breathed, winking at him, gratified to see a hint of dark color stain his cheeks.

"A picture?"

She stopped rubbing his shoulders long enough to find her own phone, snap a picture of the mark and send it to Kallan. Then she pressed herself against Hunter's back and wrapped her arms around him, tight.

"It does?" His voice quivered with strain and his spine stiffened. "Really? On the inside of your ankle?"

Katharine shut her eyes and squeezed him tighter, her cheek to the back of his shoulder, just about where the birthmark was, she realized.

His free hand landed on both of hers in the center of his chest. "Yeah, thanks, I guess...okay. I'll talk to you tomorrow. We can tell you about the Harvesters then." He thumbed the phone off.

She pressed a kiss to the mark. "It's okay.."

"Not really." He shoved forward, and she released him, watching as he rose and turned to face her, his jaw clenched.

Kat climbed off the bed and moved to stand in front of him, setting her hands on his face.

"It is. Finding out where your birth father came from doesn't automatically make you as awful as the worst of them."

He rested his forehead on hers and shut his eyes. "What if it did?"

She smiled and kissed him. "It doesn't. And it's too late now. You've already said you love me."

He opened his eyes, a slow smile curving his mouth. "True, I did." He kissed her lightly. "How are you feeling?"

She considered that for a moment. "Pretty good right now. You were right."

His smile widened. "I know."

"Maybe we should do it again. I bet it would help you, too." She winked at him.

He chuckled. "It might. Maybe you should finish your supper first. You're going to need some more energy for this." He eased back.

She sighed. "Okay, but it's probably cold by now."

"There's a small microwave next to the coffee maker." He released her and headed for the small alcove outside the bathroom. "Bring your dish here."

She obeyed, ignoring the way her stomach growled in anticipation. He was right. She smiled as she handed the dish to him. That was okay. At the moment, it was all okay.

They were alive.


HUNTER WOKE WHEN HE FELT KAT thrashing beside him. Small, panicked sounds escaped her, and she swung one arm out. He caught it before she nailed him. "Honey, wake up," he said quietly. She twisted in his grasp, gasping for breath. "Katharine." He gave her a gentle shake, and she jerked upright, suddenly awake. "You're okay."

"Oh my Gods," she wheezed, flopping back to the pillow. "I dreamed I was in the alley."

"I figured."

She rolled toward him, sliding her free hand up to wrap around his neck. "Hold onto me tighter."

He obliged, feeling her shudder, her breath too fast along his shoulder.

She tightened her grip on him. "I've never killed anyone before. I should feel bad, shouldn't I?"

He shut his eyes. "Probably still in shock," he murmured into her hair.

"He was going to kill me."

"I know. You had no choice." He rubbed one hand along her spine. At least she wasn't shaking so hard anymore.

Seeing the big man drag her into the alley made him fight harder against the other two, dirty. The throat hit to the first guy was pure desperation to even the odds. The second man had dropped like a rock when Hunter kicked him in the balls, and then Hunter bashed his head on the sidewalk until he stopped struggling, but not enough to kill him.

Hunting with back-up made sense, since they knew she wasn't alone, and especially in a city this size. Kallan had told him they'd done it before, with Andrea, but not with Philomena, mostly because they hadn't had the opportunity. Maybe their next move would be pack hunting, which they'd also attempted with Andrea. His stomach churned at that thought.

It meant they were growing desperate, and desperate people were unpredictable. Gods help them if that were the case, because he wasn't entirely certain he was up to the task of protecting her against a small army of Harvesters.

Good thing he had some back-up of his own, even if they were at a distance and he hadn't actually met either of them in person yet.

Kat shifted nearer. "I can hear you thinking," she murmured, sounding sleepy.

He pushed away thoughts of what might be—no sense in that now. "Just thinking how glad I am that you're handy with a dagger."

"Hm." She remained silent for a few seconds. "We'll need to lay low until we can get out of the city."

"Unless we can disguise ourselves." He pondered that.

"I could dye my hair. Cut it."

He stroked her damp hair. "That would be a shame."

He felt her smile against his chest. "It grows, and dye is temporary."

He grunted, frowning in the dark. Short of a mask, there wasn't much he could do to disguise himself, though.

"Maybe we can get you a wig. You could rock long hair. Some glasses, maybe."

He laughed. "That sounds awful."

She tipped her head back. "I bet you'd look hot with long hair. Didn't you ever have rock star aspirations when you were a kid?"

"I don't think so. I always wanted to be a cop like my dad." He relaxed a little. "We'll figure something out."

But no way was he letting any Harvester get their hands on Kat.

Maybe Kallan would have some ideas when they spoke in the morning. He glanced at the clock on the night stand. Only a few hours till daylight. 'In the morning' wasn't far off.

"How about you try to sleep?"

She shook her head.

"Maybe that distraction would work for you again?" He smoothed his hand down her bare back to her ass. Soft skin warmed under his fingers.

"Just hold onto me."

"I can do that." He settled her close, listening to her even breathing in the dark. He needed to work out a better plan to keep her safe.

Her plan was to take the fight to Greece.

He shut his eyes. That sounded like such a bad idea. If there were Harvesters all over the place here, surely there would be more of them there.

How could he protect her that way?

Kat kissed his collarbone. "You need to relax," she whispered.

He took a slow breath and released it just as slowly. "You, too, honey." He kissed the top of her head.

He could worry about what their next step was tomorrow. Right now, he needed to be grateful they *had* tomorrow.

# CHAPTER SIXTEEN

He didn't feel better in the morning, just tired and more worried–was his father a Harvester? Could he keep Katharine safe? How could he talk her out of going to Greece?

She wisely let him pace, and after her shower, sat at the little round table with her laptop to read from one of the journals her cousins had sent.

When his phone buzzed, he grabbed it. "Kallan, hi."

The other man chuckled. "Did you sleep?"

"Not much."

"Understandable. Sounds like you had an interesting day yesterday."

"Not sure that's the word I'd use," he muttered, continuing to circle the room.

"Tell me about the attack first. What happened?"

He told Kallan what had happened, leaving nothing out.

"It sounds like a random catch on their part, but bad luck for you two," the other man said after a few seconds. "Katharine is okay?"

"A little bruised, but otherwise, yes." He glanced over to see her watching him, her reading forgotten.

"Good. You?"

"I'm fine. A few scrapes. Nothing that will attract any attention."

"Good."

Hunter hesitated. "Have you thought about..." He couldn't bring himself to say it.

"Yes. I'm sure it's the birthmark we all have, as the Medusa's descendants all bear the snake birthmark."

He dropped onto the foot of the bed, exhaling roughly.

Kallan cleared his throat. "It means you're my cousin. That isn't a bad thing."

"Except for all of the rest of them."

A low laugh reached his ear. "True, but since I've been disavowed for my traitorous acts, I feel safe in saying you would be, too."

"Do you have any idea who...?" He couldn't even finish the thought.

"No, but I can do some digging. When you were a kid, did you have anything odd happen? Doing something you couldn't explain? Unlocking a door, or sensing someone's presence before you could see them?"

Hunter frowned. "Not that I can remember, no. Wouldn't I know if I had some weird talent like that?"

Kallan grunted. "Not necessarily. Most of us only had a little bit of it as kids, until we were around eight and started training to strengthen the talents."

"Training?"

"A bit like summer camp." Kallan huffed a

short laugh. "But instead of arts and crafts with kids we didn't know, we learned to fight with our cousins, figuring out how to do whatever we did better, to help us hunt for the Medusas. Turned into actual training as we got older. Learning how to utilize our talents in our hunt, how to fight, how to use weapons."

Kat's fingers rubbed his shoulder, and Hunter set his free hand over them. He wasn't sure what to make of this.

"Don't worry about it," the other man said. "Whatever it was, if you didn't learn how to use it, how to control it, it's likely gone now."

Hunter wasn't sure he liked that either. Some sort of supernatural talent might come in handy. Especially since he couldn't carry his gun while they wandered around New York City, and—Gods, he couldn't believe he was thinking this—considering flying to Greece, which meant going into enemy territory unarmed. Yeah, he thought some kind of magical talent would be a real plus right now.

She sat beside him and rested her hand on his leg.

"I'll see if I can find any likely parties," Kallan said. "Have you decided what you're going to do now?"

"No, not yet." He supposed he had to consider that. Now the Harvesters knew they were in the city, more would come. He should get her out ASAP.

"Stay out of sight as much as you can. They have the resources to hack the camera systems, and Ari will put more on the ground."

"We'll have to figure something out. Get out of the city."

"Let us know what you want to do. Ryder and I will help."

"Thanks." He ended the call and looked at Kat. "What?"

She smiled. "Just wanted you to know it's all right."

He sighed. "It isn't, but there's nothing I can do about it. I have no say in who donated to my DNA, right?"

Her fingers squeezed gently. "That's right. Besides, I happen to think your adoptive parents had a much bigger influence on you." Her smile widened. "I'm starving."

Hunter winced. "We'll have to order in."

"I know. Are you hungry?"

"Not especially, but I guess we should have something." He dropped his phone onto the night stand and put his arm around her. "What were you reading?"

"Margaret had quite a social life, even after she became the Medusa. Nothing useful, though." She leaned into him.

"Maybe we'll find something in one of the others. I have one waiting, too."

"Food first." She kissed his jaw and pushed to her feet. "Let's look at the menu."

He watched her go, considering their options. They could hunker down here, or in another hotel, though moving would likely put them in camera range and on the Harvesters' radar. Or they could get out of the city.

Leaving the hotel would put them on camera, even to get to the train station. Flying was out of the question since he'd have to present ID. He wondered if they could get a rental car delivered to the hotel. The Harvesters wouldn't have a way to know about that since they didn't know where he and Kat were.

It was a good possibility. But where would they go? And how could he protect her from his own...family when they got there? Family he hadn't even known he had until now.

His gut twisted. If not for his mother giving him up, he'd be among the men hunting her.

He didn't even want to consider that.

AFTER THEIR LATE BREAKFAST, THEY both dug into the journals they'd received. He felt certain Kat was skimming hers, but he read slower, hoping to find something, some little nugget of information or lore they could use to their advantage.

When his computer chimed an alert, he glanced down to see his email flag. A second later, her computer also chirped. He clicked on the icon and his email program opened, showing new email from Kallan that had an attachment.

He swallowed. The attachment could wait. He turned his attention to the email. Not just Kallan, but Ryder was included, too. He scanned back up to the top of the message.

"Hunter,

"I can't be absolutely certain, but it seems likely your birth father is one of my uncles, Alcander. His talent is sensing magic, then tracing it back to the origin, though he is not the most talented with this skill. Of more interest, though, is another of his sons, a half-brother to you, Elek. This is the cousin who's been training with Aristotle for some time now, and who is expected to take over command of the hunt when Ari dies. I've attached a photo of him from recent surveillance, and I don't know why it didn't occur to me sooner that he resembled you."

A brother. *Fuck.* Hunter took a slow breath. Not just a Harvester father, but a brother who was plotting to kill Kat. It kept getting worse.

"He is a decent strategist and has gained some respect in the family the last few years since he's been working with Ari to organize more specialized training and new methods of hunting. I don't believe he's aware of your connection, nor do I think it would matter to him. If he's as close to Ari as it seems, his bigger loyalty is to the Harvesters and the Goddess, not a newly-discovered half-sibling.

"We know the family changed tactics with Philomena, wanting to take advantage of her family to try to reach her, and since they would have killed me at Andrea's, I don't doubt they will be more than willing to sacrifice you to get to Katharine, no matter what the blood relation is. You will need to be just as careful now, perhaps more so. If they do discover your connection, they won't look kindly on your choice to be with Katharine rather than family.

"Even if I am mistaken about your father, the birthmark is a strong enough indication for me that you are a Tassos by blood, and I'm glad to have you as my cousin.

"Let me know if I can answer any questions, and let us know what help we can provide.

"Kallan and Ryder."

He swallowed. He should look at the picture, if only to see if the resemblance was as strong as Kallan thought. But he was still trying to wrap his mind around the idea of a brother. Half-brother, he corrected himself. He huffed out a quick breath and clicked on the attachment.

*Holy shit.* Hunter stared at the image on his screen.

Not quite a reflection of his own face, but close.

His half-brother, if Kallan and Ryder were right.

This was the man Ari had spent the past few years grooming to take his place, to take over the hunt for the Medusas.

He sat back in the chair. He'd gone all his life without anyone but his parents, and then with no one. He almost wished he still didn't know he had such an enormous group of relatives.

Except for Kat. He wouldn't know about them if he hadn't met Kat, and he wouldn't give her up for anything.

So he could live with knowing he had blood-ties to a group of would-be murderers, but he didn't have to embrace them, or even acknowledge them further, aside from Kallan.

*A brother.* Fuck.

He rose, pacing away from the table. He didn't even know what to do with that.

KATHARINE REREAD KALLAN'S EMAIL, frowning. No way to know for sure, but the birthmark was enough for Kallan to know they were related, and Elek certainly looked like Hunter, who paced, from the door to the bathroom to the table and back, over and over.

She rose and stepped into his path, setting her hands on his forearms to stop him when he would have set her aside. "Sit, Hunter."

"I don't want to sit."

She smiled at the growl in his tone. "Do it anyway. For me."

He glowered at her for a few seconds, then dropped onto the bed, fists on his knees.

She knelt in front of him and covered his fists with her hands. "You know family is a total accident of birth, right? And you don't have to keep it."

"Really? So you can get rid of that curse anytime you want?"

She sighed. "Except for me and mine," she said, feeling his fingers tighten under hers. "Your parents made a different family for you. You're not a Harvester just because one of them was a sperm donor. Your birth mother chose not to let them have you." She leaned closer, shifting so she was between him and whatever he was trying to glare a hole through. "You're not one of them," she said, softer. "Though Kallan isn't a bad relative to have." She touched his face, fingertips grazing his stubbled cheek. "I'm sure your birth mother would be very pleased with the man you are."

His expression shifted from anger to uncertainty in a flash. "Maybe," he allowed after a few seconds.

She smiled and set her other hand on his face, too. "Definitely. And you know I'm kind of partial to the man you are, too," she whispered, holding his gaze.

Hunter yanked her up, over him, as he tumbled back on the bed, his mouth demanding under hers.

Katharine let him take what he needed, his mouth and hands rousing her body to fever pitch in only minutes. It wasn't until after a devastating release and Hunter's own shout of triumph as he collapsed over her that she realized they were both still mostly dressed.

She panted a laugh, tugging at his shirt. "Why aren't you naked?"

"I was in a hurry. You should blame yourself for the distraction." He brushed his fingers along her jaw. "You're still bruised."

"Well, it would be convenient to heal faster like the Harvesters. I see your bruises are nearly gone already, though." She touched his cheekbone. "I guess some things don't go away."

He sighed and rolled them to their sides. "Well, you distracted me, and now you've gone and brought it back."

She leaned in to kiss him again. "Sorry, but it doesn't matter. They aren't your family. The people who raised you are your family. Now Kallan is your family."

"You're my family," he said gruffly.

Her breath caught, eyes stinging.

"You are." He held her gaze for a moment. Then her stomach growled, and he laughed, closing his eyes. "If I didn't know better, I'd think you did that on purpose to distract me."

She shook her head.

"I guess it is past lunchtime. Maybe we can get some of that really good pizza delivered, the one we had the first night."

He was as good at distraction and diversion as she was, she thought, swallowing down the lump in her throat. And she wouldn't protest it right now.

It was a long day, cooped up in their room, reading, getting food delivered, Hunter mused later. Thinking too much. At least he had. It was late when he went into the bathroom to brush his teeth. Time to call it a night.

But his attention caught on the mirror over the sink, and he stared at his reflection for a long time. He'd never known where he came from. It hadn't mattered, not with his parents.

But now...to find out his father was one of the monsters hunting Katharine... That he would be hunting her as well, if his birth mother hadn't given him up for adoption–it made him sick to his stomach.

And angry.

He hoped one of the Harvesters he'd left bloody in the alleyway was his birth father. Except none of them had been old enough.

Kat tapped at the door he'd left ajar, then opened it a bit more. "Are you okay?"

He met her worried gaze in the mirror and swallowed. "Sure," he managed.

"Liar." She shoved the door open and came in, sliding between him and the counter to put her arms around his waist.

He shut his eyes and hugged her tight.

Kat tipped her head back, and he met her gaze. "He doesn't matter," she whispered. "You aren't him."

"But I could be." It came out rough, and he cleared his throat.

Her fingers dug into his back. "But you're not. You're *mine*."

His breath caught, and he felt her flinch slightly–as if her words surprised her, too. Her eyes widened and she glanced away for a second.

He hauled her up and caught her mouth with his. He only meant it to be quick, but she lifted against him, one of her hands sliding to his nape, and before he knew it, they were half-undressed, and he was buried deep inside her.

Kat moaned a protest when he lifted his head, and she wrapped one leg around his waist.

He groaned and jerked his hips closer to hers, a move that made her body clench tighter on him.

She opened her eyes and pressed her fingers harder into the back of his neck. "Where are you going?" she whispered. The husky sound sent a fresh shot of arousal straight to his groin.

He shook his head. "Nowhere."

A faint smile touched the corners of her mouth, and she tightened her hold on him—inside and out, making him groan. "*Good.*" She guided his head down, and he kissed her, gentler this time.

By the time his brain was functional again, they were sprawled over the bed, still partially clothed, limbs tangled, drenched in sweat.

Hunter slid his hand up from her hip to the middle of her spine. "You know who'll really be pissed?"

"Who?"

"Athena."

Kat laughed, then tilted her head back to look at him, her smile fading. "I think you might be right. Two of Hers with Medusas." She stroked her fingers along his jaw, her gaze thoughtful. "We ought to tell Her when we get to Athens."

He shut his eyes. He did *not* want to think about Greece. Going right to a vengeful, grudge-holding Goddess—and then pointing out another failure of Her Harvesters–seemed a sure-fire way to be permanently slapped down. He met her gaze finally. "Haven't you ever heard the saying 'don't poke the bear'?"

Katharine grinned at him. "Sometimes the bear needs prodded." She rested her hand along his face, her smile softening. "There's no other way to end this, Hunter."

He wasn't ready to agree, but he knew he couldn't delay her much longer. Instead of protesting, he gathered her closer and rested his chin on the top of her head.

Not yet. He didn't want to lose her. Not now.

KATHARINE DECIDED THE NEXT DAY she wouldn't press Hunter today about Greece, but tomorrow... Today, she'd read this other journal of Annis's. It predated her becoming the Medusa, so it probably didn't have anything useful, but Margaret's journal was boring her to tears. Not a single mention of Harvesters for a couple of years, just lots of tea and visits with friends and family. It was useless. At least Annis was only three Medusas ago.

They had breakfast early, then settled in with their computers to read, with the usual sharing if they saw anything interesting, but mostly in silence. After a while, she got tired of the chair at the table and took her laptop to the bed, propping pillows behind her so she could keep reading. Hunter used her abandoned seat to prop his feet on.

Smiling, she dropped her gaze back to the screen.

They took a break for lunch, and afterward she returned to her comfy spot on the bed to read more. She frowned. Annis had met a young man. She paged back to check the date. Shortly before she became the Medusa. Well, too bad for her that he wasn't The One. Poor Annis.

Katharine kept reading. Their courtship was quite sweet, with gifts of flowers, very proper visits on her porch in the evenings after dinner, and it went on for quite a while. Annis thought she could fall in love with him.

That sounded promising. And bittersweet, because obviously, it hadn't worked out.

She kept reading, then started in surprise.

*Holy shit!* She leaned closer to her screen and scrolled back up to make sure she'd really read that. She reread the lines. Oh my Gods. Her beau was Iphis Tassos.

She scrolled on. The curse. Oh, no. She set one hand in the middle of her chest, recognizing Annis's shock and pain. She'd felt the shock herself, though not the same pain since she hadn't been dating anyone at the time.

But Iphis had persisted, even when she'd sent him away. How sweet. Especially since he should have been dangerous to her, not trying to woo her.

Katharine swallowed.

"I cannot persuade him to desist," Annis wrote. "And Gods help me, I don't truly want to. He knows what I am, and still he loves me. I could love him, too, if I let myself."

How sad. She took a slow breath before continuing.

"My amulet has changed from gold to silver. I know what it means. Yet what would his brother do should he discover this secret? Certainly he would not be as willing to overlook my curse, not when it is his destiny to hunt me and my family.

"Poor Iphis. I so want to be with him. Yet I have my family to protect. If I fall in love with him, this curse moves on to another cousin or aunt, stealing their hopes and dreams. I feel torn, as if I could keep it and protect them. But what about my hopes? My feelings?"

Katharine's eyes burned. Poor Annis.

A few more pages of writing about her persistent beau, and Annis's handwriting changed for the next entry, shaky, as if she were writing quickly. "The goblet has changed color again! Pink. The cursed thing is pink. I know why. It is because my attachment to Iphis grows each time I see him, each time we speak. And so does my despair."

She swallowed down a lump in her throat and kept scrolling.

"I have sent Iphis away for good," Annis wrote several weeks later. "I cannot bear to know I have selfishly passed this curse to another cousin, and I fear for what his brother

Aristotle would do to him should he learn our secret."

She tried to imagine being in Annis's place, what might have been going on in her mind. She understood not wanting to pass the curse on if she didn't have to, but she empathized with wanting her own dreams to blossom, too. She skimmed the next few days' entries, then weeks', before she found another mention of him.

"My goblet is gold again. I will grieve forever for Iphis Tassos, dead by his own hand."

"Oh my Gods." Katharine exhaled slowly and closed her eyes, trying to focus.

Annis had gotten so far through the color-changing of her tattoo, and she knew what was happening. Why wouldn't she allow it to cycle through to the end, to get rid of her curse? Could she really have been so selfless, to keep it herself and lose any hope for her future?

To protect Iphis? Her eyes popped open. Annis had worried what Ari would do to his brother if she let her heart have free rein.

Somehow, Ari knew anyway. She'd bet her life on it. Maybe Iphis's suicide note? Though, since Annis had lived to a ripe old age, Iphis couldn't have shared her name.

She straightened in her seat, mind spinning.

It meant Ari never found her. He would be equally petrified Athena would learn what Iphis had done and furious at his brother. He probably still was, since he hadn't managed to bag a Medusa.

Katharine smiled. She could share that with the Goddess, too.

Hunter already didn't like her plan to go to Greece. He definitely wouldn't like this, because it increased the chance that, in addition to being super-pissed at Ari, Athena may slap Katharine down permanently for bearing news of betrayal in addition to being the Medusa.

She thought she'd take the chance anyway.

HUNTER GLANCED UP FROM HIS READING as Katharine shifted in her spot on the bed, her gaze intent on her screen. His own reading wasn't as interesting as hers must be, lots of day-to-day tedium, with nothing he could see as useful for their situation.

"You should look at this," she said after a few minutes, bringing her laptop to him.

He frowned when he saw the scanned page in the spidery, faded writing.

"Annis's journals," Kat said. "From about a year before she became the Medusa till about two years after."

"I thought we went through her journals already." He pulled the laptop toward him.

"This one was separate, unlabeled. I don't think she meant for anyone to find this."

He raised one eyebrow. "Find what?"

"Read it." She went back to the bed and sat, pulling her knees to her chest.

Intrigued, he started to read. It took him a little while to decipher the handwriting, and then he was able to read faster.

He smiled when she wrote about her 'young man', then felt a pang of sympathy when she acquired the curse and pushed him away despite his insistence it didn't change his feelings for her. Then...he frowned, going back to reread. The cup had changed colors all the way through to pale pink–until she decided she had to rein in her emotions and send him away for good.

Hunter glanced over at Kat. "I can see why she didn't want anyone to read it–it was painful, and she probably wouldn't want anyone to know what she'd done."

"Keep reading. Just a bit more." She jerked her chin toward the laptop screen. She looked too somber, too upset.

He hunted for where he'd left off. It took him a few moments, but he got a lump in his throat when he read the tear-stained page. And then his heart stopped for a second. *Tassos.* Annis's beau was a Harvester, which meant he knew about the tattoo-goblet and never told his family before his suicide. "Holy shit." He looked at Kat. "Even after she broke his heart, he never told his family."

She shook her head. "That's what it sounds like."

He considered that. "The communication wasn't as easy or fast back then. But if he knew, he should've told them."

She bit her lip. "Maybe not."

"What am I missing?" Clearly, she knew

something else.

"He would have to explain away the betrayal of their family somehow to Ari."

"Who was he to Ari?"

"His brother."

Hunter sat back in his chair. The Aristotle mentioned in the journal entries. "Well, hell." He should've realized with the dates...

"I don't think Athena knows the whole truth. He wouldn't have wanted Her to know. Only knowing Iphis had the opportunity to kill Annis and didn't is bad enough. Knowing he betrayed not just his family, but the Goddess as well would be so much worse for Ari, if She knew. At least in Ari's mind."

And the proverbial light bulb went on. He shifted forward on his seat and set the laptop on the table. "This makes you want to go to the temple even more, doesn't it?"

"Oh, I wanted to go to Greece before this, and you know it." Kat's lips curved a tiny bit. "But I admit, it would be satisfying to make sure She's aware of his betrayal."

"Not so satisfying if She decides to do Her own dirty work," he muttered.

She swung her feet to the floor and pushed herself off the bed, taking the few steps to where he sat before dropping to her knees beside him. "I have to try." She put one hand on his where it rested on his thigh.

He knew he was running out of excuses to put off making the decision. Running out of time. "Can we wait one more day to decide?"

She smiled a little, but didn't answer. He knew she'd already decided, and he just had to wrap his head around it, like it or not.

And he definitely did not like it.

# CHAPTER SEVENTEEN

He remained there, attention settling on the screen after a few moments. "Think of all the time Kallan and Andrea could've saved if they'd known all this." He couldn't imagine Annis making that decision–a future she wanted within reach, and she'd not only given it up, but pushed it away with both hands.

Katharine frowned. "But Annis gave it up, didn't take the chance, and the goblet changed back to its original color." She tipped her head back to look at him. "So if Andi hadn't trusted Kallan, if she hadn't taken the chance, she might still be the Medusa now."

Hunter shifted his gaze from the laptop screen to her face, narrowing his eyes at her.

She touched his cheek. "Just making an observation, not getting ideas."

He searched her face, her eyes to judge the truth of her statement.

She smiled. "I don't think I'm as noble as Annis apparently was." She rose, stretching. "I need a break. My brain is too full right now."

He glanced at the clock on the night stand. Nearly suppertime. "Are you hungry?"

She shook her head. "Not yet." She moved to the window, peering out through the blinds, then turned around. "I wonder what Elek would think about this?"

"What?"

A slow smile curved her mouth. "Annis and Iphis. We should share this little tidbit with your half-brother. I wonder if Ryder and Kallan can get his email address for us."

Hunter laughed. "That's evil." And a good strategy, lobbing something mind-blowing at the enemy.

"I wonder if he'd remain so devoted to Ari if he knew the truth?" She dropped onto his lap, startling him. "His entire belief system might be shaken."

He slid his hand to her waist. "I doubt it."

"I'm going to ask if they can dig up his email anyway." She leaned in to kiss his cheek.

He noted the dark bruise along her jaw. "How does that feel?" He touched it lightly.

"It's fine."

"Throat?"

"That's fine, too." Her gaze slid to his cheek. "Yours is gone. My ribs are a bit sore, but they'll be okay, too, when the bruises fade." She leaned in to kiss him lightly again and rose, taking her laptop and moving to the seat opposite him.

While she sent off her email, he closed the journal he'd been reading. Even if he continued, he didn't believe he'd find anything as helpful as what Kat had just discovered. He opened his browser and did a quick search for area restaurants.

He hadn't meant to ask her to wait till tomorrow for him to decide about Greece. He'd hoped she might leave it alone longer than that. He still didn't think he was ready for the discussion, but it was too late now.

Hunter dragged his attention back to the restaurants he'd found.

"Any Greek on there?" she asked, setting her hands on his shoulders.

He hadn't even noticed she'd moved, he'd been so caught up in his own thoughts. "Greek?" He winced.

"I could eat some good moussaka. Maybe tzatziki, too." She leaned down to look, then laughed when she saw his face. "I'm sorry, Hunter. I didn't think about that. It just struck me that I haven't had any good Greek food lately."

He didn't say she could have real Greek food soon enough. Instead, he maneuvered her into his lap again. "I was thinking about Mexican."

"Mm. Tacos." She grinned. "I can do that, too."

He eased her closer. "I thought you weren't hungry yet," he murmured, nudging her nose with his own.

"I changed my mind." She slid one hand around his neck, her grey gaze softening. "How are you doing?"

He knew what she meant. "Okay, I guess."

"Hm." She brushed a kiss on his mouth. "What kind of tacos are on the menu?"

He let her change the subject to dinner, a little relieved. Tomorrow would be soon enough to broach difficult subjects.

Katharine watched Hunter the next morning, surreptitiously. He paced for a while, then sat, trying to focus on something on his computer screen, before he paced some more.

She didn't press. The conversation wouldn't be easy, and he was doing his best to prep. She liked that. She knew if he thought there might be another way, he'd argue for it. Which meant he had no other ideas, and he'd do this for her.

Her heart squeezed. He was such a good man, no matter who his sperm donor was.

She turned her attention to her own laptop, where she had the browser open to a map of the Acropolis. She could study satellite and street views later, to see what might be trouble spots. Right now, she just wanted to get a good feel for the whole mound.

It'd be crawling with tourists and restoration crews all day, so they'd have to go calling on Athena at night, which would be tricky. It sat above the city, lit up like the sun at night.

She definitely wanted to get on the site during the day first, so there weren't any surprises at night. She wondered if there were Harvesters on-site. Maybe. They could figure that out later. She made the map bigger. Limited entry points to the site would make it more interesting. Two entrance-slash-exits. That required some thought.

Hunter dropped into the chair opposite her with a big sigh.

She looked up, meeting his gaze.

"We have to have a plan."

She swallowed, nodding.

"I don't want to just go there and wing it. Not with your life in the balance. Though who the hell knows what Athena might do once we get there."

Katharine bit back a smile.

His blue gaze lasered in on her, making her urge to smile disappear. "We need to decide first where we are going."

"Where else? The Parthenon."

"Literally into the lion's den." He reached over to catch her hand and squeezed. "Of course." He sighed. "We couldn't go to a smaller, less-visited temple, could we?"

She smiled this time. "Direct is best." She got out of her seat and leaned over the table to kiss him lightly. "Have you ever been to Greece?"

He pulled her onto his lap. "No, I never have."

"Me neither." She wrapped her arm around his neck. "We can't plan this down to the finest detail, you know. There are too many things we won't know."

He frowned.

"I'd like a solid plan, too, but I don't think it's feasible, Hunter." Her smile faded. "We can plan loosely and leave room to wing it when we have to."

"Wing it?" His frown turned into a scowl.

She rubbed the back of his shoulder, but the tense muscles under her fingers only tightened more. "This isn't like a military operation, planned out to the nth degree, with back-up plans worked out the same way. This is going to be us, someplace unfamiliar, where we might run into people trying to stop us from what we're aiming to accomplish." She held her breath. His narrowed eyes and flat mouth told her exactly how he felt about that.

"You're not really selling me on this, Katharine," he growled.

She pushed to her feet again, taking a slow breath. "I'm sorry, I'm trying to be realistic. I'm not psychic. One of my cousins has that talent, though she tends to be a bit late with her insights. I'm trying to see all the places where things could go wrong and work from there."

"We can't go into this blind."

She started back to her seat. "We can't go into it fully prepared either."

"Then we should wait until we're more prepared."

She whirled to face him. "I am not waiting! I want my life back." She realized she was on the verge of shouting and shut her mouth, inhaling deeply before she released the breath. "I'm sorry, I didn't mean to yell." She gathered her sweater from the back of her seat, starting to fold it to distract herself from the irritation that had bubbled up. She was being stupid. He wasn't saying they weren't going.

"I can't protect you like that, just rushing blindly into Athens. Fuck, Athens. There're probably dozens of Harvesters there, since it's Her fucking city." He shoved to his feet and paced away from the table. "I can't watch them kill you. I can't watch Her kill you."

Katharine frowned at Hunter's back. "What the hell does that mean?"

One of his shoulders twitched in what she guessed was supposed to be a shrug. "You wanted not to be trapped with me. I'll call Ryder or Kallan now. You can go when they get here."

It took her a few seconds to decide he meant the growled words. And then hurt and anger boiled up in a tumbled surge. "I didn't want *you* to be trapped with *me*. Stuck with *me*. But that was before. You're not getting rid of me so easily now, you jackass."

"BEFORE WHAT?" THE WORDS WERE SO low she barely heard them.

When they registered, she saw red. She took a step toward him and swung the sweater she still held at the back of his head. It would do less damage than her fist.

He whipped around and caught her wrist, tumbling her to the bed beneath him. She didn't get her other hand up fast enough, and he caught it before she slugged him, shoving it to the mattress beside her head. She glared at him, breathing hard and blinking against sudden tears.

"Tell me," he growled.

She clamped her mouth shut.

He moved her hands over her head so he could hold both wrists in one hand, then caught her chin with his free hand, tipping her face up a little. "Tell me," he whispered.

Even if she'd wanted to answer him, the lump in her throat prevented any words from escaping, so she kept glaring at him through the tears burning in her eyes.

Holding her gaze, Hunter brushed his lips over hers, then again. When she tried to tug her hands free, his fingers tightened and he dipped in to kiss her more deeply.

Katharine felt a tear escape, scalding its way back her temple to her hair, and she squeezed her eyes shut.

"Tell me, Katharine," he rasped against her mouth, teeth grazing her lower lip so she shuddered under him.

"If you call either of them, I'll never forgive you," she managed.

His breathing hitched, and he nibbled at one corner of her mouth. "Tell me."

She turned to catch his mouth, but he lifted his head just out of reach. His eyes were shadowed and wary when she opened hers. Wounded. She swallowed around the lump. Her fault.

His thumb slid from her chin to her lower lip, brushing from one corner of her mouth to the center.

"I'm falling in love with you," she choked out.

His mouth came down again, and several more tears escaped.

She opened to him, tears scalding her face as they fell. She heard herself sob into the kiss, and Hunter released her wrists to wrap his arms around her, burying his face in her throat.

"Don't cry, Kat." He pressed open-mouthed kisses across her throat where she still bore the bruise from the attack in the alleyway. "Don't cry."

She slid her arms around him, gulping in air to try to stop the tears that kept welling up.

He lifted his head, kissing her gently. "Shh." He eased one hand from beneath her to wipe his fingers over her wet cheek.

She squeezed her eyes shut and took a big, uneven breath. It didn't help.

He rolled onto his side, keeping her tucked close, and she pressed her face into his chest. "You can't take that back now, you know," he said lightly after a few moments.

She laughed, as she was sure he meant for her to do, and tried once more to take a deep breath. Better. She repeated it several times, feeling the lump in her throat dissipate.

"Better?" He stroked her back.

"A little," she whispered.

"I guess this means I have to go to Athens."

She lifted her head to meet his somber blue gaze.

"Where you go, I go,." he rasped.

Her eyes burned again. She lifted one hand to stroke his cheek. "I'm sorry I hit you with my sweater."

A ghost of a smile touched his mouth. "I guess we need to plan as much as we can."

She nodded.

He held her gaze. "Maybe later." He tightened his arm around her.

She put her head back on his chest and shut her eyes. "Okay." She couldn't believe she'd blurted that out. She hadn't meant to, but she knew it was true. Otherwise, the amulet would still be gold instead of pink.

She just didn't want to pass this curse off to another cousin. She wanted to be the one to make it go away forever. If it meant going right to the lion's den, so be it. If it meant the end of her, well, that would suck, especially now. But if she could save the rest of her family from centuries more of this hell, she had to try.

But she had Hunter now. Which made her think this had a chance of working. Maybe a small chance, but better than nothing. Better than her family suffering for many more millennia.

She smiled, wiping her face with one hand.

This was going to work, if it killed her. She really hoped that wasn't the outcome.

HUNTER'S EYEBROWS ROSE. "YOU'RE REALLY going to email Elek?" He didn't care if she emailed his half-brother. Right now, he'd happily allow her to do *almost* anything. His heart beat faster thinking about her words earlier. He hadn't been sure she'd admit to her emotions, even seeing the color change of her amulet.

She nodded. "I want him to know what kind of man he worships."

He shook his head. "How do you think you'll persuade him you're telling the truth?"

"I'll include a screenshot of Annis's journal page."

He shut his eyes for a second. "Then what?"

She glanced up from her keyboard. "You mean after I send it?"

He waited.

"Well, if he doesn't respond, I'll decide then." A sheepish smile curved her mouth. "I'm just feeling vengeful, and if I can hurt Ari, it might be satisfying."

He held her gaze for a moment, then turned his attention back to his own screen, where a map of the Acropolis stared back at him. He couldn't believe he was actually going to do this, to go to Athens to confront a Goddess.

A fucking Goddess.

If someone had told him this a month ago, he would've thought they were insane. Now, if he told this to anyone, they'd think *he* was insane.

"Done." She looked remarkably chipper when he glanced over. Much happier now that she'd admitted to her emotions.

Almost as happy about that as he was. "Don't hold your breath."

She laughed. "I won't. What are you working on?"

He turned his laptop around so she could see the screen.

"Ah." She wisely shut her mouth.

"Did you know there are only two ways in and out?" He pulled the computer around to face him once more.

"Yes."

He studied her somber expression for a moment. "That makes this a bigger challenge."

She didn't argue.

He sighed. "So what is our loose plan?"

She closed her laptop and rested her forearms on it. "We'll need to check it out in person, in the daytime, but for what we need to do, we'll have to get in at night."

Fuck. He dropped his gaze to the screen again. "That hilltop is lit up like Christmas at night."

"I know."

"How do you propose to get around that?"

"There might be a power outage."

He narrowed his eyes at her. "What?"

She slanted a glance at him, a hint of a smile touching her lips. "I might be able to arrange for the temple to have a power problem."

He wasn't sure he wanted to know, but... "How?" He hoped he didn't regret asking.

"Oh, raise some energy and direct it to their

generators." The smile grew a bit larger.

Her casual tone set off alarm bells all through his system. "Tell me you're not talking about directing lightning."

"No, that's not how it works. Though it might look like a lightning strike when the energy hits." Her smile was a full-on grin now.

*Holy hell.* He shut his eyes. "You know you're a scary woman, right?"

She laughed.

"But I still love you." Gods, he loved her. Her outrageous courage, her determination. That wicked smile.

Her smile softened. "Good," she whispered, tipping her head to one side.

"I need a break from thinking about this. Are you hungry yet?" A distraction like supper might make the nagging throb in his head ease for a while.

"If we order now, I might be by the time food arrives. What are you hungry for?"

"Besides you?" He watched the smile flash over her face again. "Thai."

"Sounds good." She pushed to her feet, stretching, then came around the table to put her hand on his shoulder. "You can have me for dessert." She winked, then moved away.

Hunter shut his eyes. He hoped he didn't regret agreeing to go to Greece.

ELEK FROWNED AT THE EMAIL AT THE top of his in-box. "We Know About Iphis." What did that mean? And who'd sent it? The email address was a series of numbers and letters, no name.

He debated with himself for a few seconds, then clicked it open.

"We know that Iphis had a relationship with Annis Galani before and after she became the Medusa. The attachment is the proof. We know his suicide was because she spurned him after she was cursed."

He sat back for a moment, confusion mingling with anger. Iphis had died in an accident, and Ari had been grief-stricken over the loss of his brother. Everyone in the family knew it. Someone was just trying to get a reaction from him. And he certainly wouldn't download an attachment from a stranger.

He reached for the delete button, but the next line snagged his attention. "Ari knows the truth and has lied to everyone about it, including the Goddess."

His heart stopped beating for a long moment. 'Ari knows.'

He dropped his hand to the desk.

The email was unsigned.

If he sent it to Argos, his cousin could trace it. But he didn't want Argos to see this. No one should see this.

It couldn't be true. Ari would never hide something like that, never lie about his beloved brother's tragic death.

Elek's unease didn't dissipate.

Even if it were lies, someone still knew about them. About the Medusas. And they'd been able to track down his private email. Someone with resources of their own. Like his cousin Kallan and the last Medusa's man, Ryder Ware.

Which meant it was likely untrue.

But why would they concoct a story like this and send it to him?

He considered taking it to Ari–for about a second.

Even if a tiny part of it was true, Ari must have an excellent reason for keeping it secret.

He hesitated over the delete button, then simply closed the message. He could ask Ari about Iphis, but not now when there were more pressing matters.

Like finding the Medusa, killing her and taking the amulet, wherever she had it hidden.

SLEEPING ON IT DIDN'T LESSEN HIS UNEASE about their flimsy plan. Nor did a few more hours staring at computer screens, poring over maps and satellite images and photos and videos of the Acropolis. Even getting there would be no picnic. Hunter frowned out the window. They'd be lucky to get out of the city without alerting every Harvester for miles, and by now, there must be more than three of them. In their shoes, he would've called in reinforcements after the alleyway attack failure, lots of them.

"One thing at a time," Kat said lightly.

He turned to look at her. "What one thing first?" He rested one forearm on the edge of the table.

"You can't go with your own ID. You need a passport that's not connected to you."

He winced. He'd almost forgotten. "I don't know any forgers."

"Ryder will get you one." She smiled. "We need his help, not only identification for you, but travel arrangements, and probably that rental car we talked about the other day."

He let out a rough breath and reached for his phone.

The other man answered after one ring. "Hi, Hunter. You guys okay?"

"Yeah, we're fine, thanks." Hunter hesitated.

Ryder cleared his throat.

"Sorry, I'm trying to figure out how to say this without sounding like a lunatic. We need to go to Greece," he said in a rush, figuring it was best just to get it out.

Silence.

He shut his eyes, then felt Kat's warm fingers rub his nape.

"Take the fight directly to Athena, huh?" Ryder said at last.

"Yeah."

"Are you sure–"

"It's Kat's call."

She pressed a kiss on the top of his head.

Something in his tone must have given away his resignation and fear, because Ryder blew out a hard breath. "Okay, then. I can make it happen, but I'll need a couple of days to get you a clean ID, tickets, et cetera. When do you want to go?"

"As soon as possible, probably from New York or Philly. A night flight?" He was thinking out loud now. "And a rental car delivered to the hotel parking garage when it's time to go, if we can, to avoid getting ourselves on camera where they can see us."

"Okay." Ryder paused. "Do you need help in the meantime?"

"No, we're good." As good as it was possible to be with a vengeful Goddess and Her army of would-be killers hot on their heels. Yeah, maybe 'good' wasn't the word. "Staying out of sight and trying to come up with a plan that doesn't get us killed as soon as we land in Athens."

"Ah." The other man hummed for a second. "Well, let me know if I can do anything to help, but in the meantime, send me a photo, and I'll get the ball rolling on the ID, so we can get the rest of the arrangements made."

"Thanks, Ryder." He ended the call and leaned back in his chair.

Her hands shifted to his shoulders, rubbing at the tight muscles there. "It'll be fine."

He tipped his head to look up at her. "You sound pretty confident."

Her mouth curved. "I am. You and me, we can do this. Make a Goddess change Her mind after thousands of years. I mean, think how bored She must be after all this time."

He shook his head, doubt and fear twining

in his gut.

"She has to, Hunter." She leaned down to kiss his cheek. "There's no other alternative."

That he could agree with. They had to make Athena see reason. The only other option wasn't an option.

# CHAPTER EIGHTEEN

**E**lek looked almost frightened.

Aristotle blew out a hard breath. "I am not surprised your father has spawned other offspring, only that it took this long for any to surface."

And concerned that the one who had was working against them. He wondered if this man had any idea of the gravity and honor of his heritage. If he understood the sacred duty of his father's family, a destiny they must fulfill. He eased to his feet and walked from the desk to the window. He also wondered if his nephew had fathered and abandoned the child deliberately or if he was as unaware of this son as the rest of the family. Knowing Alcander, probably the latter.

He braced himself on the window frame and stared into the garden. It was shameful enough what his brother had done. Then Kallan's terrible betrayal. And now to learn *this*?

For the good of his family, the Goddess must never learn about this untrained Harvester.

He rubbed one hand over the twinge of pain in the middle of his chest. He couldn't share his own burden with Elek–Iphis's secret must die with Aristotle.

"Uncle?"

He straightened. "There is nothing you or I can do with this information, I think." He pivoted to face the younger man. "He is lost to us. Put it from your mind. We have much work to do. Argos tells me the monster has not been seen on camera in the city since Lysander's death, nor has he been able to track them to any location prior. None of the team working with Ajax has seen her or the man anywhere. We should expand our ground search. Why don't you work up a list of names to add to our group in and around New York and we can talk about it after lunch."

Elek nodded and rose, striding from the room.

Aristotle closed his eyes and bowed his head. One more failure, though this one could not be laid at his feet. How was he to know his nephew had another son out in the world when his nephew didn't even know?

Their time was running short, he felt it. *His time*. His family couldn't fail yet again.

ELEK DROPPED INTO HIS CHAIR, FROWNING. Aristotle had handled that much better than he'd expected. Maybe better than he himself had handled finding out about his half-brother.

He shook his head. He had more important things to worry about than a man helping the monster, a man who happened to share his DNA.

He turned his mind to the list Ari had requested. To expand the search, it should be a sizable group. He jotted down a few names, then a few more before coming up empty. His brain wouldn't cooperate.

To give himself time to settle, he turned to the computer and clicked open his email.

The same subject line sat at the top of his email queue, "We Know About Iphis".

Elek stared at the screen. Perhaps the email program had malfunctioned and moved the original back to new mail.

Except this had today's date on it.

He checked his old messages anyway. The first one was still there.

He sat back in his chair, uncertain. He didn't have to read it. More lies.

He opened it anyway.

Everything the first email had said, word for word, plus the attachment again, with a small addition.

"We are prepared to share this information."

With whom? Elek's pulse quickened. Athena? Surely She would know it was false.

He hesitated, then clicked on the attachment. It looked like a scan or photo of an old journal. He made it bigger so he could read it.

Spidery, feminine writing, like a pen dipped into an inkwell, dated forty years ago. He frowned. Right around the time... He cut that off and turned his attention back to the page. His gaze fell on Iphis's name, and he scanned back up the page.

She wrote about sending Iphis away, and then her grief over his death by his own hand.

Elek sat back in his chair, mind spinning. It couldn't be true.

But it would require a lot of effort to concoct a story like this, for what? To make him doubt his family? That would be foolish. Of course he didn't doubt his family.

There was the tiniest chance it could be true. Or even partially true. If so, what could he do about it now? Nothing, except upsetting his great-uncle.

Only they claimed Ari knew about it already.

He stared at the page, tear-stained from the look of it.

But she was long dead, too, this former Medusa, Annis Galani. What good would come of asking about this now?

His gaze slid to the empty doorway. Ari was so frail and so stressed right now. He'd have to seriously consider broaching the subject of Iphis with his great-uncle, but not today. Another day. Maybe after they found and killed this Medusa.

Until then...

He hit reply. "Your information is false." He hit send and closed the email program, a little surprised to note his pulse was racing. He took a measured breath and released it, concentrating on regaining his calm. After a moment, he pushed to his feet. He still needed to deal with funeral arrangements for Lysander. And to send more cousins to New York.

Perhaps he could have them remove Kallan from the world as well. But that would be for later, unless his cousin showed up in the monster's vicinity.

She was the priority right now.

K at and H unter spent most of the next day studying more maps and photos, trying to work out a loose plan.

"You'll have to leave your gun behind," she said. "We can send it to Ryder for safekeeping, but we need special packaging for that."

"We can get it without leaving our room." He added it to his list. Hunter didn't like the idea of sending his lone weapon away, but he couldn't take it on a plane into another country. But being completely unarmed? That struck him as foolish when the Harvesters might be anywhere, but it was the only option he had, and sending the gun to Ryder would ensure he got it when he returned home. If he... No, he thought, *when*. When *they* returned home.

"So with an overnight flight, we'll be there early. Hopefully we can find a hotel near the Acropolis, some place that will have good security, close enough to save ourselves time and energy. Especially for the night."

In the dark. He considered her plan to knock out the power to the complex. He wasn't sure how she could manage it. Then again, he'd never imagined curses carried down through millennia either, so if she said she could cut the electricity, he believed her.

"We'll have to check a bag, so I can have my dagger when we get there."

He glanced at her dagger, where it rested on the night stand. That definitely couldn't go in a carry-on–in spite of its sharp, sturdy blade, the dagger was pretty, feminine, as was the sheath. If security inspected their checked bag, they might simply assume it was a gift, not an actual weapon, and ignore it. "So we also need one suitcase too big to carry on the plane." He scribbled it on the list, too.

She smiled when he looked at her.

"What?"

"We'll be fine."

He wanted to believe that. He was trying to.

"I can believe for both of us," she said softly, reaching over to touch his wrist.

"I'm working on it." He flipped his hand over to catch hers.

"I know." Her smile widened. "It's a lot, especially when it's all fairly new."

He thought about that while they figured out a way to ship his gun to Ryder, and ordered a bigger suitcase to check. It *was* still fairly new. He'd known her a matter of weeks, and he was preparing to fly to Greece to take on a Goddess.

Because Kat was his.

He set his pen down. She was his, and he

was keeping her, which meant they'd go confront Athena in her temple, and they would win, period. There were no other options.

When he met her gaze again, he smiled back, squeezing her fingers in his, and something shifted in her eyes, warmed.

*His.*

WHILE HUNTER ORDERED HIS PACKING materials and a larger suitcase for their flight, she considered their options once more. She could take the easy way out–let the curse move on to another cousin and have her happy-ever-after with Hunter.

But she thought she didn't have to let another cousin suffer, and countless more after that. Knowing Annis had chosen to retain the curse was only a small part. Kat wanted her happy ending, but enough was enough. Millennia of women in her family, endless generations suffering this way was an over-the-top punishment for a girl bragging about her hair.

She knew going directly to Athena might be the end of her. But she wanted it done, and since Athena had been so angry at Ari, the time seemed right.

Not just right, but maybe the final chance to end this.

And if the Goddess didn't strike her down when she stepped into the temple, chances were fair Katharine would get her happy-ever-after.

She wanted that.

She picked up her pen. "We'll still have to take carry-ons. It would look weird not to, in case the checked bag gets lost. We can pack the laptops, some clothing. We'll have to skip toiletries in the carry-ons, though. My things are all too big for that, and so are yours, I think." She glanced over at him and blushed under his dark gaze. "What?"

"Just thinking about traveling with you. Really traveling."

"We're really traveling already, aren't we?"

He shrugged. "Flying to another country is real travel. Driving an hour, or a short train ride...those don't seem like real travel to me."

She laughed. "If you say so. For me, after staying close to home for years, this is travel." She dropped her pen and rose, stretching. Being cooped up in their room wasn't bad, but she needed to move a little. She patted Hunter's shoulder as she paced to the bathroom and back for several minutes. A couple days and they'd be on their way.

And just in time, she thought. Pretty soon, she'd have to hole up for three days, and she didn't want their trip delayed.

She wanted this confrontation over with.

"Kat."

She glanced back over her shoulder at the urgency in his tone.

"The goblet's changed again."

Her eyes widened. She knew from her cousins what the next color change was, or rather, wasn't. It would be colorless, just her skin tone within the outline of the cup. She rushed into the bathroom and twisted around to look in the mirror, pulling her tank top strap aside.

Katharine rubbed her fingers over the edge of the colorless goblet. "You need to go away from my family," she murmured, her gaze on the snake coiled around its stem. "For good."

She couldn't help thinking of the journal entry Annis had made all those years ago.

She turned away from the reflection of her tattoo. "Not for much longer," she muttered, yanking her shirt back into place. "Not if I have anything to say about it."

Hunter raised one eyebrow when she marched out of the bathroom. "Are you all right?" He closed his laptop.

"I'll be fine once we get there and do this." She reached up to undo her ponytail, then dropped the stretchy holder onto the dresser.

He caught her wrist. "We don't have to go. We can wait, make a better plan–"

"If we wait too much longer, I'll be incapacitated for three solid days," she said, turning her arm so she could grasp his. "I need to do this now, Hunter," she added more quietly. "I don't want to wait another week. In that time, the Harvesters might've found us." She took a slow breath. "It has to be now."

He nodded, then towed her in. She let him, sliding her free hand around his neck.

"It's okay, you know. I'm okay."

He looked up at her whisper and smiled. "Glad to hear it."

She was. She just needed to finish this.

THREE DAYS. IT TOOK THREE DAYS FOR Ryder to get the identification Hunter needed and make travel arrangements. The wait was excruciating, especially since they could only formulate a loose, vague 'plan' about what they'd do once they arrived. But they prepped the things they could–packing their new suitcase to check at the airport to be sure Katharine's dagger made the trip, narrowing down their hotel choices in Athens to a swanky American hotel for the security, planning for Hunter to drop his gun at the shipping store on their way to the airport.

And they talked. He told her more about his partner, about his time in the military, about his parents. She told him stories about summer visits with her cousins and aunts, where the girls learned the legend of the original Medusa, about receiving her dagger when she got her first period, about the boy who broke her heart when she was sixteen.

He wanted more of that, of them quietly talking, of seeing her face when he woke in the morning, each night before he slept.

Going to Greece was the only way he could have it. He'd resigned himself to that.

After the front desk alerted them to a package delivery, he waited at the door, watching through the peephole to be sure it was hotel staff approaching their room. The large envelope the woman carried didn't appear unusual, but it held the key to the rest of their lives. He'd barely relocked the door after accepting it before he tore it open.

Hunter studied the fake ID packet Ryder had sent. It was both impressive and frightening how real they were. He had no doubt they would pass the cursory inspection at the airport and even a closer look when they landed in Greece.

More frightening, however, was the notion that he–a former police officer, sworn to uphold the law–fully intended to use this fraudulent documentation in order to keep Katharine safe, to take her fight to the source, and he wouldn't lose sleep over it. Not to protect her.

Part of him was appalled. The rest of him just wanted the ordeal over so they could spend their lives together, without worrying these men would continue to hunt them or her family.

When she came out of the bathroom, he shut the passport and tucked the papers back into the courier envelope. "So are you ready to go on your honeymoon, Mrs. Armstrong?"

"Honeymoon, huh?" She sat beside him on the bed. "You understand, don't you?"

He put the envelope behind him and scooped her onto his lap. "I understand. If I thought there was another way, I'd never agree to this. But I can't see one. So I'll go with you." He kissed her temple. "This will be our way, and we'll end this curse." If he had to take on the Goddess Herself to keep his Kat, he would.

THE TICKETS TO GREECE WERE FOR THE following evening, leaving at six from Philadelphia. Ryder had included a note in the envelope that their car would arrive in the morning, so they could check out on time. The only thing then would be what to do half the day until their flight.

"We could ask for a late check-out," Kat said. "That would shrink the big block of time we have to kill before the flight." She didn't like the large space of time from check-out to flight time. Even knowing they had to get through security at least two hours before their flight, that left a couple hours after their check-out from the hotel, after their drive to the airport. Her stomach squeezed.

"I wish we'd thought of it earlier." Hunter rubbed the back of his neck, his mouth twisted.

"It's okay. The Harvesters aren't looking for a car. Hell, by now, they might not even think we're still in the city." She got to her feet to pace. "So we check out, get in the car and go."

"Where?"

Good question. They couldn't sit at the airport half the day, it might seem suspicious, and getting from New York to Philly wouldn't take long. She stopped at one of the windows and peered out through the blinds at the people on the street below, searching for inspiration.

"We do need to make one other stop tomorrow," he said slowly.

She glanced back over her shoulder.

"If we're honeymooning, we need rings."

She opened her mouth, then shut it again. It made sense. Most newlyweds wore shiny new rings, and if they were pretending to be on a honeymoon, it might look odd if they weren't wearing rings.

"We can find something online and pick it up tomorrow. We just have to decide where."

That would help fill some time. "Somewhere outside the city, so we don't show on a camera they're watching. Before we get to Philly, in case of more camera-watching."

He nodded. "Okay. I'll see what I can find. What's your ring size?"

She glanced down at her fingers, mind blank.

"Kat?"

She blinked, then met his gaze. "Seven and a half."

"White or yellow?"

"White."

He smiled, then lifted the lid on his laptop. "It's fine, honey."

She realized she was hung up on the idea of wearing a ring he put on her finger. How had she never considered that? He wanted forever, and she wanted it, too. Why hadn't she thought about all the details that went along with it?

Because somewhere in her mind, she realized, doubt lurked. Doubt that they could pull this off and walk out alive. Or at least that she could walk out of the Parthenon alive.

She turned back to the window, staring blindly at the surrounding buildings. She'd convinced him this was the only way, yet somehow *she* wasn't convinced. Guilt burned in her stomach. What if she'd gotten him into something that got him killed? Because she was stubborn enough, arrogant enough to think she, of all of the Medusa's descendants, could force a Goddess to change Her mind?

Her chest squeezed. If he died in Greece, it would be her fault.

She jumped when he put his hand on her shoulder.

"It's going to be okay," he murmured, stepping closer behind her.

She shut her eyes tight. "I don't want anything to happen to you."

"Where you go, I go. I want to see this through with you."

"But what if–"

"No 'what if'. We're doing this, remember? You said so."

"I've been wrong before," she whispered and turned to look up at him, chest aching.

He smiled. "Not this time." He pulled her around and into his arms. "You and me, going to break the curse. Right?"

"Gods, I hope so."

He bent to brush a kiss on her mouth. "You

go ahead and have your jitters today. Tomorrow, we go."

Katharine slid her arms around him and squeezed. "Okay, you and me. We're doing it."

HUNTER COULDN'T WAIT TO GET THROUGH security. He'd be less anxious with no weapons on the other side of the gates except the ones belonging to law enforcement. Not entirely secure, but better. And really, the day had gone perfectly–leaving the hotel in their new car, stopping at a jewelry store in an outer Philadelphia suburb to get their rings, arriving here and dropping off the rental car.

Kat stood beside him, her gaze sliding over the other travelers, tension radiating from her. He gave her hand a squeeze, and, when she glanced up at him, smiled at her.

The smile she returned was strained, so he leaned down to brush a kiss on her cheek, her mouth. "Honeymooning, remember?" he murmured.

She took a deep breath, then gave him a better smile. "Right."

"We're nearly there, sweetheart, and then you need to get some rest. I have big plans for the first day of our honeymoon," he added a bit louder when he noticed one of the wandering guards pacing toward them. The man's frown faded to a smirk as he continued past them.

Kat shut her eyes and leaned into Hunter. "Big plans, huh?"

"Yeah. You and I in that big bed in the

honeymoon suite for at least twenty-four hours." He released her hand and rubbed his own up her spine, noting the tension still tightening her muscles.

She forced a laugh. "Big talker."

They moved forward with the line, and he felt her shoulders shift beneath his hand as she tried to get rid of more of the tension before they got to the security checkpoint.

She didn't succeed, but the agents at their station wouldn't have noticed. They were too distracted by her cleavage and her smile while she talked about her honeymoon. Even when they were pulled aside for further screening since their tickets had been purchased too recently, he was the only one there who knew she was jittery and not just a new bride whose excitement was bubbling over.

They bought a few magazines after getting through security, but he couldn't focus on them while also watching for danger. By the time they boarded, Hunter's nerves were frayed.

Kallan and Ryder had put them in first class, and Kat's eyes widened when they stepped into the front of the cabin.

"Whoa," she whispered. She sat on the edge of her seat. "I could get used to this." She gave a little bounce.

He smiled. "Honeymoon perks, sweetheart," he murmured, stowing the carry-ons.

"Did someone say honeymoon?" One of the male flight attendants stopped beside them.

"Once we get going, I'll bring you some bubbly," he smiled. "To celebrate." He patted Hunter's shoulder and continued on his way into the rear of the cabin.

She smiled. "Maybe then I can sleep." Her tone suggested otherwise.

Hunter sat beside her and caught her hand in his, ignoring the cool metal bands on her finger–those were for show right now, but he'd chosen them for her, not just for now, but forever, to mark her as his so the whole world would know it. As soon as they took care of this damned curse. "How're you holding up otherwise?" He kept his voice down, leaning close. They'd look like honeymooners sharing an intimate moment, but no else needed to hear this.

Faint pink tinted her cheeks. "So far, so good."

Satisfaction made him grin. "Excellent. And if you can get a few hours of sleep, it'll help the stress." She'd said that morning she thought maybe two more days before she'd be incapacitated for three. They should be done with this before then. He hoped.

"Maybe we can join the mile-high club," she whispered, leaning to kiss him, hard.

He caught her with his free hand at her nape and pulled her back in for another. "You are a wicked woman," he breathed. "Very, very naughty."

She arched one dark brow, her grey eyes gone soft with warmth. "Naughty?"

"Very," he agreed, nipping at her lower lip. "Might need another spanking."

Color suffused her face. "I think you enjoyed that too much."

"Almost as much as you," he growled. He kissed her again–too fast, but the other seats were filling up.

She sighed and sat back. "You're a terrible tease."

He winked at her, but shut his mouth when an older couple sat in front of them.

SHE WANTED TO SLEEP. SHE KNEW SHE needed it to be functional when they got into Athens. But her brain wouldn't slow down enough. It would've helped if she'd been able to get up and pace, but that was frowned on these days.

Instead, as she stared out the window, she brooded about all the things that might happen. Hunter tightened his fingers around hers, reaching across her to close the shade. "Sweetheart, you need to rest. At least close your eyes."

She turned to look at him, noted the dark circles beneath his eyes and strain lines bracketing his mouth. She lifted her free hand to stroke his stubbled jaw. "You are the best thing that's ever happened to me," she whispered, rubbing her thumb along one of the strain lines.

He smiled faintly. "Just wait." He winked.

Her eyes burned, from the threat of tears and pure exhaustion, but she smiled anyway.

He leaned over to brush a kiss on her mouth. "Close your eyes. Please."

She did, partly to appease him and partly to hide the tears. He settled her close so her head rested on his shoulder. She knew she wouldn't sleep, but she kept her eyes shut anyhow.

HUNTER KNEW WHEN SHE FELL ASLEEP–the tension in her vanished, and he sighed. The plane was less than two hours from Athens, but it was better than nothing. He just had to make sure she got a bit more rest before they went to confront the Goddess.

He couldn't even fathom a guess about what might happen. Even if he asked Kallan or Ryder, he was certain the other men would have no idea what to expect either. After all, how many mortals actually did battle with a deity and lived to tell the story?

He realized where his mind had gone and shut that down. He needed to concentrate on firming up their plan, however sketchy it was.

First, though, they needed to scout out the temple, see potential problems, and anything they could use to their advantage.

Then they needed to rest. Kat was exhausted already. He didn't see how she could function the rest of the day without some sleep. Maybe he could talk her into waiting until tomorrow night so they had more time to plan more.

Plan what?

He frowned at the seat back in front of him.

Even if they had a week, a month, he didn't know how they could plan anything. He had no weapons besides his fists, and he'd be rusty with a knife, even if he had one. Maybe he could find a couple. Better a weapon he hadn't practiced with in a few years than none at all.

Kat's dagger was tucked into the lone suitcase they'd checked at the airport, summarily dismissed as an ornamental gift rather than the deadly weapon it truly was.

He slanted a glance to where her dark head rested on his shoulder. Maybe she'd let him borrow the dagger. Or maybe he could find somewhere to buy his own. Something he could tuck into the camera bags he'd acquired when they stopped to pick up their rings—tourists carried cameras, even now when everyone used their phones for everything, and he'd suggested it would be a good way for them to really study the complex and the temple.

It would allow them to blend in better with the other people there, make their scrutiny less suspicious to anyone watching. He thought of the baseball cap he'd tucked into the overhead along with their carry-on and camera bag. It was a pretty weak disguise, but hopefully the Harvesters wouldn't be expecting them to show up on the home field.

Which would give him and Katharine a bit of an advantage. At least to start, and he'd take any advantage he could get right now.

# CHAPTER NINETEEN

Another damned email.

Elek sat back in his seat and huffed out a breath. This was not how he wanted to end his day. Twenty more cousins sent to the city and surrounding areas, and not a cursed thing, no sign of the Medusa or the man. He didn't want to think of Phelps as his brother.

And now this?

He picked up his water and debated. He didn't have to open it. He had plenty to do.

He clicked on it. They'd replied to his email, damn them.

"Our information is true, and Ari knows it. He's hidden it all these years, lying to the Goddess and to the family. We will not hide this any longer."

What the hell did that mean?

They could hardly share it with Athena. With the family?

Kallan could assist with that, though he really didn't have access to all of them anymore. He supposed the last Medusa's man might be able to help–someone had since these emails kept landing in his inbox.

He took a slow breath. It was time to take this to his great-uncle. Then they could have

Argos block any further contact.

Aristotle sat at his desk already, his attention on his computer screen. "Good evening, Elek. Come in, come in." The old man seemed chipper.

"Is there news?" he asked, crossing the room.

"No, not yet. I am sure there will be soon." He looked up. "You are troubled. What is it?"

He debated a few seconds more whether this was the right time or not, then took a deep breath. "I have gotten several anonymous emails claiming that Iphis was romantically involved with the Medusa Annis Galani."

Ari blanched and dropped back against his chair.

Alarm tickled at the back of his mind. "They sent a journal page, claiming it is Annis's, talking about his suicide. But his accident..."

His great-uncle paled still more. "Oh, Elek, I am so sorry."

Fear knotted Elek's gut. "What do you mean?"

Ari shut his eyes for a second. "I am so sorry that you now share the burden of this secret."

It was true? *Holy Goddess!* Elek dropped onto the chair behind him, astonished.

"Iphis was a romantic fool, and Annis broke him. If she hadn't rejected him, the bloody curse would have moved on to one of her cousins and my brother wouldn't have betrayed us all."

Elek stared at the older man. "You knew? All this time?" Anger welled up under the shock, boiling away the chill in his core.

"He never mentioned her name when they were courting, and he didn't divulge it when he killed himself, only why he had done it, so I didn't know her identity until she died."

"They *know*," Elek bit out.

Ari rubbed his fingers at his temple. "I'm so sorry, Elek. I should have warned you, but I had no idea Annis had written about it. I thought only I knew now."

Elek wanted to thump his head on his great-uncle's desk. Hard. Or to throttle Ari.

He did neither. Gathering what remained of his composure, he rose. "I need to think about this," he managed. "I will come back in an hour to discuss the email."

And in the meantime, he would go pummel the stuffing out of the heavy weight bag until he couldn't see straight.

ANOTHER RENTAL CAR WAITED FOR THEM in Athens, courtesy of Ryder. Katharine tilted her head from one side to the other, trying to loosen tense muscles. She'd actually fallen asleep on the plane. That was good and bad—good because she needed it, bad because it wasn't nearly enough.

Hunter drove to the hotel they'd chosen, and because they'd made the request when Ryder made the reservation, they were able to check in right away. That meant a few hours' rest before they headed to the temple.

She looked out of the window of their room toward the Acropolis. Even now, lit by bright spotlights against the indigo sky, a partial structure, a shadow of its original self, its presence was imposing. Regal.

So close. She was so close to ending this. Or to Athena ending her.

"You need a nap." His big, warm hands landed on her shoulders.

"So do you."

"I agree." His fingers tightened slightly. "So here is the new first stage of our plan: we get a few hours of sleep, then we eat and go play tourist over there, get the lay of the land, so we're more ready for tonight."

Tonight. It seemed so far away.

"Come on, Kat." He reached out to close the curtains, then turned her toward the bed.

"I don't think I can sleep." She sat and kicked off her shoes anyway.

"I think you will. Two hours isn't enough, even when you're running on pure adrenaline and raw nerves."

Maybe she could figure out how not to die.

She managed some fitful sleep, though she shifted, half-awake, several times, trying to get comfortable, to relax, to make her brain shut off for just a while longer.

Finally, she sighed and flopped onto her back. Daylight showed around the curtains, and the clock on the night stand showed nearly eight local time. That was enough.

Hunter caught her wrist. "You didn't sleep much."

"I tried." She rolled her head on the pillow to look at him. "Too much in my head."

He rolled onto his side and leaned over to kiss her. "Okay, let's shower. I'll feel more awake then, and we can find food before we do the tour."

She smiled. "Thank you, Hunter." She touched his jaw, studying his expression. "Did I keep you awake?"

He shook his head. "My own brain did that." He kissed her again. "Come on."

THE HOTEL HAD A SMALL CAFÉ, WHERE THEY found tea and coffee and fresh yogurt and fruit. Katharine forced herself to eat every bit of food on her small plate. She needed the energy. She also drank her entire cup of sweet, floral-scented tea. It settled her nerves a bit, the tea and the ritual of the meal. She concentrated on breathing evenly, though her gaze flitted over the growing number of people passing outside the café.

Hunter ate in silence, and when they'd finished, he took her hand. "If I tell you to run, you'll go, no questions."

She studied his expression. "They don't know we're here."

"I need you to trust me to protect you, Kat."

"I do." It was true. He'd kept her safe for weeks now.

Some of the tension eased in his face.

She squeezed his fingers. "Let's hit it."

The Acropolis wasn't far, but the walk took longer than she would've liked. If it were up to her, she'd have pushed past the other pedestrians. But Hunter kept her restrained, shooting an amused glance down at her when a frustrated sigh escaped her.

"I know," she muttered, meeting his gaze for a moment.

"It's a beautiful day for a honeymoon walk." Laughter tinted his mild tone.

She didn't look up. She needed not to draw attention to herself, to them. She knew it. But they were *so close*.

The nearer they got to the entrance, the more she realized she could sense the energy of the place, vibrating over her skin. Magic. Ancient magic, eons of it, stored in the ground, the buildings, and even in the air. She inhaled deeply and smiled.

Hunter's glance was full of questions.

She leaned closer to him. "So much old magic here."

He smiled and shook his head.

"I really want to kick off my shoes and sit on the ground. There's so much energy in the air, I bet sitting on the Earth would give me a serious buzz."

He released her hand, then wrapped his arm around her shoulders. "I'll take your word for that." His gaze slid away, moving over the people.

Watching for Harvesters.

She slid her arm to his waist and gave him a squeeze. "Let's go scope out the battlefield."

He slanted a warning glance down at her. "I don't think I like that phrase."

She smiled again. "Come on."

He let her move him, but as they joined the line of tourists waiting to purchase their tickets or to be admitted to the site, he remained alert.

So did Kat, but she hid it better. Anyone who looked at Hunter would know he was on a mission, his blue gaze intense and focused.

Because they'd arrived early, their wait wasn't long. She glanced back from the ticket station and breathed a sigh of relief that they weren't in the line that stretched out of sight now. He linked their fingers, and she glanced up, noting the stress lines fanning out from his eyes.

"We're fine," she murmured, squeezing his hand.

"Let's get in before it's too crowded."

She nodded her agreement, letting him tow her along to the mound.

*Look out, Athena, here we come.*


HUNTER TOOK MENTAL NOTES AS they walked, potential hiding places for enemies, for them if they needed them, routes around obstacles, to the two exits. Kat took photos, lots of photos, which was probably just as good–they could study them when they got back to their hotel.

When they reached the temple, he stood for

a moment, impressed. It must have been truly awe-inspiring when it was first built. He counted steps, noted locations of the equipment the restorers were using. And hoped like hell they came out of this ruin alive tonight.

He turned to Kat, then realized she'd moved away a few steps to get more pictures from another angle. Her full attention was on her task, her shoulders set. He admitted to himself how strong she was. He just didn't know if either of them were strong enough to face down a Goddess. She believed they had a chance.

Because he was sure she wouldn't let the curse pass on to another cousin, this really was their only shot, because he had no intention of letting her go.

She glanced over and smiled, and he forced himself to relax a little, smiling back at her. He loved her, period. This wasn't just her fight, but his as well.

They took their time wandering the perimeter, studying. To any stranger's eye, they'd be like the rest of the tourists, he thought, wanting to see and record every detail for their keepsakes and scrapbooks. He doubted any other tourists were imagining a battle on the site, though.

Finally, they went to the temple, and she tipped her head back to look up. The restored columns stood tall and strong, befitting the temple of a Goddess.

"There is so much power here," she

whispered. "I don't even need to take off my shoes or sit on the ground." Her eyes closed, lips curving. "I can feel it all around me, around us. It's incredible."

He pondered that. He didn't sense anything different. Maybe if he'd been raised in the Tassos family that wouldn't be the case. Kallan had told him some of the cousins had the ability to sense and undo spells. Right now, he'd settle for some super-human strength to deal with whatever came tonight.

She touched one of the marble columns, her eyes closing again, and gasped. "Oh, how lovely. I can see how this looked originally. So beautiful. Better than the reconstruction images we saw online. So ornate." She met his gaze. "I wish you could see it, too."

He bent to kiss her lightly. "That'd be nice." He glanced around. "Let's walk as much of the rest as we can."

She let him move her, going around other tourists, and kept snapping pictures while he studied, hoping for some inspiration to strike.

Finally, satisfied they'd seen everything, he turned one last time. "Are you hungry?"

"A bit. We could go down the hill to the Plaka. Lots of places to eat there. Also great views of the Acropolis, so we can study more." She set one hand on his chest, over his heart. "I'm glad you're here with me."

He bent to kiss her, lingering this time. "I wouldn't be anywhere else," he whispered against her mouth, holding her grey gaze.

She smiled. "Shall we walk to the other entry point? In case we need that route later?"

He nodded and turned her. The more information they had, the better.

The Plaka was more crowded than he liked. Too many people to watch everyone, to study expressions for intentions. So he settled for holding tighter to her hand, keeping her close in the hot crush of people. They walked slowly, looking at the cafés and shops along the way, pausing to study menus a couple of times.

"*Teras!* Monster!"

Hunter turned to see where the shout had come from, pulse quickening.

A tall, dark man stood on a balcony over a café, eyes narrowed on Hunter and Kat.

*Shit.* Hunter turned her in the crowd to retrace their steps. "We need to get out of here," he growled.

They wove among the other tourists, and he dared a glance back over his shoulder. The man was no longer on the balcony.

"Fuck. This way." He tugged her into a narrow alleyway between two buildings, shaded from the midday sun and any casual glances behind some stacked crates and baskets. "Be quiet and don't move."

A moment later, he heard people muttering or calling out, and the man shoved past their hiding spot.

Hunter held his breath and eased forward a tiny bit so he could see the street.

The man had stopped several doors down,

panic in his expression when he turned around. He craned his neck to peer over the people heading in the direction they'd been going, then moved a few steps forward before he stopped, shoulders slumping. He turned to scan the crowd, peeking in a shop window and at the outdoor tables at one of the small restaurants. He turned a full three-sixty to be sure they weren't still here. His lips moved, and Hunter almost wished he was close enough to hear the Harvester's curse.

Reluctance lined the man's face as he pulled out his cell to call someone. The conversation was short, but when he stuffed his phone back into his pocket, the Harvester's face was flushed, mouth set in sulky lines, and eyes narrowed with anger.

He was in trouble and not happy about it. *Tough.*

When she shifted behind him, Hunter gave Kat's hand a squeeze, silently willing her to stop before she revealed them. She stilled, and he breathed a silent sigh of relief.

The Harvester finally moved, back toward where he'd come from, not nearly as alert now, but Hunter kept his grip on Katharine well after the other man had vanished into the crowd.

He felt her relax behind him.

"Nice moves, Mr. Phelps," she murmured.

"You'd never've survived military life," he teased. "You don't take orders well."

She smiled when he turned to face her. "You're just bossy."

He slid one hand around her back and drew her close. "Maybe." He shut his eyes and took a steadying breath. "Let's go find food elsewhere." He steered her ahead of him, keeping a careful eye on the crowd to be sure the Harvester hadn't returned, and that no one else was lurking. He wasn't really hungry now, but he needed to keep them both occupied for a while.

It was a long time until dark, and he didn't plan to waste energy by spending those hours on the run from Harvesters. Maybe room service would be better, though it wouldn't give them more time on the ground.

"Uncle, the monster is here."

Aristotle's heart stopped for a moment. "What?"

"I saw her, just now, in the Plaka." Xenos sounded breathless.

He swallowed, mouth dry. "Is she alone?"

"No, Uncle, the man is with her."

Aristotle was so angry, he shook. He couldn't even lift his water glass without the liquid sloshing over the edge. "Are you following them?"

Xenos hesitated. "No, sir, they got away by the time I reached the street."

"Search again. Find them! They cannot escape." He disconnected the call and put his phone down so he could use both hands to lift his water, to wet his parched throat.

Why was the monster in Greece? How *dare*

she?

His chest pinched with pain, but he ignored it to pace away from his desk. For a moment, he considered flying there now. He could be there overnight. Find her. Confront her himself.

No. The boys would get her this time.

He turned back to his desk and reached for the phone. "Kyril, you need to gather your brothers and cousins–Acrisius, Urian, Rasmus, Myron. The monster is in Athens, and you must get there, kill her." He hung up, then rubbed his hand over his heart. "We will not fail You this time, my Lady," he murmured. They *could not*.

# CHAPTER TWENTY

Hunter kept her hand in his as they took an indirect route toward the hotel, scanning the surrounding crowd.

*"Teras!"*

*Son of a bitch.* That word again. He tugged on Kat's hand and pushed his way through the people ahead of them, gripping her fingers hard.

There were too many people for them to run, dammit. He shoved past another group of tourists.

*"Teras!"*

This time, the shout was closer, and Kat's hand jerked free of his. Her yell was cut off, and he turned in time to see a man dragging her backward–one arm banding hers to her sides, and his other hand covering her mouth–then into a narrow opening between buildings.

*Fuck.*

People turned to see what the commotion was, but he noticed as he pushed past them that no one went after the man. On the other hand, it would be hard to explain this to any of the tourists, he thought. Better to deal with it himself.

He heard Kat cry out again as he barreled into the alleyway. She hit the wall of the building on the right and slid down it, and he charged at the guy, who seemed reluctant to give up his prize. Hunter punched him in the side of the head, and the Harvester released her arm to swing blindly at Hunter, landing a lucky blow to the jaw.

Hunter gathered his breath and put his fist directly into the Harvester's face this time. The man's head rocked back against the building on the left, and he dropped. Hard. When he didn't move, Hunter ran to where Kat had pushed to her feet, using the building behind her as a brace. She held her dagger in one hand and the other hand gingerly along the side of her face.

"We need to move." He slid his arm behind her and half-carried her toward the opposite end of the alley. "Put your dagger away."

"I'm going to have a black eye," she said unsteadily.

"It'll go with your fat lip," he teased gruffly. His heart still beat so hard in his chest, it ached. "Do me a favor."

"What?" She glanced over as they crept along the alley.

"Let's not do that again."

She laughed. "Stick in the mud."

"Yeah, that's me. I could do with a bit less excitement, especially when it means seeing you hurt."

"I don't think I hit hard enough for a concussion. Only a lump."

Much as he wanted to check now, he didn't, just hauled her out of the alleyway to join the crush of tourists on the street.

"We can't wait," she said after they'd been walking for a few minutes. "Ready or not, it has to be tonight."

Hunter didn't like that, but he couldn't argue. The Harvesters would only keep coming now they knew Kat was here, and they had home field advantage. A surprise charge was best. "I know," he said finally. "Let's cut across this street here. It'll be longer, but we can make sure no one else is following us if we take the indirect route." What he really wanted to do was rush her back to the hotel and keep her there.

More than that, he wanted this over with, so he would go with her to the Parthenon tonight, and they would do battle with the Goddess, and whoever else happened to be there.

And he meant to win.

"LET'S STOP HERE FOR A FEW MINUTES," SHE said when they got to a small patch of green. It looked like a tiny park, and it had a good view of the Acropolis.

Hunter frowned but didn't protest even though she knew he wanted to.

Her head throbbed, from the lump she could feel on the back of her scalp to the swelling at her cheekbone. The Harvester hadn't been gentle. But she wasn't dead, so that was a plus. She sat, cross-legged, on the ground, smiling up at Hunter, who shifted his gaze to the sparser foot-traffic on this street and moved to stand between her and the view of the mound.

Still on full-alert. That was okay. She could use that for a few minutes.

Katharine took a deep breath, then another, concentrating on settling her pulse to a slower beat, her mind to a more relaxed state, seeing herself connecting to the Earth beneath her.

The energy she sought was warm, soothing, healing. She concentrated on it, got a firm grip on it, saw herself capturing it, drawing it upward–only what she thought she needed–then wrapping it around Hunter, to protect him from whatever came at them. Bright, warm. She made sure it encircled him completely, leaving no part of him unprotected–the mistake Achilles's mother had made with her beloved boy. She held onto a small bit for herself, letting it soothe the ache in her head and face. Satisfied, she grounded the rest of the energy, releasing it back into the Earth. "Thank you, Mother," she breathed, opening her eyes.

Hunter turned around and narrowed his eyes. "What did you do?"

She blinked. "What?" He was too far away to hear her whisper.

"I just got about ten degrees warmer, all over. What did you do?"

*Interesting.* "Just a little protective energy," she said, studying him. "Warmer?"

He nodded and walked back toward her. "Why can I feel it?"

"Good question. Maybe you're more

susceptible because of your father? Maybe you've been hanging around me too long," she teased when he dropped to the ground beside her.

"Not nearly long enough," he shot back.

"How does it look?"

"Insanely busy." He propped himself on one elbow and scanned the hilltop. "How long before they clear everyone out?"

"Hours." They'd already discussed this, so she knew he was getting antsy.

"Then we should get some food and rest." He shifted his gaze back to her. "Run through our really thin plan again."

Katharine nodded. "All right."

He frowned. "Are you placating me?"

"No, I'm agreeing with you." She pushed to her feet and held out one hand to him. "We've hardly slept since the night before last, and we're both running on nerves."

He didn't appear convinced, but he shoved off his elbow and caught her hand, coming to his feet in one smooth motion.

"Hm." Her already-revved hormones kicked into higher gear.

Hunter laughed and wrapped both arms around her. "So we'll take a nap *after*."

"I can take care of myself," she teased.

He growled. "I can take care of you better." The last word touched her lips half a second before his mouth.

Indeed, he could, and she would let him.

When they got into their room, she closed

the curtains against the light, then pulled off her blouse.

Hunter stood stock-still near the door, his blue eyes wide and dark.

She smiled and stripped off the rest of her clothes. "Come take a shower with me."

His throat worked as he swallowed, but he followed her into the smaller room.

She turned the water on in the big shower, then she tugged at the hem of his shirt. He caught it and whipped it over his head, then unbuckled his belt, kicking off his shoes.

She smiled as she turned to step in the shower. By the time he joined her, she'd lathered her hands with the herby-smelling hotel soap. "Turn around."

His chest rose and fell faster.

"Turn." She waited.

He finally released a slow breath and pivoted, presenting her with his back.

Katharine wiped her soapy hands across his wide shoulders, her gaze sliding from the short, pale scar on the back of his left arm to the faint birthmark on the back of his shoulder, to the muscles flexing beneath her touch as she washed his back.

"Is it my turn yet?" he asked gruffly.

"Not even close," she said, gliding her fingers lower, to his narrow waist.

"You know I'll make you pay for the torture, right?"

"Can't wait." She stroked suds lower, over the taut muscles of his ass, enjoying his sharp inhalation. Then she reached around with one hand to capture his erection, and he groaned, slapping his hands against the shower wall.

"Katharine." Her name was a low rumble, sending goosebumps up her arms.

She smiled again, stroking him, and stepped closer so her aching breasts rubbed his back. He felt good. Solid, strong, warm. And he loved her. She shut her eyes against the burn. They had to do this tonight, but before that... Before that, she needed to make sure he knew how she felt, even if she couldn't tell him yet. Not until they'd gotten Athena to remove the curse, until she knew it was over. In case she didn't get the opportunity to say the words.

His muscles quivered, and then she found herself pressed to the cool tile shower wall, the wide head of his cock nudging into her wet folds.

She blinked up at him, putting her hands on his shoulders to steady herself.

"Enough torture for now," he growled, his hips easing closer so he slid inside her.

Her breath caught, and she wrapped her legs around his waist, letting him sink fully into her. "Oh."

His smile flashed briefly, before he bent to catch her mouth with his. And he began to move, slow and steady, kicking up her own desire several notches.

He wouldn't be rushed either, not even when she tried to rock against him. He simply pressed her tight between himself and the tiles, kissing her endlessly until she couldn't think.

Then he began again, slow, hard thrusts that set off mini-releases deep inside her, making her tremble in his arms. And when his pace finally quickened, she held on tight. Anything he wanted, she would do it. Her heart beat an erratic tattoo under her ribs, 'love him, love him, love him', in counterpoint to her ragged breathing and his rough groans. The next orgasm was massive, leaving her limp and teary.

He dragged in a slow breath after a long time, then reached behind himself to shut off the water. "I love you, Katharine."

Her eyes burned, but she smiled at him anyway, sliding one hand into the wet hair at his nape to draw him down for another kiss. Lingering, tender.

Eventually, they climbed out and dried off. She deliberately kept her attention on the present moment, not allowing thoughts of the coming night to distract her from him.

"Your eye looks better," he said, picking her up to carry her into the bedroom.

"A little healing energy after I made sure you'll be protected tonight. Hopefully enough to get rid of the shiner."

"I don't think anyone would notice it now if they didn't know it was there. It's pretty faint." He put her in the middle of the bed. "You need to rest."

"Yes. So do you." Katharine rolled onto her side to face him as he pulled the sheet up.

"I'm going to set an alarm. Not that I think we'll need it."

She watched him retrieve his phone from his pants, then return to the bed, sliding under the sheet to face her.

"Close your eyes."

"I'm just looking." She obeyed anyway, taking a slow, deep breath.

"No thinking."

She laughed. "I'll try."

He pulled her closer, sliding one arm under her pillow. "Try hard. We both need a nap or we'll never be functional up there." He pressed a kiss on her forehead. "Sleep, honey."

She concentrated on breathing, redirecting her thoughts when something tried to intrude. Until her brain finally cooperated.

She woke some time later, and without looking toward the window, she knew it was dusky out. The room was darker now.

She didn't think Hunter had dozed, he was too alert, but she let him have his silence. He needed to think about what was coming, too. She'd already thought about it enough. She knew what she needed to do. The only thing she couldn't know was the outcome–ending the curse, or death by Goddess.

So she didn't think any further than the next step–making sure they remained unseen, by taking out the power to the temple mound. From a safe distance.

ARISTOTLE POPPED ANOTHER OF THE TINY pills and tucked the box back into his pocket with a shaking hand.

"Uncle Ari, why don't you lie down for a few hours?" Elek said, worry wrinkling his forehead.

"I don't have time to rest while the monster is still walking and breathing, and in our Lady's city." He ignored the stabbing pain in his chest to glare at his nephews. "The Goddess has charged us with a duty, and we are failing Her!"

Elek and Argos stared at him, wide-eyed.

Aristotle realized he'd shouted, and took a slow, measured breath. "Forgive me," he said after a moment. "I fear my time is short, and I would have an end to these monsters, once and for all. We *must* get the amulet and kill the Medusa, and we must do so quickly."

Argos studied him for a few more seconds. "We do understand, Uncle, but while we wait for word from Kyril, you should rest. There is nothing you can do until then."

Aristotle knew his nephews were right, but he shook his head. "I cannot rest until we have word." He paced away from his desk, resolutely ignoring the pain in his chest. Too much stress, the doctor had said, perhaps he should think about retiring. Aristotle clenched his fist at his side. He could not until he succeeded in ridding the world of these monsters.

This was his final chance, and he could not

fail.

"WE SHOULD'VE BROUGHT SOME FOOD back with us. Snacks or something." Hunter turned his head on his pillow to look at her. "We never got lunch."

"I can't eat anything." She smiled over at him, her grey eyes clear.

He didn't think he could either, but it would fill time before they headed out.

"We can get room service when we get back. It's available twenty-four-seven." She rolled to face him and stretched to touch his jaw with warm fingers. "We'll be starving then."

Assuming they weren't dead in the Parthenon. He frowned. No, they wouldn't be dead. They were going to do this.

"You should have taken one of my pills. You might have actually slept," she teased.

He scowled. "And left you unprotected? No. It isn't the first time I've gone without sleep on a case." But it had been a while, and even with the anticipation and adrenaline in his system, he wished he'd slept a little more. He needed to be alert, ready for... For what? He had no idea. Harvesters, for sure. But what else? Well, he supposed they'd find out.

He hadn't had time to find a weapon. Hell, he'd be happy with a steak knife right now.

"You should have my dagger tonight."

He looked over at her again. "Don't you think you'll need it?"

"My fight is with Athena, and a dagger won't help me there." Her lips curved slightly. "You take it."

He pondered that, turning his gaze to the shadowed ceiling. He had no idea what she'd have to do to convince Athena to remove the curse, what argument she could make that would be persuasive enough. If he had to fight off a few Harvesters, his battle would be far easier than hers, he thought, gut twisting. He reached out blindly for her hand, lacing their fingers tightly.

He could hold off some Harvesters for her, no matter how many arrived. He would.

ELEK SKIPPED LUNCH WITH HIS great-uncle and Argos. His stomach churned in time with the thunder and lightning that had blown in a couple of hours ago. The last word they'd received from Athens was that Phelps had stopped Acrisius from getting her. Acrisius had a mild concussion and would be fine by morning.

But the Medusa had escaped once more.

Ari had taken the news badly, his fury putting bright spots of red onto his cheeks in an otherwise pale face, and he'd popped yet another of his little white pills. This stress must be taking a toll on his already-ailing heart.

Elek frowned, propping his chin on his fist. His great-uncle's health was declining, and the evidence of it was visible to anyone with eyes. Other cousins had asked recently, and he'd brushed their inquiries aside, but he wouldn't be able to do that much longer, not when the older man grew frailer each day.

*He had known.*

Elek shut his eyes. All those years, and Ari had known about his brother and the Medusa, and lied to the entire family. *To the Goddess.*

Perhaps the Goddess *should* know the secret Ari had kept all this time.

It was disloyal to consider, but hadn't Ari done worse all these years, betraying the Goddess to whom they owed all loyalty?

He shoved to his feet and strode to the window. The rain had lightened to a heavy mist, but occasional lightning still flashed in the distance.

Perhaps if he disclosed this secret to Athena, She wouldn't hold him responsible for the current fiasco. She would be too furious at Ari.

Then again, he could be mistaken.

He shut his eyes. This required more consideration, more than his exhausted mind could manage currently. He'd hardly slept all night, between the need to wait for word from his cousins in Athens, and his mind racing over what he now knew about Iphis, over his half-brother, over what he should do about all of it. Yet he had no answers, to any of it.

The main thing he needed to deal with right now was the monster in Athens.

He turned from the window and returned to his desk. Earlier he'd asked another half dozen cousins and uncles to get to Athens as soon as possible. He glanced at the clock on his computer. It was late there now. They couldn't hunt her in the dark with no idea where to begin, but when they arrived, they would stand guard at the temple, walk the Plaka.

He couldn't imagine why the Medusa had thought going to Athens would help her cause.

No, this would be the end of her.

Possibly of his half-brother as well.

He didn't like that. Mostly, he didn't like that Ari was fine with it. Any collateral damage at this point was fine with him as long as they killed the Medusa and got the amulet.

Elek scowled. They didn't even know where the cursed amulet was. All these years, all the Medusas his family had managed to track down and kill, and no one had ever found the thing.

If he didn't know better, he'd think it was a legend and nothing more. Except Medusa's daughters exhibited no signs of the curse, other than the one who was the current Medusa.

No, he mused, it was real. He wondered if Ari knew more about that, too, that he'd kept secret. Surely not. If he knew anything, he would've told them, and the quest would be ended.

He took a slow breath and opened the family's private website. He found looking at the old images and artifacts soothing. Like the sculpture of Perseus holding up the severed head of the monster as a trophy. It meant victory for his family.

It felt like a never-ending quest, one they could never achieve.

Sighing, he clicked to the next page. A platter decorated with an image of the young Medusa, still living, beautiful, even with the viperous snakes on her head. He scrolled down. An urn with another depiction of the Medusa, more mature, draped in a classical gown, snakes for her hair, and... He frowned, leaning nearer to the screen. A goblet on her thigh.

He scrolled back up. Not on the platter. He scrolled further down the page, pausing to study each image, each object. None of the ones showing her as a younger woman had the goblet, at least not that he could see. But not all of the mature Medusa images had it either.

It might be just an idea one artist had that spread to others who knew of the true story.

Or it might be the cursed amulet, in front of them all this time.

His heart beat faster. If the amulet was the goblet, that meant it was *on* the Medusa, not hidden away somewhere. It would explain why they'd never found it. It must transfer from one to the next.

*Holy Goddess.* He squeezed his eyes shut. If that was true, he didn't see how they could ever get it. It really would be a never-ending quest, dooming them to eternal failure.

What if he was wrong? What if it was just a symbol used by ancient familial artists?

He still had to share his idea with Uncle

Ari. If it was the amulet, his cousins needed to know. Even if there was only a tiny possibility it was the amulet, they couldn't kill this Medusa until they took the amulet. And taking the goblet would likely be the death of her.

He shoved to his feet and ran from his office to Ari's, not allowing himself to think about how much more gruesome their task might have become.

# CHAPTER TWENTY-ONE

Hunter tried to call on his years of experience on the force to gather some calm, to settle his thoughts and focus, but not knowing what they'd face made that challenging. He worked with her dagger, refreshing his memory on moves that were unfamiliar after all this time.

"You're too tense," she said from her seat at the small table, where she'd been studying the pictures they'd taken that morning on her laptop screen. "You need to feel the dagger as an extension of your arm, of your hand, a part of you."

"I know. I'm rusty." He sighed and took a slow breath, then released it and started over. Repeating the movements. Once more. Again. Until it felt more natural. Not like when he was fully practiced, but better than when he'd started. He debated another round, then his phone alarm chimed.

He turned toward Kat. She closed the laptop and got to her feet, stretching her arms over her head. She smiled. "It's going to be fine."

She'd repeated it so many times in the last few days, he was almost convinced she believed it.

Even though it'd been seasonally hot earlier, they'd agreed that wearing dark clothes and long pants would be better for their trek tonight, in case anyone happened to be watching. Less exposed skin in the dark meant less chance of being spotted. She already had on dark jeans and her boots, and now pulled on her black hoodie over her dark green tank.

Hunter tucked the dagger into her sheath, now attached to his belt. The darkest shirt he'd packed was royal blue, and he pulled his own hoodie on over that. He let out a slow breath, concentrating on easing his pulse. After a moment, he turned back to her and held out one hand.

She took it, her fingers warm.

*Go time.*

Outside, the first quarter moon played hide and seek with thick clouds, some scudding by quickly and others taking longer. He wished there were more of the slow-movers. They walked in silence, and he listened to the sounds of the city, the laughter of a group somewhere nearby, faint chatter, car engines farther away.

It was late, nearing midnight, and the city would be settling in. Less eyes on them. The Harvesters knew they were here, so he remained alert, watching ahead, glancing back, listening for the sound of footsteps.

When they finally reached the spot they'd decided on earlier, Hunter eyed the enormous ruin. "You're absolutely sure?"

Katharine nodded, her own gaze stuck fast

on the Parthenon. "Enough is enough."

He wasn't as certain, but he couldn't think of any other solution. His heart beat faster.

She started forward, and he caught her wrist. She gave him a reassuring smile.

"No matter what happens here tonight," he said hoarsely, "remember I love you."

Her smile widened. "That's why I have to do this." She stretched up and kissed him lightly. "Ready to take on a Goddess?"

"For you? Sure." He knew his attempt at keeping his tone casual failed, but she leaned in anyway to kiss him again, longer this time.

Her warm fingers touched his cheek. "Thank you, Hunter." Her gaze held his in the dark. "Not just for this. For all of it."

He knew what she meant. What she was really saying. For a moment, fear clogged his throat. A goodbye, in case... He swallowed it down. "A little longer, and you'll be home free," he said, forcing some lightness into his tone.

Her eyes sparkled with tears, and then she blinked. "That's right, we will. Let's do it."

He squeezed her hand once more before he released her. "Okay." Breathe slow and steady, he reminded himself.

Time to kick some Harvester and Goddess ass.


KATHARINE GLANCED OVER HER SHOULDER to make sure he'd stayed behind her far enough, then she stood for a few moments, clearing her mind. She concentrated on the energy of the Earth beneath her. On drawing it up, through her feet, up her legs, to her spine, pooling in her center, expanding, warming. It made her feel lighter, almost giddy, but she held onto it while she drew more, still more.

When she couldn't hold it any longer, she directed the energy at the powerful generators that flooded the Acropolis grounds with light. The energy burst sent arcs of hot red and white sparks high into the air like fireworks, and she continued to direct the Earth's energy there until all of the lights went out, until the generators were toast. Then she released her connection, grounding what remained back into the earth, along with some of her own nervous energy.

"Holy shit."

Hunter's whisper made her smile, and she turned, finding him nearer.

"Way to go, Katharine," he breathed close to her ear.

She caught his hand and gestured ahead of them.

He nodded, and they crept through the dark cautiously, Hunter's hand tight on hers. She tried to use the filtered moonlight to step carefully as they climbed the hill, but the clouds made it a challenge, flitting across the moon in giant billows of shadow, as if the Gods themselves had taken flight.

She didn't mind the Gods, but she had business with one particular Goddess, and a little cloud cover wouldn't stop her.

The trek up seemed to take forever, but finally, they reached the end of the *Propylaia* and would get a clear view of the Parthenon in a second. She gave Hunter's fingers a squeeze, and he squeezed back.

The clouds parted for a couple seconds, just long enough for Katharine to see the large man standing on the steps of the Parthenon.

One Harvester wouldn't stop her either.

Especially when she had her own Harvester to help her.

Hunter gave her hand a light squeeze, and when she turned to him in the dark, he leaned closer. "Big guy," he breathed in her ear.

She nodded. Her heart beat steadily. Grounding had been a good idea. Otherwise, she'd be extra-nervous right now, even with Hunter at her side. She considered their options. The most direct route from where they stood in the shadows of the *Propylaia* would be safest in the dark, but the Harvester would see them coming as soon as they stepped out of their hidden spot here.

She glanced to the side, to the steps there. But those didn't lead to a clear path, only rough terrain and rocky rubble between them and the footpath on that side. She'd hate to stumble over something that would alert the Harvester to their presence, or to break her ankle before they even reached the temple. She took a shallow breath, debating.

When he squeezed her hand, she glanced

up to see him jerk his chin at the direct path. She frowned, then looked toward the temple again. The Harvester had turned to walk inside. She returned the squeeze to Hunter's hand and they crept down the steps and onto the path.

Each cautious step made her pulse quicken. Closer, yet not close enough, and the Harvester could come back out any second. The clouds overhead skittered away from the moon, and they froze. She glanced up, dismayed not to see another big cloud moving in to replace it.

He tugged on her hand, and she met his gaze. He gestured forward.

It would be easier to go faster now that they could see the path ahead. She let him pull her along, careful to step as quietly as she could. They'd nearly reached the Parthenon when she heard footsteps on stone, and they froze.

The Harvester emerged from the interior of the temple, paused and muttered something she didn't understand right before he charged toward them.

Hunter released her hand and raced to meet the other man.

A muffled thud sounded as they collided, and she held her breath for a moment, then realized she should be going inside. Hunter would be fine. She skirted around the pair as they grappled for control, hurrying into the shadows.

The energy of the ancient magic shimmered in the air, especially inside the structure. She felt it beneath her feet, like a heartbeat in the very ground. She heard a bigger thud from outside, and she smiled. Hunter had taken the Harvester down. She just knew.

*Weird.*

She took another step inside, the stones amplifying the sound.

"Kat," Hunter breathed from behind her.

She held out her hand, and his warm fingers wrapped around hers. "Athena," she began, her voice steady, "I have come to ask You to remove Your curse from my family."

Silence answered her.

She took a quick breath, then lifted her chin. "Athena," she called out.

The ground rumbled under their feet, and his fingers clenched on hers.

A moment later, she found herself looking at the Goddess.

Athena stared down at them, Her grey eyes stormy. "How dare you enter my temple and summon me?"

Katharine squared her shoulders. "I have done nothing to You."

"You live."

*Ouch.* Hunter's fingers squeezed. "Then You should have killed the first Medusa, instead of cursing her."

The Goddess's eyes flashed, but She remained silent.

Running footsteps sounded outside, and Katharine glanced up at Hunter. "I've got this," she breathed. "You deal with that."

He wanted to say 'no'. It was etched on his

face. But he didn't, instead leaning in to touch his lips to her forehead. "I love you." He turned and strode from the temple.

Now she could focus on Athena. "I've come to ask You to remove Your curse from my family," she repeated.

The Goddess laughed, the sound making the temple shudder. "Your arrogance rivals the first Medusa's."

"She bragged about her hair. I'm here to beg for my family's lives. Not quite the same."

Athena arched one eyebrow. "I see no begging."

The sounds of a scuffle came now from outside. Another damned Harvester.

Katharine did her best to ignore what Hunter might be doing. "You want me on my knees? Fine." She dropped onto the cool stone floor. "Please, Athena, please remove Your curse from my family." She bowed her head, half-expecting to be struck down.

Instead, the Goddess was silent.

ATHENA NARROWED HER EYES AS SHE studied the Medusa. She had the look of the first one, though her eyes were grey instead of blue, and her shiny black hair was shorter than her ancestor's thigh-length curls had been. But this one was braver than the original, braver than any since, coming directly to Her temple this way, with a man. No doubt it was a man who loved her despite the curse.

He had also proven his bravery, even

before their arrival in Greece. More of Her Harvesters were dead between the pair of them.

It seemed the last worthy Harvester had fallen in love several Medusas ago. Kallan Tassos had even killed his own to protect his Medusa.

HUNTER'S BREATH LEFT HIS LUNGS IN A rush when the other guy's fist plowed into his gut. He should've seen that coming. He reared back and rammed his head into the Harvester's throat. It caught the man off-guard and had him choking, struggling for air.

Hunter took advantage to pummel the guy until he fell first to his knees, then crumpled, unconscious, to the ancient stones beneath them. Now back to Kat.

Except heavy footsteps pounded toward him on the pathway.

"Son of a bitch," he muttered, panting. "Of course he didn't come alone." He straightened, swiping one hand across his bloody lip, and turned to face the new guy, while the temple rumbled behind him.

This one was larger, maybe an inch taller, but more heavily-built, wide across the chest, and Hunter thought he'd have a bigger challenge now. All he wanted was to get back inside and be sure Katharine was safe, but he'd do his part while she dealt with the Goddess.

The Harvester wasted no time, lowering his head and charging toward Hunter like a bull. Hunter waited, then sidestepped at the last second, catching the guy's arm and knocking his legs out from under him with one good kick. An ominous crack sounded when the Harvester's head hit the stone, and he stayed down, too.

But he wasn't the last.

Katharine's pulse hammered in her veins, and the grunts and thuds from Hunter's fight with the Harvesters outside carried into the temple. She even imagined she could hear the sounds the ancient rocks made as they stood against the night. While she held her breath, waiting for Athena to decide what to do with her.

"You have much courage," the Goddess said finally, "to come here this way. What prompts this?"

She decided honesty was best. "Love for my family. Anger at Your curse. Love for the man here with me."

Another pause. "This man loves you in spite of my curse?"

"Yes. And I believe he is a Tassos. One of Yours."

Athena frowned again. "What do you mean?"

"His mother gave him up for adoption and never told his father about him. He bears the birthmark."

The Goddess pondered that for several moments. So...two worthy Harvesters in recent years, and both protecting their Medusas. How curious. Even odder that the second had no idea of his legacy his entire life and still wound up with a Medusa.

"I SENSE THERE IS MORE," THE Goddess said.

She had been silent so long, Katherine expected to be struck down in a fury. She debated with herself for a few seconds. Should she? Should she withhold her knowledge? Would it do anyone any good at this point? "Another of Yours also loved a Medusa," she started. "I discovered her journal recently. Annis. She met a young man not long before the curse fell on her, and he continued to court her even after, but she feared for him, because of who his brother is." She hesitated.

"Which of mine loved her?"

"Iphis Tassos."

The temple shook again, a stronger quake than the previous tremor. "That is untrue."

Pain clenched her chest, hot and sharp, and Katharine gasped. "It is true, my Lady. After she'd turned him away, she wept over her journal as she wrote of his suicide. He didn't know she did it to protect him from Aristotle."

Another rumble under her knees, and Katharine hoped the stones around them stayed where they were. She panted through the pressure around her heart.

"Aristotle knew?" The Goddess's tone was low and ominous.

The pain increased, and she sucked in a

quick breath to steady herself. "He didn't know who Annis was until her death many years later because Iphis did not divulge her name, but he knew why his brother killed himself." She concentrated on breathing through the pain, ignoring the warning voice in her head trying to make itself heard in the furious silence from Athena. Piss off a Goddess and die. *Shit, that hurt.*

The sounds of the fight outside carried clearly, the heavy scuff of footsteps, the more muted thuds of fists meeting flesh. Katharine hoped that last groan she'd heard had come from a Harvester.

"I will admit to a modicum of admiration for your ancestor," Athena said at last. "I never imagined she would be able to protect her family for so long. Or perhaps I over-estimated my Harvesters. They have grown weaker over the years, despite my blessings. And now I learn the one I trusted most has betrayed me."

The hot stabbing in her chest eased, and she exhaled roughly, focusing on the floor beneath her knees. Maybe she wouldn't die here.

"Goddess, help me!" The shout came from outside.

Athena sighed. "Weak," she muttered. "You are foolhardy, coming to my temple this way, Medusa. I can kill you now myself."

The pressure around her heart increased a little again. Hunter had warned her...

"You knew that, did you not?"

"Yes, my Lady," she gasped around sharper

pain.

"You would die for your family, to end my curse? You would die to save this man who loves you?"

Katharine squeezed her eyes shut as unimaginable pain stabbed into her chest, spreading into her extremities. Until it was all she knew. Hot, sharp blades along her nerves, into her heart, her belly, her head.

"Would you die for them?"

To keep Hunter alive? Her family? "Yes," she ground out, unable to breathe now.

Light flashed, white and hot, and the pain vanished.

She sucked in a slow breath. Not dead. Yet.

"Goddess, help!" the man shouted again.

The Goddess made a sound of disgust. "So weak, these Harvesters of mine. Rise, Medusa," she said more loudly.

Katharine pushed to her feet, keeping her gaze on the floor as she tried to breathe evenly.

"You and your family are forgiven. My curse on your ancestor is no more."

A fiery burning from her tattoo made Kat bite her lip to stifle a moan. "Thank You, my Lady," she whispered through gritted teeth. Sweat popped out on her forehead and the back of her neck, down her spine under the layers of her sweater and tank top. *Holy shit, that hurt.* Even more than the squeezing in her chest a few moments earlier, searing heat through her skin.

The Goddess clapped Her hands, and the

entire temple rocked even more. "Since there is no longer a Medusa–" Her voice echoed in the hall–"I no longer require Harvesters. All of the gifts I have bestowed upon you are now revoked." She clapped Her hands once more, and the pain in Katharine's shoulder vanished. A brush of cool air touched the side of her face, as if someone had just swept by, though there were no accompanying footsteps.

The Goddess had gone.

Kat took a deeper breath and opened her eyes.

"Kat?" Hunter's quick footsteps came from the entry, and she turned to meet him.

"It's over." She realized she was smiling. And crying.

He pulled her into his arms, kissing the top of her head, her cheek, wherever he could reach. "I didn't want to leave you with Her."

"Let's go outside. I need some air." Never mind that the temple was open to the night on all sides.

When they reached the steps, several Harvesters lay sprawled outside, unconscious.

Hunter's fingers tightened around hers.

"They can't hurt us anymore," she whispered, tugging him down the steps with her.

He let her, though when he glanced back over his shoulder, he looked as if he wanted to go back and finish the job.

By the time they reached the bottom of the hill, Kat's legs shook so hard, she fell to her knees. "Oh my G-Gods," she got out through chattering teeth. Adrenaline, she thought.

Hunter dropped to his knees beside her and pulled her close. "How did I let you talk me into this?"

She turned her face so it rested against his throat. "The c-curse is g-gone. After all this t-time."

He kissed the top of her head. "You can go anywhere you want now. Do anything you like."

She pushed away far enough to look into his shadowed face. "I just want to go home, with you."

He sucked in a quick breath. "That might be kind of boring after all this."

She brushed her lips along his. "Never." She smiled at him, tears burning her face. "I can't think of anything better."

"Then you should know those rings are for real, honey." He kissed her harder.

She laughed against his mouth, heart racing, but not painfully this time. "I love you."

He groaned and shoved to his feet. "Let's get out of here before anyone else shows up, and they haven't gotten the memo yet that they've fallen from favor with the Goddess."

Katharine let him tug her up, heart light. She couldn't ever remember experiencing this joy, not even before the curse landed on her. She swung their joined hands between them, laughing. "I love you, Hunter."

He chuckled, pulling her to his side. "You

can show me how much when we get back to our room."

AT THE FLASH OF BRIGHT LIGHT, ARISTOTLE tumbled from his chair to the floor, narrowly missing the corner of the desk. "My Lady," he said hoarsely as he bowed his head. He heard his nephews dropping to their knees across the room.

"I no longer require your services," the Goddess said after a long moment.

Aristotle's heart thumped painfully inside his ribs. "My Lady, we believe we have learned the secret of their amulet. I have someone preparing to kill her now. In Greece.."

"Not any longer. There is no Medusa."

He swayed on his knees, pain shooting from his chest to his left arm. "My Lady?" he managed.

"I have forgiven the Medusas and removed the curse. And since there is no longer a Medusa, there are no longer Harvesters."

His nephews gasped at the same time. Aristotle's vision greyed around the edges.

"And because of your betrayal, the Tassos family no longer carries My favor."

He clutched his fingers at his sides. "My Lady, I beg Your pardon–"

"I am weary of your begging, Aristotle. It is unbecoming, as are your lies."

The vise clamped around his heart squeezed tighter, and he slipped sideways, thumping his shoulder against the table.

Someone shouted, "Uncle Ari," but he couldn't tell which of his great-nephews it was.

"You served me well for a long time," the Goddess murmured, "but you will wander Erebus for your betrayal."

Aristotle shut his eyes for a few moments as the pain and shock stole his breath. "My...life for You, my Lady," he gasped, forcing his eyes open.

But She was gone, and the last thing he saw were the pale, worried faces of his nephews.

HUNTER DIDN'T WASTE TIME IN THE morning, changing their flight to the first one out of Athens, just in case anyone in the Tassos family hadn't gotten the news they were no longer on a mission for Athena. While he did that, Kat alerted her family. He wondered if the Harvesters all knew right away they'd lost their talents.

He studied Kat's tattoo while she stuffed their clothes into the suitcases. The goblet and snake were gone, the tattoo was now nothing more than a bouquet of bright flowers. She glanced over her shoulder, as if making sure she hadn't forgotten anything, and caught him staring.

She grinned. "No more Medusas, no need for an amulet." She straightened.

"I know." He still had his birthmark, though, he'd noted earlier.

She zipped up the big suitcase, and then the carry-on. "Let's get out of here."

"I want to meet your parents."

She laughed. "I think we can safely do that now."

"And your sisters."

She crossed the room to him and slid her hands around the back of his neck. "You can meet my whole damn family," she said softly.

He lifted her up and brushed a kiss on her mouth. "Let's go catch our flight."

She actually slept on the plane.

He couldn't quite relax enough for that, but he'd make up for it when they got home. He thought he could probably sleep for a week. Or at least a solid eight hours.

Ryder met them at the baggage claim, a wide smile on his face. "Congratulations."

Kat rushed to hug the woman at his side, and Hunter guessed it must be Philomena. He shook hands with the other man. "Thanks. Nice to meet you finally."

"We came to give you guys a lift home since I had your car, and we didn't want you to have to deal with travel arrangements. You had a long couple of days."

Hunter chuckled. "You could say that."

"I'll wait to ask for details. The drive isn't long enough for a debrief." Ryder turned to the women. "Do you have everything?"

Hunter gestured to the suitcases at his side. "We're set." Bemused, he followed the others out of the terminal to the short-term parking. Kat and her cousin climbed into the backseat of a dark SUV, chatting and crying.

It must be overwhelming, he mused. After all this time.

Ryder started the engine. "Are you both all right?"

"Nothing more than a few scrapes and bruises." He relaxed back into his seat. "Just tired."

"We'll want a full report, you know, me and Kallan," the other man said with a grin.

"I figured. Maybe we can have a get-together in a few weeks, once we're settled."

Ryder shot an assessing glance at him. "You'll have to meet everyone, you know, eventually."

Hunter nodded. "I'm okay with that." He was. He'd just acquired an enormous family with Kat. He glanced into the backseat and winked at her, gratified by the color blooming in her cheeks.

"Good. I hope you're prepared."

He would be by then.

He wasn't prepared, though, for what waited at his house. His pulse skipped a beat and then sped up at the sight of the man on his front porch.

Eyes narrowing, Ryder eased the car to a stop. "What the fuck is *he* doing here?"

"I think it's okay," Hunter said slowly.

"Are you sure?"

He nodded and unfastened his seat belt, then opened the door.

Kat shoved her door open, too, and he took her hand.

He watched the man who stepped off the porch and approached them. It wasn't quite like looking at his reflection, but uncannily similar.

"You are Hunter?" The other man started to put out his right hand, then hesitated. "I am Elek. Your...brother. Half-brother."

Kat gave Hunter's hand a squeeze, then released it, stepping back.

Hunter shot her a quick glance, and she smiled, tipping her chin up. He turned toward the Harvester again. His half-brother. He couldn't quite bring himself to shake the man's hand. After all, this man had had a part in hunting Katharine, her cousins before her.

Elek cleared his throat. "I know you weren't expecting to see me, and to be honest, I didn't plan to come here. But since I wound up here, I wanted to apologize."

He blinked. "For what?"

The other man laughed shortly. "It's quite a list, but I'll start with Uncle Ari and his lies and secrets. Had the Goddess known about Iphis and Annis, who knows what would have happened."

"She knows."

Elek's eyes widened a little. "Ah. Well, that explains her visit to him last night right before he died."

"He's dead?" Hunter's own eyes widened. "Holy shit." He shut his mouth. "I'm sorry, that was insensitive."

One of Elek's shoulders twitched in a sketch of a shrug. "It's all right. He admitted to me he'd known about them. I'm glad She knows." His bright gaze searched Hunter's face. "I won't stay, you look like you need to rest, but I...well, I guess I wanted to see you. To know if it was true. That we're brothers. I can see it is. And I want to apologize for our father. He is...indiscriminate. Always has been."

"I had good parents," Hunter said before the other man could continue. "I'm glad they adopted me."

Elek nodded. "Perhaps we can talk more another time." He glanced past Hunter. "Ryder Ware doesn't seem happy to see me here."

He grinned. "He isn't. As long as you agree there is no more conflict between the Medusa's descendants and the Tassos family, I'm sure things will be fine. Eventually."

The other man smiled faintly. "There is no more conflict. The Goddess has revoked all of her favors and gifts. I think we will spend a long time working our way back into her good graces." He met Hunter's gaze again. "You can reach me when, or if, you want to talk further. When you're ready."

Hunter nodded. "Thanks." He watched the other man walk away, climbing into a dark sedan parked near the corner.

Kat's hand slid down his arm. "Are you okay?"

He smiled, turning to her. "I am." He studied her for a few seconds. "You look like you're ready to drop. Let's get in the house."

Ryder had their bags and wheeled them to the front door. "We'll let you guys get some sleep, but let's plan to talk sooner than a few weeks from now." He clapped Hunter's shoulder. "Welcome home, and welcome to the family."

Inside, Hunter kicked the mail aside and shut the door, resetting the alarm.

Kat leaned against the door, her grey eyes crinkled at the corners.

"This feels familiar," he said slowly.

Her mouth curved. "Does it?"

He stepped closer. "It does." He set his hands on her waist. "Wrap your legs around me." He lifted her up.

She obeyed. "Hm, this does seem familiar." She slid her hands around his neck.

"Do you want a drink? You didn't get to finish yours?"

She grinned. "No, thanks."

"I want to marry you, for real."

Her smile softened. "I want that, too."

His heart thundered in his chest, excitement and emotion expanding. "Let's go start the honeymoon now."

She laughed as he turned toward the steps.

# EPILOGUE

K at frowned as she hefted the box on the porch. She hadn't ordered anything lately. She carried it and the rest of the mail inside with her. Maybe from her editor?

She set it on the kitchen table and started sorting through the rest of the mail when her phone rang. Philomena. She thumbed it on. "Hi, how's the baby?"

"Hungry every two hours."

Kat laughed. "Poor Philomena."

"You laugh now. Wait till it's your turn."

"Not for a long time, thanks."

"We'll see." Her cousin made a shushing noise. "I sent you some pictures this afternoon. Oh, and a link to an article you need to read. Have you opened your email?"

"No, I just walked in the door with the snail mail."

"It's an obituary I think you'll appreciate seeing."

While they finished their chat, Hunter came in, sliding his hands around her waist from behind so he could nuzzle her nape. "Bye, Philomena," Kat murmured, shutting off her phone and leaning back against him. "Hello there, husband."

His teeth closed gently on a sensitive spot for a second. "Hello, wife. How's the baby?"

"An insomniac, apparently." She turned and went up on tiptoe to kiss him.

"What'd we get?" His chin lifted toward the table.

"Beats me."

He released her. "It's addressed to you." He lifted it carefully. "No rattling. It's not heavy."

"So let's just open it."

"You notice there's no return address?"

She sighed. "Yes. But I still want to know what's in it."

"Of course you do." He pulled a pocket knife out to slit the sealing tape, then hesitated.

"No more Harvesters, remember?" She reached over and lifted one flap on the top of the box. "Come on."

His mouth curved, and he flipped the other side, pulled out a piece of foam. "*Whoa.*"

Kat shifted her gaze from his hand to the contents of the box. "Oh...my." She reached in and wrapped her fingers around the gold stem of a delicate goblet.

Etched into the shiny surface were swirls and flowers, and a snake wound around the stem, its eyes sparkling emeralds set near the bowl of the goblet.

Kat shot a sidelong glance at Hunter, whose eyes were wide. "Is there a card?" Not that she needed a card or return address to know Who had sent it.

He pulled a fine parchment envelope from

inside the box and handed it over. In exchange, she handed him the goblet.

"Katharine, My congratulations on your marriage. In honor of that happy occasion, and to mark a new beginning for your family, I thought perhaps this goblet, in the design of your ancestor for your protection, and now indicating My protection, would serve as a reminder to Us all of a better future. A."

For a long moment, she stared at the note. "Huh."

Hunter laughed and slid his free hand around her waist. "It's a hell of a wedding present, but I think it needs to be in a safe."

She shook her head. "No, I think She meant it to be seen regularly. In the living room, I believe."

He pressed a light kiss at her temple. "Good thing we have a state-of-the-art security system."

Kat carried the goblet and its case into the other room and set it on the mantel. "Perfect." She turned back to Hunter, sliding her hands up his chest to lock her fingers together at his nape. "I'm suddenly feeling like Greek food. What do you think, husband?"

"I'm not sure that's exactly what Athena was going for, but okay."

She tugged his head down and gave him a fast, smacking kiss. "Even when you're a smart ass, I still love you."

He suddenly gathered her close, startling a yelp out of her. "You'd better," he growled, landing a stinging swat on her ass.

Kat's pulse quickened as heat spread from that point of contact. "Mm. Maybe the Greek food can wait a little while," she murmured.

His eyes darkened, and he gave her a slow grin that made her hormones sit up and beg. "Really?" He slid his hand lower to cup her ass. "Wrap your legs around me, sweetheart. We can delay supper as long as you like."

She laughed as she obeyed. "I like."

"I love," he whispered against her mouth.

"I love you, too."

"Even if you aren't the Medusa anymore," he teased.

Thank you for reading this story! It's been some time in the making, and I really do appreciate the readers who've waited for it. Once upon a time, a long time ago...okay, in 2014, *Hunting Medusa*, the first book in this trilogy, was released in ebook format. It's been a long journey from that release to this one, and I'm thankful for all the support I've had along the way from the readers who picked that up and waited to finish the trilogy. **You all rock!** If you loved this story, it would be awesome if you said that in a review at your bookseller of choice. Those kind words can make an author's day. If you're not into writing reviews even for books you love, but you'll suggest those books to your reader friends, we love that, too!

# About the Author

Elizabeth Andrews has been a book lover since she was old enough to read. She read her copies of *Little Women* and the *Little House* series so many times, the books fell apart. As an adult, her book habit continues. She has a room overflowing with her literary collection right now, and still more spreading into other rooms.

Almost as long as she's been reading great stories, she's been attempting to write her own. Thanks to a fifth grade teacher who started the class on creative writing, Elizabeth went from writing creative sentences to short stories and eventually full-length novels. Her father saved her poor, callused fingers from permanent damage when he brought home a used typewriter for her.

Elizabeth found her mother's stash of romance novels as a teenager, and—though she loves horror—romance became her favorite genre, making writing romances a natural progression.

Along with her enormous book stash, Elizabeth lives with her husband of thirty years, with two adult sons nearby, though no one else in the family reads the way she does. When she's not at work or buried in books or writing, there is a garden outside full of herbs, flowers and vegetables that requires occasional attention.

You can find out more at her home on the web at www.elizabethandrewswrites.com

## Also by this author:

### <u>Light the Way Home</u>
*A Common Elements Romance Project novella*

Single dad Nate Baxter has his hands full with his son and his haunted lighthouse. He doesn't have time to spend with a woman...especially one who won't stick around, like his ex-wife.

But Lucie Russo's not like other women Nate's met. She's sweet and sexy, and his mouth waters every time he's around her.

Will a family emergency cause him to break his relationship rules? And if he does, will his heart be broken too?

### <u>Hunting Medusa</u>
*The Medusa's Daughters Trilogy, Book 1*
*One murderous mission. One killer case of*
*PMS. Who said "the curse" was a myth?*

Ever since the original Medusa ticked off Athena by bragging about her beauty, her cursed daughters have been paying for that mistake. To this day, successive Medusas play cat and mouse with the descendants of Perseus, known as the Harvesters.

When Kallan Tassos tracks down the

current Medusa, he expects to find a monster. Instead he finds a wary, beautiful woman, shielded by a complicated web of spells that foils his plans for a quick kill and retrieval of her protective amulet.

Andrea Rosakis expects the handsome Harvester to go for the kill. Instead, his attempt to take the amulet imprinted on her skin without harming her takes her completely by surprise. And ends with the two of them in a magical bind—together.

Though their attraction is combustible, her impending PMS (Pre Magical-Curse Syndrome) puts a real damper on any chance of a relationship. But Kallan isn't the only Harvester tracking Andi, and they must cooperate to stay at least one step ahead of a ruthless killer before they can have any future, together or apart.

Warning: A hunter who's fallen for the woman he's bound to kill, a Medusa who must trust him with her life, and a magical curse only love can break.

## <u>Protecting Medusa</u>
The Medusa's Daughters Trilogy, Book 2

Being the Medusa puts a real crimp in a woman's social life. Lucky for Philomena Gregory, she gave up on men long before

Athena's curse landed on her head—she learned as a child men don't stay, a lesson reinforced as a lovesick teenager. The hot naked man in her bathroom won't change her mind.

Ryder Ware has waited six years to meet Mena in person. She's managed to avoid him every time he's visited his son, her nephew. Flirting on the phone and via email is no substitute when a man is so intrigued. But now that Athena's Harvesters have found her, Mena has no choice but to let him keep her safe—and close, *very* close.

Philomena may have to accept his protection, but, even with chemistry hotter than Hades, she won't change her mind about a relationship, even after a little sex. Or even a lot of sex. Good thing Ryder's a patient man. After waiting years, what's a few more weeks to convince the woman of his dreams he wants forever? All he has to do is keep them ahead of the Harvesters long enough to prove he'll be there when she needs him.